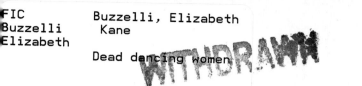

FORTHCOMING BY ELIZABETH KANE BUZZELLI

Dead Floating Lovers

An
Emily Kincaid
Mystery

DEAD
DANCING
WOMEN

Elizabeth Kane Buzzelli

MIDNIGHT INK
WOODBURY, MINNESOTA

MIDNIGHT
INK

FIRST EDITION
First Printing, 2008

Book design by Donna Burch
Cover design by Ellen Dahl
Editing by Rosemary Wallner

E. Weick, "no strings attached literature," E.W. Ink, 2004. eweick@atlanticbb.net

"Reckoning" written by Ani DiFranco
© 2007 RIGHTEOUS BABE MUSIC (BMI) Administered by BUG
All Rights Reserved. Used By Permission.

Midnight Ink, an imprint of Llewellyn Publications

Library of Congress Cataloging-in-Publication Data
Buzzelli, Elizabeth Kane, 1946–
    Dead dancing women / Elizabeth Kane Buzzelli.—1st ed.
        p. cm.—(An Emily Kincaid mystery ; #1)
    ISBN 978-0-7387-1266-6
    1. Women journalists—Michigan—Fiction. 2. Women police—Michigan—Fiction. 3. City and town life—Michigan—Fiction. 4. Michigan—Fiction. I. Title.
    PS3602.U985D43 2008
    813'.6—dc22

                                                                    2008020922

Midnight Ink
Llewellyn Publications
2143 Woodale Drive, Dept. 978-0-7387-1266-6
Woodbury, MN 55125-2989, U.S.A.
www.midnightinkbooks.com

Printed in the United States of America

For the International Women's Writing Guild,
especially Hannelore Hahn,
mother and patient protector of all women writers.
And for Rainelle Burton, one of the finest
writers at work today, and a wonderful friend.
As is Annick Hivert Carthew.

For the Mule Team: Linda Savard and Dr. Ruth Lerman.

For the Detroit Women Writers,
especially my good friend, artist, writer Carolyn Hall
who, beyond all common sense, continues to encourage me.

And for my friends and students:
Anne Noble, Lisa Walmsley, and Cindy Kochis,
who not only have learned from me but have now surpassed me.

And, as always, for Tony.

ONE

THIS MONDAY WAS LIKE all Mondays up in northern Michigan. No better. No worse.

Another garbage day where first I lugged the battered can a black bear'd been tossing around for the last few weeks up the drive, then back down again. In between I hunted for the lid and fought off the scavenger crows. Spring, summer, winter, autumn, some things didn't get any better no matter how you tried your best to overcome them.

Some days things got worse.

I knew I was in for it. I could feel that "something" around me in the woods as I climbed up to Willow Lake Road to get that fought-over garbage can. I could feel it in the traitorous, looming, late September air, with needles of cold at its heart. Autumn. Prelude to death, I thought morosely as I climbed. Garden going to die: the ferns, grasses, and the last of the purple knapweed clinging to sheltered places on the hills—soon all gone.

Autumn depressed me, despite all the raging color in the woods.

It was autumn when I first arrived up here, three years ago. Brought by serendipity; a few wrong turns; a mad desire to get away from my ex-husband, Jackson Rinaldi, back in Ann Arbor; a need to breathe air a million people hadn't breathed before me; a sudden, if unwanted, infusion of cash from my dead father—all those things and more.

I found my little house on its wild lake by driving north after clearing out my father's home, coming upon photographs of happy childhood times I could barely remember, selling off furniture his hands had made, and closing more doors on my past than I'd known existed. It seemed natural to turn north at Grand Blanc, toward the woods, to take my tears where they didn't require explanation. Getting lost was the serendipitous part. Wrong turn after wrong turn brought me to a faded for-sale sign and a driveway angling downhill; to my little golden house standing empty then, alone in its sandy plot with the beginnings of a garden at the back and a sea of bent bronzed ferns at the front. I'd explored around the house, peeking in windows, following a narrow path through the ferns down to a wild lake where geese honked angrily at me and a beaver surfaced to eye me. I returned to Ann Arbor only to quit my job at the *Ann Arbor Times* and claim my division of the spoils from my marriage to poor Jackson, who still didn't understand what I'd gotten so angry about.

I had this new place where I wasn't certain I belonged. This new writing life that wasn't getting me anywhere—fast. And a lot of time leftover to feel grateful for the quiet, sometimes too lonely, life I led.

I was halfway up the drive when I heard the crows. They'd be waiting, screeching because I dared to snatch my garbage can back before they'd finished picking every morsel they could gather. I'd learned quickly to resent the beady-eyed birds that attacked anything left dangling from the can; attacked boxes I dared set on the ground; and tore at black plastic bags with their pointed beaks, then squawked and squeaked at me, making me feel as if, but for a technicality—being alive rather than dead—I'd do as well as any bloodied meat wrappings.

Corvus Americanus. Forked tongues, bristling nostrils, convex beaks, and all. I'd researched them because I believed one must know thine enemies. They would wait like thugs to hassle and harass me, though the eternal dispute was only about my empty garbage can.

I climbed through an Ottoman mosaic, a patchwork of brown and dying ferns bent like weeping ladies, through bright red sumac, through the smells of autumn—of fallen leaves, rotting weeds, damp air. Off to my right I could see my little lake between the trees: a flat, slate-colored oval of water. Above my head, the dark sky hung close and huge, threatening rain at any moment. The day was muddy gray, but still the pretty part of fall, before the leaves turned dark and old; before icy winds knocked them down, leaving gray branches bare and vulnerable; before somebody turned on the north wind and let loose the tons of snow that would lock me in the house for days, pacing and muttering about unhappy women who left good jobs and a not-so-bad husband (except for that one bad habit), and went to live on an iceberg.

I took deep breaths of cool air that tasted like water and reluctantly reached the top of the drive.

As I suspected, more crows than usual. Crows in the trees and sitting on overhead wires. Crows in the road. A convention of crows. A conglomeration of crows staring without shame, without blinking. I was the thing caught in the headlights, frozen for the first minute before I waved my arms wildly, trying to scare them off because they scared the heck out of me.

A few of the black menaces flew up to perch on low, bloody, maple branches. Some hopped into a thicket beneath pines. Some strutted aggressively from the center of the road, toward me rather than away. Their beady black eyes bulged. They made rude, angry noises, telling me to get lost, get off their turf: *buzz off, lady.* I stood and gave them as good as they gave me, muttering, making comments about their funny gait, about their ruffled feathers.

"Carrion eaters," I grumbled and scuffed the toe of one tennis shoe in the gravel beside the road.

I figured I'd better grab my garbage can and get out of there fast, though I couldn't help waving my arms one more time and yelling "Shoo!" like an old lady running kids off her lawn. It did little good. The crows flapped their shaggy wings right back and leaped, startled and irate, into the air. The cawing, squalling noise was deafening.

A dead possum lay on the far side of the road, salt and pepper furred testament to an attempt to cross in widening headlights the night before. Maybe the possum was the real cause of the morning's crow chaos, I thought. But the crows weren't bothering with the possum. It was me they kept their glazed eyes on, and my garbage can. They cawed in unison, commenting, I was sure, on my crummy jeans, my University of Michigan sweatshirt, my hair that hadn't seen a Traverse City beautician's hand since July. They laughed at my dirty tennis shoes, muddy from working in the garden grabbing slugs off my late tomatoes, dropping them to dissolve in a plastic carton of kosher salt. And maybe they made a comment or two on my supposed sex life, or my abortive mystery novels that always brought letters from agents like, "This book just doesn't excite me enough to offer representation. In fact, there is a familiar ring to the story. Sorry. Try us again with your next book." As if I churned out a book a week and they would remember my name or care if I showed up with another book or not. As if they cared that I was beginning to be a laughingstock among my few acquaintances up here who knew how hard I worked to turn out these things—each one a masterpiece. Or maybe not a laughingstock, because northern Michigan people were too kind. Maybe they just pitied me since they would see me at the top of the drive, pull their pickups or their SUVs over to have a talk, and offer me a mystery plot that "just might do the trick for you, Emily," though it always came from a TV show they'd watched the night before.

Maybe crows can't know that much, but bright or not, these particular crows were daunting. I was making a grab for the empty garbage can when Simon, my mailman, drove around the curve, yellow flasher pulsing on top of his yellow Jeep. He aimed his vehicle toward me, pretending he was going to run me down. I, in turn, pretended panic and jumped out of his way. Simon threw back his head of long, thick, blond hair and laughed.

"Morning, Emily," he called out his open window and bent to collect my mail from the seat beside him. I took the two official-looking letters—one a bill from Top O'Michigan Rural Electric Company, the other from a department store in Traverse City, and asked him how he was doing. I had time to talk. It was either Simon or a chapter of yet another mystery in which I killed off a poor soul at the beginning—a lot of carnage for nothing since the books didn't sell.

I leaned in his window.

"How ya doin'?" Simon lowered his head and reared back, away from me. I intimidated Simon. He knew I was some kind of writer or painter or something because I got a lot of mail from arts and literary agencies and had books sent to me from bookstores. Being a female artist alone in the Michigan woods meant one of two things to him: I was nuts or I was a man hater. Either way, Simon, who was all of twenty-three, wasn't willing to take his chances.

"Got a lotta crows today." He squinted his pale blue eyes at the birds leaving the trees to creep along the ground. "Don't think I've ever seen so many all at once. What you got in your garbage, Emily? Big Macs?" He laughed and bent down, coming up with a squirming, black and white puppy in his large, cupped hands.

"See what I found wandering out on Double Lake Road? Over near Arnold's Swamp. Not a house anywhere. Somebody must've dropped him off. Couldn't leave him like that."

A darling puppy. Big brown eyes. A tiny pink tongue sticking out. He looked at me, blinked a few times, and woofed a sad woof.

"You keeping him?" I asked.

Simon looked down at the black and white mottled face. The puppy woofed again, almost to himself.

"Got six dogs." Simon shook his head. "I was thinking about you. I never seen a dog with you. And being all alone, well, I thought maybe you'd need one."

I shook my head. Every thwarted instinct in me quivered. What I wanted was certainly a dog, I wanted to tell him, a little alive thing greeting me when I came into my empty house, or sitting at my feet out in my studio. Something to talk to other than myself, though I did a lot of that.

But what I couldn't allow into my life right then was anything needing care. I had enough trouble caring for me, getting my life straight, learning what that life was going to include. No. I looked away from "puppy" who, I swear, smiled at me.

Nope, I told myself. Nothing demanding food and water and needing to go out nights. I'd left Jackson over stuff like that and wasn't about to fall into that trap so soon again.

"I don't think so," I told Simon and backed away quickly before the puppy could snag me with his sad, black and white face. *If things had been different. If my books sold. If I were at all sure of my future…*

"Better to have a dog," Simon said, and he shook his own shaggy head. "Could be killed in your bed some night. A dog gives you warning."

"Really? Anybody been murdered lately up here?"

"Nope. None yet. But you never know. There's old Mrs. Poet, from in town. Ain't been seen in about a month. Had it on the TV. Still can't find her. Then there's escaped criminals coming down from up in Marquette. There's men that go bonkers. Plenty of reason to have a good dog in the house. Look at old Harry, over there. You never know when old Harry might decide to go off."

He pointed across the road toward the narrow, overgrown, dirt driveway headed with a battered, black mailbox standing on a half-rotten, leaning post. The vague path led back through two rows of mossy elm trees to where Harry Mockerman lived. Harry might not have pulled down a Nobel Prize for brain power, but he was savvy enough to scrounge work cutting trees, selling wood, doing odd chores for "ladies of the woods" (as he called me and any others around like me, of which there were a few).

"Nothing wrong with Harry." I stood up for Harry because he taught me how to identify morels in May and puffballs in August and find wild leeks all summer, and other things too, like tiny milk-weed pods, which, when cooked in three boiling waters, drained, and fried in butter, tasted like, oh, maybe chicken.

Simon curled his lip at me and shook his head as if I'd just confirmed how nuts I was, trusting a shuffling old guy who wore a shiny black funeral suit to cut down trees in case one fell on him and killed him and nobody knew where to find his burying suit. Or, sometimes, brought over a Mason jar of his woodchuck stew as a neighborly gesture. Stew made from a woodchuck he'd killed with a slingshot (he bragged to me one time). "Ya jist add a whole tamata, one patata, a onion, some peppa, a little bit a salt, an' a lot a watta."

Simon'd once mentioned finding a jar of stew sitting under the mailbox with the name "Mailman" written across the lid. He said he took the stew and left a thank you, but when he got home and offered it to his dogs they howled and backed away.

Well, I thought Harry's stew was delicious, and in return I'd baked Harry a loaf of bread, which probably sent Harry howling and backing away, but still he was kind enough to thank me for the neighborly gesture.

"No sale," I said, pointing toward the dog.

"I'll keep trying to find a home for him." Simon sighed and put his car in gear. "If you change your mind, just leave a note in the box and I'll bring him down."

I patted the soft, round puppy head, endured a long-suffering look and a few sweet licks at my hand. I reluctantly backed away, waving goodbye as Simon drove off.

The sky got darker now. Wind picking up. The maples and the pines in my woods began to dance the way they do during storms. Dance, and sometimes fall ungracefully into heaps, which occasioned my notes in Harry's mailbox to bring his chain saw and come see me because I had a job for him.

The breeze was already wet, as if it had been raining elsewhere and I was getting the residue, a dampness leftover from Lake Michigan storms, serious storms that headed up toward Lake Superior to worry ships, wreak havoc, and cause gloomy songs to be written.

I stood still for a few minutes, waiting to see if anyone else would stop by and have a word or two, keep me from going back down the hill to my writing studio and the new novel about a New York writer who was suspected of a murder because a friend of hers was killed in the same manner the writer used to kill off a character in a book. I was having strange, mystical feelings of déjà vu, as if I'd heard the plot before, and hoping I hadn't taken it from one of my neighbors and was rewriting an old *Murder She Wrote* rerun, or an *Alias* episode.

I looked down Willow Lake Road in one direction, then the other. Nobody was going to come and save me from working on the book, or on the article I'd agreed to write for a local magazine, about a group of Survivalists living back in the woods down the road from me. I had to make phone calls. An interview to arrange. I wasn't exactly looking forward to doing either.

The trees along the road waved and bent in the wind. Clouds scudded by in brightly lighted puffs. Crows leaped about or hunkered down along the telephone wires, their thick plumage poking straight up in the damp wind.

I gave an involuntary shiver as I made a move for the garbage can. Willy, the garbage guy, had uncharacteristically put the lid back on instead of leading me on my usual treasure hunt to retrieve it. I wrapped my arms around the can and lifted. The can had an odd, off-balanced feel to it. Something left inside. I tipped it one way, then the other, causing whatever was in there to roll like a basketball

TWO

I DID AN AMAZING dance. A leap in the air, a twirl, all the while holding the lid in my hand, and yelping words I didn't know I knew. I must have kicked the garbage can at one point in my dance because it fell over and away from me, causing the head to roll out onto the pavement, wild gray hair moving in a clotted clump. The head came to rest with the dead face turned toward me, on its side, eyes looking directly into mine.

I took a lot of deep breaths and moved closer to the slightly rocking head. It wasn't pretty. The smell I'd been ignoring got to me now, making my stomach do things I didn't want it to do. I hadn't paid attention to the smell but the crows sure had, and were going crazy around me. Crows in the air, wings flapping. Crows leaping up and down in the road. Crows. Crows. Crows. Rain falling. Trees going crazy ...

A rocking head ...

I took a lot of deep gulps of air, hoping to hold my breakfast down. This wasn't a thing to be alone with. I stepped back a lot of quick steps, away from the ... thing, looking straight at me. I had

11

to think. The police, of course. I'd go back down to my studio and call Police Chief Lucky Barnard in Leetsville. And Bill Corcoran. I had to call Bill, editor at the paper I did freelance work for, and let him know what happened out here. Geez—how many dead heads turned up in garbage cans?

Still, I couldn't leave the head in the road. Alone. There was something beyond pathetic about it—the poor woman. Dead. Unreal. But ... not alone. A car might come by. Or those damn birds might make off with it. I wasn't about to touch her ... er ... "it," so I carefully retrieved my garbage can and set it upside down over the head, figuring no one would drive into the poor thing that way.

I ran down the drive to my studio. I fooled around with the temperamental lock, ran in, grabbed up my phone. I got the number and called the police chief in Leetsville.

At first, Lucky Barnard didn't believe me.

"Having a little joke on me, Ms. Kincaid?" he asked when I said there was a dead head lying on Willow Lake Road, at the top of my drive, under my garbage can. "Something for one of your books?"

I sighed and looked around my writing space for solace. "No, Mr. Barnard ... er ... Chief. I mean, I've got a dead head under my garbage can. I think you'd better get out here."

I took in the smiling photo of Georgia O'Keeffe hanging beside my desk. She was flirting with Stieglitz, her husband, this woman who lived by her own standards, everything going into her work, her amazing photographs. My saving places: O'Keeffe; the Jim Harrison poem, framed and hung beside her; my Erica Weick poem; my lithograph of Emily Dickinson's house; my painting of Flannery O'Connor. All part of my coterie of artists who sustained me.

"Hmm," Lucky said.

I threw in a little more detail, hoping to interest him, desperate to be taken seriously. "Very dead, chief. An old woman's head ..."

"Hmm," he said again. I heard him turn from the phone and ask someone a question.

"OK, Ms. Kincaid. My deputy is somewhere out there right now. I'll have her stop by."

Relieved at first, because I'd gotten to the point where I was thinking I'd have to bury the head and forget it, I then remembered who he was talking about: Deputy Dolly Wakowski, scourge of the backwoods roads, a squat little woman with the thin but strident voice of a marionette. Deputy Dolly wore her police uniform like a suit that didn't quite fit. She'd stand beside your car, staring you down, shrugging her way around in her ill-fitting blue shirt, shifting her drooping gun belt back and forth, and then give you a ticket and a lecture because the back, two-lane roads up here were dangerous, but also empty most of the time, easy to speed on, and Deputy Dolly was determined to keep us all alive.

Deputy Dolly, a lot like Barney Fife, only not as pretty. I'd heard she was condemned to work the back roads forever since she smashed one of the two Leetsville police cars while chasing a teenaged candy-store bandit. She was a little gnat of a woman who had already given me three speeding tickets, leading the people down at Buster's Bar, where I sometimes went for the fish fry on Friday nights, to let me in on the flash-your-headlights warning if Dolly was spotted in the area.

Sure thing—I would be thrilled as thrilled could be to show her my dead head. Still, at that point, even Deputy Dolly looked good to me. Anybody. Just so I didn't have to go back up there and be alone with ... that ... poor woman.

"I'll be right on out, too, and I'll put a call in to Doc Stevenson, Kalkaska County Coroner. You go back to the road, OK? Watch that garbage can, and wait for the deputy."

When I got back to the top of my drive, there was a white and gold police car parked across the road, red lights flashing. The crows were gone. Deputy Dolly was bent over, the rear of her, with gun belt dangling, turned my way. She was gingerly lifting one side of the garbage can and peeking underneath.

"It's there all right," I called out.

She gave a whoop and dumped the can over, exposing the head as she jumped back with one hand on her chest and one hand flying to her gun.

"You scared the hell out of me!" Dolly chirped, dancing in my direction, frowning and angry.

I hunkered down in my denim jacket, hands clenched in my pockets, ponytail dripping down my back. I kept my eyes on her. It was a lot colder now. Light rain still falling. I looked over at the poor head in the road and had the urge to take my jacket off and cover it.

"You're Emily Kincaid," Deputy Dolly said. She came closer, slowing down, frowning hard at me. "I remember you."

I choked out something about being happy to see her, which was asinine under the circumstances, and would have been asinine anyway, since I would never be happy to see her.

Dolly whipped out a small notebook, felt in her shirt pocket for a pen, then in her pants pocket, came up with one, and frowned at me again. This, I was thinking, is a formidable woman.

She asked questions and wrote down my answers. A car approached. Dolly ran into the road and furiously waved the car back, motioning for the old man behind the wheel to turn around, to get out of there.

"Have to get this road blocked off as soon as the chief gets here," she called out as she gave what passed for a thin smile. She was walking toward me when I noticed a flash of movement across the road, somewhere down Harry Mockerman's drive. A flash of black, like the shadow of an animal, or just a wave of leaves in the growing wind. I took a step into the road and raised my arm to hail Harry, but there was no one there. Nerves, I told myself. Between the head in the road and this deputy, no wonder I was seeing things.

A blue sedan came sedately around the far curve. No flashers. No sirens. Nothing to denote any eagerness or urgency. The car pulled to the side of the road across from where we waited, not talking to each other. Chief Lucky Barnard, a big, sturdy man in a trim blue and white uniform, got out. "Where is it?" he called, coming toward us slowly.

Dolly pointed to the place in the road where the head lay. He walked over, bent down, and looked the poor thing squarely in the face. He straightened fast and came to where we waited.

"Recognize who it is?" the chief said to Dolly.

She nodded.

He nodded, too.

"Who?" I asked, tired of their silent cop routine.

"Might as well know, I suppose. Everybody's going to, soon as word gets out. Old Mrs. Poet. Ruby Poet. Disappeared, oh, back a few weeks. Had a big search for her. Did everything we could. Always thought she got lost in the woods. Old, ya know. Probably got disoriented. But, how the hell did her head end up in your garbage can?" He shook his own head again. "I just don't see …"

"Probably some animal found it," Dolly said. The two stood looking over at the dead Mrs. Poet. They toed the ground awhile, chewing things over, ruminating.

"Some animal?" I said, just a little incredulous. "Found it and put it in my garbage?"

"Well, I guess not," the chief said. "But, then there's got to be an explanation."

"Yup," I said.

"We'll just wait for Doc Stevenson," the chief said. "He'll be able to give us a better idea of what happened to the poor old soul." He reared back on his heels and chewed awhile at his bottom lip.

The chief was a big man. Once a Marine, I'd heard. He fixed me with a long, suspicious look now. "How're the mysteries coming? I read a lot of mysteries. Haven't read one of yours, have I?"

I shrugged and shook my head, leaving it at that, though my face was burning. He knew damned well none of my books had been published. Everybody up here knew everything about everybody. Well, almost everything. I'd always imagined there were a lot of secrets buried in the blank-windowed, backwoods houses, and behind the facades of the ginger-breaded, Victorian houses in town.

"This wouldn't be something from a book you're writing, would it?"

"I don't dig up dead people just to see what'll happen," I said, being as inane as he was.

A long blue Oldsmobile came up the road and parked behind the chief's car. An elderly man in a windbreaker over a rumpled blue suit got out.

"That's Doc Stevenson," the chief said. "We'll have him take a look and tell us what he thinks. Why don't you go on back down to your house now, Ms. Kincaid? Use the day to rest and come on into town in the morning, tell us what happened out here. Help a lot if you'd do that. Dolly would be glad to give you a ride, if you need one. Wouldn't you Dolly?"

She made a face at him.

Rather than see an argument break out over me, I assured Chief Barnard I could get into town on my own. We agreed on ten o'clock and I started down my drive, happy to get out of the rain that was falling harder now, and hoping, somehow, to get the vision of that poor woman's dead head out of my mind.

"Oh, Miss Kincaid … er … Emily," the chief yelled after me. "We'll be taking your garbage can along with us. Hope you got another one."

I nodded. "Take it," I called back. It wasn't a trophy I'd planned on keeping.

Time to buy that black bear a new can to kick around.

THREE

I SHUDDERED AS I stepped into my tiny, overcrowded living room. It was depressing to think of that poor woman, Mrs. Poet. I didn't know her, but the name was familiar, probably from that search a few weeks back. For a few days, local TV reporters followed police into the woods before being shooed away, left standing with camera rolling, microphone in hand, explaining why they couldn't go into the woods, trying to make a story where there was none. I hadn't paid much attention at the time, since I didn't report on it, but the name was an odd one.

I ran water into a flowered cup at my sink. Now that everything was out of my hands, I found I was shaking. Tea was what I needed. A good and strong Earl Grey.

I set the cup into my microwave, made my tea when the microwave dinged, and went over to my living room desk to call Bill Corcoran at the *Northern Statesman*.

When he answered, Bill sounded hurried. There was the usual noise of telephones and reporters' voices behind him. Traverse City was a growing resort town and his paper one of the biggest dailies in the North Country, right behind the *Record Eagle*. He was always pressed for time, slightly out of breath, on a perpetual deadline. I wondered if he figured on all of this when he'd moved up here from Detroit to run the paper.

"Something happened out here this morning, Bill," I said, trying to keep my voice steady.

"Yeah, Emily? What's going on?"

"I found a human head in my garbage can."

"A human what?"

"Head."

"Well, eh, how'd you know?"

"Know what?"

"Er … nothing. I guess you'd know a human head if you saw one." He sounded like I was feeling.

"The police from Leetsville came out and took it away."

"Wow! I mean … that's something. Where'd they take it?"

"Coroner."

"So … they know who it belongs to?"

"'Belonged,'" I corrected. "I think so. That Mrs. Poet they were looking for. Remember they searched the woods out here for almost a week? She never turned up."

He was quiet a minute. "Yeah, I remember."

"That's it."

"So, you follow the story for us?"

"Sure. I guess I'm kind of at the middle of it."

"Talk to the police …"

"They want me there in the morning—to make a statement."

"Yeah, that's Leetsville. Morning's soon enough. I'll get something in tomorrow's paper, whatever you've got. I'll need details for Wednesday. See who takes jurisdiction, probably be the state

19

boys, but I'll bet Lucky Barnard keeps his hand in. That's his town. He protects his turf. See what you can find on the woman and her family; what people in town think—things like that."

"Sure."

"And, Emily. Must've been a shock. You OK?"

"Well, it wasn't pleasant. But I'm OK."

"So... make sure I get something in time for tomorrow. TV people will be all over you, I suppose."

"I'll handle it."

"Good. Eh, Emily, you sure you're all right?"

I said I'd be just fine. Veteran reporter—all that stuff. I hung up and felt better. He'd sounded almost like a friend. I was assigned the story. I could follow up, find out who Mrs. Poet was, what happened to her.

I sipped my tea and stared at the wall. I needed to talk to somebody. Any friendly voice to knock out the memory of what I'd found up there at the road. There was Jackson, of course. In a way we were still friends. If you didn't have to be married to him, Jackson wasn't a bad guy. Funny. Bright. Good looking. The kind of friend you have fun with but not the kind you end up marrying. Unless you suffer a severe lapse in judgment during a weekend trip with him in New York City—which you shouldn't have gone on in the first place.

No, not Jackson. I'd called him when I got mad at the beaver for scaring me with those tail slaps and it was really funny when I slapped the water right back at him ... well, I thought it was funny. Jackson was (as they say of the queen) "not amused."

So, maybe not a dead head story either.

I put on a James Taylor CD to soothe me. There was something I'd been avoiding here. A thought I didn't want to think. Someone

20

put Mrs. Poet where I found her. Certainly it was no accident. No storm washed her up and plunked her into place. No wild animal, as Chief Barnard suggested, unless coyotes and bears were getting smarter than I wanted to know about. And then there was the thought I'd *really* been avoiding: someone disliked me enough to put that poor woman's head in my garbage can.

When the phone rang I decided I no longer was in a hurry to talk to anyone. I let the machine get it. A TV reporter wanted to know what happened out here, and if I would pose for pictures with my garbage can, up at the road where I'd found the dead woman's head. I answered and told the woman to call the Leetsville Police, that I had nothing to pose with since Lucky Barnard took my can with him.

I hung up and sat down at the living room desk. I leaned over the teacup, taking in the fumes, restoring my soul. The best thing I could do, I told myself, was get to work. That meant the story waiting out in my studio, or the article on Survivalists Jan Romanoff, at *Northern Pines Magazine,* had asked for.

"Don't piss 'em off," she'd warned me. "Just follow 'em around for a day. You know, through the woods. They say they live off the land, but I know the guy's at least got a listed phone number. Do a kind of 'back to nature' piece. Get some recipes for raccoon or bear. You know. A little bit tongue in cheek. A little bit serious. No political stuff. He said they weren't into antigovernment crap, just living through the coming end of the world." She laughed, then laughed harder when I thanked her for the assignment.

"I know you came up here to get away from it all, Emily," she said when she stopped laughing. "Figured you'd be the one to pick up grinding your own corn and jerking your own beef—or whatever it is they do to it."

I agreed that I was certainly the one for the story.

Better than nothing.

I dialed the number Jan had given me.

"Yah," a deep-voiced man grunted.

"Ah..." I squinted at my handwriting in my notebook. "Dave Rombart?"

"Yes, ma'am, that's me."

I told him who I was and that Jan Romanoff asked me to call and set up an appointment to come out and meet him, talk about his "lifestyle."

"Well now." He wasn't sounding as enthused as I'd expected. "I kinda thought she'd send a man. You know, because there's a lot of trekking through the woods involved. And shooting. And stuff."

I assured him I could trek, and shoot—if I had to. "Just want to follow you. How many of you are there?"

"'Bout eleven. Give or take a couple. Me and the wife, mostly. We got ourselves a nice place out here." He told me where to find them, a few miles down the road from me. A place I'd always wondered about, with a huge, metal gate, and big KEEP OUT signs.

"And we got to talkin' the other night that maybe others should know how to take care a theirselves out in the woods. For when the big one drops. Can't be too ready. And it seemed kind of... well... selfish not to share what we learned. Could mean the difference between surviving and being melted."

On that happy note, I assured him he was doing the world a favor, and set up a time to meet on Thursday, out by the gate. He said he'd be waiting and he knew Sharon, "the wife," would just love to give me her recipe for venison stew with corn bread muffins.

Since it was now past lunchtime, I made myself a tuna sandwich and opened a cold Diet Coke. I arranged some apple slices around my sandwich, feeling the need for feminine frills right then, and took the whole thing down to the lake.

Willow Lake could have been called a pond, I suppose. It was small, elliptical, with a sandy bottom where bass laid their eggs in swirling circles every early summer. Nice beach, sky blue water out to the place the water darkened and deepened at the drop-off. I liked the thought of it as a whole lake. My lake. Me, and a couple of loons, and those noisy ducks, and that damned beaver, who stayed busy knocking over trees with his two front teeth.

Actually willow trees did ring the lake, unusual for this far north. They hung long branches of yellowing leaves into the water. Trees and sky doubled on the lake's calm surface, so the whole place was a painting, repeated and repeated.

I sat in a lawn chair on my wobbly dock, ate my sandwich, drank my Coke, and lounged in what had become a half sunny, half overcast, day. With watery sun on my back, and the soft lapping of water at my feet, I began to feel cleaner, braver, almost as if that morning hadn't happened.

This was what I'd come to the North Country for: peace, mindless nature, and not many people. I was here to heal and find a new way to live. Kind of like the Survivalists.

I looked back at the sand path leading to my north-facing house. I'd already had the privilege of learning survival up close and personal. My first summer here a storm out of the west gobbled up the sky, moved black and thick across the lake, obliterated everything: water, sky, woods. I remembered how the walls of my house shook. The windows shook. Geraniums, in clay pots I'd set along the front deck, went flying off banister posts, and off the steps. I went flying too, into the bathroom. I closed the door and climbed into the tub, where I'd cowered with a pineapple-printed shower curtain wrapped around me, and a bath mat on my head, until the house stopped shaking and quivering like something out of *The Wizard of Oz*.

It was at that moment living alone in the woods lost all sense of romance and bravado. This was real life I discovered in those long minutes in my bathroom, not a Disney movie with birdies flitting on my shoulders as I sang a pretty song.

During that storm, I learned to live alone. Bears shaking my garbage can at night didn't bother me. Trees falling on my house didn't bother me. Snow so deep I had to shovel out my windows didn't bother me. Quiet bothered me. Sometimes loneliness bothered me.

But finding part of a poor old woman in my garbage can… well… there were some things in life you could never be prepared for.

I set the diet soda at my feet. I must've moved too fast. I surprised the beaver swimming out from the dock, coming from his growing twig house back in the reeds. He slapped the water hard with his tail, sending a huge spray of lake water over me. I leaped out of my chair.

He really got me, my summer's nemesis. I was still unnerved by the morning's events and he'd caught me off-guard. We were in a knock-down battle—him taking down the soft woods around the lake, and me hoping to scare him away.

I wasn't in the mood for the game right then. I grabbed my dish and soda can and headed back to the house, muttering that I was going to talk to old Harry about getting rid of the beaver, save my lake, free the world from one more nuisance. Let the creature end up as a beaver stew. Maybe the Survivalists had it right.

FOUR

I woke up at six the next morning feeling as if I'd been hit on the head. I took a tepid shower and shook my hair dry, pretending to glamour with my head of streaky blond hair that had grown too long and too wild. I put on a clean yellow cotton sweater and a pair of jeans, and jumped into my yellow Jeep, heading into Leetsville where beavers and crows wouldn't taunt me, and people wouldn't try to scare me to death.

Leetsville was twenty minutes in by some of the worst potholed roads I'd ever driven. It took a lot longer than it should have to get there because of going slow to dodge the holes and stopping for a flock of turkeys. I stopped for the turkeys to be courteous, giving them the right of way. One jenny shook her head at me, scolded, and made as though she was going to attack my Jeep. Disgruntled, I supposed, that I was in her road, that I leaned my head out the window asking them to hurry it up, that I happened to be alive that morning.

Except for the turkeys and the potholes, my drive to town was fairly tranquil.

Leetsville is a mid-sized village. Two grocery stores, one an IGA and the other a Whitney's Discount Foods. A library. A Guns and Ammo store where you can get a Michigan Lotto ticket and a Traverse City *Northern Statesman* (to check last week's Lotto numbers), right along with your shotgun shells, flies for fishing, Pinconning Cheese, and cartons of night crawlers.

I loved planning my trips to town. Maybe it wasn't Ann Arbor—no art, no galleries, no downtown, no lectures, no professors, no visiting writers, no Zingerman's for corned beef sandwiches; but we did have Fuller's EATS, the only restaurant for miles around, owned by Eugenia Fuller, a big, motherly woman who fed everybody in town whether they had the money to pay or not. EATS was where the locals gathered and gossiped and socialized, and where everybody tried to dodge Eugenia when she was on a tear about some relative of hers she'd just discovered. She was a fanatic about her family genealogy. The five-by-five foyer of Fuller's was pasted with charts of Eugenia's family tree. She liked to keep them there so people could watch how far back in time she'd managed to wade. Unfortunately, most of Eugenia's ancestors had been either hung or tarred and feathered, or they had died in jail; but that didn't deter her from tracing them, nor squelch her pride in the whole bunch.

EATS was where most of the town politicking and character assassination took place; where news was spread: someone in need, someone's loss, someone's misfortune. It was the place where money was collected for groceries and clothes after a fire out at the mobile home park on the state road. It was the very place the preachers from the town's three churches came for breakfast after Sunday morning sermons, still bristling with their topic of the week, trying to outdo each other from the center of their flock, and giving blessings over stacks of blueberry pancakes.

Then, there was George's Candy Shoppe (but George's wasn't so busy anymore since Lucky Barnard busted him for selling porn out of the back of the store). At least the front of the store wasn't busy anymore.

Over on the corner of Griffith and Mitchell, a block off the main highway running straight through the middle of town, stood Murphy's Funeral Home—a big, white, peeling, house with leaning pillars across the front. The widow Murphy carried on the family business downstairs, while living above the store with her two dim sons, Gilbert and Sullivan.

Gertie's Shoppe de Beauté was behind Murphy's Funeral Home, on Mitchell. I didn't trust Gertie, that's why I went into Traverse City to have my hair done. Gertie's own hair was very red, a kind of mahogany with orange highlights. And it was very thin. Gertie's scalp shone through all that mahogany hair like a sandy beach with a few patches of sea grass.

Across from Gertie's was Bob's Barber Shop—a decaying storefront so thick with smoke you couldn't see in the windows and, I heard, the magazine racks were filled with Michigan Militia literature, so the place scared me a little, just looking at the cramped little building with a wooden Indian standing at the door, carved from a single log, announcing how retro and politically incorrect the place was. Personally, with the Native American casinos fast making the tribes some of the wealthiest and most powerful people in the state, I wouldn't have set that wooden effigy out there to draw attention to my politics—or lack of them. But then, in Leetsville, like out in the woods, people took pride in their independence of thought, right along with the busted couches sitting on their front porches, their pickups with full gun racks, and their groaning deer pole every November.

And they took pride in their two-minute-long Labor Day Parade for which they elected a Miss Leetsville and invested in a rhinestone crown, which, that past year, was trampled in the beer tent when Miss Leetsville got drunk and lost badly in an arm wrestling contest.

To round out the shops, there was Bailey's Feed and Seed, where I could buy bag balm and hog wash—if I should ever need such items. There was Ernie Henry's small-engine repair, Spinski's Five and Dime, and a resale shop. There was Pansy's bakery, the U.S. post office, and Jamison's Wood Products where most of the town's people worked. The Skunk Saloon. Tom's bowling alley. A few other stores and, for the most part, houses. There was a Catholic church and a Baptist church and a Church of the Contented Flock, which didn't belong to any denomination I'd ever heard of. There were a few municipal offices, and not much else. A bank—but I wasn't happy with the bank because their ATM ate my card without reason and the bank manager, Willy Jensen, wouldn't give it back to me because I could be a wanted fugitive, he said—after knowing me for three years. Anyway, that ATM wouldn't take my deposits either so I figured it wasn't much good and instead saved my banking for Traverse City.

The combined Leetsville Police and Fire Station was just past the Baptist church, on Divinity Drive. I pulled up to the front of the stone building and parked my Jeep. I could see Chief Barnard and Deputy Dolly inside, in earnest conversation with a state police officer.

The two men stood as I entered. Nice, old-fashioned chivalry. Dolly leaned forward in her chair, hat in her hands, a worried look on her face. She glanced up and nodded curtly.

"Emily Kincaid, this is Officer Brent with the state police. He'll be looking into Mrs. Poet's death, along with me and Dolly here.

The sheriff's going to do what he can to help, too. It's just that everybody's stretched kind of thin right now," the chief said, introducing me to a tall officer with a shaved head and a unibrow that took up the middle of his face. The man nodded curtly as I took the only chair left in the room.

"Emily's our local writer," the chief said, and he gave a smile that never got beyond his tight mouth. "She's the one found poor Miz Poet's head in her garbage can." He turned to me. "I've been telling Officer Brent, here, what happened."

"You break the news to her family?" I asked, pulling at a notebook from my purse.

The chief nodded and looked unhappy. "Of course. Did that right away. Only got the one daughter, Amanda."

"How'd she take it?"

"How'd you imagine a daughter would take that kind of news?"

"You tell her it was just the head?"

"Well, not directly. Just said part of her mother turned up."

"Tell her where?"

"No need for that much information. Amanda fainted dead away and we had to get a neighbor lady over to take care of her. Amanda's a refined woman. Delicate, I'd say. Very delicate. We'll call on her again this afternoon. Should tell you, too, Emily, Officer Brent and a bunch of us are going to be out by your place tomorrow morning, combing those woods for the rest of Miz Poet. Figure the body—or whatever's left—can't be far."

"Any idea, yet, who did it?"

He stuck out his bottom lip and shook his head.

"Any idea where, exactly, you'll be searching?" I persisted.

"Around your woods. Cover the whole area, I imagine." He looked at Officer Brent who stared, frozen-faced, at the ceiling.

29

I took a deep breath. "I should tell you, Bill Corcoran asked me to cover the story for the *Northern Statesman*. Thought I ought to let you know." I smiled my best smile all around, though nobody smiled back.

"In that case, Ms. Kincaid," the very straight-backed officer spoke up, after clearing his throat, "I think we'll keep this interview to what happened out at your place. Everything else will have to come from Gaylord."

I nodded. What I expected anyway. Gaylord was the main state police post in the area.

"If you'll just go over for me..." Officer Brent took a notebook and pen from his jacket pocket and waited for me to begin. I waited for a question. He looked up, surprised, and not too friendly. "Any idea where the head came from? Anybody have it in for you? Did you know Ruby Poet? Know any reason somebody would want to kill her and put her head in your garbage can?"

I sat back and answered all of his questions, stopping only when Dolly sniffed and twirled her hat.

"You know, Officer Brent," she said, her mouth drawn down, her eyes looking away from his face. "You're going to have problems with the folks around here talking to you. They're friendly people, all right, but not with strangers. Now, me and Chief Barnard, well, we know 'em. We knew Ruby Poet and her daughter, Amanda. We know their friends." She shook her head. "Be a lot easier if you let us do most of the checking around."

"Well now, Dolly...," Chief Barnard began but was stopped when Dolly turned toward him, her face tied in an unpleasant knot.

"Chief, I know you've got your hands full, what with Charlie going to the hospital and all. I wasn't trying to make your job harder.

It's just that I know the town and the people. I know the folks out there in the woods, too, near where Emily lives."

"Given all of us a lot of tickets," I said, nodding in agreement with Dolly. "You sure do know us."

"Be a lot easier for me . . . ," she went on, ignoring me.

"Thank you, Officer Wakowski. We'd appreciate all the help you can give us," the officer said, and he smiled a cool smile at her. "Got a shoot-out in Petoskey. Bar fight turned ugly." He made a face and blew air out through his pursed lips. "Appreciate whatever you find out. No reason we can't share information." He shifted around on his feet, ran a hand over his bald head, then relaxed enough to grin at me. "You, too, Ms. Kincaid. Appreciate any help the press can provide."

Deputy Dolly nodded and sniffed. She slid down in her chair and twirled her hat between her hands as Officer Brent finished questioning me.

Before I walked out of the office, I told Chief Barnard that I had to call my story in that afternoon. I asked if Amanda Poet had any idea why her mother, or part of her, should be as far out as my place? I asked him what the next move by the police would be, any leads?

Chief Barnard spread his hands. "You'll have to get most of your information from Gaylord, Emily. Sorry, that's the way it is right now. We'll be working with 'em but I won't be able to tell you much. Better you hear it straight from the state boys."

I nodded to the wooden state cop, to a disgruntled Dolly, to a red-faced chief of police, and walked out. I knew one place in town that would be buzzing with information; one place where the people wouldn't be afraid to talk to me; one place where I could get a warm reception along with a cup of thick black coffee: Fuller's

EATS. Before the chief or the state boys learned anything; before a confession could be heard; before the miscreant acknowledged guilt, even to himself; the regulars at Fuller's EATS would know; would have worked out a tragic childhood, bad parentage, and bad lineage. "*Goes back to 'is great-grandfather, Chilton. I remember the man. Tipped over the Johnson's outhouse one Halloween and never had the gumption to admit to it. Bad, right from then on. Coward, you might say. Fun is fun, but telling the truth is something else...*"

Fuller's EATS folks would explain the whole thing to me; tell me what happened and why; and probably what was coming next.

I might not get anything I could put in my story for Bill Corcoran, but I'd sure get a lot more than the police were giving out.

FIVE

THE DARK-PANELED VESTIBULE OF Fuller's featured an expanding genealogy chart with new sheets tacked up in tilted prominence, like movie posters. You couldn't miss the Johnny-come-lately dead relatives with big misshapen gold stars stuck around them, bringing attention to yet another of Eugenia's ill-fated ancestors. This one was an uncle—a John Holliday. I read it fast because I was keeping a kind of tally in my head: how many of her relatives had been to jail, how many were hung. It was 41 to 9 so far.

All Eugenia's relatives got equal space on the wall, but the ones who had been hung got just a little more room. Eugenia said it was only fair since they'd been royally screwed in life.

"Hey, Emily, how ya doin'?" Eugenia called as I entered the dark, smoky, low-ceilinged restaurant. She waved her fly swatter in greeting. She stood behind the cash register, keeping an eye on a poor fly just about to land on the counter. For a big woman, Eugenia could bring herself to a breath-holding halt when in pursuit of one of our slow, late September flies; the kind that hung lazily in the air as if they had no idea where to land next. This one had little will to live and was squashed quickly with one of Eugenia's mighty blows.

She delicately scooped up the remains with a napkin and deposited it into the basket behind the counter. "Hate those buggers," she said, and made a face at me, then quickly changed over to sympathy. "Heard what happened out to your place yesterday. Terrible thing, about Miz Poet. Must've got lost in the woods, there by you. You know how they get when they're old. Think the coyotes got her?" She leaned over the counter, getting closer so she could lower her voice and not upset the appetites of her customers. The woman's small eyes, lost in a nest of smoker's wrinkles, glistened. "You heard about the cougar got a horse not long ago? Somewhere over by Manistee, I think it was. Could've been a cougar got 'er. Who would've thought something like this could happen to such a sweet soul? If you're interested, I mean, like it's something you want to write about, you could go talk to Joslyn Henry. She's right down the road from you and she was a close friend to poor Miz Poet. Those two were closer than jelly donuts."

Eugenia shook her head, clucking over the loss. I agreed. Maybe I'd go talk to my neighbor, Mrs. Henry, and get a human interest angle on the dead woman. I eased away from Eugenia because when she started talking she could keep you standing for a long time, and her talk always got around to her family tree, to what some long-dead uncle had done—or been accused of doing—since Eugenia had a family filled with innocent and wronged people.

I took a seat in a corner booth. Gloria, Eugenia's youngest and prettiest waitress, came hurrying over. She knelt on the seat across from me, and slapped her order pad on the table, then leaned forward far enough to show the cleavage male customers came in for. "I'm telling you, Emily. A girl isn't safe in her bed anymore. It's those people from down below, you know, in the cities. They're coming up here and killing us off. That's the plan, Simon says. Kill all of us off and take our property."

"Do you have property, Gloria?" I asked as I buried my nose in the menu I already knew by heart.

"Well, no, but me and Simon are planning on it soon. We're going to build a house out to his father's farm but back in the woods where nothing's been cleared yet." Her face lit up with her plan; a small, round face with red cheeks and a sweet, innocent smile. Gloria was engaged to my mailman, Simon.

Too early for lunch. To kill time, I ordered a coffee. I sure didn't feel like going back to my house yet. I had to call Bill Corcoran at the paper and I'd gotten nothing from the police. Not an auspicious beginning for my crime-reporting career.

There were only a few customers in EATS, but I could feel the eyes of every one of them on me. Most of the customers waved or nodded when I looked their way, then bent into whispered conversations. I was the talk of the town. Just as long as they didn't get around to deciding I was the murderer, I thought. People in Leetsville didn't like frustratingly oblique answers to things. A duck was a duck was a duck—to their way of thinking. I just didn't want to become the duck they settled on.

Gloria brought my coffee, a napkin, and a spoon. She pushed the sugar shaker over toward me, though I virtuously pushed it back and settled on drinking the thick brew black and straight up.

Normally Gloria was a whirl of energy, bustling around the restaurant, greeting everyone, filling sugar holders and creamers, and taking swipes at a crumby table. This afternoon she hovered across from me, staring up at the ceiling, then down at the toe of one of her tennis shoes. I sipped my coffee, though it was very hot, and waited, smiling at her every now and then, wondering what was coming.

It didn't take long to find out. Gloria leaned over and pretended my napkin holder needed straightening. Her small face worked with whatever she had to say.

"You know, Emily," she whispered. "I belong to the Church of the Contented Flock. Well, I don't like to speak ill of the dead, but awhile ago Pastor Runcival preached a whole sermon on people worshipping the devil and bringing evil into our midst."

"What's that got to do with Ruby Poet?" I sat back, startled. You never quite knew what folks up here might fixate on. I wasn't sure about Gloria's opening but at least this was something beyond everybody moaning over "Poor old Miz Poet."

"Probably nothing, but there has been talk. Now, don't get me wrong. You know I don't gossip like Eugenia does. Still, it's hard to work here and not pick up on a thing or two. I heard that Miz Poet and a group of her friends got themselves involved in nature worship, or some such thing. They meet in the woods, out by you, at Miz Henry's. Don't ask me what it's all about. I only heard this from somebody saying something in here. Amanda Poet, Miz Poet's daughter, caught what was said—was what I heard—and she got up and flounced right out. Caused a big stink. I asked Eugenia what it was about and she said just a bunch of old ladies dancing out in the woods because it made them feel young, or it made them happy, or something. Called themselves Women of the Moon. Eugenia didn't seem to think there was anything wrong with it…" She hesitated, looking around to see who was watching or listening. She lowered her voice, "But then, Eugenia's no chicken herself. She thinks anything old ladies do is all right."

I looked around, too, and would have said everybody was watching—and not watching. They were certainly straining their ears toward us, over what I imagined were cold cups of coffee.

"Well, that was the first I understood what Pastor Runcival was mad about. You know, like there were witches loose in town or something."

"Witches!" I shook my head at Gloria. "That's crazy."

"Now, Emily. The reverend says we don't know everything that goes on back in the woods. Those people aren't like town people. I mean, you know, some of them are really odd."

"I live out in the woods."

Gloria had the good grace to blush. "I know you do. Well, of course, I know that. But you're new up here ..."

"Three years."

"Phew, that's nothing. My mother came from Grand Rapids thirty-two years ago and they still call her 'the Grand Rapids girl.'"

"So, you think maybe your pastor had it in for Mrs. Poet?"

Gloria's jaw dropped. Her dark eyes grew huge. "I wasn't saying anything of the kind, Emily. I was just saying, because of the gossip about Miz Poet and her friends ... well ... who knows what got into somebody's brain. I just thought I'd share that with you because I didn't want to say anything to Lucky Barnard. I don't want to get anybody in trouble ..."

She was going to go on with her disclaimers but Deputy Dolly Wakowski walked in and the whole restaurant went silent. The only sound was the angry buzz of one fly beating hard against a smoke-fogged window.

Dolly stood in the doorway, looking around, hunching her shoulders up, hands clutching on to her drooping gun belt. She searched the place, table by table, until her eyes fell on Gloria and me. With a dip of her head, as if she'd found what she was looking for, Dolly walked over, excused herself to Gloria, and slid into the seat across from me.

Gloria was off like a shot with Dolly calling after her that she wanted tea. Dark and straight up.

"Saw your car in the lot." She stared back at the people staring at us, then sniffed, and took her hat off, setting it on the table beside her. She had bad, dirty-blond, hat hair.

"Well, what did you think of that?" she demanded in what passed as a whisper for Dolly. Her eyes gleamed. A little too bright for comfort. She dipped her head, gave me a conspiratorial smirk, and thumped her broad hands on the tabletop.

"Of what?" I asked.

"Of the state boys taking over."

I shrugged. "They're not. Officer Brent said they don't have the time, though I'd say they've got more resources than you and Lucky."

"Comes to the same thing. You watch. They'll be breathing down our necks. Like they could do it without us. Like they know the people around here. They don't have a clue where to begin. Who to talk to. They went out to see Amanda again, poor woman—like she didn't have enough on her hands already. Then what? They won't know where to go next unless we tell 'em."

"Well, you will, won't you? I mean, you'll all work together. They're trained investigators, after all. You and the chief—well, you're not really used to murder."

Dolly scowled heavily at me. "You think I'm not a trained investigator? You think the chief and me don't handle all kinds of things? Why, just last winter there was a shooting down at the Skunk. Got

38

the guy right away because we know who's fighting who. We went right out and apprehended the culprit…" She hesitated, giving me a hard look. "Anything I say to you here is not for publication. Hope we got that clear right here at the beginning."

I nodded, wondering where she was going with all of this.

"I was thinking." She dipped her head and glared at me. "Because of your problems selling those books of yours, and working for the paper, well, maybe we could, well, kind of work together. The two of us could find out who did this to poor Miz Poet in about half the time it would take alone. I mean, you know old Harry Mockerman, out by you. You got other neighbors. I know the people here in town. I've got some ideas already…"

I smiled. "So you think this experience will sharpen my detective skills? Maybe I'll get a book out of it?"

"I don't know about that." She looked wary now. "And no matter what comes of this, don't you ever put me in one of your damned books. That's not what I mean. I just figured with my detecting skills and your reporting skills—and maybe because you've got the education—we could look into this tragedy and find out what in hell happened to Ruby Poet."

Dolly looked fierce, and dedicated. I wanted to laugh but the little woman was serious.

"Where would we begin?" I asked, willing to hear her out because I was a little short of ideas myself and had to come up with something for Bill.

"I thought maybe we'd start with old Harry, across from you. He'd never give me the time of day if I went there alone, but with you—maybe he saw something, or heard something. He'd tell you, wouldn't he? I mean, I hear he works for you from time to time, so he trusts you."

I nodded then made a decision. It didn't look as though the state police relished giving me information and I wouldn't get much on my own. Maybe, with Deputy Dolly...I sighed. There weren't a lot of choices.

I leaned close after Gloria set a cup of tea in front of Dolly and sauntered off. I was determined to hold up my end, if we were going to do this together. "Gloria was just telling me there's gossip in town about Ruby Poet. That she was some kind of nature worshipper. I guess the pastor at the Church of the Contented Flock preached against what she was doing back sometime this summer. Just before she disappeared."

Dolly only nodded at my news. "I heard all of that gossip. Tempest in a teapot. Ruby Poet didn't even belong to that church. Amanda does, though, and I guess she was incensed for a while, then she and the pastor made peace."

Dolly glanced up at a couple in the next booth who'd been listening. She narrowed one eye at them. They looked away, embarrassed.

Dolly hunkered lower in her seat. "From what I heard Ruby and some friends of hers had a little thing going where they'd gather together in the woods at different times of the year and give thanks to the trees and the clouds and such."

"Like Druidic worship," I said, shaking my head.

"Whatever." Dolly shrugged. "Anyway. Harmless stuff a bunch of old ladies might do. Lucky wanted me to go talk to Miz Poet after Parson Runcival started the uproar with that sermon, but I didn't think it was my place. This is a free country, despite what some people might like to think. The women can do whatever they want out in the woods, as far as I'm concerned. Then Miz Poet wandered off and didn't come back and we figured it was all over anyway."

"What do you think now?" I asked.

40

"Maybe we should go talk to Ruby's friends."

"You know who they are?"

"Maybe one of 'em."

"Look, before I go anywhere with you I've got to call the news-paper."

"But you don't give 'em any of what we've been talking about here. I need to know I can trust you." She narrowed her small eyes at me.

"Just the things I know for sure. Where the head was found. What the woman's name was. Next of kin. Who's working on the case. Facts about the search for her."

"And as we find out things, you're not giving any of it to the paper until we've got it wrapped up. Is that a deal?"

I thought awhile. "I'll have to turn in stories as I go along."

She nodded. "That's fine with me. Just nothing we're working on."

"Dolly," I warned, "I've got a job to do."

Her face turned red. "Me too," she said and then stared down into her tea.

"So, OK," I said.

She nodded, looked up, and stuck her hand across the tabletop at me. "Guess we're partners."

I took the short-fingered hand and shook it one quick time. "Guess so," I said. "We'll start with old Harry. Should go over and warn him anyway, that there'll be men in the woods tomorrow, searching for the rest of Mrs. Poet. He doesn't like strangers in his woods. We don't want him siccing those dogs of his on the police."

"Then there's your other neighbor. Over to Ruffle Pond. Joslyn Henry. We could go talk to her, too."

"Joslyn helped me with my garden my first year up here. She lives with her son, doesn't she? Isn't that Ernie Henry, from the small-engine repair shop?"

"Yup. So, guess we'd better talk to Ernie, too. He can be an odd one. You know, still living at home. In his late thirties. Maybe he didn't like his mother messing with this nature worship stuff. You never know up here. People get to brooding when the winter goes on too long. End up doing things they'd never do otherwise. You'd be surprised at the effects of a bad winter. Seen 'em go stark staring mad from too much snow."

"But this happened in the fall. Or maybe she was killed in the summer."

Dolly shrugged off this brush with logic. "Still, with some it takes a long time to work up the nerve to do what they've been stewing over for months."

"OK." I stretched back and yawned. "I'd like to see Mrs. Henry. When I lost most of my lilies to something I thought were worms I called the local extension agent, down in Kalkaska, and he suggested I drop over and visit Mrs. Henry. 'Retired librarian and gardener par excellence,' he told me. Said she'd help out about the skunks digging in my compost heap and deer eating my roses. I went over there and got a severe case of flower envy when I saw her garden."

"Been there. Beautiful. She's done it for years. Was the president of our local garden club at one time."

"Told me to give those worms—that were really slugs—a mixture of yeast and beer. Told me better yet was to pick 'em off, one by one, and drop them into a can of kosher salt. That's what I've been doing ever since. She told me to plant nasturtiums and foxglove and spiky things the deer don't bother. And she said to use cayenne pepper that would make them sneeze, or buy some fine netting to drape over the flower buds. And she said for me to give up on growing tulips. Deer eat them. She said to try crocuses and daffodils. Nobody eats daffodils. And she told me how to build a wooden fence around my compost."

I'd followed Joslyn Henry's advice and the next year my spring garden fairly glowed with daffodils and crocuses. I didn't go back to see Mrs. Henry after that. I had the feeling she didn't welcome visitors too often and I didn't want to impose. Our only conversations took place when she stopped to talk while I was collecting my mail, or out for a walk. She'd ask about my garden. I'd ask about hers. That was it, though I invited her to drop down any day she wanted. She never had, as far as I knew.

"As I said, she's a friend of Ruby Poet," Dolly was saying. "One of the woods ladies. If she hasn't heard about Ruby Poet yet, well, it will be a favor to break it to her. And just maybe she can tell us more about what was going on in Ruby's life when she disappeared."

I nodded. So, right under my nose: nature worship, firebrand preaching, town taking sides for and against Mrs. Poet. I'd thought I was more a part of Leetsville and life out in the woods than I was. I knew nothing about anything. I wasn't sure how much help I was going to be to Deputy Dolly, but it felt right to be working on a story, and it felt good to stay away from my house until all those bad spirits swirling around out there settled down.

"Let me call in my story," I said, picking up the check for the drinks. "I'll meet you by Harry's driveway in what—half an hour?"

I paid the bill and got a wave and a curious look from Eugenia. There was going to be wild speculation about what was going on after Dolly and I left.

Outside the restaurant, Dolly stuck her hand out to take mine again. I guessed we were sealing our deal though I was already feeling a little uncomfortable.

She waited, hand in the air. I had no choice. I took the hand sticking out too far from the frayed jacket cuff, and shook it solemnly.

"Should we exchange blood?" I asked, though I figured she was too straight arrow to get it.

Dolly frowned, I guess to impress me with the seriousness of our joint undertaking. "Let's hope nobody's going to be losing any more blood. I'll protect you the best I can."

I smiled gratefully. Now I felt safe and secure. Deputy Dolly— my protector. Odd that small chills ran up and down my back, and that the hair along my arms stood on end as she pulled open the sprung door of her police car, got in and drove off, back toward our secret meeting place, a couple of clanks and a cloud of exhaust marking where she'd been.

SIX

OLD HARRY'S DRIVE WAS little more than a wide dirt path through a double row of dead and dying elms; an overgrown lane lined with lethal raspberry bushes, arching branches reaching out to grab at our jackets and tug at our hair. Harry didn't use the driveway for more than walking out to the road, as far as I knew. He owned a vehicle—of sorts. A kind of half-breed he'd put together himself from spare parts, with a black pickup cab for a front, and a flatbed he'd built on the back. He drove over to my place in it when he came to take out a fallen tree, or get a wasp's nest from under my eaves; but always avoiding main roads, taking the old logging roads so Dolly couldn't catch him. On the flatbed of his unique vehicle, Harry kept chain saws and oilcans and rags and even a beekeeper's veiled hat. He was a man equipped at all times to take on any disaster I came up with.

"I've seen Harry's car," Dolly said, as we walked along through a new layer of fallen leaves. "Always gets away before I can check to see if he's got a license on it. Can't be coming in and out this way though. Take a look at this drive."

I was taking a look. Close up, bent halfway over, eyeing the thorns on the branches, burrs on the bushes.

I didn't answer Dolly because I was sure Harry didn't fool with licenses for anything he owned. Not his dogs. Not his hunting. And certainly not that old, slapped-together car. But I wasn't going to help Deputy Dolly look into it. Our partnership stretched only so far. "Lots of last-century logging roads back in the woods for him to get in and out on," I said. "And Shell Oil put in roads to get to the rigs and the pumps they've got going back in these woods. Some of the roads must run behind his property."

"Didn't find oil on your property, did they?" Dolly grinned over her shoulder at me. "You'd be a millionaire if they did. Making millionaires out of some of the damnedest people."

"Don't own the mineral rights," I said. "I think Shell does."

"Yeah, most don't own 'em. Old mining company bought 'em up years ago. Sold 'em to Shell. But you'd be amazed what some of the scrub and sand land is bringing folks who didn't sell out."

While we walked, cussing a few times when the brambles got us, the weather turned again, with the sun going behind the clouds, leaving fumes of cold to scuttle along the ground like tiny goblins. More shadows than I cared to think about slipped in and out around us. I shivered in my denim jacket and told myself it was time for warmer clothes. Sooner than I cared to think about, it would be time to trot out the down jacket, knee-high boots, and the wool cap I pulled over my ears on below-zero mornings when my breath froze into cartoon balloons in front of me.

I'd never been to Harry Mockerman's house. I always left notes in his mailbox, asking him to come repair a screen or a window; come cut a fallen tree. There was something about Harry that didn't invite cozy friendliness. Maybe it was that dead-looking black suit and yellowed shirt he wore day in and day out, season after season. Harry in that funeral suit—with his long gray hair and grizzled face, with almost opaque eyes—could be intimidating. He was old, and skinny as a razor's edge. Never looked at me when he spoke, only down at the ground, always hunting earnestly for something. He'd stand dead still a minute then walk away to examine a thing he'd spotted. When he wandered back, he'd have a leaf in his hand, or a stone, or a piece of some unidentifiable item I didn't want to put a name to. He'd look up at me with his sad, faded blue eyes that were almost lost in his face, folded back in among fossilized wrinkles, and he'd give me a look that was pure question. As in: *Who are you? How'd you get here? Where are we?*

Harry's stubbled chin would start to work then. He chewed thoughts over in his head, and in his mouth. His furry eyebrows would knit together. After a long time maybe I'd get a drawn-out, "*Welllllll now…*"

He looked as if he'd been carved from a single piece of wood, not made of flesh and bone. There was something fixed about him, as if he'd always looked just this way, and there'd never been a different Harry Mockerman. Never a young Harry Mockerman. No past. No future. Just an old man living deep in the woods.

He had, he once told me in a long, drawn-out story that took him the better part of an hour to get out, worked for the Leetsville Logging Company back in the '20s, when he was just a boy. Which would make him close to ninety, I figured. He'd been a log skidder, he'd told me, and went on to tell me things about the lumber camps, with Indians camping on one side, loggers on the other, big stories that took him a long time to get out. A couple of the stories stretched over a two-day job, when he was fixing my dock.

47

Maybe his stories were true. Maybe he was lying, taking pleasure in fooling the city girl, as so many did up here. I'd heard some fantastic tales—ghosts and witches and murder. Through all of them I'd stood in proper appreciation and wonderment, wide-eyed, playing the role I'd been handed.

Harry's dogs, penned up somewhere beyond the house, began to bark wildly when Dolly and I broke out of the bushes and into the clearing where the house stood. Dolly cursed under her breath and pulled brown pickers from her uniform pants. I figured I'd do mine later, when I wouldn't have to be bent over, exposing my vulnerable backside to an empty clearing with dogs barking beyond.

Harry's house was small, tarpapered, and leaning. The front door and sill didn't quite meet. The screen door hung halfway open. Behind the house—what I could see from where I stood—was a group of buildings, each in worse shape than the other. I spotted his hybrid vehicle parked back there beside one of the sheds.

"Think he's home?" Dolly straightened and looked at me. She scrunched her face, then tapped at one of her ears, meaning the barking was too loud.

I shrugged. "Who knows? If he doesn't want to see us, he's long gone by now."

Dolly reached up and slapped, flat-handed, on Harry's screen door. Her knock formed a kind of vacuum with the closed inner door, muting her knocks, making the screen bounce.

"Harry?" I leaned around and called through the screen door with dozens of small tears in it, useless at keeping out our no-see-ums, our mosquitoes, and our killer flies.

"Harry?" I called again. "It's me. Your neighbor, Emily Kincaid. From across the road. Could you come out here a minute? There's been some trouble over at my place and I have a deputy with me.

48

She wants to ask you a few questions. See if you noticed anything or anyone out on the road yester..."

The inner door had opened soundlessly and Harry stood there, framed behind the screen. I stepped back, choking on the words I'd been about to say.

"Geez, Harry," I said, recovering, forcing a smile. "This is Deputy Dolly, with the Leetsville Police. She wants to ask you a few questions. I came along because..."

He pushed the screen door open. Not a word out of Harry. He stood with his head down, examining the cracked linoleum at his feet.

Harry wore his usual shiny black suit, but now he'd wrapped a big white towel around his middle, protecting the suit from something. The strange thing about Harry and that suit of his was that the suit didn't smell. If there'd ever been an odor to Harry it was always a kind of smoked smell, woodsy, like someone who lived year-round with a blazing fire.

Harry held the crooked door wider. Dolly stepped through first, with me behind her. He led the way, without speaking, back through a cluttered but not unclean living room, into the room beyond, a tiny alcove of a kitchen where a simmering enameled pot on a white gas stove sat with its lid bouncing, letting out little vents of good-smelling steam. It was a tiny room. Cluttered, like the living room, but not dirty. Everything in it was old and well used, with either a crack or a yellow patina of age. There was an old-fashioned icebox, with a pan underneath it catching slow drips from melting ice; a white metal table with two ladder-backed chairs; and a single open cupboard made of bare boards and metal uprights. The cupboard held a few dishes, a couple of cups, two pots, and a dozen or more Mason jars.

Harry motioned for us to sit down while he went to the back door, stuck his head out, and yelled "Shut up" at his dogs, who quieted immediately with only an occasional complaining bark or two.

Dolly nervously adjusted her gun belt back and forth, trying to get comfortable on the wooden chair with a cracked seat. "Miz Kincaid here found something pretty awful in her garbage can yesterday morning, Mr. Mockerman." She launched into our reason for coming.

Harry nodded a time or two without looking at her. He picked up a big spoon, went to the stove, and stirred whatever was cooking there. The smell in the room was good. Onions and herbs. He didn't turn around, just stirred, keeping his back hunched over as he minded his pot. We waited.

I knew Harry to be a quiet man, but not this quiet. There seemed something too still about the bent back he kept turned. Harry was afraid. That was obvious. Maybe of us or maybe any woman who dared come into his home. There'd been a professor at U of M like that, a friend of Jackson's. Totally afraid of women, unless he met them out of doors, where he could run. God knows how he managed his classes. Poetry, for heaven's sakes. Of course—because he was good-looking—the class was filled to overflowing with dewy-eyed sprites clutching their spit-worn Emily Dickinsons to fluttering bosoms.

I'm a kind of spit-worn Emily Dickinson, all by myself, since I was named for her, which pretty well sealed my fate, though I married and never wrote poetry and left my father's house when I was eighteen to go away to college. Still—I'd decided early in life that there was something tragic about me, too. I just couldn't quite put my finger on what that tragic thing was since I always seemed so disgustingly ordinary.

Harry stirred. We sat. Dolly sniffed from time to time.

I figured, finally, that it was Dolly and the uniform that were getting to Harry.

"I found a head, Harry," I said as gently as I could. "Somebody put it in my garbage can."

"Don't say." Harry pulled his shoulders up tight to his ears. From time to time, he changed the spoon, one hand to the other, then wiped his free hand on the towel wrapped around his middle.

Dolly cleared her throat. "You see anything up at the road yesterday?"

Harry made a noise and stirred faster, spirals of steam rising around him, spots of liquid flying from the pot, hitting the surface of the stove with soft sizzles, hitting the towel that covered the prized suit.

That stew did smell good. I was willing to bet he'd put some wild leeks in there, and maybe a little wild parsley. If you couldn't say much else for Harry, you had to admit he was a good cook. My mouth was watering.

"Anyway," she said, not admitting defeat. "You know Miz Poet from town? Ruby Poet? Sure you know her, Mr. Mockerman. You grew up around here. You must know just about everybody."

Harry shook his head then. "Nope. Don't know her," he said.

"Come on, Mr. Mockerman." Dolly gave a little, insincere laugh. "After living your whole life here, on this piece of property, in this particular house not five miles out of Leetsville? Why, that's hard to believe."

He shook his head again. Harder this time.

"Harry, you had to know her," I said, keeping my voice very soft. "She disappeared a few weeks ago. It was in the papers and on TV."

"Don't get the paper. Don't got no TV." His voice was gruff, sulky.

"Well, anyway, you knew Ruby Poet." Dolly was exasperated. She got up and stretched as tall as she could get. I got up, too, because it was hard to sit and be as nervous as I was feeling. "Everybody knew her. It was her head, though she had no business turning up in Emily's garbage can."

"Oh," was all she managed to get out of him.

"You see anybody around Emily's garbage can yesterday after the truck went by? You up by the road at all?"

A very slow, thoughtful shake of Harry's head.

"Strange cars around? Somebody out walking?"

Harry appeared to think hard again, as if he was really trying to help, then shook his head. "Seen nothing. Weren't up to the road all day yesterday. Nope. Nowhere near the road. Not all day. I was busy here, in my house."

"Garbage day," I said.

"Forgot to take my bag out," he said.

"I thought I saw you, or somebody, in your drive …"

Harry whipped his head around to give me a long, hard look. I supposed I was breaking some kind of code of the woods, saying anything, bringing trouble to his door. I stopped and added feebly, "I'm probably wrong. A bird or something …"

"Lots a crows," he agreed as he moved away from the stove to the open shelf and took down a quart Mason jar. He got himself a big metal ladle, went back to the stove, and began dipping the soup or stew or whatever into the jar in his hand. When the jar

52

was full, he found a metal screw top and lid and set those in place. He screwed the jar shut as Dolly and I waited, at a loss for words, while he pulled a dishtowel from the table and carefully wiped the jar dry.

"What are you making?" I motioned toward the pot, sensing we'd better prepare to leave or end up standing there all day staring at Harry's silent back.

"Possum stew," he said, turning and holding the jar out to me. "I would a brought it over later."

I took it, reluctantly. "You get a possum this morning?"

Harry nodded and gave a fleeting, crooked smile. "Yup."

"So, you been out hunting?" Dolly drew herself up to full height.

"Nope. Don't hunt outta season. It came to the door. They sometimes do that." Harry shook his head emphatically but he still didn't look either one of us in the eye. "Sometimes walk right up here and drop dead."

The jar in my hands was hot. I set one palm on top of the lid and slid the corner of my jacket under the bottom. I had to get out fast or I'd end up burned. I backed across the room, thanking Harry as I went. Dolly, though she wasn't happy about learning nothing, followed me through the living room and out the screen door, Harry trailing along behind. The dogs, in back, began to bark again. I could imagine them straining at their leashes, teeth bared, mouths foaming.

In the doorway, Dolly turned as if remembering something. "Oh," she said over the barking. She gave Harry a big smile. "Just to warn you. There'll be men out here searching the woods tomorrow. Don't want you to be surprised if you see a lot of people wandering around."

Harry looked Dolly straight in the face. His eyes popped wide. "Searching for what?" he demanded.

"For the rest of Miz Poet, of course. Got to be more of her somewhere. These woods the logical place now."

Harry didn't say another word. He wasn't happy with the thought of men in his woods. In the spring Harry was busy, from the middle of May until late June, chasing mushroom hunters off his property. Now he was faced with the prospect of hordes of men, in uniform, stepping on his illegal traps and stomping over his mushroom grounds. We left an unhappy Harry Mockerman behind us.

Out in the weedy drive, I juggled the jar of stew from hand to hand. Dolly leaned toward me and whispered, "Harry's lying, you know."

"About knowing Mrs. Poet? Well, of course. Living here all his life, he had to ..."

"No, I mean about not being out to the road."

"What do you mean?"

She pointed at the jar I was clutching. "Possum," she said. "There was one beside the road when I got here yesterday. Remember?"

"But that was yesterday. The crows got it by now."

Dolly gave me a look. "You want to bet? I know these old woodsmen. That possum cooking in that pot didn't walk right up and drop dead at his door." She shook her head and dodged a huge raspberry bush. "And about the crows. He said 'lots of crows.' How'd he know if he wasn't out to the road some time or other?"

"He could've heard them."

"Way back there?" she motioned over her shoulder, back toward the house. "Un-uh. I think he saw 'em."

"Shy man. Maybe he just doesn't want anything to do with the whole business. Lots of people like that up here." I didn't like thinking ill of Harry.

We stepped out from the bushes to the pavement. Dolly gestured toward the empty road. No crows. No head. No garbage can. No possum.

"See," she said, giving me a knowing look. "Possum's gone."

"Crows got it," was all I said. I turned to look back toward Harry's place. There was a shadow down the path again. Not a deer. Not a bird. Something. Definitely something.

I looked at the jar in my hands and decided I wouldn't be eating this stew. It had smelled good, cooking back there in Harry's kitchen, but now I had an idea where it came from, and just the thought— the dead possum on one side of the road, dead Ruby Poet on the other—took my appetite away.

SEVEN

OUR NEXT STOP WAS Joslyn and Ernie Henry's house. Mother and son. Down the road about a mile, and another half mile in. Close by Ruffle Pond.

The narrow lane into their house ran through daylight turned golden by tall yellow and red maples swaying like hula dancers in the mild, southern wind. As Dolly drove closer, glints of sunlight sparkled off the pond.

Dolly negotiated the ruts and mud holes in the curving road with precision. I guessed she didn't want to damage another police car. All that was left for her to patrol, should she get in trouble again, were the two-track logging roads deep in the woods.

The pond was wild and shallow, almost circular, with a sandy shore. We passed along the far side, the road circling around toward the Henry's tall, plain farmhouse.

We lurched past the south edge of the pond just as a flock of geese lifted off the water, honking their hearts out as they headed up and over the trees. I couldn't help mumbling something about rats leaving the sinking ship. I loved to see the birds return in spring, but fall was another thing entirely. I saw it as desertion. As the worst kind of cowardice.

Joslyn Henry's house was as I remembered it, standing in an open space surrounded by woods. The house itself was as simple as an Amish farmer. Pale green, with a long and wide front porch where three rockers stood in a line, all rocking slightly in a non-existent breeze. Around the house were gardens: wide beds; some forked over and raked; some filled with bright and dull, yellow and rust, mums; some with purple asters. We parked and walked straight up through the center of the garden, up broad green steps to the porch. Dolly knocked.

I saw the lace door curtain twitch back, then fall into place. I hadn't seen a face looking out, but there was definitely someone home.

Dolly knocked again. This time the inner door opened and Joslyn Henry stood there, half hidden behind the door, peering out at us through the screen. The woman frowned, hung back. Not a bit friendly. If anything, I would have said Joslyn Henry was wary of me and my uniformed friend.

"Yes?" she said, and opened the door a bit wider when she saw who it was. There was still no invitation in her voice, no smile on her long, wary face.

Her hair was piled up into a loose, floppy topknot. She wore a flowered house dress with a coat sweater over it. Today she looked her seventy or so years, unlike the vital Joslyn Henry I'd met before.

"What can I help you with?" Mrs. Henry said, as if we were Jehovah's Witnesses.

"It's me," I said. "Emily Kincaid. Your neighbor." I leaned around Dolly and smiled wide to show how harmless I was.

"Sure, I know you, Emily. Not senile yet."

The screen door stayed closed. I stood with an inane smile pasted on my face. "This is Deputy Dolly ... eh ..."

"Wakowski." Dolly leaned forward and gave her last name. "We met before, Miz Henry. I think I gave your son Ernie a ticket once. Came here 'cause he got mad and tore it up and I didn't want his temper getting him in trouble. But that's neither here nor there. Thing is, Emily, here, found something strange in her garbage can yesterday morning and we're kind of going around to the neighbors, wondering if you saw anything odd out by the road. Some person not supposed to be hanging around."

"What was it, Emily?" Mrs. Henry asked me, ignoring Dolly. I got the impression that what I had to say wasn't going to come as a surprise. From her frozen face and icy voice, I figured Mrs. Henry knew about Ruby Poet and had already been crying.

"It was a human head, Mrs. Henry," I said, though I was still talking through her screen door and wondering why. Must be Dolly's uniform again, I thought. We were going to have to split up to talk to people, or Dolly was going to have to think about a wardrobe change.

Mrs. Henry caught her breath and put a hand to her mouth. She put her other hand out to steady herself in the doorway, forcing the door open a little more. If she would only have unlocked the damned screen, I could have helped her. Whatever her reason for the unfriendly behavior, she was on her own handling her surprise—if it was a surprise.

"Whose head was it?" she asked when she could take a deep breath again.

58

"Ruby Poet's," Dolly said with a bluntness that made me uncomfortable. "You must've known Miz Poet, didn't you?"

Again, Mrs. Henry had to hold on to the doorjamb. She made a noise and shook her head, as if she were clearing it. "Oh, no," she said. "So it's true. Poor Ruby. Oh my. Who would do such a thing to our beloved Ruby? Oh dear. Oh dear." She put both hands to her mouth and really cried.

"Now, come on, Ma." Ernie, a short, thick, little man who usually wore overalls with an oily rag sticking from the back pocket, appeared from somewhere behind her and clucked first at her, then at me and Dolly. "Flora Coy called earlier about Miz Poet. Ma's really upset. Maybe you better come around another time."

"Well, now, Ernie, could you answer a couple of questions?" Dolly pushed on.

"Neither one of us saw a thing." Ernie, hanging behind in the shadows, shook his head. Joslyn Henry stepped back. She was bent almost in half, sobbing.

"If you'd let us in ..."

"Come on, Deputy. You can see for yourself this isn't a good time. I'd better take care of my mother. Miz Poet was her friend. You need to know anything, you come back another day, OK?"

"Of course," I said, putting a hand on Dolly's arm. She was pretty stiff and determined.

"Were you out to the road yesterday morning, Ernie?" Dolly whipped out her notebook and tried looking official, while pulling away from me.

"Yes, I was. Putting out the garbage. That's all. We've got a wire cage by the road. That way I don't have to fool with garbage cans, just drive the bags out."

"You see anybody? Anything different? See somebody hanging around?" Dolly said.

Ernie shook his head and took a swipe at his nose. "Not a soul." His voice was shaky. The woman behind him moved out of sight. I could hear her sobbing and felt sorry for both son and mother. I wanted to get out of there.

"Anybody in the area been acting strange lately?" Dolly was pressing on. I grabbed her arm again. "What about that time Parson Runcival, took exception to what was goin'..."

I pulled hard now. She glared at me. I glared back.

"That was nothing. Ma's got friends, is all. Maybe you should go talk to Mary Margaret over to the funeral home. She was in the group with Ma. Or even Flora Coy. There's another one."

"Sorry, Ernie," I said. "Tell your mother I feel bad for her trouble. We'll come back another time, if you don't mind. When your mother's doing better."

Ernie nodded. "Sure. If that's necessary. Terrible thing that's happened. Probably some awful accident. Happens to old people I guess. That's why I'm always warning Ma about being out by the pond, the way they are. Never know."

We backed off the porch and down the steps, Dolly sputtering at me, and warning me to take my hand off of her.

"By the way," Ernie called after us, holding the outer door wider now. "If you go see Amanda, tell her we got the news and that we're sorry for her loss. Tell her we'll be in to visit when things calm down out here. OK? Will you do that for us?"

I waved, assuring Ernie we'd deliver his message if we could.

The inner door closed slowly on Ernie Henry. I heard the lock click behind him. Both of the Henrys weren't feeling hospitable and I didn't blame them. After all, these people didn't have reporters and police coming to their door every day. I understood their reluctance to talk. I hoped everybody up here wouldn't feel the same, or Dolly and I were going to get nowhere.

EIGHT

"Probably one of the dying ones," Dolly said, shaking her head as we walked back through Mrs. Henry's garden, to the car. She pointed to a tall, old maple at the edge of the woods. "If you know anything about trees, the ones that are going to die will be the best and brightest one year and the next they're nothing but sticks. Guess if you're gonna go that's the best way. One last blast of color."

I agreed, though I found nothing particularly encouraging about going out in a blast of color, or any other way, for that matter. Not at that moment, when death seemed to be our only topic of conversation. Deputy Dolly Wakowski certainly had a dark side to her.

"Lots of women like Miz Henry, up here," Dolly was saying very low and confidentially, as we climbed back into her police car. "Widowed early. Left with her son, Ernie ... geez, the guy must be almost forty. Never married. Stays home with mama. I hear he's kind of tight with a dollar. Probably doesn't want a wife."

"They're both afraid of something," I said.

"Whew," Dolly whistled. "You can say that again. All of 'em. Harry Mockerman. These folks. Something's really spooked 'em.

Never know. People who live alone back in these woods...well, you just never know. They get funny, being alone too much."

"I live alone back in these woods," I said, yet one more time, taking umbrage at her blanket judgment of us all. "Only sensible way to get along. Keep to yourself."

"I suppose you'd feel like that," Dolly said, watching the rear-view mirror as she backed her way out to a turnaround. "You've got that in you. Probably end like the rest of them: old, eccentric, a little nutty. Or, maybe you'll get it in gear and write a good mystery for a change."

"And maybe you'll stop crashing police cars; and get off patrolling these back roads; and do something better with your life than chase innocent people, and give them tickets."

Dolly made a face and gave me what I could only describe as a malevolent smile. Her washed-out blue eyes crinkled with tiny lines at their corners. For a thirty-some-year-old woman, Dolly was already getting the skin of middle-age. Too much frowning, I thought. Too many long faces. Too much sauntering up to pulled-over cars and smiling tight, mean smiles.

"Sorry if I touched a nerve." Dolly braked, and turned full at me, one small hand flying up. Her slightly cock-eyed, blue eyes looked polished. "I don't know when to shut my mouth. Emily, you're helping me out here and I know it. What you do with your life is none of my damned business. It's just me. That's the way I am. Not that I want to be like this. I wish to God I could learn to shut up. But I don't think people should be alone all the time."

"Now that you've gone through all of that, you'd better be ready to tell me you live a happy life with husband and kids," I grumbled. "You better live where the birds sing and butterflies flit, and hummingbirds sit on your shoulder."

She gave me a look, then threw back her head and laughed. "Yup. That's it. You just described my life."

She let the brake up and headed back to my place.

"I'll bet you're a really good writer, Emily," she said as we neared my drive. "I mean, I've never known anybody who wrote anything but letters and checks before. You're probably a lot smarter than I am. Maybe that's my problem with you. It's like you're looking down at me. I've only been out of Leetsville a couple of times in my life. I don't know…eh…the things you know. I didn't go to college, like you."

Taken by surprise, I began to laugh. Being with Dolly Wakowski was like traveling on a very wild conversational roller coaster. Up. Down. All over the place.

"What do you mean 'looking down at you'?" I asked. "I'm trying to keep up with you. I don't even know what we're doing. I should be working on my next really awful mystery. Instead, here I am annoying my neighbors. Probably just made enemies for life, thanks to you."

She gave a small chuckle, the most mirth I'd seen from her since our first traffic ticket together. She stopped behind where I'd left my car and leaned over the steering wheel. "So what've we got?" she asked.

"A lying Harry Mockerman and a frightened Joslyn Henry. Oh, and a very nervous Ernie Henry," I said.

"What's it all about, do you think?"

I shrugged. "An old woman's been killed. Will Chief Barnard tell you what the coroner says about the head? I mean, what he finds—how she was killed, how long ago?"

Dolly nodded. "The chief'll tell us whatever they tell him. He'd be doing this himself if it wasn't for Charlie, his little boy. He's in

Munson Hospital, in Traverse. An operation, though the kid's only seven. Some heart thing he was born with. So, the chief's busy and we're it. Anyway, he told me he's afraid it won't end with old Miz Poet. I mean, no reason for her to be killed. None in the world. But somebody's taken exception to something the lady did. And if it's this dancing in the woods stuff, well, there's others that could be in trouble."

"I doubt that has anything ..."

"You don't know though, do you?" Dolly snapped around to look hard at me. "You don't know and I don't know and the chief doesn't know and we're charged with keeping the people safe. That's our job."

I nodded. Well, that was her job. As for me, maybe I'd just as soon leave it to the state police investigators. I'd already pissed off three of my neighbors by prying. Now I wanted to get back to my house, put on some good music, cook an omelet for dinner, open a bottle of white wine, and lull myself into oblivion.

"Mind if I come with you?" Dolly motioned toward my drive. She watched me, maybe reading my mind and knowing I wanted to get rid of her.

"I've got to pee bad," she said, and she gave me a pained look so I'd believe her.

That wasn't the kind of request you denied, so I got out and drove down ahead of her. I parked next to the house and motioned Dolly in next to my car.

She surprised me by peeing and leaving right afterward.

"I'll call you in the morning with anything I find out," she said, standing with one foot in the police car. "If you're still interested by then."

I left it there. I had to call the state police to get what they were giving out to the press, and call another story into Bill. Maybe that would be the extent of my involvement from here on, I thought. I was beginning to feel a little silly—doing this sleuthing thing with my girl chum, Deputy Dolly. Maybe it was time to get back to my real purpose in life—writing the crappy mystery. Wasn't that enough to handle? I asked myself, as I stood waving to Dolly, who backed up and out my driveway too fast through my fragile birch trees.

I went in to check my machine for messages and discovered a message from Jackson Rinaldi. Yuck, I thought as I listened to the familiar affected drone. "Emily. It's Jackson. Give me a call when you get in, will you? I've something to ask you. A favor—maybe— if you can find it in your heart ..."

Here he gave a phony little laugh, as if I could deny him, would deny him; as if any woman could. "Well, it will be wonderful to speak to you anyway. It's been a long time. I've always thought of us as friends, no matter how difficult you made things ..." I hit the button and cut him off.

Drivel. Enough for more than a single phone message. Jackson took up more time and more space than a decent person should. Hell if I'd call him. Let him call me. No, better yet—let him not call me and live with the fact I didn't care enough to pay attention.

I stomped around the house long enough to cool off then went to the phone and got the number of the Michigan State Police in Gaylord, over toward the middle of the state. Officer Brent wasn't there but I was referred to an Officer Chamberlain who gave me the pat story of the Poet investigation—everything I already knew. I hung up and called Lucky Barnard but he wasn't in either, at least

66

nobody was answering the Leetsville Police Department's phone, which seemed strange since he and Dolly were the only law for many miles around. I made some notes, then called the paper, and gave Bill Corcoran all the information I had—not very much. I did put in a few quotes from Harry Mockerman and one from Ernie Henry. Just the usual about being shocked; how wonderful a woman Mrs. Poet was. That sort of thing. He was still concerned enough about me to offer to come out if I needed help. I said I didn't, that I'd be fine. When I hung up, my duty done, I sat looking down at the phone awhile then picked it up and dialed the familiar number of my old house in Ann Arbor. I waited through three rings and then came his voice on the machine, asking me to please leave him a message and he would get back to me as soon as time permitted.

"Bastard," I muttered under my breath, half hoping the machine caught it. "This is Emily returning your call." Bang. Nothing else. No message. No encouragement. No *"Call me, please, oh please, oh please, will ya, huh?"*

I had at least an hour before I'd be starving and, since I was deeply depressed, I didn't want to let myself eat until it was safe. If I opened the refrigerator at that moment I'd gobble everything in sight then head back to Leetsville, to the nearest market, and buy more to gobble. It wasn't that I put on weight after these binges, I usually didn't. It was that I made myself sick. Instead, I planned a lovely omelet dinner and a jug of wine, a hunk of bread ... though, blissfully, there was no *"thou, beside me. Singing in the wilderness."*

I went out to my studio to work awhile on the book, which loomed larger and larger in my consciousness. I'd decided to focus on writing, and not think about dead heads, and strange-acting

67

neighbors, and certainly not odd little female deputies with gun belts.

My studio was the size of a small garage. Plain. Undecorated. Wooden. A single open room with windows looking out on a small meadow where I could watch deer chase each other; and once I'd seen a coyote passing through; and once a mother fox with her kits. It was a good place to work and a good place to do nothing but stand at the window and look out—a thing I did a lot of, calling it "mental writing."

Elbows on the window sill was a terrific position, I'd found, for musing. My best stuff came from watching the meadow, and sometimes observing a spider weave a web in a corner of the window, and sometimes lying on my back on my ragged old futon, watching the ceiling, hoping inspiration would droppeth like "*the gentle rain from heaven.*"

During this hour, when it wasn't dark yet, in the still time before the sun went down, when the world held its breath and noises were embarrassing and alien, I decided my New York writer needed a male detective to counter her. Maybe they'd even fall in love. Martin Gorman, his name would be, I told myself, while lying on my futon contemplating nothing. He would be a man with a checkered past. A man with one divorce and a few troubles in his work. I would get him in deep with the seductive writer he'd be investigating. I needed a bar scene. Maybe Martin was going to take up drinking again, or he would have a fight with somebody. I wanted him to appear more and more unstable so people thought he wasn't to be trusted.

I didn't feel like putting myself into a smoky bar right then. Anyway, my troubles with the dead head and with my neighbors seemed a whole lot worse than Martin Gorman's. I was in no mood to write. All I seemed capable of was listening to the trees make a buzzing sound like electricity running through wires. But maybe it was only my ears, and the quiet of being so alone.

NINE

When the phone on my desk rang, I was grateful. Anybody—I didn't care who was on the other end of the line. Somebody to bring me out of my dark funk. I got up from the futon where I'd been lying for over an hour and picked up the phone.

"Emily?"

Oh Lord, I'd forgotten about Jackson. I should have amended my wish: anybody but Jackson Rinaldi.

"Jackson here. Emily. This is you, right?"

Jackson's voice tended to rise when he got miffed, which, with me, had been most of the time, because I tended not to play along with his latest illusion of himself. Today he was sounding terribly, terribly British.

"Yes, Jackson," I muttered. "It's me."

"Oh, yes, so good to hear your voice. How are you?"

"Fine. And you?" As if I gave a rat's...

"Fine, too. I saw Sylvia King the other day, and she asked for you, and I was ashamed to say I hadn't spoken to you in a while. I've been remiss in checking on you, haven't I? I mean, up there in the wilds, alone, the way you are. I'm really very sorry I haven't been in touch. I was in England for most of the summer. You recall I wrote you I was going? Went with two friends. Do you remember Wilfred and Margaret Fletcher? I don't think you knew them. They came after the divorce. Anyway, Will and Margaret and I traveled together ... "

I knew of the Fletchers, all right. He in psychology and she in history. A kind of *Who's Afraid of Virginia Woolf* couple. I couldn't have wished Jackson better traveling companions. *Oh, what a fun trio*, was all I could think.

Jackson went on about his trip to England and I zoned out, watching the trees outside my window do a kind of tethered dance when the wind sprang up after the quiet time. Leaves blew around in manic dances. The voice at the other end became a kind of wire-buzz, something beyond the scope of human hearing. Instead, I heard Nina Simone singing that Bob Dylan song about breaking like a little girl. What a haunting voice that woman had. Like a saw against my skin, along my nerves, diving into memory.

"Keats country, of course," Jackson went on. "'*When I have fears that I may cease to be; Before my pen has glean'd my teeming brain; Before high piled books, in charact'ry; Hold like rich garters the full-ripen'd grain ...*'"

"That's 'garners,' Jackson. Not 'garters,'" I corrected him, and heard myself sigh.

"Of course. Of course. Misspoke myself." He gave a strained laugh. "And how's your writing going? Still working on one of your little books?"

You know how sometimes your back teeth can ache? Like you're getting a long needle into your gums? That's how Jackson's conde-scension got to me. I knew better than to call him on it or we'd be on the phone for hours with him apologizing and going on about his own work on Chaucer and "Of course the world needs lighter work, too, Emily. Like yours. I didn't mean …"

Some circles are worn so deep into the mud you only hit bedrock. I'd struck bedrock a long time ago with Jackson.

"Anyway," he nervously covered my long silence, "I was wondering if you might be up to a little company next weekend?"

"Who?"

"*Emily*." He sounded hurt. "Me, of course."

"Why?"

"Because I've missed you. Because it's about time …"

"And?" I demanded, knowing we hadn't gotten anywhere near his real reason as yet.

"Well, I'm taking a sabbatical and thought of locating up there. You always seemed to think it the best writing territory. I mean, look at Jim Harrison, after all."

The tendency was to snap, *You're no Jim Harrison.* But I didn't.

"I'll be doing my Chaucer book and will definitely need a place where nothing goes on."

Hmmm, I thought. This might not be that place …

"Maybe you can help me find a cottage to rent. I mean—six months or so."

"You don't mean close to me!"

"I wouldn't camp on your doorstep, if that's what you're afraid of." He sounded deeply hurt. My female guilt stirred.

"I'll call Saturday, from Grayling, for directions. Two-ish, OK?"

I agreed, hung up, and thought: OK, Saturday. *Two-ish.*

I got down to writing but found I was doing some very nasty things to Martin Gorman. In fact, I had him falling off the wagon so hard he was out for a couple of days and when he awoke, *His head feels like a pumpkin the day after Halloween; like somebody's been carving on it, making a jack-o'-lantern out of him.*

And I thought, *Yes, oh yes.* That's exactly how Mr. Gorman should be feeling. And then I wondered if I should let him live at the end of the book. Hmm. Or maybe something else. The ultimate threat. Castration. What a dandy word. Martin Gorman as eunuch. I had to stop myself before I'd drawn and quartered poor Gorman, because I'd made him look too much like Jackson. I went back to the window where I could look out on the wild leaves blowing in the wind and get the evil meanness out of my soul—yet again.

The thermometer attached to the outside of the window said thirty-nine degrees. It looked as though the benign part of fall was almost over. Next came the first blasts of winter—maybe even a little snow. And then a few warm days before the real cold settled in with a vengeance. Ice storms. Snow piled up over the window sills. I hugged myself and shivered, though the little gas fireplace in the room behind me kept me fairly warm.

Over the last week, I'd heard predictions in town of a bad winter, snow, ice, wind that would howl and curse every human being in its path. Thinking of the predictions depressed me even more than Jackson and Martin Gorman did. Each year in autumn I made myself miserable worrying about the electricity going out and me freezing to death; or ice on the drive so I couldn't get to buy food—and me starving to death. I thought of long dark days, seeing nobody, hearing from nobody, me going crazy. I stood there and felt sorry for myself. Poor me—all alone. Jackson coming to visit. Dead heads in my garbage cans. Could life get any worse?

Emily Dickinson knew it . . .

> *There's a certain slant of light,*
> *on winter afternoons,*

73

> *That oppresses, like the weight*
> *of cathedral tunes…*

Oh yes—that *certain slant of light. Cathedral tunes…*
And Jackson Rinaldi.
Truly oppressive.

I took a really deep sigh, one that could be the beginning of a series of sighs. I thought thoughts Dolly had planted—about growing old alone, becoming like Mrs. Henry, tending my flowers, watching soap operas, speculating about the weather, reacting with fear to strangers. Then I thought of my Brazilian friend, Erica Weick's, poem:

> *As it stands,*
> *I do not wish to have a nation in me*
>   *no more.*
>
> *As it stands,*
> *I do not wish to be a city*
> *(urban legends to soothe me)*
>   *no more.*
>
> *Brick on brick I wish for open ended walls*
> *to meet the breeze on swaying grasses,*
>   *in open fields*
>   *the sweat and speed of common labor,*
> *the piercing thought of thought in common,*
>   *the common bond*
>   *the common beat of human heart.*
>
> *And given that I will then create*
>   *a nation of one with my surroundings…*

Her words often roamed around in my head. She was so right. "... *a nation of one* ..."

Something so much deeper than Jackson or the newspaper. Something atavistic. What is it really that can drive a woman away from others? Maybe a low tolerance for disappointment. Maybe a need to think without interruption. Sometimes living like a rock isn't a bad thing. Three years now of rock living and still I hadn't had my fill. I was where I needed to be. Maybe in the next few years, when my money got low. Maybe then.

But not yet. "*I do not wish to be a city ... no more.*"

How I missed friends like Erica, since I'd moved up here and she had moved to Maryland; but how I would miss this place, should I ever have to leave.

Back up at the house, while my omelet formed in the pan, a glass of wine sat waiting, and my slice of nutty bread, from Bay Bakery in Traverse City, rested on a pink place mat on the counter, I put on Mozart's *Requiem*. Long, slow, mordant music. Perfect for my mood.

I sat at the counter and ate to the "Kyrie." On to the "Sequentia," as I sat on the couch with a second glass of wine. "Offertorium." "Sanctus." "Benedictus." Third glass. "Agnus Dei." "Communio." Fourth glass.

After that I must have closed my eyes for a minute or two because it was 3 a.m. by the kitchen wall clock when I awoke. There was a noise on my porch, a scuffling, a thud—as if something had been thrown at my door. Then nothing.

It took a few seconds to locate where the noise came from, then another few minutes to get up and walk straight. I flipped on the porch light and looked out. Nothing, though I thought I saw a figure scuttling off behind my car. An animal. Dark was the time of the animals—when they wandered close to houses looking for food. But not a time when they knocked, I told myself as I carefully opened the door. I was going to step outside, holler at whoever or whatever was in the drive, and chase them off. Maybe a bear, I warned myself, not opening the door too far. Maybe a raccoon—those guys were bold enough to knock.

I was looking for something small and furry when I glanced down at the porch. Something alive and hungry, at the least. I didn't expect what I saw. I didn't expect a long, naked arm with the hand turned up, cupped and begging.

TEN

My house was full of cops. More people than I'd ever had in there, like a party I didn't want to throw. Local cops. State cops. The sheriff. Even Dolly came when the chief called her because, he said, he thought I might need a woman around after what had been happening to me.

It wasn't a "Dolly" kind of woman I felt the need of right then. More a mother, a nurturer, I was wanting. Some calm soul who would put her arms around me and say, *Don't worry, dear. Everything's going to be all right.* Somebody who would pat my back and commiserate with me, then turn to all the big, insensitive men and ask them to, *Please, have some consideration here.*

But I got Dolly, who growled, in that thin voice of hers, about getting out of bed in the middle of the night to come hold my hand just because I found another body part, and she didn't see that it mattered all that much anyway, because hadn't I already discovered a head in my garbage can and, was it only her, or did it seem I either attracted strange objects to me, or maybe I was mixed up in this in some way I didn't realize? Which irritated me. I forgot to be feminine and distraught and afraid, so maybe her form of consoling was better for me after all.

"I'd say somebody was pulling an awful joke on you," Lucky Barnard said when he was back in my living room, assuring me the "thing" was gone from my side porch. "Except that the other … er … part belonged to Miz Poet, I'd think for sure it was some sicko digging up graves. But we know it's not that."

"You don't think this is a sicko?" I demanded, incredulous.

"The chief didn't mean that exactly." Dolly stuck her two cents in. She was dressed in her full, ill-fitting uniform although it was now about 4 a.m. I could visualize her leaping out of bed when she got the call and into her police uniform—standing in the corner—then flying out her door.

"No, Emily, what I was saying was it looks like somebody's targeting you for a reason. Beyond me. You know anybody up here who might have it in for you?"

"Me and Ruby Poet?"

"Well, she's dead. You're still alive," he said.

Oh, nice encouraging thought.

"Usually I hear about feuds back here in the woods." Dolly shook her head. "Never heard of anybody didn't like Emily."

She sucked at her bottom lip and thought some more. I smiled, grateful for this much—to know I wasn't generally known as a pariah.

"Er, Emily…" The chief rubbed his hands together, very uncomfortable. "We heard back from the coroner. I don't like even saying this right now—with what's happened to you here tonight—but I think I've got to. If you write it in the paper, well, that's up to you. I suppose you have to. Anyway, Channel 9 and 10's been on it already."

I waited, curled up at one end of my sofa, covered with an afghan because I'd been shivering and shaking since the gruesome discovery on my porch. I sensed more bad news was coming and looked over to Dolly who sat across from me, head down, hands clasped between her knees.

"It seems that the idea I had, you know, about Miz Poet maybe being found in the woods by an animal, after wandering off and dying? Well, I wasn't completely right on that one."

"We know that." I frowned at him. "No animal put the damned thing in my garbage can."

"Well, yes, that's true." The man stretched his neck, trying to make himself comfortable enough to deliver his next bad news. "Anyway, the coroner said there were teeth marks in the skin. Something—a coyote maybe—dug it up 'cause there's evidence of burial. But, well, this is the hard part. Though he can't tell the cause of death—so maybe it's still natural causes—well, it seems the head itself was cut from the body with what he thinks was a saw. Definite saw marks on the spinal column. Couldn't tell anything from the skin itself—too decayed . . ."

I put up my hand. I had all the details I could tolerate.

He shrugged. "Won't know about the arm until the coroner looks it over. Their lab will do fingerprints—if they can. Don't imagine it's anybody else's but Miz Poet's. Seems parts of her are going to keep turning up."

"This is crazy," I said. I was scared out of my mind. "A maniac killer's running around out there and now he's focused on me."

"Well," Chief Barnard lowered his voice, tucked his chin into his shirt collar, and gave me a direct and earnest look. "Deputy Wakowski, here, is going to stay with you the rest of tonight. She'll go on staying as long as you need her."

"Until I can sell my house and leave, you mean," I said.

"Emily." Dolly reached down and patted me on one covered knee in what I took to be the height of commiseration. "We're going to get whoever's doing this, and find out what really happened to Ruby Poet."

"I hope nobody thinks I had anything to do with her death." The thought struck me that even I'd be somewhat suspicious of me by now.

"Of course not. Not at all." Maybe Dolly was just a little too soothing.

I nodded, inexplicably grateful for her offer to stay. I definitely didn't want to be left alone and vulnerable to another noise at my door, another present left, maybe in my shed or in my car.

Dolly saw the chief and the other men out the door to their cars. I was alone after that, with every light in the house on, plus the radio and the TV—which was only buzzing, and all the shades and blinds and drapes pulled tight across the windows.

Dolly walked back in and the house was suddenly much too quiet. Her heavy boots echoed across my wood floor. She clanked as I'd never noticed her clanking. But the noise and clanking were good things—meant shit-kicking boots and a gun. If I was going to remain cowering on the sofa—as I had every intention of doing—somebody had better be on duty.

"You want coffee or something?" Dolly stood halfway between the living room and the kitchen, obviously uncomfortable now that she was out of her police role and into that of caretaker or, God forbid, friend.

I thought tea would be the thing and, wanting to save myself the effort of explaining where everything was, got up and made tea for both of us. I brought out a package of Mama Ida's biscotti.

Even tragedy and fear called for some form of sugar. Dolly settled herself on a stool with only a little fine-tuning of her holster. Her plain face was blank. There was plenty going on behind it.

I set the teapot between us, along with the only matching cups and saucers I had. My mother's china had taken a beating the night I told Jackson to go screw himself (instead of his eighteen-year-old student), and threw most of it at his head, fortunately missing with these few cups and saucers.

I poured. Dolly lifted her cup and sipped delicately, little finger in the air, which I found ludicrous considering the hardware she was packing and the big metal badge stuck on her dumpy chest.

"Ya know, Emily." She looked up slyly. "I sure wish you liked me better. Ya know, trusted me more."

"I like you, Dolly," I lied. "I've been under a big strain here. If I'm not wildly friendly, well…"

"Nah, I think it's those three tickets I gave you."

"Well…," I said.

"You probably think I should've given you a warning. At least the first time."

I shrugged and sipped at the tea, happy to hide behind a wisp of steam.

"Yes," I finally said. "You should've. At least the first time. You are a little overbearing, you know."

I expected an angry comeback. Dolly sipped her tea. She said nothing, just sat there, a small woman pretending to be a big woman.

Since I was shivering, despite the hot tea, I went over and got the Christmas afghan, with Father Christmas on it, and wrapped myself up again. The kind of cold I felt sank right into my bones. Nothing to do with temperature. My house was plenty warm. More to do with the places fear could burrow.

"Are you married, Dolly?" I asked, from my afghan nest, realizing I'd spent an entire day with her and knew nothing about her life.

"No, I'm not." She shook her head. "Was once. When I was nineteen. Lasted a few months and he was gone. Never did hear where he got to. I think we're still married, unless there's a statute of limitations or something. Wouldn't know him if I saw him tomorrow. How about you?"

"Was once."

"That's what I heard," she said. "To some professor at U of M who cheated on you with his students. Sounds like a lousy bastard."

Hmm, I thought. Some kind of special intelligence gathering system up here. I tried to recall anybody I'd told this much to and couldn't. Maybe Simon had divined all this information from my mail. Maybe the garbage guy—from my garbage. Maybe some old friend, coming through town, had confided in everybody at Fuller's EATS. Amazing, I thought, not in resentment, but in awe. It was like living among the fairies. Life among the Little Folk. I would have hummed something from *Finian's Rainbow* if I knew any of the music.

"He's coming to visit this weekend," I said before I knew I was going to say anything.

"Why?" She turned toward me and made a face. "You're divorced, right?"

I nodded. "He's looking for a place up here in the woods. Something isolated, alone, to rent. He's taking a sabbatical to write a book."

"Geez. You're all writing books. Is that all you people know how to do?"

I let that go. "If you know of somebody willing to rent…"

82

"Why're you helping him?"

I shrugged. "He didn't give me a chance to think."

"Probably how he got you to marry him." Dolly laughed. Her shoulders kept shaking after the laughter stopped. She turned and gave me the eye. "You should do something about your hair. You don't want him to think you let yourself go to seed."

"As if I cared."

"Sure, you care. If my ex came back tomorrow I'd want him to see something special, make him sorry for what he left behind."

"That's you."

"Naw, that's every woman."

"I'm not going to go nuts fixing myself up for …"

"I went to beauty school for a while."

Well, this news knocked me back a few feet. Dolly? Beauty school? Not three words I would have thought to put together.

"I'll fix your hair for you, and show you a few makeup tips."

It was my turn to give her a look, like: Who's kidding who here?

"You know," she went on. "What the chief said, about me staying here with you awhile? That's not a bad idea. If he can't work it so I'm off patrol, well still, I could be here a lot of the time, and we could go on doing the investigating we've been doing. Get to the bottom of this so you're not afraid."

I narrowed my eyes and looked hard at Deputy Dolly. Did I want to spend a lot of time with her? Did I want her around at all? Did I need someone here with me when Jackson came to visit? Hmm.

"And you know what else?" Dolly was perking up, sitting straighter. Her light eyes were wide open as if she'd been struck by a perfect thought. "Get yourself a dog. If you had a dog nobody'd dare bother you. Trust me. Creeps don't like barking dogs. Everybody up here in the woods keeps at least one of 'em. Look at old Harry. He must have a dozen dogs back there. Don't see anybody fooling with him."

First positive idea I'd heard. A dog. A sweet little black and white face leaped into my head. Simon's puppy. Perfect. The little guy would have a home. I'd be safe.

With Deputy Dolly and a puppy, who'd dare come after me?

ELEVEN

BEING ALONE WASN'T AS alluring as it once was. In the morning, after Dolly left to go to work, the walls crept closer. I felt as if I couldn't breathe; couldn't get my own stale air down far enough into my lungs because I'd breathed that same air before, tasted it before, was so overly familiar with that air I'd become allergic to it. And the sound of my refrigerator thumping and buzzing, my damned birdcall clock I'd thought so charming when I bought it—all of it was driving me crazy. My ears hurt at times, from the quiet that fell in between the mechanical sounds. My skin ached for the presence of another human being. Not to be made love to—it wasn't a deep down yearning sex thing. More a need to feel the floor shiver with movement I didn't make myself, to have a laugh or a word travel toward me, to share an emotion, draw a response, be given a touch of solace. For the first time in three years—I was more alone than I could stand.

I liked the idea of getting a dog. Dolly'd made fun of the idea of a puppy protecting me from anything. She said I should visit the shelter in Traverse and get an older dog that needed a home, who knew how to bark and tear a stranger's leg off. Old/young—I figured it didn't matter much since I'd never had a dog before and I'd be starting from scratch either way. Better to begin with a young one that wouldn't sense my inexperience and give me trouble. It seemed to me, with an old dog, it would be like Jackson—I'd be jumping through hoops for him within days. Not to say that I'm a wimp. More that it takes a lot of energy to control people and things. I never had that kind of energy.

Only enough to call Gaylord and talk to Officer Brent. I needed to know what was happening on the state police end. I had to write a follow-up for Bill. Getting to work felt like plugging into a stream of energy, tapping into things and people in motion. Better than standing at a window watching a quiet lake and a couple of loons, and doing nothing.

Brent was up in Mackinaw City, working on a case. Again, I got another officer.

"We don't know a lot at this point, Miss Kincaid." The policeman's voice went deep and official.

"The arm and the head, they're from the same person?" I needed at least that much from him. Not two disparate bodies. Certainly not *two* of them.

"I think we can assume the … eh … appendages are from the same person. That would be all right to say." This man was nothing if not cautious.

"Mrs. Poet then?"

A long pause. "You could say that."

I squirmed. Pulling this man's fingernails out one at a time would be easier, I thought.

"So, you're investigating a murder."

"Hmm, yes, you could say that."

"Have fingerprints been taken?"

"Well now, that's up to our forensics lab in Grayling. We should be hearing soon, but since the head was hers, well, I think it's safe to say the arm belongs to her, too."

"And the way the arm was … eh … removed from the body? They said the head had been sawed off. Is that true of the arm?" Talking about these things made my stomach do a slow rolling dive, but I had to ask the questions.

"Let's leave matters like that until we hear from the lab. They'll have a lot more to tell us."

"I heard they found teeth marks on the head. So some animal found her after all."

"I believe that's true. Maybe you need to get this from Officer Brent."

"But no animal put her in my garbage can."

"I rather doubt that was the case. Unless you've got yourself some homicidal chipmunks out your way." His voice didn't change, not by a single quiver, but I knew he was making fun of me.

I forged ahead. "Any suspects yet?"

He cleared his throat. "You mean who murdered her?"

I wanted to scream. Getting anything from this guy was like pulling weeds with never-ending roots.

"Just put down that we're looking into a number of suspects. That an arrest is imminent."

"Really? Can you name names?" I knew he had no one in mind and no arrest was imminent, but I couldn't help testing.

"You'll get that information as it becomes available. As I said, you should talk to Officer Brent."

Sure. Enough of that party line, I told myself, and I hung up.

I called the paper.

Bill Corcoran was concerned even more for me when I told him about the arm. "You going to be all right?" His deep voice was worried and that made me feel good. A long time since a man had sounded like that about me. "Something really dangerous going on out there, Emily. I don't know if you should hang around or if you should keep working on the story. Maybe somebody else ... ?"

"Why? They'd just have to interview me, 'cause I'm not going anywhere."

"You might want to rethink that, consider making yourself scarce over there for a while. Sounds like somebody's got it in for you. If you need a place to stay, I've got a spare room."

"Hmm, as attractive as that is ..."

"I didn't mean ..." He was flustered.

I wanted to laugh but didn't. "I'll be fine, Bill. Couldn't be in better hands."

"And whose would those be? Lucky Barnard's?"

"Well, the chief and his deputy. They're taking very good care of me."

"That would be Deputy Dolly right? Heard of her. Why don't I feel reassured?" he asked and hung up.

I spent the next hour standing at the front window, hugging my arms to my body and shivering. I stared out at the lake where the loons dipped and dove and popped up in unexpected places. Even they would soon be gone. I couldn't go out to my studio; writing was out of the question. No concentrating today. No sitting quietly in an empty room without the feel of eyes boring into my back, without my skin crawling at the slightest sound beyond the studio walls. I watched the loons until it was time to put my body in motion.

I had to meet Dolly in town in a couple of hours. We'd decided I should call back at Harry Mockerman's house; see if he'd tell me anything without the uniform present. And Joslyn Henry's, too. We thought maybe she and Ernie would be less nervous without Dolly there. Maybe Joslyn would ask me in, tell me what bothered her so much she'd been afraid to open the door to us.

First I had dog business to see to. I hurriedly scrawled a note to Simon, asking him to drop by with the puppy. Then I grabbed up my car keys and purse and drove to the top of my drive where I left my car.

Putting Simon's note into my mailbox meant pulling the mailbox door open. I'm not a slow learner. I already knew what could happen when you lifted lids and opened doors. A beating heart or an upright foot, anything could be in there. It took all I had to open the mailbox, stick the note inside without looking, then slam the door shut. Whoever was doing this to me knew what they were doing. Everywhere I turned seemed treacherous now—the woods too dark, trees too close. Willow Lake Road was too empty—there should be cars, traffic, people walking. What I'd loved about this North Country before—the emptiness and quiet—seemed a trap. Any misstep into a dark shallow of weeds and saplings could mean death.

I stood for a moment trying to recapture my place, my woods, my northern world. Sun and warmth and blue sky. It could be summer again. A day to work in my garden, cut back the iris and the lilies, tear out the tomatoes, rake a few of the beds, empty clay pots I would store in the shed until next spring. What a great day for getting my hands dirty, doing a last weeding of all my beds. Anything but tracking a murderer with Deputy Dolly. Anything but thinking about dead things.

I hesitated at the edge of the road, putting off walking up Harry's overgrown drive alone. Nothing was as friendly nor as accessible as it once was. With this change, with my small world made dangerous, I didn't feel I belonged up here the way I had.

Voices came from some place off in the woods. Male voices, calling one to the other. Men, where they weren't supposed to be. It frightened me, until I remembered—the police, hunting for more of Ruby Poet—whatever was left of her to find. I felt a little safer, knowing the police were in the woods along with whatever else was out there. Nobody was going to sling a leg or some other body part at me with the cops around. I started up Harry's dark path just a little braver than I'd been before.

The first thing I looked for was Harry's old black car/truck, but it wasn't behind the house. No one answered the door either. No smells met me. The house had the empty, nobody-home feeling that houses can get. I listened for Harry's chain saw off in the woods, but all I heard was a muffled call from one of the searchers. I walked around back, in case he was in the kennel. Nobody there but his dozen or more dogs, who went crazy, barking at the sight of me and leaping at the chainlink fence. I imagined the men searching the woods for Ruby Poet could hear and maybe the noise would draw them this way. Harry would hate that. Probably why he was gone—because he couldn't tolerate the thought of the police in his woods. Harry was a very private man. I'd violated his privacy enough already. I didn't want to be the cause of men swarming over his property.

I went back the way I'd gone in, and walked on down to Joslyn Henry's house. A couple of police officers, standing by the road, nodded as I passed, then went on talking, bending over a map they'd spread across the hood of their patrol car.

It felt good—the walking, getting some exercise. I didn't mind the half mile in to Joslyn Henry's house either. I was sure the police had been there before me, probably asking the same questions I was going to ask, but Dolly and I agreed we had to cover a lot of ground again and again, if we were going to get anywhere.

Another closed door. No answer to my knock or my, "Yoo-hoo. Mrs. Henry!"

Nobody home there either. I couldn't help but take a little time to walk around Joslyn Henry's flower beds and admire the configuration of circles and squares and ellipses she'd achieved. At that time of year, there wasn't much left in the way of vegetation, some dank-looking mums, a couple of bowing asters, but the layout of the garden was interesting, best seen when the beds were empty. It was a mathematical equation—a place of basic shapes. The woman, whether she knew it or not, was quite a garden designer. If this all worked out, and my neighbors were still speaking to me next spring, I decided I'd ask her to help me design a new plot of beds I'd been thinking about, up the hill at the back of the house. Nothing there now but bracken and a few wild raspberries. It could be pretty, laid out like this. Maybe a rose bed, though I'd have to order winter hardy bushes from Canada, because it could get down as low as thirty below. Maybe a back bed of double hollyhocks, with some tall lupine in front, and annuals in front of them. In my head, my garden was always perfect. In my head, no animal ever came to browse. In my head, there was never a bug on my flowers. Nobody ate a single bud. A storm never beat down the blossoms. In my head … ooh … like most of my life, much of my garden was lost inside my head.

TWELVE

Dolly's patrol car was outside the restaurant when I got there. I stopped in the vestibule to look at Eugenia's latest outlaw relative before entering. It didn't do to let Eugenia think you ignored her genealogical charts—might get very cold soup for a week or so.

There were a couple of new sheets. One on a Harry Longabaugh, who'd fled the country with the law hot on his tail, and another one named Robert LeRoy Parker. The last name struck some kind of chord, but I figured Parker was a common enough name. Odd, I thought, how few of her relatives were named Fuller. I supposed they all came from the female side, lots of name changing. I leafed through the older charts to see if anything else rang a bell. Ned Christie, Pearl Bywater, Etta Place. Not a Fuller among them.

Eugenia was busy cutting pies and portioning them out onto plates. She smiled and nodded, but looked lost in thought over her pie work, so I was safe from genealogical comment. The restaurant was full, maybe it was the excitement in town or maybe because they were all hungry at the same time. The air quivered with smoke. I never found out where Eugenia's "No Smoking" section was. Probably lost in the fog.

Dolly was seated in a corner booth. I headed her way, cutting between chairs set at the end of filled tables. I spotted Doc Crimson, the town veterinarian, at a table under the air filter that kept snapping like a bug catcher. Just the man I needed to see. I waved and went over to stand by his table, as everybody did sooner or later, to ask what I should do about a new puppy.

"Just bring him on in when you get him. We'll give him his shots." He shook his shaggy head of long white hair at me and held his fork, filled with crusty apple pie, just below his mouth, signaling this had better be a short consultation.

"Anything I need to know? I mean, about taking care of him." I was on shaky ground with a young animal, or any other living, breathing thing. There had to be dietary requirements and sleep requirements and vitamins and all that stuff.

"He'll teach you." His eyes danced, and I knew I was being had.

"Yeah," I said. "That's what I'm afraid of. But what do I feed him?"

"Pick up a bag of puppy chow and read the label."

"OK." I nodded, sure I wasn't getting the whole story. "That's it?"

"About it. Maybe you'll need a bed for 'im. Maybe some toys—to keep him from chewing up the house. But you come on in and see me. We'll talk about it."

Smart man, I thought, as I made my way to the corner booth near the front windows where Dolly sat. The vet wasn't giving me a lot of information for free when I might as well be paying for his time.

"Nobody home at Harry's or Mrs. Henry's house either," I said to Dolly as I slid in across from her, keeping my voice low because I had the feeling we were the center of attention again. No one stared directly, but you can sense when ears are turned toward you, like a roof full of antennas.

"It was Miz Poet's arm all right," Dolly half-whispered back. "Teeth marks, but nobody thinks a cougar dropped this one on you either."

The Murphy boys from the funeral home were at the table across from us. I only knew one of them, Gilbert, the reported gambler in the family, a short, rotund, fortyish man who liked to stand outside the funeral home, over on Griffith Street, watch the cars go by, and smoke a foot-long cigar. In my first year up here, I met him while doing a story on a woman who'd sworn she'd seen a panther stalking a funeral party. Gilbert had laughed at the woman and wised me up to a few of the people in town who liked to come up with bizarre stories to keep the juices flowing, and the others in a state of panic.

I nodded to Gilbert and supposed the man with him was Sullivan, his twin. I couldn't go wrong in that assumption since the other guy looked exactly like Gilbert, only a little dimmed, as if he were fading into a smaller, shadowy version of his brother.

"Should we talk to them?" I mumbled to Dolly after the coffee we ordered arrived. Dolly glanced over my shrugging shoulders and shook her head.

"Not yet. Their mother, Mary Margaret, first, I'd guess. Those guys are both full of crap. Gilbert there's a gambler. His brother's a drinker. All kinds of stories about that pair." She took off her hat and set it on the table between us. Her head looked like there'd been a bowl sitting on it. A flounce of damp hair stood out from her hat ring.

There were plenty of people in the restaurant today, sitting primly with their hands folded, waiting for service as they avoided looking directly at me and Dolly.

Gertie, of Gertie's Shoppe de Beauté, leaned out from a front booth and waved. She eyed my ragged, skunk-striped hair and gave a sad shrug. Dolly noticed and smirked. "We'll do something about your hair before Saturday," she said. "I'll pick up some Clairol. But you'll have to pay me back."

I agreed. Dolly pulled out a flip-up notebook and studied the notes she'd made. "I've been thinking," she said, glancing up. "Let's outline this so we don't miss anything."

"Good," I said. "That's the way I write my mysteries."

She gave me a non-supportive, skeptical look and made more notes. "What do you think of talking to Amanda Poet next? If anybody knows anything about her mother, it should be her."

"Then the other women in Ruby's religious group—or whatever it was. Mary Margaret Murphy. We should see her right away. Maybe we could call Joslyn Henry and set up an appointment. Or go over and talk to Ernie at his repair shop."

"The other lady, too," Dolly said. "Flora Coy. I know Miz Coy pretty well from helping the garden club plant petunias down Main Street last spring, and before that she was with the Welcome Wagon and brought me a bunch of leftover free stuff one time."

I nodded. Sounded like a plan.

"Don't forget the pastor at that church." I motioned for her to write him down.

She nodded, wrote, then held the notebook up to look at our list in the light from the flyspecked window. She flipped the notebook shut and stuck it in her shirt pocket, looking satisfied. "That's a good start. I've already got a feeling we're onto something . . ."

"What would that be?" I asked, not sharing her confidence.

"Well, I mean, you know, it's got to be somebody here in Leetsville and right there the field is limited."

"Why Leetsville? Remember how Harry Mockerman lied about being out at the road? And Ruby Poet's body is coming from somewhere in our woods. Harry's my neighbor. What's to say Harry didn't have a hand in this whole thing?"

"He said he didn't even know Miz Poet," she argued, frowning at me, wrinkling her nose.

"And you said he was lying."

"Hmm," was all Dolly came up with. I had the sinking feeling neither of us had a clue how to go about finding the murderer of a harmless old, nature-worshipping lady.

We got up to leave and were stopped at one table after another by people asking if it was true we were looking into "poor" Ruby's murder. So much for that big secret, I thought, and couldn't help but shake my head and wonder how the heck a murderer expected to get away with keeping such a thing as doing a murder from all these folks. They didn't need cops and reporters in Leetsville. All they needed was somebody to make the rounds at Fuller's EATS and take notes.

Dolly smirked at people and kept pushing her way out. I stayed close behind, like a ship after a tug.

———

We drove both our cars the four blocks over to Amanda Poet's house and parked behind a blue Dodge Dart on the street.

I'd noticed the Poet's house before. A tiny place. A gingerbread house, barely large enough for two grown women, it had a peaked roof with carved trim and a tiny porch, where a child's rocking horse rocked. I'd thought it a playhouse the first time I drove through town, three houses down from Bailey's Feed and Seed, across the street from the Church of the Contented Flock.

The garden was always beautifully kept. In the spring, it was filled with tulips and jonquils. In the summer, the beds were a blast of color behind the low picket fence. I hadn't realized this was the house of the old woman who'd disappeared. Now, standing behind Dolly as she knocked at the door, I looked around. The garden was an unkempt tangle. No one had pulled the late summer weeds or deadheaded the last of the daisies. The daughter, Amanda, had obviously let the whole thing go. Probably distraught over her mother's disappearance, but why Ruby Poet's gardening friend, Joslyn Henry, or one of the other nature-loving women hadn't leaped in to save her friend's garden, I didn't understand.

There is something especially poignant about an abandoned garden. Maybe because you know it had been loved and tended once. I took a lot of joy in planting and watering and tending. I always imagined, in some sloppy sentimental way, that my plants were like a nursery full of children, needing care and constant supervision, rewarding me with beauty.

I hung behind Dolly, not certain what we were going to use as an excuse for being there, intruding on Amanda's grief. I figured Dolly'd come up with something, but when the door opened all she did was turn to me and roll her eyes.

Amanda Poet was a tiny woman, extremely thin, quite pretty in a fainting Truman Capote way. She had an anxious face and nervous eyes that flicked from Dolly to me and back to Dolly. She took in Dolly's uniform inch by inch before smiling wanly. "Yes?"

Dolly told her who we were and that we were looking into her mother's death. The woman, in her early forties with blond-going-to-faded hair piled on her head and caught with big combs at the top, had a waif-like air to her. Big-eyed, and still smiling without comprehension, Amanda tilted her head and said sweetly again, "Yes?"

"Could we come in, Amanda?" Dolly asked, reaching for the edge of the door. Dolly was impatient with this fey little woman.

"Why, of course." Amanda Poet pushed the door open, inviting us into a tiny living room that must once have been a lot neater than it was now. I had a feeling that when Ruby Poet was alive her house never looked quite this messy. The living room was one of those faux country rooms, cute enough to give you a queasy feeling. There were metal moose picture frames on the tables, and tiny stuffed animals sitting on the chairs. Tabbed cambric curtains hung at the low front window and rag throw rugs were laid at odd angles over the floor. A plate rail near the ceiling held a collection of hand-painted flower plates. On a pie-crust table someone had gathered apple-head dolls into a little village. A rumpled Raggedy Ann sprawled face down in a bent wood rocker.

Newspapers lay everywhere around the room, open, spread on the rag rugs. A gold crocheted afghan hung half off a La-Z-Boy chair. Dirty glasses and pop cans sat in the tableau of apple dolls so it looked like a skewed Mr. Bill advertisement for Coke.

Just standing there, feeling overly large in a room meant for small people and small things, I knew that if Ruby Poet walked back in right now she would be appalled. It was that kind of house, where you could predict the reactions of the owner. If I knew anything about Ruby, from the garden she used to keep, I knew she wouldn't have liked what her daughter had let happen to their life.

Obviously Amanda Poet hadn't inherited her mother's penchant for order—inside or out. She looked to me like the kind of woman who never quite grew up, who stayed at least partially dependent forever, and sucked the life out of the poor soul elected to be her keeper.

But maybe that wasn't fair. She seemed nice enough, scurrying around picking up the newspapers, though she dropped them in another spot without improving the look of the room.

"How can I help you, officer?" Amanda gave up her efforts at straightening and sank into the rocker, squashing poor Raggedy Ann. The woman looked exhausted, as if she'd just run a mile or two. Next, she might put the back of her hand to her forehead and faint dead away—she was that kind of person. I'd once known just such a woman back in Ann Arbor. I'd interviewed her when her husband came up missing and was ever so sorry for her, going way out of my way to help, posting missing-person bulletins on lampposts and fences and basking in her feinting thank-yous and quiet tears—until her husband was found floating in Lake Erie with forty-two knife wounds in his back, and a couple who'd been making out under a tree nearby identified my poor-soul lady as the person they'd seen drive down to the lake and pull a body from the trunk of her car. I'd learned then about getting too close to the people I wrote about.

"I'm with the *Northern Statesman*," I said, wanting my role here straightforward so I didn't feel as if I was taking advantage of poor distraught Amanda Poet.

She smiled.

"And your … er … mother was found out by my house."

"*Your* garbage can?" She looked incredulous.

I nodded.

"My, my, my. Isn't this just the most terrible thing you've ever heard of?" She looked at the purse I'd set beside me on the floor and waited.

"Aren't you going to take notes?" she finally asked, eyebrows up.

Surprised, I hurried to flush a notebook from my purse, then hunted for a pen. Dolly handed me hers.

"I mean, my poor mother never hurt a soul on this earth and look what's been done to her." Amanda took a swipe at her left eye and waited until I'd written down what she said.

"Do you know if there's anyone who was angry with her?"

"With my mother?" Amanda gave a limp sweep of her hand, whisking away such thoughts. "No one. And, you know..." She looked directly at Dolly. "Other officers, from the state police, have been here asking the same things. I told them there's never been anybody who didn't just love my mother. If you talk to them, I'm sure they'll tell you what I said. I didn't know a thing that could help them."

"What about Pastor Runcival?"

Amanda sat back. Her face got a little stiff. "You don't mean that silly sermon of his, do you? That was a long time ago..."

"Summer," Dolly said.

"Yes, well. He told me he didn't mean anything by what he preached in church. It was just that he was using my mother and her friends as an example of how people can get off the straight path to heaven. I explained to him that what Mother and her friends were doing was nothing. They're such gardeners, is all. Everything in nature was special to them. No sinister Pagan stuff, the way he made it sound at the time. A little dancing out of doors—for health reasons, of course. That's it. Nothing to get excited about."

Dolly nodded. I waited, though I had questions of my own.

"Pastor and I are very good friends," Amanda added, giving a smirk that I could have sworn was meant to imply something more than mere friendship. "He wouldn't do anything to embarrass me. It was a misunderstanding, soon cleared up. He didn't wish my mother any harm, that's for certain."

"What about the other parishioners?" Dolly said. "Maybe somebody went over the edge. Took it that the women worshipped Satan out there at Miz Henry's house. Maybe one of them's just a little too religious. Can you think of anybody like that? I mean, it's possible that some guy heard the sermon and thought he'd be doing God's work, killing your mother."

Amanda considered for a moment, then shook her head. "No. Nobody like that."

"Your mother ever mention somebody here in town she didn't get along with?" Dolly pressed on.

Again, Amanda shook her head.

"Did she know Harry Mockerman? He lives out on Willow Lake Road, across from me."

She thought awhile. "I've certainly heard of Harry Mockerman. I think he and Mother went to school together, but then everybody who lived here their whole life long knows everybody else. She didn't talk about him. Not that I remember. Unless..."

Amanda screwed her face up. "Oh yes. I do too remember something. She bought wood from him for the stove. Probably last winter. If I remember correctly, Mother said he asked for one price when she first talked to him, then wanted more money when he delivered the wood. She wouldn't pay it. All I recall is her saying she'd get her wood elsewhere come this next winter. I don't know if that's anything," she said, giving us a hopeful look.

"What about money?" Dolly shot out. "Who inherits from your mother?"

It seemed a personal question, but then I wasn't used to police interrogation, and was beginning to feel I wasn't really very good at it.

"Why," Amanda sat up and frowned deeply, "I don't see what …"

"Is there just you?"

"Yes, just me and Mother. My father died years ago. I hardly remember him."

"And you've always lived here with your mother?" I asked quickly before this stream of information dried up.

"All my life."

"You never married."

She shook her head and smiled sweetly. "Never had the opportunity. Mother needed seeing to. I wasn't free to up and leave her."

Dolly stood. I followed her lead. We thanked Amanda and asked if we could call back if we needed more information.

At the front door, Amanda, with suspicion in her voice, asked, "Why are you and the state police both investigating what happened to my mother?"

"We always work together like this." Dolly smiled.

"Well, I certainly hope you find out who did this and put him away for the rest of his life. I never imagined … not here in Leetsville. Down in Detroit, or in Grand Rapids, well, there's always murder going on there, but not here. Not in our sweet little town."

"Doesn't seem so sweet right now," Dolly said.

I told Amanda to call if I could be of any help.

"I'm having a ceremony beginning of next week." Amanda stopped us on the steps. She brushed a stray lock of hair from her forehead. "Just a small remembrance ceremony at the church. Pastor and I are planning it. You're welcome to come. It will be very refined. Seems the least I can do for her."

"Don't you want to wait until … well … until they find the rest of her?" Dolly asked. "They're out there searching right now. I'd wait if I were you."

"Whatever," Amanda said, dismissing the idea. "Pastor can do a nice little ceremony over just the … whatever we have, you know. And the ladies are going to serve tea and cakes in the church basement. I thought I should let everybody come and express their sympathy like that. I mean, it's only right after all."

I didn't see the sense to what she was planning. Why rush at this point? But who's going to argue with a grieving daughter? Whatever it takes, I said to myself.

"By the way," Dolly turned in the middle of the narrow front walk, "Ernie Henry sends his condolences, if you haven't talked to him yet. Said to say how sorry for your loss he and his mother are. But maybe you've already heard from him?" Dolly waited.

The woman's face turned a brilliant red. She shook her head. "Nothing yet, but I expect everybody will come to the service we're …"

She stopped talking and looked hard toward a car pulling into place behind mine at the curb. "Why, speak of the devil. Here's Joslyn Henry now. Poor soul. She's probably as distraught as I am." Amanda smiled wanly and leaned against the doorjamb.

As we watched, an unhappy-looking Joslyn Henry got out of her car, head down. She came through the gate and started up the walk, almost running into us.

"Miz Henry," Dolly said, putting a hand up as if she were going to tip her hat.

"I was just over to your place," I said with false heartiness.

103

Joslyn Henry, tall and straight, stopped abruptly, looked up, and frowned at me as if she couldn't place who I was. "What for?" she demanded.

"I needed some information about Ruby Poet. I heard you two were friends and I wanted some background for a story I'm doing…"

Joslyn Henry waved a hand, dismissing me. She spotted Amanda on her porch and pushed on past. "I'll talk to you later, Emily. First I've got to see Amanda.

"Amanda," she called toward the woman on the porch. "There's something we have to discuss…"

"Come on in, Miz Henry," Amanda trilled, cutting her short. "I was hoping to see you."

"Well, there's something you need to know…"

"Come right on in, now."

Joslyn Henry was up the steps and into the house before another word could be said. The door closed behind them.

Dolly and I looked at each other. In the car, Dolly underlined Joslyn Henry's name in her notebook. We definitely had to have a talk with her, find out what had upset her.

"And Pastor Runcival, too," Dolly said, writing down his name again. "Gotta talk to him."

"We'd better divide 'em up," I said, glancing at the list of people. "Or we'll never get through it. And we don't know how the state police are doing. Maybe they're way ahead of us."

Dolly fixed me with a stern look and adjusted her hat firmly to her small, oblong head. "This isn't a race, Emily. We're not in competition. No contest, remember? You said that yourself. But if it's between them and us, people will want to talk to us."

"Like Joslyn Henry just did?" I asked, raising an eyebrow at her.

I picked Pastor Runcival and Joslyn Henry from our list. Dolly got Mary Margaret Murphy and Flora Coy. We came up with a set of questions for each of them.

"Don't forget we're talking about almost a month ago," Dolly reminded me. "That's about when she was killed. So ask them what was going on back then. What they remember involving Ruby Poet. And Pastor Runcival, you ask him where he heard about the women, and what he said, and if anybody in his church was especially upset over them."

"Should we wait for Joslyn Henry?" I asked.

Dolly made a face and shook her head. "Nah. We'll get her tomorrow, when she's settled down. She was sure upset about something, don't you think? By tonight, tomorrow, maybe then she'll be ready to talk to us. It's more than her friend dying, I'd say."

"More like she was intent on something," I said.

Dolly looked thoughtful. "Better to wait until later," she said.

Fine with me. I'd had enough of bearding lions for one day, and waiting seemed like a good idea at the time.

THIRTEEN

DIRECTLY ACROSS THE STREET from the Poets' house, The Church of the Contented Flock sat like an orphaned chick beneath tall maples and taller pines. The yellow, bluntly squared-off, wood building had a peak at the exact middle, with a plain brown crucifix nailed at the highest point. There was something forlorn about the little church, a rundown look to it like an old A-frame back in the woods.

Pastor Runcival raked leaves on the front lawn. He wore a dark blue crewneck sweater and jeans. Very casual, though his wispy brown hair was combed back with almost painful precision, each hair in perfect alignment with the hair next to it. A cheap toupee, I thought, hoping it wasn't one, not liking the vision in my head of this small man with stooped shoulders and tight mouth also cursed with baldness.

I strolled over to introduce myself and watched the disappointment on the small man's face as he realized he didn't have a new believer, only a reporter wanting a quote or two about Ruby Poet.

"Haven't seen you around before, have I? A Catholic?" He leaned on his rake, and sniffed. He eyed me speculatively.

I shook my head.

"Pentecostal? Methodist? Presbyterian?" His tight face got tighter as he scrolled through possibilities. I shook my head at each. Finally, he gave up when he'd ticked off every acceptable church he could think of.

"Well, Miss Kincaid. What can I do for you?"

I explained about helping Deputy Dolly Wakowski look into Mrs. Poet's death.

"Have you spoken to Amanda?" he motioned impatiently toward the Poet house. His round face, behind small round glasses, labored into a narrow smile. "She'd be the one to ask."

"Just came from there," I said, smiling my best good-girl-trying-to-be-liked smile. "Naturally she's upset about what happened to her mother, and she wants whoever did this caught right away ..."

"As do we all." The pastor leaned harder on his rake and slowly bobbled his head. "As do we all. Never heard of anything so cruel. But then, there's evil loose in the world. Let in by our media. The TV and you newspaper people, of course. Report it all the time. Give it the form it's been hunting. Think about it." He bent closer to me, the rake a staff between us. "Before the printing press, what was there? News didn't spread. It was contained; wasn't copied and magnified. We'd all be better off without too much information. You have to take responsibility, you know." He was nodding and motioning with his rake—though not a hair moved on his bouncing little head.

Hmm—an attack I wasn't prepared for. I thought as fast as I could and stammered a lame, "What about the persecution of Christians? The Sack of Rome. What about the Middle Ages, horrible executions ..." I tried desperately to come up with more from my meager store of historical knowledge. "All without the help of a single newspaper to spread the word."

Pastor Runcival bent backward, then forward again, fixing me with bright, arrogant, little eyes. "Before the printing press—we knew nothing of any of that."

"But your own Bible ..."

"We don't rely on any book at the Church of the Contented Flock. We're 'Content' in our secure and direct knowledge of God. Think of the confusion brought by the printed word."

"What about school—the kids?" I was too astounded by this Luddite view of the world to do more than grab for words.

"Ah, yes, education." He nodded wisely. "A necessary evil. Because of the state. If I had my way, well, the children would all be taught at home, by their parents and the church. Their heads wouldn't be filled with ideas that pull young minds in a million wrong directions ..."

"Everybody in your church believes the way you do?"

"Well, not yet. Not all. But they're coming to it." He smiled and dipped his head a time or two. "Many find it difficult to undo what years of education have wrought."

"And Mrs. Poet?"

"Misguided woman. A constant source of regret to poor Amanda. Amanda, contrary to most of nature, was the child trying to lead the mother, rather than the other way around."

"Amanda's got newspapers all over her house. I was just there."

The reverend brushed that aside. "An aberration. We all have our failings, though we keep trying. We keep trying, my dear. Perfection is not within the scope of man. Only striving. We strive, therefore we are." He smiled and passed a hand over his pasted hair.

I think, therefore I am ...

I figured the man had to have read a book sometime to know René Descartes. Hypocrite? I wondered. Or a man simpler, and wiser, than I was capable of comprehending.

"I heard you'd preached against Mrs. Poet and some of her friends. Maybe your sermon set off something. There are other ways of spreading evil. Ill-considered words, that sort of thing."

The pastor's face moved into an expression of deep distaste. "Don't try shifting blame to God's people, young woman. Old business. That was way back, oh, over a month ago now. I'm sure my little chide to the women had nothing to do ..."

He smiled a nervous smile. A contrite smile. So, he did have a conscience. I wasn't saying anything he hadn't already taken up with himself. I thought about hair shirts and knotted whips then thought, instead, of how we all try to get along, make a place for ourselves in the world. This was the reverend's gnawed-out niche. Who was I to attack the man for finding his own place?

"The police are looking into all angles," I said by way of sympathy. "Could have been any number of things ..."

"As well they should look into it," he agreed, then began slowly raking leaves again, his head down, eyes averted. "Poor soul probably got lost. You know, at that age ..."

"She was dismembered."

"Animals, no doubt."

I didn't go into my not-in-my-garbage-can speech. No use. These people, like so many others I'd met before, would have things as they wanted them to be. I was tired of demanding intellectual honesty from anyone.

"What was it you preached against?" I pressed, as much as I felt I could.

"You're with the newspaper, you said. I don't give answers that might appear in print."

"I'm also helping the local police in their investigation."

"Really?" His eyebrows shot up.

"We're determined to discover who committed this terrible crime…" I had nothing against shrugging on self-importance if it helped. I didn't know this man from… well, from Adam. Maybe he was an ecclesiastical murderer—if there was such a thing. Maybe he'd killed Ruby Poet because she read the *Northern Statesman*, and then slipped her head into my garbage can as a warning to a reporter. And threw her arm on my porch…

Much as I didn't care for this self-puffed person, I wasn't picking up desperate murderer from him.

"As are we all," the pastor said yet again, and shook his head with exaggerated sorrow.

"If you could just think back. What were the women doing that you objected to?"

"Hmm." The gigantic pile of leaves between us stirred. He stopped raking, grew thoughtful, his faded eyes looking off. "What I objected to at the time was the fact that some of our leading citizens, these very women, were taking up a form of religious practice that was in no way in line with the teachings of our church. Or any church, for that matter. From what was being said around town, it sounded like Druidic practice. All that dancing in the woods, holding ceremonies out there at Joslyn Henry's on Pagan feast days. A number of my parishioners came to me with complaints about what they'd heard."

"Did you ever witness the dancing?"

"Of course not, but I was told what was going on."

"By whom?"

"I'd rather not say. Shall we simply say it was brought to my attention? More than one person, now that I think about it."

"Surely you can say who complained? It would help."

He shook his head again.

"Anyone express their unhappiness with the women about anything else?"

He thought a moment.

"Any fanatics in your church the sermon might have set off? You know, somebody who would kill an old woman because of her beliefs?"

The parson pursed his lips. "No one in my church. We don't have that kind of parishioner in the Church of the Contented Flock. We are simple people with a simple faith."

"If you think of anything, or think of who complained to you about Ruby Poet and the others, I'd appreciate a call. Emily Kincaid, out on Willow Lake Road."

"You in the book?" he asked with a straight face, not considering what he was saying.

I nodded but couldn't hide my silly smile. "Yes, I'm in 'the book.'"

"Maybe some Sunday you'd like to stop in for services." The parson was all brightness and light now that the inquisition was over. "We're got a lively group here. If I say so myself, I do preach an interesting sermon. You should give us a try. Might lead you to a more honorable profession."

I promised that one day I might do just that. Sure thing, I thought. I'll give up the evils of the written word—soon as he got a decent haircut. I left Pastor to his raking.

Joslyn Henry hadn't come out of Amanda Poet's house while I was talking to the pastor, so there was nothing more for me to do but go home. It wasn't hard to talk myself into it. I had research on the Survivalists to do that evening, and I wanted to make lists of what I'd learned so far about this Poet business to share with Dolly. Anyway, I was tired of talking to people who weren't really interested in talking back to me.

As I drove past Murphy's Funeral Home, I saw Dolly's patrol car parked at the curb, behind a black, shining hearse with Murphy's Funeral Home inscribed on the door in small gold letters. I hoped she was getting more information than I was. So far, we seemed to have nothing but a group of people who all loved sweet old Mrs. Poet, or at least were only concerned about her soul, and wouldn't harm a hair on her head. Notwithstanding, that the head was loose and very, very dead.

———————

Simon's yellow SUV was parked down next to my house when I got back. I now had a dog, I imagined. Something to care for me and love me unconditionally. And if he ever ran after another female I'd get him fixed, I pledged as my first act of dog ownership. I was telling myself all of this while parking and waving to Simon and his girlfriend, Gloria, the waitress I knew from EATS. They were down by Willow Lake, romping in the ferns with my new puppy.

The first to notice me was the little dog, who came happily bouncing up the path, tongue lolling out of his black and white face, paws barely touching the earth as he leaped into the air and hit me squarely in the stomach.

The dog had grown in the two days since I'd last seen him. What I hadn't noticed when Simon held him on his lap were his huge, shaggy feet.

I righted myself and held the squirming animal down with one hand on the flat of his head as I greeted Simon, then Gloria, who looked different out of her waitressing outfit. She was in jeans and a long purple sweater, her brown hair caught back in a ponytail. We talked while the dog leaped around us in circles, yelping and carrying on, though he was being ignored.

"I knew you couldn't turn him down," Simon grinned and shouted over the noise.

"Is he always this … happy?" I asked, one eye on the wild figure leaping and flipping in the air.

"Just like this." Simon nodded as if it were a good thing.

I asked them into the house for a Coke or a cup of coffee, and we traipsed back up the sand path with the dog running circles around us.

In the house Dog settled down; even seemed a little cowed by four walls and a roof. Timidly, he sniffed each piece of furniture and nudged up my rugs with his nose. Gloria helped me find a water bowl for him—an old plastic container—then we sat at the counter to talk dog food and the responsibilities of pet ownership.

I shouldn't have gotten too deeply into the discussion. I should have noticed that Dog was walking funny, but I didn't, and Gloria and Simon were busy looking over my house while discussing the finer points of doggie raising. Dog squatted in the middle of one of my better carpets; one my dad said came from Turkey, and left me a pile of steaming shit.

Simon laughed and Gloria admonished the puppy with a few sad mews and clucks. I got paper towels and scooped the pile into a plastic garbage bag that I set outside the door, all the while gagging and holding my nose. I got a rag and some spray cleaner, and did the best I could for the carpet.

First thing was going to be toilet training. I thought some kind of litter box, but Simon said I had the wrong animal. I had to train Dog to go outside to do his business.

"You can keep him on the screen porch when you're not here," Gloria said. "Little puddles and stuff won't hurt the wood out there."

I looked at the size of the dog, growing before my eyes, and speculated on the size of those puddles and piles. OK, I told myself. It's my fault that I don't know anything about caring for him. I'd learn. He'd learn. And we'd live happily ever after. I figured it was kind of like a marriage. First was attraction—when everything seemed OK. Then came living together, and reality. And finally came acceptance, or at least sufferance.

"So," Simon said from his stool at my counter, after Dog had fallen into a sleeping stupor in the living room. "You and Deputy Dolly learn anything about what happened to Miz Poet?"

I smiled an inscrutable smile.

As if I would inform the town criers of our progress.

"Gloria said she told you about Pastor Runcival, and that sermon he preached last summer. Everybody knew who he was talking about. A bunch of harmless old ladies. No devil worship and stuff like that going on, from what Ernie told me. Just some ladies taking to the woods and baking cookies and having a kind of party out there."

"And you know what else?" Gloria leaned in close to whisper. "I heard that Amanda Poet stands to inherit a sum of money. Seems her mom had property that had been in the family a hundred years and she just recently signed oil leases on it. Lots of people doing that now, on what everybody thought was worthless land. Could be a lot of money. That's a reason to do a poor old soul in."

"Where'd you hear that?" I wanted to know, envying those with access to the jungle drumming.

"Oh, it's just going around. And some are saying that those Survivalists, down the road here, had a run-in with Miz Henry because they were doing something on her property, where the women have their little meetings. Maybe they took it out on poor Miz Poet."

"Hmm," was all I said. These two had picked up more than Dolly and I, just by gossiping around town. So much for our logical and ordered investigation.

"Anything else you come across?" I asked.

"Well there's old Harry. He had a fight about some wood with Miz Poet last winter."

"I heard that one."

"And," Simon leaned in close. "To tell you the truth, I don't trust Ernie Henry so much. There's been stories about him. Things I don't like to say…"

I waited, knowing he would "say" soon enough.

"He makes these trips out of town. Nobody knows where he goes and who he sees, though there's talk that it's some CIA thing he's got himself into. He knows a lot about machines and motors and there's been some speculation that Ernie's helping the government."

I kind of dismissed that one.

"Do you know anything about Mrs. Murphy and her sons?" I was being shameless.

"You know that Gilbert gambles away everything he can get his hands on? Poor Mrs. Murphy is at her wits' end, Eugenia told me, with him losing every dime to the Indians, up there at the casino in Petoskey. It's not like he wins or anything. That's why she can't make repairs to the funeral home. Roof's leaking. Basement's sinking. The front porch needs shoring up."

"What about the other one? Sullivan."

Gloria rolled her eyes. "That one. He's a drinker. What his brother doesn't lose at the casino, Sullivan pours down his throat."

"None of that gives anybody a reason to kill Mrs. Poet."

Gloria shrugged. "You never know. Soon as I heard there was money involved I told Simon, 'Could be anybody who thought there was a chance of doing poor Amanda out of some cash.' You just watch Gilbert and Sullivan go after her now. Or Ernie—for that matter. Ernie's so cheap he squeaks when he's got to pull out a dollar. He talks about expanding that small-engine repair shop of his, but I can't see him taking anything out of his own pocket. Gives him a reason. Or even Pastor Runcival—though I'd hate to think it. I know Amanda's been a devout church member, doing more than a little to help the pastor out. Maybe he was mad about the old lady. She wasn't into organized religion, you know. And Miz Henry, well, she used to be a librarian so you can guess what she's been saying about the pastor. People who read get funny ideas. And the pastor's dead set against reading and such."

I didn't buy into Simon and Gloria's dramatic scenarios. A little too much overheated imagination going on here. What I needed most, I realized, was to talk to Joslyn Henry. Dolly was talking to Flora Coy, who I didn't know at all, and Mary Margaret Murphy. When we learned what went on out there in the woods, maybe we'd understand what had happened to Ruby Poet, and why.

In the meantime, I had to get back into town for dog food, some dog toys, and get Dog to Doc Crimson. And I had to come up with a name other than Dog. Then I had to put some questions together for my Survivalist story. Work had to come into my life somewhere in here.

On his way out the door, Simon stopped long enough to run a new plot he'd thought up by me. "How about this?" he asked. "Seems there's this bunch of people on a fancy train somewhere in Europe." His eyes wandered as he thought. "Somebody turns up dead and come to find out everybody on the train hated him. It'll turn out that he was murdered by all of them. Sound good?"

I assured Simon I would think about it. I said it had possibilities. Distinct possibilities. Agatha Christie hadn't done badly with it. Why not me?

FOURTEEN

You can doubt anything, if you think about it long
enough, 'cuz what happened always adjusts to fit what
happened after that, and it's hard to feel like you are
free, when all you seem to do is referee... *

ANI DIFRANCO'S WORDS KEPT running through my head.

My best friend—though she doesn't know me from...well...
from anybody.

It's because I was there, in Chicago, at one of her amazing con-
certs. And when I'm feeling down, or lost, or feeling just about
anything, I think of ani and what her life must have been like, and
the battles she keeps on fighting and...well...

I was getting my brain revved to face the Survivalists. In order
to do things I don't want to do, I think of things that make me
happy and secure. Places and people in the world where I know
everything's all right and not crazy and not out at some edge of
anger.

* from "Reckoning" by ani difranco

I needed ani to get me through this interview. Maybe to get me through my life.

I'd had a bad night with Dog. He'd whined and scratched at the inside door when I put him in a box out on the porch, the way Doc Crimson told me to. I let him in, and he stood beside my bed barking at me. Then he peed and pooped. I stepped in it the first thing when I got up.

All in all, not a good start for a day when I had to do an interview I was dreading. Something would have to be done about Dog. Now that he'd had his shots he was really, officially, my dog, and deserved his own name. I would start there. And some kind of cage for him. A sleeping place. Or maybe we'd just get used to each other and things would all work out. But that was what I'd told myself when I married Jackson Rinaldi.

So I was driving down a very bad two-track—though my Jeep was taking it just fine—and thinking of all the strong female spirits, like ani, I kept around me and wondering if that made me strange. Druidic, as the pastor said of Ruby Poet. And if I was strange, why did it feel so good to call on living and dead predecessors in my time of moral and psychological need? Wasn't that like calling on a saint? Wasn't that like calling on your own family? Wasn't I, after all, of the family of women fighting their way through the world— big and small, short and tall, brave and … well … me.

And I was thinking about Dolly's phone call the night before. They'd found the rest of Mrs. Poet—out in a shallow grave in the woods. Her cut-up body had been dumped into a hole in the ground and covered over. The grave had been disturbed. Parts of her, as I well knew, were missing—but only those parts that had already turned up at my house.

I'd felt irrationally happy when she told me. No more pieces of Ruby Poet appearing in unexpected places. I could open my mailbox again without fear of finding a small body part.

"Do they know how she died?" I'd asked.

"Not yet. Doc said maybe we'd never know. No blunt trauma to the head, but can't tell if there was strangulation because the neck was severed. Maybe something in her system, or on the rest of the body. The lab at Grayling's going over everything they found out there."

That was all I wanted to know. We made plans to meet at my house after she got off work and I was back from my interview. I'd called Gaylord to get official news of the body find. Then called Bill with the story. I was hoping, as I drove, that Dolly would come over late enough to let me work on my mystery before it dwindled off like quicksilver, and I'd never get it finished.

The two-track I was on ended at a wide metal gate with warning signs posted next to it and over it, and in the trees to each side of it. KEEP OUT was the nicest of the signs. Others warned that parts of my anatomy might be in danger if I didn't turn around and get going. I stopped my car and tested my belief in signs. Did I get out and open the gate? Or did I sit there, meekly, and wait for somebody to come get me?

I parked, got out to stand within the safety of my open door, and looked down the road on the other side of the gate. Nobody. "Oh well," I was telling myself. "I tried," I was thinking, when a square-bodied woman dressed in fatigues and a red hunting hat with ear flaps and with a gun held over her left arm stepped out from behind a tree and called to me.

"You Emily Kincaid, from that magazine?" she demanded and I nodded, not giving it much enthusiasm because I wasn't sure of my welcome.

She walked over and unlocked the gate; then unwound some protective wire from the bars and held the gate wide enough for me to barely get through.

"Sharon Rombart, Dave's wife." She held her hand out for me to shake. I did. The hand was calloused, as I expected.

"We're going to go back by the Center and talk. Dave calls it Operations Center, but you don't have to pay a lot of attention to him." She turned, gun swinging along at her side, and took off down the overgrown trail at a slow lope. I stumbled to keep up, through dead Queen Anne's Lace, through bronzed joe-pye weed, through bowed mullein and faintly golden goldenrod. Burrs stuck to my jeans. I tripped in animal holes. All the while I bumbled after her, I tried to ask questions.

"So, you mean you don't go along with this Survivalist stuff?" I called out merrily at the back lumping up and down ahead of me.

She stopped and turned to face me squarely, the gun slipping through her hand to stand, stock down, in the dried weeds. Her feet were spread wide. Her face was cold, eyes the kind you might see just before they pulled the switch on the chair you were sitting in. "What the hell do you mean 'stuff'? This ain't no 'stuff' we're doing here. This is real. We know what's coming, even if you Liberals don't have the brains to see it. Don't come in here thinking you're going to laugh and call it 'stuff.'"

I kept my eyes on the gun, then on her face, which was flat and empty. "You said not to pay attention to Dave..."

She turned and was off again, with me behind her. She called over her shoulder. "I just meant that Dave's not up on the latest information the way I am. If you really want to know what's going on, you ask me. If you want to know what Dave thinks, you ask him."

We stepped from the trees into a wide clearing. Five men in ragtag camouflage ringed the perimeter of the clearing, leaning on guns, or squatting with their backs hunched, heads settled down into their camouflage jackets.

A few nodded. I nodded back.

"Don't mind them," Sharon said, turning to me. "They didn't think it was a good idea, bringing the press out here. But Dave's a good man and wants to spread the word of Survival."

I smiled the tightest smile I could force. Sure enough, I wouldn't talk to any of the bearded guys with suspicious eyes, as long as they didn't dare talk to me. I pulled out my notebook and made some notes.

There was no house to speak of, only a doorway built into the side of a hill. The door was painted khaki brown. Everything there seemed to be khaki brown. Just the feeling I got. Brown world. Brown people. Brown sky. Brown trees. Brown earth.

Sharon stopped dead in front of the hillside door. "I'm going to leave most of it for Dave to tell you." She smiled a broad smile at me and turned to knock hard at the door.

I was beginning to like this little woman with the big attitude. I hadn't met Dave yet, but I thought maybe he was a lucky man.

"Hey Dave!" she called. "The lady from the magazine's here. You better come on out before I tell her all wrong."

The brown door opened and a tall man with a long black beard stepped out, shrugging on a camouflage jacket over a white tee shirt.

"Mr. Rombart." I walked toward him.

"Dave." He dipped his head, fumbled for the hand I held toward him, shook it, then glanced at his wife. "Sharon taking care of you?"

"Yes, sir. But I've got a lot of questions."

"Figures." He grinned at Sharon, who grinned back. He chewed at his lower lip. "I'm going to show you some things. Hope you brought a good camera. These are things folks should know, and soon." He motioned me to follow him and Sharon, and we set off.

We marched our way back into the woods and down another trail. We went through some wet places, picking our way carefully around rocks and fallen trees. I followed along, with Sharon bringing up the rear. I called questions after Dave Rombart, when I was sure I could take my eyes off the ground for a minute. I asked about the group and their philosophy, swallowing hard in order to catch my breath. Once, Dave stopped dead, turned, and launched into a long speech I tried my best to write down. When he turned away, he didn't say another word until we were in a large, round clearing, where something like a moonshine still stood.

Huge, round, made of stainless steel with pipes sticking out, it looked like a silo or a big whiskey maker. Dave stood next to it, cleared his throat, clasped his hands behind his back, and delivered his canned speech.

"We believe bad times are coming and people have forgotten how to take care of themselves. Always depending on grocery stores and 'lectric companies and gas companies. Relying on that foreign oil that turns us into hostages." He shook his head and turned to give his big machine a few loving pats. "Government's trying to take our weapons away from us, while getting us into trouble everywhere around the world. There's threat of nuclear holocaust from all directions, and nobody's protecting us." He stuck out his neck. His face turned a vague red shade. There were mumbles of approval from Sharon. "There's danger, Emily. That's what I want you to write. There's danger, and people have to get back to the basics. You know, women back to the kitchens. Men back to farmin'."

I nodded and waited. I wasn't sensing menace here, more a man with a fixation, and a woman who loved him. He was interesting, and sincere, in an obsessed way. How could I say he was wrong? Or right? Only time would tell. In the meantime I decided maybe I'd write about some great ways people could save money by doing things for themselves. That kind of article always drew interest. Maybe it wouldn't be exactly what Dave and Sharon wanted, but, as I tried to do with most of the stories I wrote, everybody could get at least something from it.

"Got this water purifier, in case all the ground water's contaminated. Made it myself." He patted the stainless steel machine again. "Got our own sawmill. We've got a grain mill to grind the millet we grow. We've got our vitamins, our food stocks. Could live out anything. Got stores, back where we came from, in the house. Rooms with water and food enough to last us three months."

At that, the two of them tramped out of that clearing and on to another, where wide, cleared fields opened in two directions.

"Grow everything we eat. Kill the rest of what we need," Dave bragged, pointing to two deer foraging at the far end of the field.

I took photographs. More photos at the sawmill. More inside a huge metal barn where hay was stored. Dave and Sharon, after the first half hour, weren't nearly as intimidating as I'd expected, maybe a little obsessive, but not bad people. They'd chosen a way they wanted to live, and found reasons to live in just that way. Many people were like that. Most, in fact. Some for not nearly as good a reason as Dave and Sharon had found.

Since I was here, and we'd gotten to the point of joking about the time Sharon's canning jars had exploded, and the time Dave fell off his horse-drawn tractor headfirst into the mud, I said I'd heard there was some trouble between them and their neighbor, Joslyn Henry. I asked if they thought she was against what they believed in.

We'd just come from a tour of an underground bunker with high shelves stacked with jars and cans and huge tanks for water. Dave shot me a look, then shook his head as if he wished I hadn't brought up trouble.

"That's not her they found dead ... er ... some part of her?" Dave asked.

"No. That was a woman from town. But she was a friend of Mrs. Henry's."

"Terrible thing," Sharon said. "Just awful."

Dave frowned. "That one. That Joslyn Henry." He shook his head. "Crazy as a bedbug."

"So, you did have trouble with her," I said.

Dave shrugged. "Didn't exactly have trouble with Mrs. Henry. It was just that she thought I was peeping at them, I think—the old ladies dancing out there around a campfire they built. Mrs. Henry called the law from town and that police chief came out. He saw there was nothing to it. I didn't like she called the cops on me, though. That's not neighborly and there are times you don't want the law to take notice of what you're doing." He winked at me. "You know, Emily, me and my people here, we stay above the law. I'm tellin' you, way above the law. Still, if people get it into their head I'm shooting deer outta season, or anything like that, well, it's just best not to have the law hanging around. If you know what I mean."

I nodded, fully understanding.

"I didn't say nothing to anybody about what the women did out there. Just some dancing and singing. Kind of like old girl scouts, you know. But I sure didn't like her calling the cops on me."

"So Mrs. Henry caught you…saw you over in your own woods and called the police on you?" I clucked my sympathy. "That's awful."

He shook his head. "Still, I shouldn't of done what I did. I was mad, is all. Next time they was out there dancing and acting foolish I yelled right at 'em that if they ever tried a trick like calling the authorities on us again I'd be delivering a load of buckshot right where they didn't want to get it. That's what people are talkin' about."

"Where did they have their bonfire? Out by the pond, or over by Mrs. Henry's house, or …?"

"I said, right out by the pond. They've got some kind of place set up. Maybe it's an altar. I don't know what you'd call it."

"That was all? No more trouble with the women after that one time?"

"Ain't seen 'em since," Dave said. "And I didn't have anything to do with none of them dying. Hope they don't think I did. I wouldn't hurt a fly. Never meant them old ladies any harm. It was just what they did … wasn't buckshot she died of, was it?"

I shook my head. "Not that I've heard."

"No, of course not. People don't die of a little buckshot in the ass."

Sharon walked me back out to my car, sharing her recipe for venison stew on the way. I promised to try it and get back to her. Just as soon as I got myself a gun and some ammunition, learned to load the gun, then to shoot the gun, obtained a hunting license and a bright red jacket, went out into the woods on a freezing November day, and shot myself a deer.

FIFTEEN

Dog was running with his tail between his legs, looking over his shoulder at me as if I'd gone mad, which I had. I ran after him, arms flailing, screaming like a crazy person.

While I was out he'd chewed an enormous hole in the drywall of the back bedroom where I'd put him instead of out on the porch, which I thought was too cold for such a young dog. It served me right, I thought as I chased him. Now he'd done this terrible thing to the room where I was going to put my ex-husband. I wanted Jackson Rinaldi to envy me my perfect little house in my perfect little woods—just a little bit. But now my perfect house had this huge, amoeba-shaped hole in the wall of the very room where he would be staying.

I stopped running and screaming when I got out of breath and when I realized I was maddest because I would look like a failure in Jackson's eyes. Why, I asked myself, hands on my head, did I care what Jackson thought of me? Wasn't I over vying for his attention, hoping for a good grade on my hair, my intelligence, my very being?

Dog taught me I wasn't as blasé about this visit as I was pretending. Awful, knowing there were pockets of my mind harboring ideas completely at odds with the rest of me. Like having nasty demons living in my brain cells. Surely, I didn't still have hopes where Jackson Rinaldi was concerned? Some women never learned. I sighed, and apologized to Dog.

Poor Dog, he didn't understand a woman losing it over a two-bit time filler, a simple: I'm-bored-guess-I'll-chew-the-wall decision. *Geez, lady—it's a hole!* He stopped running when I stopped, and turned to look back at me, dark round eyes troubled. I fell into a heap on the floor, buried my face in my hands, and howled. All too much for me: Dog, home repairs, dead body parts, ex-husbands coming to visit with God-only-knew what intent. Maybe, I told myself between sobs, I was covering my feelings for him and maybe I was tired of living by myself here in the woods and tired of being a failed mystery writer everybody—and I was sure of this—just everybody for miles around made fun of. And maybe all my helpful neighbors and friends, coming to me with their obviously purloined mystery plots, weren't the naive ones after all.

I was having a good wallow when Dog decided it was safe to come over and put his face close to mine. He nuzzled my cheek. I threw my arms around him, held on, and howled all the louder. He stood very still, his body braced, and let me cry out my misery against his neck. What a friend I had in Dog. What a divine consoler. After a while I pulled back and looked him straight in the eye. His face was sad and contrite. Maybe he thought he was the sole cause of all this grief. Maybe he didn't care, but consolation was his job.

It came to me then that Dog had a name, from *The Hotel New Hampshire*, a wonderful book by John Irving. I remembered that dog so well. Best animal in literary history, I'd always thought. The dog's name had been Sorrow, and when his dead, stuffed body fell off a ship bound for Europe, the family looked back to see him floating along behind for hundreds of miles. "Sorrow floats," someone observed.

Sorrow.

Why not?

"Sorrow." I called him by name to see what he thought, and he licked my face. Our deal was sealed. Whatever he called himself wasn't important. He was Sorrow from then on, and with me as his housemate I thought he'd better be able to float.

It was time to get some work done before Dolly showed up. So, out to the studio to get at the mystery, or to write the Survivalist story—such as it was. Or, I could stand at the window with my elbows on the sill and stare at the glowing afternoon for a couple of hours, and listen to the trees rustling their last rustle before the leaves dropped.

It was a slow walk. The afternoon was perfect, a day of warmth and slight chill, of sun and brilliant white clouds, of blue sky. No shadow of danger. My walk led toward the meadow, golden with tall grasses, and then to my little studio—half a garage really—under a stand of old oaks, surrounded now with fallen acorns. A gray squirrel sat on my roof ridge like a dark weathervane.

Sorrow trotted beside me, not running off, but keeping up a good little black and white pace. Inside, he settled at my feet while I made phone calls to Gaylord and then to the newspaper.

"Hey Emily, I'm coming to see you this weekend," Bill Corcoran greeted me. "Kind of like to take a look around myself."

Bill's voice was overly cheerful. I thought about letting him come out, then remembered I had Jackson for the weekend—or however long he was staying.

"I'm having company, Bill."

"That's good. Very good. Glad you won't be alone. Still, I'd like to take a drive over, maybe Sunday afternoon. If you're there, fine. If not, well, I'll just feel better."

"Why?"

"Just will. I don't know 'why.' Just ... better."

"Then come on out. But Bill, call first, OK? I'll take you around myself. Show you the important parts, like where my garbage can sat."

He agreed he would call. I figured it would be an early warning, though why I was worried about Bill visiting while Jackson was there, I hadn't a clue.

"Stay with the story, Emily. Unless you feel threatened in any way. I mean, with all those body parts turning up."

"I'll stay with it. Interviewed a Survivalist guy today, who says he saw them dancing in the woods—all the women."

"Go see the others then. Go after it from that way."

"I'm working pretty closely with Deputy Dolly Wakowski. The state police are in charge but she thinks together we'll have more luck getting people in town to talk."

"She might be right. Still, be careful. I take it nobody knows much of anything yet."

I promised follow-ups as soon as I had information.

Because of Sorrow's wild morning, and because I knew inside repairs were beyond Crazy Harry's capability, I had to find a handyman in town who would come out and fix my wall. The only one listed in the local phone book had an answering machine that let me know "John" would be away all week hunting squirrel, try him next week. I decided I'd see about moving the furniture around in the room, maybe I could pull the dresser across the hole.

I gave up housekeeping thoughts and went back to work on *Creative Murder*, the working title of my novel.

Sorrow stayed settled by the little green fireplace while I got back to writing. I felt confident that, with Sorrow at my feet, I'd turn out superior work. He wasn't going to be just a dog. He would be my muse, my good luck talisman. Sorrow could carry the gloom in my life while I was free to soar.

I made progress and was feeling good about it when I saw Dolly's car zip down the hill, pass the studio, and come to a gravel-throwing stop by my house. I turned off my computer. Sorrow and I went out to greet her. Me, with grace and decorum. Sorrow, with huge leaps and jumps and yelps of joy. Dolly fended off the leaping dog, then grabbed him in a bear hug that calmed him, or scared him.

I made tea for both of us, because it was the thing to do in the late afternoon. Jackson had always loved a proper English high tea, cucumber sandwiches with the crust trimmed off, and little cakes, and pots and pots of tea. I was thinking I'd have to get into town and buy some cakes, or something besides a grocery store sponge cake, then I thought I'd rather put Jackson's arrival out of my head. I'd rather plan no menus, have nothing in the house.

I'll think about that tomorrow, I told myself with proper Southern inflection.

Dolly had more important things than tea parties on her mind.

"Didn't get much out of Mary Margaret or Flora Coy." She blew at the hot tea and settled her elbows on the counter after mov-

132

ing her gun belt around so it didn't catch on the arm of the stool. "Flora Coy wouldn't say a word. Wrote out that she had laryngitis, though I'm not convinced that's what was wrong with her. The woman looked really nervous. And in a big hurry to get me out of her house. Just like Miz Henry. Mary Margaret Murphy, too. Didn't have much to say and usually you can't stop that one from talking. Most people avoid Mary Margaret for that. Not because she's the town undertaker, but for her talking and talking and talking. Something's up with all of them. I'll tell you, Emily, I sure wish I knew what it was. I'd like to ask Miz Henry about that business at Amanda's yesterday, too. You get anything from Pastor Runcival?"

"Not much. He preached against what he called their 'Druidic' rites in the woods. Said parishioners had come to him complaining. That's why he preached that sermon. Kind of outing the ladies. He wouldn't tell me who'd complained. What was that you asked Amanda? About who inherited? Gloria and Simon were saying something about Mrs. Poet renting out family land. Oil leases. Sounds as if there could be money. That's always a motive for murder."

Dolly gave me a pained look. "Like I don't know a motive for murder when I see one," she said. "There's been talk in town for the last six months about Miz Poet and some property that's been in her family for like a hundred years or more. Maybe she made some money from Shell Oil, selling off her oil and mineral rights, or leasing them, or something. Most of the property around here, the rights were sold off years ago. Shell Oil could come in anywhere almost and drill without anybody having a thing to say. But not on this property Miz Poet owned. It looks as if there's something there. Don't know what she got. What kind of money we're talking. Could be, if they bring in oil, Amanda stands to make a good bit. So much per barrel, is what I heard. Depends on the deal her mother struck. But that's all gossip anyway. Don't know anything for certain. Still, even the smell of money sometimes stirs people to do things they wouldn't have thought up otherwise."

Dolly stretched her neck a little. "I was thinking there'd have to be a will. Everybody knows about probate. Nobody up here is stupid, you know. I'm sure Ruby Poet knew how to take care of her assets. The first thing you look for in an investigation is who benefits. You knew that didn't you? Hmm … You've got a lot to learn, Emily. Lucky for you we've hooked up. I'll make a mystery writer out of you yet."

"Should we go back and see this Mrs. Coy?" I asked. "Maybe together. Anyway, I'd like to talk to her. Bill wants me to follow the story. Keep on it."

"Couldn't hurt. Guess we'll save Miz Henry for later."

I tied Sorrow to the wall on the side porch with a long piece of clothesline, and we were ready to go. Off again, this time in Dolly's police car, which smelled like an old house that'd been closed up for about twenty years, with a dead body inside.

———————

Mrs. Coy's farmhouse was on Oak Street, two blocks down from Main. At one time it must have stood alone, in the middle of large fields. Leetsville had grown around it until now there were houses lined up and down both sides of Oak. The house could've used a coat of white paint. The front porch leaned a little to the left. Still, it had the feeling of a home somebody loved. Cement flower pots lined the steps though now they held only dead flowers. There were neatly curved and turned flower beds across both sides of the front. Another gardener, I thought, and began to wonder if gardening was a killing offense up here.

When Mrs. Coy opened her door, her eyes did a literal bulge behind pink framed glasses, at the sight of Dolly back so soon. Obviously, we weren't going to be welcomed guests.

Flora Coy was a small woman with white sprightly hair curled, or frizzed, around her face. The thick lenses in her glasses magnified her eyes and gave her a startled look.

"Hello Mrs. Coy." Dolly bent at the waist, obsequious, not like Dolly.

The little woman frowned and pointed to her throat—her laryngitis, she was telling us.

"I know," Dolly said. "I just wanted to bring my friend, Emily Kincaid, over to see you. She's with the *Northern Statesman*, kind of following up on Miz Poet's death. We thought maybe there was something you'd like everybody to know. I mean about Miz Poet, about your women's group. Things like that."

The woman's face didn't move. Her thin lips were pursed. She wasn't pleased to see us and nothing Dolly said was going to change that fact. Dolly stepped into the house, backing Mrs. Coy into her living room.

Grudgingly, Mrs. Coy motioned to the sofa, indicating we should sit. She took a rocking chair, with what looked like one of Ruby Poet's crocheted Afghans over the back and sat with her legs crossed at the ankles, hands holding each other in her lap.

From somewhere back in the house I heard a bird clock cheeping, except it didn't stop. It kept on peeping and calling. I figured Mrs. Coy had the real thing. Live birds.

"I know you can't talk," Dolly began, then stopped and looked at me.

"Officer Wakowski, here, is worried about you." I stepped into a kind of good cop/bad cop routine. "She thinks you're not talking because you're afraid of something. We'd like very much to help. I know it must be awful, losing a friend like Ruby Poet, but if there's anything you could tell us, could lead to who did this to her—well, please…"

The woman frowned and pointed to her throat.

"You can't say a word?" I asked. "Not even croak out a yes or no?"

She shook her head.

"Could you write down what you want us to know about Ruby? Anything that might help in the murder investigation," Dolly said.

At the word "murder" Mrs. Coy grimaced and seemed to shrink, her shoulders slumping, back bent.

I fumbled in my purse for my notebook, then held it out to her, along with a pen. She took both, but only held them in her lap. After a while she started to write, then held the notebook up for us to see.

> I THINK YOU'D BETTER LEAVE NOW. I'VE GOT
> NOTHING TO SAY ABOUT ANYTHING. POOR
> RUBY. NOTHING WILL BRING HER BACK . I'M
> GRIEVING AND I ASK THAT YOU RESPECT MY
> FEELINGS.

"Well, yes." I was embarrassed. We'd pushed too hard. I didn't like being a part of this whole thing and would rather just write what people told me than wring it out of them. I got up. Dolly was slower. She sat, looking straight at Mrs. Coy, until the woman's naturally bright pink cheeks went a brazen red. Dolly got up then because I was motioning at her to come on, don't bother this woman anymore. Mrs. Coy rose, and was about to follow us to the door, obviously relieved to think she was seeing the end of us, when she tripped on one of her rag throw rugs and stumbled. Her hands flew out in front of her. She flailed around, trying to right herself.

"Oh my, no . . . ," she said clearly, in a surprisingly deep voice, as she grabbed for the back of a chair.

Dolly turned to face her. She said nothing. I already had my hand on the doorknob but I stood still, too. So much for laryngitis, I thought, and waited to see what would happen next.

Mrs. Coy righted herself, shook her head a few times. She blinked her eyes and straightened the pink glasses that had fallen down her nose. "Well," she said, looking angry, probably at herself. "Guess my throat's not as bad as I thought it was."

She didn't bother looking embarrassed about the lie. She heaved a sigh and stood, waiting for what was coming next.

"I'm very sad about our poor Ruby," she said, her deep voice grudging. She had her bright eyes on me, avoiding Dolly. "Don't think I need to even come out and say it. We've been friends since we were five years old. Started school together. The thing is . . . well." She looked nervous, not angry. "The thing is I've been warned not to talk to anybody."

"Who warned you to do that? The state police?"

Mrs. Coy shook her head fast, setting her white frizz to quivering around her head, like an electric halo. She held up a finger for us to wait, and went back through a tall archway. We heard her footsteps along an uncarpeted hallway and heard what must've been a drawer open, then close.

When she walked back in, she carried a folded piece of pink paper. "Found this in my mailbox yesterday morning," she said and then handed the letter to Dolly.

Dolly shook the letter open and read. I looked over her shoulder.

YOU'LL STOP YOUR PAGAN WAYS OR FACE
AN AVENGING GOD DON'T GO TALKING TO
ANYBODY ANYMORE OR THIS WON'T STOP
WITH RUBY POET YOU KNOW WHAT I MEAN
GET YOUR HEATHEN SELF BACK TO THE
CHURCH AND YOU'LL BE SAVED
    OR ELSE

"Guess I was being stupid, being afraid like that." She sniffed now, one hand wiping angrily at her nose. She sat back down and wrapped the brightly colored afghan around her. She rocked as fast as she could get the chair to go, talking more to herself than to us.

"Anybody else get anything like this?" Dolly asked.

"I don't know. Haven't called either Mary Margaret or Joslyn and they haven't called me. That's not usual, so I kind of think something's going on with them, too. I'm an old woman." She looked up and there were tears in the bright blue eyes, shining all the brighter for the thick lenses. "I've never had anyone threaten me before. Why, I can't imagine. Why would anybody want to hurt any of us? We don't do anything wrong. We get together for the solstices and a few other celebrations. All in fun. Ruby said if we got more in tune with nature our gardens would do better. She said what we were doing had nothing to do with religion, just a way of thanking the earth ... you know ..." She spread her hands and shrugged. "It wasn't anything that hurt anybody. We'd bake cookies in the shape of suns and moons and sometimes make little goddesses out of them. We'd have hot chocolate or lemonade; take it out to the fire. Joslyn played the flute and I brought my violin. We'd play music, and then we'd dance, if we felt like it. Nothing strange. We'd wave our arms and dance around and laugh and sing. What's so terrible about having a little fun? Is it just because we're old women? Is that it? People can't stand to see us acting young, and laughing, and enjoying ourselves? A shame. An awful shame, I'll tell you."

"Any idea, at all, who might've sent this?" Dolly held the letter by one corner.

Mrs. Coy shrugged her shoulders, then made a face. The rocking chair slowed, the thumping sound against the floor dropped in tempo. "You know, I heard Pastor Runcival, over to the Church of the Contented Flock, preached out against us. Or, not us exactly, but what he called New Age people dancing in the woods. As if we'd call ourselves 'New Age.' Or new anything, for that matter. More 'old age,' I'd say. We never did a thing to hurt him or his flock. Amanda goes to that very church. I can't imagine a pastor sending a letter like that. Not in a million years. Still …"

"We'll look into it," Dolly said. "Get it to the state police to go over. I'll show the chief. Maybe Dorothy at the post office. She'll remember somebody bringing it in, if she saw 'em. It's Butch who brings around your mail, isn't it? I'll talk to him, too."

Dolly folded the letter carefully and slipped it into her shirt pocket. She turned to me. "Maybe we'd better get over to see Mary Margaret." Dolly scrunched her face so I couldn't tell if she was uncomfortable or angry.

"Dave Rombart told me there was trouble between him and you ladies. You don't think he would do something like this to Mrs. Poet do you?" I asked.

"Hmmp. That Rombart man. He would've shot Joslyn, if you ask me, not gone after poor Ruby. He thinks he's got rights nobody else has got because that wife of his put it into his head that they're different from the rest of us, don't have to obey the laws of this country. I don't think he's got it in him to really hurt anybody. Dave grew up right here in town. We all knew him from when he was little. I remember him running the streets in a diaper, one hand down on his back cheek, nose running." She shook her head. "Sad little boy. But how can you know what goes on in a man's heart and mind? Why, there's no way of knowing anything. I'm as confused by all of this as you are. If I thought … well … I'm not one to get anybody in trouble. I'd have to be awfully sure …"

We waited. I was hoping she was going to come up with something but there was reluctance written across her face. Mrs. Coy was one of those delicate ladies who didn't wish to cause anyone trouble. Whether that delicacy stretched to people who'd murdered her friend and threatened her, we'd have to wait and see.

"You aren't afraid to be alone or anything, are you?" Dolly turned back to Mrs. Coy as we were leaving.

The woman shook her head. "Lived here all my life. Not going to be scared now. Must be some kids or some nut who wants to be in on the excitement that sent me the letter. Not many murders in Leetsville, as you well know. It's just so … very … unsettling."

"If you're worried, you call the station. The chief will get a hold of me," Dolly said.

"Or me," I added and wrote my name and number down in my notebook then tore it out and handed her the paper. "Any time. I'd be glad to have you come stay with me if need be. Don't be afraid to ask."

"How neighborly. Thank you both." Mrs. Coy didn't seem as nervous now. "You make me feel a whole lot better. I'm sure I'll be just fine. But could you tell Mary Margaret to give me a call? I'll feel better knowing she isn't getting threatening letters, too. Joslyn, too—if you see her. I sure hope it's only me."

We left her, walked out to the car, then drove over to the big crumbling funeral home at the corner of Griffith and Mitchell streets.

SIXTEEN

MARY MARGARET MURPHY WAS not the kind of well-tailored, plastic-smile funeral director you might expect. She was more the motherly sort, big, blowzy, with a malleable face that went from throw-back-your-head-and-laugh to Poor-Dear, so-sad, in a nanosecond. Dressed in her un-funereal, large-flowered, polyester dress cinched in under her big breasts by an invisible belt, she stood across from me and Dolly in the front hall of her funeral home wringing her hands and shaking her head sadly. "Our precious Ruby. Who'd ever have thought she'd be the first to go."

Around us were dusty red velvet draperies, a red Axminster carpet, and huge gold-framed mirrors, leading me to wonder why funeral homes and houses of prostitution went in for the same decor.

Every time I'd seen Mary Margaret before, usually at EATS, she'd never seemed a woman to look dejected—despite her profession. She was more an upbeat person, back-patting and cheering. Now she listed to the left, the way the building listed. Her left leg was stuck out, her head was tilted, and her hands were gathered at her left hip. I felt off-kilter, the way you feel in one of those mystery spots where the rooms are built wrong, as if I might fall over if I didn't rearrange my body. I stuck my right leg out, tilted my head to the right and felt better.

"Sure," she answered a question Dolly asked. She frowned briefly, before her face automatically drew back to a tepid smile. "I got one of those letters. Don't tell me Flora's worried. Nonsense—all of that. Everybody knows our precious Ruby got herself lost out there in the woods. She went hunting for weeds. Well, she called 'em herbs. Always traipsing around hunting for a mushroom that only grew there by you, or for some wildflower in danger of becoming extinct. Not that I can tell one weed from another." She leaned forward at the waist and chuckled. "Still our Ruby was the one into all of that and it was important to her. And you know what, Dolly? If she died out there where she was happiest, then so be it. Better we all go like that than in some cold hospital with tubes stuck up our butts."

"Wasn't natural causes," Dolly said.

"Well," Mary Margaret waved a hand, dismissing details. "Whatever took her out there, she'd have wanted it that way."

"Not the way she went," Dolly went on doggedly.

"Why? What do you mean? Nobody said anything to me."

"I'm surprised you haven't heard," I said, knowing that by now all of Fuller's EATS had to be buzzing with the news.

"So?" Mary Margaret frowned in earnest, her lips puffed out, her painted eyebrows drawn up, then down, into jagged angle irons.

"Ruby Poet was murdered, or at least her body was cut up after death. With a saw," Dolly said.

Mary Margaret's hand flew to her mouth. Her eyes shot wide. "You don't say. I don't believe it. Not up here. Down below—well, they act like that. But not up here." She shook her head. "No sir, I just won't believe it of anybody from up here. Except, maybe one of those kooks from back in the words. Maybe one of those. We had an incident with Dave Rombart out by Joslyn not too long ago. Man thinks he's a general or something. He and his wife, they live out there beyond Joslyn. Behind barbed wire, if you can believe it. Live off the land, they call it. That sort of thing. You never know. If one of that kind went nuts, well, oh dear, but not our precious Ruby—the least among us. The dearest. The gentlest. Well, wouldn't you just know it? This world isn't fit for good people like Ruby Poet."

"That's why we're concerned about those letters you women got," Dolly said. "Can we see it—the letter?"

"I tore the thing up and threw it away. You've always got your religious nuts, no matter where you go. I didn't think anything of it. There's not one of us doing wrong. We get together and have a bonfire and sometimes we sing songs Ruby comes … er … came up with. And we'd do a little dancing around the fire—just to make our bodies feel good. I mean, it really felt good being out there in the woods with friends. We'd take out thermoses of hot tea and some fancy cups and cookies. Somebody always made cookies. Kind of a competition between us, who came up with the best cookies. One time I made these orange butter cookies that beat everything else. But the cookies and stuff wasn't the point. It was being there under the trees, with the fire going. That was it. Made you feel connected to the earth. I think Ruby, more than the rest of us, had a connection to what she called the Goddess spirit. Maybe that's what made people angry, when she talked about the feminine spirit in the woods. But she didn't mean it in any religious sense. You understand?

"I mean, it was just that she felt it was closer to all that's real about life, being there with the wind and stars and fire and earth. All

144

the elements. Like Ruby said: we came from the elements and that's what we should be thanking for our lives. I don't know if I bought into all that so much. It was just fun to be with my old friends and laugh and dance and sing and feel young, like I had no worries about my boys or about this place. That's what we all said and were grateful to Ruby for organizing the meetings. Just a few hours, maybe every month or so, to be together like we used to be when we were kids and be doing something... I don't know... something other people didn't know about. Though I guess they did."

She stopped talking and readjusted her body, listing farther left. "Hope that wasn't it. That somebody took offense enough to kill our precious Ruby. Terrible thought. Don't know if I can stay in a place that would do something like this..."

"It wasn't the town," Dolly said with more thoughtfulness than I'd imagined her capable of. "Just one person. Could be anywhere. Evil can spring up any place, any time."

"Got that right." Mary Margaret sighed.

"Well, if there's nothing you can add. No ideas about who might've done this to Miz Poet?"

Mary Margaret shook her head slowly. "Can't come up with a thing."

"What about those oil leases of hers?" Dolly asked. I watched the woman's face closely. If anyone would know if there was truth to the rumors, I imagined a close friend would.

"Well, yes. She mentioned something about signing papers. Said it might bring her some money. Said she hoped she could do good with that money—if she got any. That was all. Just that much. We never talked about business, or our kids, or even about our lives. Not when we were out at Joslyn's. That was kind of kept sacred, you understand. Like there was one place where the everyday stuff couldn't get us. We all have our trouble, I can tell you. But we had that one place. I wonder what we'll do now. Ruby was our spark plug. I'll have to talk to Joslyn and Flora. Maybe after the funeral. I'd like to see us keep going, myself. But maybe they'll be afraid. Not that I'd blame them. Still. Oh my." Her hands flew up to cover her mouth. "The coroner'll bring Ruby here. He didn't call … but … oh dear. Pieces? Gilbert will have to handle it. Why, I just couldn't. Not my dear precious Ruby."

I got a few strained quotes from her about Ruby Poet, how they were best friends. "Gave each other words of encouragement, you know. Sometimes a little poem. Sometimes just a note to buck each other up. Always there with a kind word. Especially Ruby. Why, I've got a note from her now. Gave us each one—something for the bad times, she said. I think that's what she said. Haven't given it a thought until now. Gotta find it. Open it, when I can read her words without bawling my eyes out."

Dolly told the tearful Mary Margaret to call either one of us if she thought of anything at all. Something Ruby had said, somebody she was afraid of or worried about, anything that could help find who did this terrible thing to Ruby Poet. Mary Margaret assured us she'd be keeping her ears open and searching back in her head for anything that should have warned her there was danger.

We left with Mary Margaret calling after us as we stepped across the sloping, veranda-like, front porch, "I'm going to get ahold of Flora right now and maybe ask her to come stay here until after the funeral, if she's worried. I tried getting Joslyn on the phone, but no luck. I think this is her day to go shopping into Traverse. I'll call again this evening."

Dolly and I took a look at the tilting, weathered porch of the decaying funeral home and looked at each other, both doubting Flora Coy would come there for a safe haven.

Dolly pulled into a parking place directly in front of the Leetsville police station, beside Lucky Barnard's dark sedan. The chief was in his office and motioned me to sit, leaving Dolly to balance herself with one hip on his desk, her gun belt clanking against the metal top.

"How's Charlie doing?" she asked as she thumbed through papers neatly piled at the corner of Lucky Barnard's desk.

"Really good, looks like," the chief said, and he reached out to straighten his papers. Dolly sat up and folded her hands in her lap. "I've got to get back there right away. Just came in to make sure things were going OK. Tried to raise you but you had the radio shut off."

His big face was stern. This wasn't the way he ran his department. Maybe Dolly was making up too many of her own rules.

Dolly nodded. "Me and Emily were in talking to Mrs. Coy and then to Mary Margaret, over at the funeral home." She leaned back and drew Mrs. Coy's letter from her pocket. She handed it to Chief Barnard. He read it. His face didn't change.

"I'll turn this over to the state police right away. They'll want the lab in Grayling to go over it for fingerprints ..." He held the letter gingerly away from him as if he could decontaminate it now. "Probably won't get much beyond you and Mrs. Coy, and now me."

Dolly shrugged.

"Mary Margaret get one?" Lucky asked.

Dolly nodded.

"What about Mrs. Henry? Check with her yet?"

"Can't get her."

He nodded.

"Why don't you go on over there? I'll see Mrs. Coy and get the envelope, then I'll stop at the post office and talk to Dorothy, see if she remembers anything about it. You know Dorothy, she recognizes everybody in town by their handwriting, even by their typing. She might be some help. Or even Butch, he delivers around here. He might know who sent it. I'll radio you with what I get. You keep that radio on, you hear?" His voice and face were stern. Dolly didn't seem to notice. She got up and stretched.

"Eh, Chief," I jumped in, "Dave Rombart told me he had a run-in with the women in the woods during one of their dancing sessions—or whatever you want to call it. He says you went out there to talk to him. Did they accuse him of peeping at them, or was it something else? He seemed to think they were just causing trouble."

Chief Barnard gave me a rueful smile and shook his head. "You meet his wife?" He shook his head again. "She's the real source of trouble. Every time there's a run-in out there it's something Sharon instigated. Maybe not this time. I talked to her after the women complained. I think what Dave was doing was poaching on Mrs. Henry's property. He kills quail and rabbit. Pretty sure some deer, too. We know it, but you have to catch him in the act, or with the dead animal. So far that hasn't happened. Mrs. Henry told me she'd keep calling, every time she saw Dave on her property. That's what it was about—him hunting her woods. Those women are against hunting to begin with. Lots of signs all over the Henrys' place, but Dave Rombart doesn't obey signs. Says they have nothing to do with him, that you can't own land and keep people from hunting on it, but you try stepping a foot on their property and they're out there with guns pointed. I warned Dave, more than once, not to hunt any place out of season. It's Sharon that's always running her mouth, saying they don't have to follow laws they don't believe in. If you ask me, she's nuttier than Dave is. And that's pretty nutty."

"Then you don't think he might have been holding a grudge against the women?" I said.

Lucky thought a moment and made a face. "If that was the case, Dave would have a grudge against just about everybody living out your way. He and Harry Mockerman had to-dos about Harry's going onto Dave's property. Harry thinks nothing of letting his dogs run. Makes a lot of your neighbors over there mad. I do my best for people, but you have to realize that some been living here their whole life and you can't ask them to change everything just because we've got newcomers."

"Dave's not a newcomer."

"No, but since he holed up and put those signs around his property—well, he's been acting like he's the army and everything on his place is top secret."

"Maybe it is," I said. "Maybe the women found out something he didn't want them to know. Or maybe they saw something and don't even know it."

Dave shrugged. "All you can do is ask," he said.

Dolly took my arm and pulled me toward the door.

"You've got to get back to the hospital," she said to the chief. "Give Charlie my love and tell him to get better real fast."

Lucky nodded and stood as we left his office. He promised to stay in touch, especially if he found out anything at the PO. Dolly promised to leave her radio on.

I would have sworn Eugenia was waiting to pounce on us when we walked into Fuller's EATS for a quick dinner before going back out to my place. "You two hear those ladies were being threatened?" Eugenia hissed at us before we were barely in the front door.

Dolly glowered at her. My mouth fell open. "How'd you know?" I asked. "We just found out a little while ago."

"Sullivan Murphy came in. Said his mother got a letter threatening her if she didn't stop whatever those women were doing out in the woods. Now, why in hell would anybody care what a bunch of old ladies was doing on their own property, having a little fun, or whatever it was? Just terrible. Like we've got Nazis moved in, telling us what we can do." Eugenia's face was red with anger. "They better not try anything like that with me. I've still got the rifle Rodney left me. I'll use it faster than they can say 'bite me.' I'm not afraid to stand up to any of those crazies. You just watch."

"Don't forget one of those ladies is already dead," Dolly said, and she shook her head at Eugenia. "I'd say everybody better be careful what they say and who they say it to."

"You two gonna find out who did this? Seems that we've got you and the state police on this and nothing's happening." Eugenia was getting herself worked up. I knew how she was feeling. I understood what it was like to feel targeted and not know by whom, or why.

"We're trying," Dolly said. "We need people in town to report anything funny they might have noticed, anything they heard. It's going to take the whole town to stop whoever this crazy man is. You just pass that along now, OK? You tell everybody to give me, or Chief Barnard, a call if they know anything, because this is no joke. One woman's dead. At least two more have been threatened. We don't know where this is going to stop."

Eugenia's eyes grew huge while Dolly talked, as if the enormity and seriousness were just sinking in. She nodded again and again. "You can depend on me. You know if somebody's whispering anything, anywhere in this town, it gets talked about in here. I'll be listening, and I'll call you." She nodded to me and then to Dolly.

We made our way to the table Eugenia pointed to.

"Hey Emily," she called after me. "How's your new dog working out? You named him Sorrow? How come? Sorrow. Seems like a sad name for a puppy. You ever heard of calling a dog Spot or Rover? Those are real dog names."

I nodded, waved, and smiled. "I'll think about it," I called back, deciding I should have named him Mud because that's what his name was going to be if there was any more chewing in my house. I felt immediately contrite. The poor thing had been home alone for ages now, tied up on the porch. I'd named him well. Living with me—a person who could forget him for hours on end—wasn't going to be easy. Sorrow it was, and Sorrow it would remain.

SEVENTEEN

JOSLYN HENRY'S HOUSE WAS as still and unoccupied as it had been when I'd gone by earlier. Leaves blew across the front porch, collecting against the east railing. It seemed to me Joslyn Henry wouldn't allow leaves to gather. While other gardeners—like me—let things go because winter was coming and next spring would be soon enough to clean up, Joslyn Henry had been at work, doing the things we were supposed to do, spreading winter mulch and weeding. As I recalled, standing with Dolly, knocking for the fourth time, when I'd seen her there was a kind of precision about her. Not in how she dressed, that was always casual enough, more in how she stood and looked straight into your eyes, and in the way she spoke, kind of leaning back away, tucking her chin down to form a nest of three, and looking down her nose. But who knew? After a friend was killed the way her friend was killed, she might be too upset to notice things like leaves collecting on her porch, or that a pot of mums had fallen from the railing and lay broken, dirt spilling down the front steps.

I peeked in one of the front windows, half expecting someone to peek back; someone not wanting to answer the door. I was beginning to feel like a true *persona non grata* around there. I couldn't blame it on being with Deputy Dolly any longer. They were avoiding me because I was me.

"What should we do?" I whispered to Dolly, feeling like a kid on Halloween when the homeowner is hiding inside, in the dark, and doesn't want to bother passing out a piece of penny candy to a scruffy kid. I didn't know whether to tiptoe off the porch or stomp and yell.

Dolly shrugged. "Let's leave a note. Ask Miz Henry or Ernie to call. Can't think of anything else."

I scrambled in my purse for my notebook and pen, then scribbled out a note complete with greeting and compliments on getting her beds in order so early. I wrote that I'd be happy if she called me, or called Officer Dolly Wakowski at the police station in town. We had some questions about Ruby Poet's death, and were working hard to find out who'd done this awful thing.

Dolly read the note, then stuck it in the screen door.

On the way back down the steps, I picked up the broken pot pieces, collecting them into a little pile. I swept the spilled soil away with my foot and took the mum, dug a little hole with my fingers beside the steps, and stuck the flower into the hole, patting the soil around it. There, I thought. That's what one neighbor does for another. Not ignore a friend's garden. I still couldn't understand why Joslyn Henry hadn't done something about Ruby Poet's garden. Why let it go? If Amanda didn't care, certainly Joslyn Henry did. Or Mary Margaret, who seemed to value Ruby Poet above the others. Or Flora Coy, herself a gardener. None of the women were so old they couldn't have kept Ruby's garden in order. If I'd known, I would have done it. It was always such a shame to see a garden go wild.

Dolly was coming back to stay with me. She had all the stuff in her car to do my makeover, and she had her pj's, too, for sleeping on my couch. She figured her job on me was going to take a long time, and anyway, she told me, while she worked we could put the pieces we had, so far, together, seeing what we needed to do next.

I figured I could use the makeover and the help moving furniture in the room where Jackson would sleep. I had that hole to hide, and I wanted to get the dust bunnies out from under the bed and spruce things up a little. I wasn't sure how. Maybe I could get some flowers at the IGA in town. Flowers always made a room look festive, and Jackson liked it when I put flowers on the table, or in the bathroom. Or maybe I'd just pick some dead flowers. A kind of symbol.

All the way from the Henrys' to my house, I whined to Dolly that I shouldn't have left Sorrow alone so long, that it probably wasn't good for young dogs to be tied up, that I'd probably pay with psychological damage that would cost me plenty to rectify—in training and attention.

Sorrow sat in the middle of the drive, tongue lolling out to one side, ears up at attention. He saw me and galloped for the Jeep, leaping in the air like a doggie Lotto winner. When I got out, he was all over me, as if I'd been lost and now was found; as if he'd left me someplace and was so very grateful I'd found my way home again.

On the porch I discovered how he'd gotten loose. Chewed through the piece of clothesline.

"Better get him some chain," Dolly said as I stood examining first the chewed clothesline then the place in the door where Sorrow had gone straight out, tearing the screen into a bent flap. Sorrow stuck his nose where I pushed at the screen, as if trying to figure out who could have done this dastardly deed. His innocence didn't fool me. I swore under my breath and quickly started thinking of punishments for him. None I could come up with fit the crime.

"I'm not going to start chaining an animal," I growled at Dolly.

"Then get him trained better," she said, going back inside.

"What do you mean 'better'? He's not trained at all," I shouted after her.

"Then get him into a class," she called back. "I'm going to telephone Ernie's shop. See if he knows where his mother is."

I sat alone with my puppy, facing my inability to care for him properly.

"Cage," I hissed at his puzzled face. "As soon as I can, I'm getting into Traverse and finding a cage I can leave you in when I'm gone."

Sorrow looked closely at me since I was kneeling and he could stare directly in my eyes. "You are a terrible animal," I said.

He licked my nose. The damned thing loved me. He wasn't mad at me, though I'd been gone all day. He'd occupied himself. Wouldn't I have done the same? Did I expect more of a being from another species than I did of myself? Some kind of bigotry working in my head. I had to come up with new ways of dealing with Sorrow. Something no one had thought of before. I was, after all, a very bright woman. Surely I could outsmart a puppy. Surely I could come to terms with his needs and my own needs and learn to live with this warm, mischievous, little being.

Surely...

Maybe.

I fed him and gave him water, since he'd turned over his dish. After deep, incriminating gulps (though he'd had the whole lake in front of him), he followed me into the house and flopped on the floor. He was sound asleep in a minute. Who knew where he'd been all day? With whom? I could have lost him. Somebody could have picked him up—the way Simon did to begin with. I squatted beside the sleeping dog, now rolled into a black and white circlet, and petted his soft head. He had me, all right. I was hooked. Madly in love with this pathetic little creature.

"Nobody answers at Ernie's shop, either." Dolly stood behind me, watching, hands on her hips. "They must have gone someplace together. Maybe Miz Henry needed a new dress for Ruby's services. That's what women always do when things get bad. They go shopping. Nobody up here any different than down below, where there's all those malls. They need new dresses for the big occasions, too."

After a while she heaved a sigh. "Might as well get started on you," she said. "I'll go get the stuff from my car. Bought a great color for your hair."

"What about the Henrys? Should we call anybody else?"

She shrugged and reached to unfasten her gun belt. I supposed this was her signal that she was off duty. "We'll go down there first thing in the morning. They should be back by then."

She put her gun on the counter. "Keep it close by," she said as she patted her holster. "Never know when you're going to need it."

She took her tie off and hung it over a chair back, then loosened her blue shirt at the neck. Dolly was now off duty and ready to begin her beauty salvage work.

On the way out to her car, she said, "I brought a sleeping bag. I'll sleep on the couch."

"Oh," was all I could think to say. Not exactly welcoming, but not unhappy either.

I would have gone out to help her bring in her bags and boxes and sleeping bag, but the phone rang just then. Jackson. I was almost happy to hear from him.

"Yes," he said. "We'll be there just past noon, if that's all right? Don't worry about lunch. We'll stop somewhere along the road. I'll call you from Grayling and get the exact directions. I'm looking forward to seeing you, Emily. Hope you're not too unhappy to see me again. I'd hate to think we couldn't be friends."

What could I do but assure him I looked forward to his visit. I was almost convinced it was true until what he'd said sank in. "We'll be there . . . ," he'd said. "We'll stop . . ."

Before I could ask who this "we" was, he was gone with a merry, "See you on Saturday."

"Damn him." I slammed the receiver down and stood leaning against the desk chair.

"What's wrong?" Dolly was back, plastic store bags dangling from her fingers. The screen door banged shut behind her.

"Jackson's bringing someone with him."

"Hmm," she said. "Didn't you ask who it was?"

"He was gone before I realized what he'd said."

"Call him back. I would. I'd ask him who the hell he's bringing."

"Yeah, and I'd better ask where I'm supposed to put his friend? I've only got the one extra bedroom."

"Maybe he thinks he's sleeping with you and his friend can take the bedroom."

"Like hell." I glared at her over my shoulder.

"Then call and ask." She set her packages on the counter. "We'll work right here, OK? The light's good and the sink's close to rinse the color out of your hair. And …" She bent down, hunting the wall for something. "Yeah, there's an outlet right here for the dryer."

"Well, I'm not calling," I said, following her around the kitchen. "I'll just tell him when he gets here. His friend can go find a motel. Or they both can. Of all the damned nerve. I should have known he'd pull something."

"Maybe it's a surprise for you. Somebody who wanted to see you. Somebody you both used to know." She was taking things out of bags and setting them along the counter. Little brushes and little bottles and packages. It had never taken that much to fix me up before. I figured I must really be a fright if Dolly thought all of this was necessary.

I concentrated a minute. Could be Sam Larson, another English professor, who was coming with him. I used to like Sam. He wasn't an impossible snob like most of Jackson's friends. Could be Sam wanted to ride along. I wouldn't mind him. Or even somebody from the paper where I used to work. Maybe somebody with family up here. That was probably it. People moved up permanently, like I did, or they had summer places. A great time of year to visit. I decided I'd made too much of Jackson's "we" and began to look over the things Dolly'd brought to beautify me.

"Want me to fix you up after you've finished with me?" I asked, eager to get my hands on those makeup brushes, experiment with the liner pencils.

"No thanks. This is your night. We're going to get you so beautiful Jackson will be sorry for the rest of his life that he ever let you go."

I had to laugh. A lofty goal here. An unnecessary goal. Still, it was nice of Dolly to care. She was showing surprising sides I'd never imagined. Not just our dumpy, mean, speeder-chasing, Deputy Dolly. She was cheering me up and giving me a weapon against my ex-husband.

Before we started, I asked for her help moving the furniture in Jackson's room. I showed her the hole Sorrow had chewed in the drywall. She agreed the only thing to do was move the dresser in front of it. Once we'd pulled the dresser over we couldn't open the door all the way but at least the hole was covered. Dolly decided that the room needed color since the walls were white and the bedspread was an old white chenille. She gathered colorful leaves out in the garden and stuck them in a cloisonné vase the previous owners had left behind. The vase and leaves, sitting on the night stand, brightened the room. Next she found a Mexican throw in the linen closet and spread it over the bed. Now the room looked at least a little sophisticated, brighter and more cheerful.

"Needs pictures," Dolly mumbled as we stood in the hallway looking in.

"It's just Jackson. He won't be here long."

"Still," she said. "You gotta see my place. Pictures all over the walls. Couldn't stand not to have pictures. Like windows looking out on different places. Cut 'em out of magazines, if I have to. All over my walls. You should come over sometime and see my place."

I agreed I'd have to do that, and got her off the subject of wall hangings.

"I hope you like the color I bought…" Her little face brightened as she opened a box of Clairol, took out the applicator and the color vial.

I struggled to smile. "You're really going to color my hair?"

She stood at the sink, held still, and frowned. "You weren't going to leave it those three shades of mud you've got going now, were you?"

Naw. I shook my head. Of course not. I'd be any shade Dolly'd chosen for me. Some nice fire-engine red, maybe. A chorus girl blond. I didn't have the heart to fight her. If she wanted me beautiful, then who was I to get in the way? I made tea for us and set out a plate of cookies.

"What color'd you get?" I dared ask as she stood frowning over the directions.

"Hmm." She pulled at her lips and narrowed her eyes. "Something called 'Mousey Brown.'"

"No," I said, appalled.

"Kidding." She laughed hard. "It's Deep Mink."

"Hmm," I said back. "Sounds expensive."

I fingered the bottles she'd set along the counter. Some of them looked a little worn, old. I wondered if makeup got rancid, got diseased, caused death. I hoped I wasn't headed for some exotic illness they'd never trace to ancient makeup samples picked up in defunct department stores.

My hair didn't take long, and after it was dried I thought she was very right—I did look a lot better with a single shade of brown. She trimmed off about four inches and poufed it so my face didn't seem so long and drawn. Dolly's magic was working. I was beginning to relish a makeover. I wanted to see what Dolly had up her sleeve for my face.

She rubbed cream into my skin as I sat with my eyes closed, letting myself enjoy the attention. She rubbed makeup on, though she cleansed it right back off when we both decided that shade of orange wasn't for me. She outlined my eyes and patted my cheeks with blush and put some stuff on my eyelids with small brushes. I was feeling very glamorous by the time I'd puckered and squinted and bunched up my cheeks for her.

When she finished and stood back to examine me, her face took on a self-satisfied smirk. She held a hand mirror up for me to see myself. I looked like a woman in a magazine. My hair shone and turned under slightly, just beneath my ears. It was too short, now, to pull back into a ponytail, but maybe that was a good thing. The makeup made me colorful, and pretty. Well, I told myself, won't Jackson be surprised.

Next, I insisted on doing Dolly's face, though the makeup looked funny on her. She was too down-to-earth. Makeup on a face that frowns deeply and crunches into crevice-like scowls, well, it just sat there looking as if it could roll off by itself, in one, wide, single sheet. She washed her face because we both agreed she was pretty enough without it.

EIGHTEEN

NEXT MORNING NO ONE answered the door again at the tall, plain, Henry house. No car in the drive or behind the house. No one inside. I cupped my hands at the front window and looked hard, but the drapes were drawn across the window now.

"Somebody's been home," I said. "The drapes were open last night and our note's gone."

Dolly shrugged. "Must've had some place else to go today."

"Obviously," I said, peeved that Dolly found it necessary to state the obvious.

"So, what now?" I asked, stepping back from the front window, looking over the neat garden.

"While we're out here I'd at least like to see the place where the women danced," Dolly said.

"Dave Rombart said their bonfire was out by the pond."

Dolly nodded. "If somebody killed Ruby because of the nature stuff, we'd better have a look at where it went on. Might give us some idea who could get back there and who'd be familiar enough with the territory to spy on the ladies. So far I'd say Dave Rombart and Harry Mockerman, and Ernie. All of them know these woods like the back of their hand."

As we headed down the steps, I noticed the pile of pot shards was just as I'd left it the day before.

The walk, from the Henry house out to Ruffle Pond, was beautiful, the sandy ground covered with orange and yellow leaves. Lining the path in thick clumps, the sumac had turned a vivid red. Dead ferns, now bronze, fell over, catching at our legs as we passed. In the sunlit patches, the world had taken on a golden glow. Magic. Dolly and I didn't talk. This was one of those places that called for silence. One of those days.

Ahead, down the path, I could see the milky white and blue of Ruffle Pond.

We walked the beach, scruffy with tall weeds, and looked out over the water, to the trees on the other side, most still in full fall dress, some already blown bare. I dug my toe into the sand, recognizing the pointed prints of a couple of deer; the small footprints of a raccoon, around us.

"I'd like to dance out here, too," I said and half meant it. A peaceful place. I could imagine a fire on the shore. I could imagine singing. Even the dancing. In my head, I was sure I could see four old women with their arms in the air, their bodies surprisingly lithe and limber—swaying to their own music. I could hear muted laughter coming over water.

"Where do you think they had their … altar, or whatever it was?" Dolly turned, her hand up to shade her eyes. She scanned the trees and beach behind us, looking hard at the open places where the land curved up to the tall grass, then to the trees.

I turned to look with her.

She pointed. "Over there. Looks like log seats in a circle. That would be the place, around a campfire. Like a bunch of Girl Scouts. Don't see why anybody would object to anything they did out here, on their own land."

She shook her head and started off toward the circle of cut logs. I followed. It was a little way down the beach and up the curve of sand. We could see the blackened remnants of a log fire and something just beyond the fire pit, stretched out on the ground. I thought it might be their altar. A mound, close to the earth.

Dolly picked up speed. I ran along behind.

"Christ's sakes!" she exploded just about the time I let out a long and painful breath.

We could see the mound better. Not an altar. Not a site of worship. A body, laid out in a long black coat. The head was back, salt-and-pepper hair arranged perfectly around her.

Joslyn Henry. As obviously dead as she was ever going to get.

Dolly stopped me, stretching her arms wide.

"It's her all right," she said. "We've got to get back to the car and call the chief. If he isn't there, we'll call Gaylord. We don't want to mess anything up here. Maybe, after this, we'd better butt out completely. I hate to think this happened because we've been asking too many questions." She was shaking her head. I thought I saw tears in her eyes.

Somebody's got to ask those questions, I thought, but I knew how Dolly felt. What I wanted to do now was stay as far as I could from Joslyn Henry. Stay away from the other poor deluded women who thought they were hurting no one with their joyous dances in the woods. What I wanted to do most was run home, post Sorrow at the door, crawl into bed, stick my head under the blankets, and come out when this was over.

The chief was with his son in Traverse City so the state police drove over from Gaylord. Officer Brent was the first to arrive, his long face sad, the single eyebrow immobilized.

He walked by without acknowledging us. He knelt down, seemed to be poking and prodding, then got up, whisked his hands together and came back to where we waited.

"Dead all right," he said. "You want to tell me how you found the body?"

He gave me a long, hard look.

Dolly spoke up. "We were looking for her. She hasn't been seen in a few days. Her son, Ernie, either. No one home so we came out here to find where the women had been holding their … eh … meetings, and there she was."

He nodded, then nodded again. We all stood looking over toward where the body lay.

"Marks on her neck. I'd say she was strangled. Looks like she'd been sitting on that log and fell over after she was attacked. Probably didn't even see the attacker."

I reached in my shoulder bag for my notebook, but he gave me a withering look. "Don't you write anything down yet, Emily. I'm not talking for the record here. That was only speculation I was giving. You'll have to get official word later."

I closed my purse.

"You know, maybe you two better pull back, let us take the lead out here. Looking really bad. Another one. Serious business going on."

Dolly nodded. We all fell silent. I toed a pile of leaves at my feet, all dead cupped hands. All around me were these dark brown, pleading hands.

After a while, Brent turned casually to face Dolly. "Got anything I should know? With your investigation?"

Dolly nodded, then shrugged, giving nothing away.

"Don't imagine you know any more than we do," he said. "If you find out anything, you'll give me a call, right? Come on in and we'll have a talk."

"We found that letter Mrs. Coy got," she said, squinting up at him. "Thought it might be important."

"We're looking into it. See if anything comes of the typing, the stationery. Maybe fingerprints other than Mrs. Coy's, yours, and the chief's. We've got the resources for that kind of thing."

"You look into Ruby Poet's oil leases yet?"

Brent looked confused for a minute. He said nothing.

"Shell Oil," Dolly said. "She was coming into money."

Brent nodded. "Thanks."

"See about her will, too," she said.

He fit his hat on his slickly shaved head. "Do that," he said and then stalked off to greet men from the sheriff's department, who'd just driven in and walked up the slope side by side, like a posse.

"Good thing we had this talk," Dolly called after him.

We heard motors pulling in along the other side of the pond and made our way back to the Henrys' house. More cops. As soon as the men were busy out by the fire pit, we were free to go.

We drove to my house, where Dolly said we'd better double up our efforts before somebody else got hurt.

"I thought Brent was kind of warning us off."

"Yeah, sure." She gave me a full face of disgust.

"That's what I figured," I said. "So, what now?"

"We've got to find Ernie," Dolly said. "That's where we start. While they're busy out there, we just keep getting ahead of them. Got to find Ernie. If he isn't dead, too, where the hell is he?"

NINETEEN

We didn't find Ernie though we checked his engine repair shop in town. Big CLOSED sign in the window. Not at Fuller's either, though there were a lot of townspeople there, buzzing about another murder. Neither of us felt like staying and hashing over this latest tragedy.

Ernie wasn't at the Skunk Saloon, across Main Street from Fuller's, and not at the bowling alley. I was tired enough to give up caring. Considering what we'd been through in the last few days, and what was ahead of me—with Jackson and the mystery "We" coming the next afternoon—I was beyond needing to be the one to save Ernie Henry from the shock of his mother's awful death.

"I'm going home," I said. "And I don't want to hear anything about anybody dying for at least twenty-four hours."

We stood in the bowling alley parking lot among red and rusty pickups, one with a yellow-eyed black lab tied in the bed.

"You going to poop out now? Right when we need to be working hardest on this?" Dolly reared back and fixed her eyes on me. "What about the other two women? They're all that's left."

"We haven't exactly been saving anybody," I said, one foot in my car.

"And we sure won't by giving up."

"Bull!" I was really tired of being talked into things. I didn't want to be bullied anymore by this stub of a woman. "Let the state police handle it."

"They save anybody yet?"

"You don't get it, Dolly. I don't care right now. I've got stuff in my own life. I've had enough shocks for a while. OK?"

"You out of it completely?" Her thumbs were twined around her gun belt. She closed one eye against the sun and looked up at me.

"I don't know," I said, giving an honest answer. I didn't know what I wanted to do. At the moment, I just needed to be away from her, away from death, away from trouble, and away from Leetsville, with all its shabby sadness.

She gave me one last, long look. "Then piss off," she said, turned her back, got in her squad car, and drove away.

I went home, called in the story, and settled down to a long day of quiet reading, eating when and what I pleased, and finally falling asleep without a thought to anybody tossing anything at my door or of stumbling on one more dead body.

It was a thrill to have my house to myself the next morning— me and Sorrow. Not that I'd minded having Dolly there with me. She'd actually been good company. Now that I was rested, I was feeling guilty that I'd walked out on her the way I had. I figured I should call her, but I couldn't bring myself to pick up the phone. I liked having my life back. I liked my house empty. All that was left me were a few hours of peace before Jackson got there. I didn't see a need to call and make up with Deputy Dolly right then.

I hummed as I boiled myself an egg and pushed an English muffin into the toaster. I'd been over Jackson's room again, straightening the rug, pulling the Mexican throw from the bed, then putting it back on. The dresser looked funny, pulled so close to the door when there was plenty of empty wall space beyond it. Still, it was better than having that gaping chew-hole show.

I was happy for the peaceful morning. Sorrow'd discovered he loved licking my bare feet so I had to give up going barefoot. It was demeaning to have him that grateful for a home, though he was still insistent, chasing me, nipping at my fluffy slippers.

We were getting along better, I thought. And he was protective. Barked when Simon pulled down the drive to deliver a book I'd ordered, barked at birds flying in front of the windows, and barked when a squirrel scampered over the roof. Well, and barked if I closed the door too hard. And barked when I dropped a spoon...

Still, I had hopes for our future together.

The morning lay ahead of me. The house was as clean as it was going to get. I didn't have to worry about lunch since Jackson said he'd eat somewhere along I-75. Dinner was iffy. I didn't want to make plans that took anything for granted. For all I knew he would have appointments to look at cottages all afternoon. Better not to presume he was coming to see me and would be hanging around. Better to prepare myself for disappointment, an emotion I knew well from the years of our marriage.

But disappointment was dippy, I told myself. No disappointment because I had no expectations—despite my new hair, and the makeup I wasn't sure I was going to apply. Disappointment was for girls who didn't get asked to the senior prom, or women waiting breathlessly for that hoped-for phone call. How could you disappoint a woman who'd bought whole-hog into that "ever after" stuff, and lost?

Sorrow broke up all that useless reverie with his whining at the door. I let him out. I'd discovered he didn't run away but spent a lot of time sitting on the porch, waiting for the door to open again, like a kid afraid of getting lost if he went too far.

After breakfast, I cleaned up and wiped the sink until it was dry and shining, I dressed in ancient sweats to go out and work in the garden. There were the last of the weeds to pull before they dropped their seed for next year, which I knew was dumb because they would have dropped those errant seeds weeks before. There were marigolds and hollyhocks to cut back. There were roses to begin mounding. I had daffodils to plant. Straw to spread. So much to do. I looked forward to a half day of heavy work. It would keep my mind occupied. I wouldn't sit in my office avoiding writing. I wouldn't stand staring out the window, hoping for inspiration to strike me. I wouldn't think about dead people. In gardening there was the benefit of mindless work; digging in dirt, a kind of hypnosis. Worm-mind, I called it. No thought. No worry. No self-pity. Just dig and burrow and edge forward with scavenging fingers.

I shrugged on a ripped jacket, which would do well for working outside on a half chilly/half warm late September day. Before I could get out of the house, the phone rang.

"It's me," Dolly said.

I was happy to hear her voice. "Hi," I said, just a little too cheerful. That final "Piss off" yesterday melted away.

"You coming into town? We've got to keep moving on this."

"You forget Jackson's getting here this afternoon? I can't go anywhere."

171

"Yeah. But later. I mean, this isn't something we can sit on. Good Lord, now we've got two dead women and we don't even know why. You think the state boys are entertaining company?"

"I thought I was kind of … well … out of it," I said.

"You were tired. You're not a quitter. You said you wanted to find out who was doing this."

"Yes," I said, half flattered, half knowing I was being had.

"This is serious, Emily."

"I know," I said, anger bubbling, slightly. Here I was, being pushed all over again.

"So? How about this afternoon? You get him settled in and let him go out looking for a house to rent."

"OK," I said, keeping my lips tight.

"Great." Her squeaky voice lifted as if everything was settled between us. "Or tell 'im you've got work to do. He'll be glad of it. You know flatlanders; they get worn out just from the drive up here. I'll call you after a while. Or you call me. Whatever. Now, can I fill you in on what's been happening?" Dolly had said her piece without drawing a breath. I guessed our quarrel was over. Funny, my part in it seemed so negligible.

She gulped in air, and began as if reading from notes.

"Here's what the chief got out of Officer Brent. You can take it down and give as much to the paper as you want to, OK? Number one: Miz Henry was strangled, just like Officer Brent said. It's not official yet but they think she was killed on Thursday sometime.

"There, that's that." She mumbled to herself, then burst out, "Oh, oh, yeah. Ernie. Drove in right after we left, I guess. He was at a tractor pull over in Leland. Said he hadn't talked to his mother since Wednesday. Ernie said he didn't have any idea who would want to hurt his mother. He's all broken up, poor guy. Feels responsible, for being away. Said he's always taken good care of her. An awful thing. Lived his whole life with her, and he's almost forty. Shame. Some men never grow up. He's kidding himself, that he was taking care of her. More the other way around. Anyway, he drove in just as the coroner was taking his mother's body away."

"Then Mrs. Henry must've been home all that time. I mean, when I was over there knocking. But wait—if she was killed Thursday she must've been dead when we were there that night. So who closed the drapes after that? Something's wrong here."

"Well, listen to this. The house was ransacked. The chief said there wasn't a dish left in the cupboards, not a piece of clothing in any of the closets. Just a mess. All torn up."

"Any idea who did it?"

"Had to be whoever killed her."

A shiver ran through my body.

"Whoever did it took the note we left on the door."

"And closed the drapes in case we came back." She stopped. I heard her sniff. "I'm going over to warn Mary Margaret and Flora Coy now." Dolly sounded pretty sick. "Wish I could take 'em into custody. God only knows what's going on here."

"Could they get out of town for a while, you think? Just until this is over?"

"They'd never leave. People in this town don't get scared off easy."

"Well, at least tell them to be careful. Flora Coy should get somebody in that house with her."

"Yeah. Mary Margaret's got Gilbert and Sullivan, though I'm not sure those two boys would be much help in a pinch."

"Hmm," I said, thinking how I would feel if my two friends had just been murdered. Speaking solely for myself, I think I'd get the hell out of town as fast as my wheels could carry me.

"Oh, speaking of those letters, the chief went to see Dorothy at the post office and she remembered letters going to Flora Coy and Mary Margaret. Says she's sure Joslyn Henry got one, too. They were all the same, small pink envelopes, like birthday cards. She noticed they were typed and there was no return address on any of them. She said they came in right there at the post office drop box. She took them out of mail collection herself but she didn't know who put them there, and she didn't recognize the type on the envelopes. Says she didn't think about it at the time.

"Ya know, Emily, if we can't talk to Ernie we've got to get over and talk to Amanda. We really need to find out what was on Miz Henry's mind that day she called on her. It seems like that's got something to do with what happened. I'll come get you, if you want. Say five o'clock? I'm on duty today anyway so I won't be free until about then. Would that be OK?"

"I'll meet you in town," I said, feeling that maybe Dolly was more than a little curious to get a look at Jackson. "Let's ask, too, when they're having services for both women. I'd like to see who comes to those, wouldn't you?"

"Everybody will be there. That's the way the town is. What about your neighbor? Old Harry. I've still got a feeling he knows something. Didn't you get that feeling?"

I had to admit Harry hadn't been forthcoming. It had been awhile since I'd seen him. Time to drop by. He was always out in the woods. Maybe he saw something over at the Henrys' place. We agreed we had to talk to Harry.

"So, if you don't want me to come get you, where'd you want to meet?"

"How about the parking lot of the IGA? You know if we go to Fuller's we'll be bombarded with questions."

"Yeah, but that goes the other way, too. That's where we get answers we didn't know we needed."

"We'll start at Fuller's, then. Five thirty? I might have to bring Jackson with me."

"Geez, Emily. What'll we do with him?"

"You'll like him, Dolly. Jackson can be very charming."

"I don't care what he is. We don't need him in the way right now."

"He could be here for some time."

"You're not letting him stay with you, are you?"

"Well, maybe … until he finds his own place to write."

"I don't know, Emily. He might try to put something over on you, move in until he gets his book done. What better than to have you cooking and cleaning all over again, while he sits and writes his dumb book nobody's going to read anyway."

"Now, Dolly. You don't even know Jackson. And his work is important."

"Yeah, what'd you say it was on?"

"Chaucer."

"See what I mean? How high is that on the bestseller list?"

"That's not the point with scholarship …"

"Don't start the nose-thumbing at me, Emily. I'm just saying, don't be a patsy and let him move in on you. You know you'll only be sorry. And if you ask me, you're a little too nice sometimes."

"Don't worry. It's just until he gets settled," I said with my teeth gritted.

"Then I hope he gets settled right away. You want me to start calling Realtors for him? I could get them going. Know a few houses for rent myself. I'll write down numbers and directions. The sooner he gets out of your hair the better for you. You've got that mystery to finish. That's important."

I laughed at the thought of *Creative Murder* being important, especially now, with Jackson doing his lofty study of a Middle English writer. Inwardly, I groaned. I'd have to hear every tiny detail as he made his way through Chaucer, one cheery or dreary character at a time. I liked Chaucer well enough. Especially the Wife of Bath, who was my kind of woman. Still, Jackson knew how to drain the life out of any subject, how to vampirize good writing until it lay on the page like a consumptive: anemic, *in extremis*.

Before we hung up I got the last word. "And, Dolly," I said. "I am not too nice. Don't ever call me that again.

"Hmmp," I said to the phone as I put the receiver down. That fixed her.

TWENTY

JACKSON CALLED JUST AFTER one o'clock, cheerful and hyped about being up north, smelling the fresh air, feeling invigorated already. I gave him directions from Grayling. It would take him about half an hour. Half an hour to scrub the dirt from my hands and face, comb my hair into my fancy new "do," and slap on a little of Dolly's makeup. I figured jeans and a sweater would be fine. After all, this wasn't one of Thoreau's occasions requiring new clothes. It was Jackson. And while he intimidated others, he couldn't do it to me. Not anymore. We were equals and it was my house, my dog, my garden, my lake, my furniture, my dishes . . .

I was getting myself worked up. I took a couple of gulps of "my" fresh air, then stood decorously in the garden, leaning on a leaf rake, pretending I'd been working in my white cable-stitched sweater and pressed jeans.

Sorrow was my early warning system. He barked and whirled in circles when the car came down the drive. I waved. A white Jaguar. White, of course, I thought, for purity of thought and action . . .

Enough of that, I told myself and pasted on a smile as I set my rake aside and strolled rube-like, dog bounding ahead of me, around through the arbor to greet Jackson.

Both car doors opened. Jackson got out, bent to pat Sorrow's head, then leaned in to speak to his passenger. He stood, stretched, waved. Dark hair, long enough to be fashionable but not scruffy, enough of a Pierce Brosnan five o'clock shadow to be sexy, and wearing the perfect, blue cashmere sweater over precisely tailored trousers. Awful, but despite everything, he still looked good to me. I might have been immune to being conned by him, but not immune to how damned well put together Jackson always was.

He shouted, "My God, Emily, how on earth did you ever find this place? This is the end of nowhere. I didn't for a moment think I was on the right road."

He chuckled, held his arms wide, and walked toward me. I was more interested in the long pair of very female legs coming out of the other side of the car, then the head, with big sunglasses and long blond hair, that jutted above the car door. All of this was followed by a long body, and then a bare arm stuck up in the air, waving at me.

Jackson hugged hard though I had my hands out, against his chest, pushing him away.

"You didn't bring one of your students with you?" I hissed at him.

Jackson held me, then leaned back, and looked down into my face, astonished. He smelled of mint. Aftershave, maybe, or mouthwash. "Emily, Jennifer's my assistant. Her family lives up here. She knows people. She's going to find a place for me, and help later. With the typing. You know what a project like mine entails. She's not staying. You don't imagine . . . well, of course not." He looked hurt, and then bemused. "I'm driving her to her parents in Northport this afternoon. I could have stayed there, too, but I thought this might give us the opportunity to, well, mend a few fences."

I nodded through all of this, taking in what he was saying, and also the gorgeous, model-cum-beauty queen who walked toward me with her hand stuck out like a rudder and a big smile stuck on her perfect face.

"Emily!" she said. "Jack's been telling me so much about you. For goodness sakes." She pulled off her sunglasses, exposing wide, round blue eyes. She dropped her mouth open and took in my garden and the woods beyond in one direction, the lake in the other. "No wonder you moved up here. This is so very beautiful. I grew up in Northport and I miss it so."

Hmm. I took the hand—a wily, live thing—in mine, and decided she couldn't be too bad. Very young. Too pretty. Just Jackson's type, but with a glimmer of intelligence. Could be a friend after all; an assistant, or an eager grad student helping out. Looking from her to Jackson, who the last three years hadn't been kind to, I began to hope, for her sake, that was all she was.

Up close, I noticed Jackson's hair had lost the black sheen it used to have, like something dimming without the proper light. His skin was pocked, rougher than I remembered, tanned but splotched with red patches, like healing sunburn. Dark pouches sagged beneath his eyes. He was forty-three, but looking older, unless he'd lied to me to begin with, back when we met at that party in Ann Arbor. "*Well, well,*" he'd said sometime during that evening. "*A true journalist. I've read you often though I have to take you to task...*" And we'd been off, arguing local politics, wrangling over university policy, eventually disagreeing on sexual politics. Why on earth, I wondered as I stood with his arm around me, keeping me in place, had we thought disagreement forged a marriage bond?

"You're certainly looking well," Jackson said as I reveled in how crappy he appeared. He took in my hair, my makeup, assessing what his advantage was here. Had I fixed myself up for him? Did this give him some kind of power over me? A true man to play the angles, Jackson was sizing me up. But I was only imagining, being sulky because this lovely Jennifer had appeared when I'd expected a walk down a memory lane that never existed.

I led them up the brick path to my house and offered coffee. Jackson brought in his bags while I got the coffee going. I heard him trying to push the door to the bedroom open and banging into the dresser. I didn't care. Jennifer smiled down at Sorrow, who melted, falling with a plop right over on his back. She giggled at my love-struck dog, patted his head, and cooed at him.

I shot Sorrow a dirty look, thinking of all I'd been through with him, and how easily he was seduced from me. I excused myself and went into the bathroom where I took a swipe at my lipstick with a tissue and tried to gather my hair into a pony tail. Too short to gather, I settled for a clean face.

"Well, well, well." Jackson was back, straddling a kitchen counter stool and grinning. "So this is where you've gone to hide? Writing going well, is it?"

I nodded.

"I'll soon be deep into Middle English," he smirked at me and then at Jennifer. "I'll need a quiet place, like this one. But one closer to a city, I think. Traverse City, if I remember, is a big town. Maybe closer to Traverse. What do you think, Jennifer? I will need a decent library. And restaurants, of course, since I won't have time for cooking."

"Sounds like Ann Arbor. Maybe you should've stayed there," I said, and smiled to show I wasn't being mean.

"You know how it is, Emily. Too many friends. Phone always ringing. Students who keep calling, even when you ask them not to."

"Ah yes," I said. "I remember it well."

His smile grew strained. Jennifer leaned down to pat Sorrow, then asked if she could take him for a walk. I got his leash, reluctantly, as this meant being left alone with Jackson—what I'd expected to begin with, but now dreaded.

Jackson leaped up to hold her stool as she got down. He took her arm familiarly and warned her not to go too far, not to get lost.

I'd been had yet again, I realized. There was, in his concern and in her body language, signals of intimacy. What made me angriest was that he felt he had to hide it from me, as if some old reflex had kicked in. And even worse—this woman, this "Jennifer," was going along with it. *Let's all fool the little ex-wifey...*

But Sorrow liked her and I reminded myself that who Jackson slept with now was none of my business.

I smiled at Jennifer after attaching the leash to Sorrow's collar.

"You don't have to leave today," I said, out to prove I knew what was going on, that they weren't fooling me, that I was a great deal smarter than both of them. And wasn't I just the best sport in the world? "Jackson and I aren't married. You don't have to pretend anything with me. I really couldn't care less."

I got a brilliant smile in return. I took back the "intelligent" assessment; even that tiny glimmer I'd credited to her. Maybe there was something to that "blond" thing, I thought, grateful for my all-brown hair.

"That's really ... eh ... understanding of you. Jack was afraid that you might harbor some feelings for ..."

I laughed hard. "He's always had a tendency to flatter himself," I said, giving Jackson a forgiving look.

"Then, if you really don't mind," Jennifer turned from me to Jackson, who looked a little sick, "I don't see why I can't stay a few days. What do you think, Jack? Emily's a terrific person. I mean, not jealous at all ..."

She looked at me again. "I'll bet you've got someone of your own. Am I right? I'll bet anything that's it. Why, you could have him over, if you like."

Smiling was getting harder. Oh Lord, I'd backed myself into a corner. How to get out of all of this?

"He's away," I said. "Some other time."

"See," she crowed. "I told you."

"Well, well," Jackson said, leaning over his coffee, blowing though the coffee had to be cold by that time. "A country boy, Emily? How lucky for you."

"Actually, a journalist," I said.

"Oh? Another writer? You do go for writers, don't you?"

My stomach took a bounce.

"You must tell me about England?" I changed the subject, hoping to get him off into one of his long self-aggrandizing ruminations. "I thought I detected a bit of an accent on the phone. You must have been there a long time."

"Well, yes," he said. "A month. Hardly enough time to pick up an accent. Though you know what a good ear I have."

Jennifer excused herself and took off with Sorrow. I was left to endure two hours of *Jackson in England* and the places his research took him and the people he met who encouraged him to certainly write yet another scholarly work on Chaucer. An American, after all. Who better? Just what the British would embrace. He went on with no inkling of the irony to his tales. Nothing made a dent in his self-satisfaction. After a while I settled back, put my interested smile in place, and let my mind wander to where Dolly and I should begin later, who to see, and then back to a part of the puzzle we'd been missing: why had I been brought into it? Why were pieces of Ruby Poet dropped into my world? Was it because I was a journalist? What would that have to do with anything? Was there something we were missing here? A murderer who wanted it known that Mrs. Poet was dead?

All too much for me. We needed more information. Maybe I could get something out of the state police.

"And then, of course, I went to Canterbury..." Jackson was well into his travels as I got down from my stool, excused myself, mumbled something about remembering a story I had to follow up on, and walked out to my studio as Jennifer came flying down the hill toward me, screaming at Sorrow to "Stop! Stop!"

The poor dog was struggling to get to me, his leash entangled around Jennifer's wrist. The two of them loped downward. A long stream of obscenities spewed from lovely Jennifer's pretty mouth. I let Sorrow leap into my arms and staggered under the weight of him. My sweet puppy. Jennifer fell full tilt into us and then indecorously to the ground, legs in the air. Unfortunately, there was no underwear in sight. I averted my eyes as I find nothing remotely interesting, or pretty, about that particular part of the female body—not even my own.

Jennifer's mouth hung open. Her eyes were huge. Having misplaced her charm while falling to her back, legs pumping the air,

TWENTY-ONE

THE LATEST RELATIVE WAS somebody named Martha Jane Cannary. Pretty name for an old aunt. I didn't take the time to read what havoc Aunt Martha had wreaked on the world, just made a note of the name in case she came up in Eugenia's conversation.

Gloria, with the sweet smell of cinnamon and cloves to her, brought our turkey dinners to the table and leaned in close, fussing with where she put the plates and where to set side dishes of canned, creamed corn.

"Everybody's getting worried," she whispered, eyes huge. "Eugenia doesn't want me gossiping about it because she thinks maybe we better just calm people down from here on in. But I've got to tell you, word's around that Flora Coy's sure she's next. And Mary Margaret's keeping the boys as close as they'll stay to home, to protect her. Something awful's going on. A few of the folks have been thinking it's Harry Mockerman that's been doing this, killing the women. Some crazy idea in his head, who knows? And he did have a fight with Ruby Poet. You heard about that?"

Dolly and I nodded in unison.

"Well, from what's being said, he yelled at Ruby that he was going to kill her because she wouldn't pay him for a load of wood and ..."

"That's not what happened," I whispered up at her. "She didn't like the price and wasn't going to buy from him next year. That's all. People are talking way too much. They're getting worked up over the wrong things. Just because we don't know what happened yet doesn't mean they've got to make up stories." I shook my head.

"Lord, lord." Dolly rolled her eyes after Gloria was gone. "Next thing we'll have a lynch party."

"Poor Harry," I said, and dug into my mountain of mashed potatoes with thick yellow gravy.

Dolly was quiet during dinner. Over Strawberry Jell-O with bananas and Cool Whip, she wrinkled her nose at me. "You know, let's consider Harry. I mean, just between us. He lives out there by you, so that's handy for dropping body parts at your house. And none of these people have alibis. Nobody knows where they were on any particular day."

"Because of a load of wood? He's going to murder the woman? What about Mrs. Henry? What reason did he have to kill her?"

"Now, just think about it," she said, quieting me. "If you don't have a lot going on in your life, small things can get awfully big. We had a man shot his wife because she hung up on his mother. Another one we had was a father shot his son because the kid didn't bring back his circular saw when he said he would. I mean, small things can get you killed up here."

"You notice you talk about people shooting other people? It seems to me people up here don't strangle each other, and they certainly don't try to hide the bodies, or get rid of them one piece at a time."

"Miz Henry was in plain sight."

"If you knew where to look. And she was strangled."

Over coffee, we thought about that and came up with nothing.

On our way out, Eugenia stopped us in the vestibule where she was hanging a bright gold star near a new great-grand uncle she'd stumbled across, she said, while researching a group of thirteen men all hung on the same day in Abilene. I was beginning to have my doubts about Eugenia's family tree, but I didn't say anything while she kept us standing, listening to her ancestor's list of misdeeds.

"On another subject," she cleared her throat, got awkwardly down off her step stool, and leaned close, "you ladies ever consider the Mitchell boys, out to Scykull Lake? There's a bad bunch if I ever saw one. Could be some of their work."

"I know the Mitchell boys," Dolly said. "They spray-painted their names on buildings—not thinking we'd identify them that way. They were the ones stole from the five-and-ten, and Rodney, the oldest, dropped his driver's license in the store. They're the boys who were shooting out car windows last Halloween and shot out their own father's side window. He turned them in. Not the brightest bulbs in the bunch. I don't think this is their kind of thing."

"Just offering it up as an idea." Eugenia was a bit peeved with Dolly. She wasn't a woman who got put in her place often. She sniffed and drew herself up tall, working her shoulders back. Her wrinkled face drew in on itself. "I'm kind of a criminal expert, you might say. Considering what I come from. I consider blood to be a thing that makes you smarter than just schooling.

"Oh, and another thing you should know." She tapped one finger on the end of her nose as if playing charades. Dolly wasn't going to get a word in and I could see her sputtering over the "smarter than just schooling" remark. "Flora and Mary Margaret are scared to death. Everybody in town's sure one of them's going to get it next. Don't you think they should have some kind of protection or something?"

"Wish we could do that." Dolly shook her head slower than was called for. "It's just me and Lucky Barnard here in town. Sheriff's overextended. I don't know about the state police. I'll call 'em right away, but I don't think so. What if Flora Coy moved in with one of you?" Dolly looked at her out of the side of her eyes, as if delivering a knock-out punch.

"Hell's bells, Dolly, you expect me or Gloria to fight off somebody coming to kill one of them?" Eugenia made a face, then reached out to straighten a relative's sheet that had gone crooked.

"How about Simon? Isn't he staying over at Gloria's a lot of the time? He could keep an eye on the ladies."

"Don't say that around Gloria. She thinks nobody knows Simon stays with her."

Dolly nodded, promised to look into it, and we left. I was glad to get out of there before those two bristling women went after each other.

———

Amanda Poet answered the door but seemed reluctant to let us in. It was only Dolly pushing the door and stepping inside that got us into the living room where Ernie Henry sat at the edge of the recliner, a surprised look on his drawn-in face. Both of them seemed nervous, as if we'd interrupted something private. But then, I imagined death was a very private thing.

"Ernie's here to plan the funeral. We figured we might as well have a double," Amanda said, and she waved at the couch, asking us to sit down. She was done up in a frilly pink robe, her tousled hair wrapped haphazardly in a pink turban. I noticed her nails had been done recently, bright pink. Odd, I thought, for a grieving daughter to care that much how her nails looked.

Dolly and I mumbled "Sorry" in Ernie's direction. He hung his head.

There were more newspapers spread around today—probably one for every day since we'd last visited. Pop cans had overpowered the tableau of apple-head dolls. Two of the dolls lay on the floor, their wizened faces smashed.

"Don't mind the mess," Amanda said. "I've been too busy to give a thought to cleaning. So many kind people stopping by. Now the funeral. And poor Ernie here."

Ernie nodded again and got up. I didn't know if it was a gentlemanly gesture or an urge to flee so many women in the same room at once.

"No, no, now you stay where you are, Ernie. These women won't be here long. I imagine they want to ask us a few questions." She turned to me and Dolly. "Pastor wants us to get together the music we'd like for the funerals, and a few things we want him to say."

She smirked. I swear, it was a smirk. Something told me Amanda Poet liked being at the center of a tragedy. She might be mourning, but there was a part of her that basked in limelight.

"You found Mother, eh?" Ernie shook his head at us. His long face was sad, his eyes rimmed with red. "Can't imagine who'd want to do something like that. Never hurt a flea. And if it's this stuff going around town, you know, about them worshipping the devil out at our place, or anything like that, well, that's crazy. They never did anything of the sort. If you ask me, you find out who's crazy enough to believe such stuff, and you'll find who did this."

"When's the funeral, Ernie?" Dolly asked.

Amanda chirped right in, hands clasped at her chest, eyes slightly off, as if she was watching a future event unfold. "That's what we're planning right now. Looks like the memorials will be at Murphy's next week. They're being cremated, you know. Then the funerals will be on Wednesday morning. First at the funeral home, then over to our church."

"I didn't think the women belonged to the Church of the Contented Flock," I said, catching an unhappy look on Ernie Henry's face.

"Well, not technically, but Pastor is doing me and Ernie a favor. He's having the service there, and the ladies are doing a lovely luncheon afterward. It's the best we could think to do, under the circumstances."

"But neither of them was religious, in that sense," Dolly said. "Wouldn't they be happier having their ashes scattered out in the woods?"

"That's just awful, Dolly." Amanda looked shocked, then saddened at Dolly's insensitivity. "Neither I, nor Ernie, would let such a thing happen. It was just that they were old, you know. People get confused when they get old. We're having a nice urn for each of them. Something tasteful."

Dolly made a noise that could mean a storm to follow.

I turned to Amanda. "Mrs. Henry was here the day before she died. Remember? She seemed upset. Do you mind if I ask what that was all about?"

Amanda tucked her chin down into her robe, and hesitated. "Well, not if you're going to put it in the paper. Me and Ernie don't want publicity. Last thing we want is our mothers' names being besmirched."

"I'm here helping the deputy for the most part," I said. "We just want to put an end to whatever's going on, and get the guilty man in jail."

"The state police officer already asked me a hundred questions." She made a face and waved a limp hand at us.

"We're all looking into it," Dolly stepped in. "We want this stopped, and whoever does that is fine with me and the chief."

Amanda nodded, then sniffed. "Well." She gave Ernie a look. "Mrs. Henry came over because she was mad as could be at me for letting my mother's garden go the way I did. Isn't that right, Ernie?" She gave a little giggle. Ernie shrugged and spread his hands. "Ernie here can tell you how they all take care of their gardens. Mother said it had something to do with her soul. She wouldn't go over to the church with me, but she'd put hours in that garden, even on Sunday mornings. It got to be a sore spot between us, that the garden came before God. After she went missing, I just took it as a sign that you don't put false gods before the real Lord, and I let it go kind of wild. It wasn't nice of me. Not the sort of thing a good Christian woman does, but I was angry. I thought for a while Mother had taken off to spite me. When Mrs. Coy and Mrs. Henry and Mary Margaret came over and wanted to work on it—and it was on a Sunday morning they came, too—well, I just said they should leave well enough alone. If God thought our garden was that important, I was sure he'd see to it. Just like I was sure he would bring Mother back to me safe and sound."

Amanda rolled her eyes at Ernie Henry who sat with his head down, saying nothing.

"Of course, if I'd known how important it was to your mother, I would have let them come on in and weed away," she said in Ernie's direction.

His face got red. He didn't look at Amanda or over at us. He pushed his hands into the pockets of his old corduroy jacket. A slightly oily rag dangled from one back pocket. The man must have come over from his repair shop or his oily rag was his security blanket.

"I'll be going now." He stood and headed for the door. "You go on and plan what you like for the funerals, Amanda. Whatever you choose will be fine with me. Just remember, I don't want to spend a whole lot of money. They're gone. That's that."

Then he was gone, too. Amanda gave a couple of clucks of her tongue and tightened her narrow nostrils. "Poor man. He doesn't understand there are times you can't pinch pennies. People will expect something nice of us. I mean ..." She sighed. "Well, our mothers were pillars of the community, despite what people say."

She stopped and sighed again, then smiled and batted her eyelashes at us. "He doesn't have a clue how to act without a woman to tell 'im. That's the trouble when a boy doesn't leave his mother at the right time. They stay as dependent as babies. Now, a woman, on the other hand, why, I've never had trouble making a life for myself. Right now I have plans to move to a new place. You won't catch me staying here in Leetsville. Not with all these terrible memories."

"Where you moving to, Amanda?" I asked.

"Oh, just up to Charlevoix, I think. I've been looking at some very pretty places ..."

Dolly whistled. "That's money over there, Amanda."

Amanda smirked. "I know. But with the life insurance and this oil money I just found out about, well, I figure it's something I should do to honor my mother's name."

Dolly gave her an odd look. "Your mother loved this town. All her friends were here. How would you be honoring her by moving away?"

"Now, Dolly Wakowski." She put on her hurt look. I was catching on to Amanda Poet. She had a set of faces she switched to for differing emotions. Seemed a good way to handle things, not having to think too much. Just push the button—new face. I kind of liked the idea of getting away with being on automatic pilot. But then I had to slide out of my self-satisfaction and smug criticism when I realized that was about the way I treated Jackson.

"You know very well my mother'd always hoped to move someplace else. There's gardening clubs over to Charlevoix and Elk Rapids. They'd have been thrilled to have a lady like my mother join them. She would've been so happy among people of her own kind."

"Miz Henry and Flora Coy and Mary Margaret were her own kind." Dolly scowled and let her small voice get even smaller, and tighter.

"I don't mean anything against the ladies, but you know my mother came from cultured people…"

"Your grandfather was a dirt farmer out by Camden Road," Dolly said from between clenched teeth. "Your mother never could sell the farm because it was such poor ground, and that's the same property where they're bringing in oil and gas now."

"That's what you get for listening to gossip, Dolly Wakowski." She flounced around to face me. "Don't you put a word of what she said in the paper. We came from refined people, despite what the deputy here wants to think."

"Not a word," I assured her.

TWENTY-TWO

WHILE DOLLY WENT OVER to talk to Flora Coy about getting someone to stay with her, I went back home, my sense of hospitality
overcoming my antipathy to the visiting duo.

Sorrow didn't greet me when I got out of the car. I missed being bowled over, and suddenly longed to reach down to touch his
eager little head. Something about a dog that could make the rest
of the world a better place, just by their joy at being a part of it.
I figured he was either banned to the screened porch, or sound
asleep inside.

I walked under the arbor and stopped to pick a last climbing
Blaze rose. I tucked an errant branch back through the lattice and
patted it in place, then pulled a big thorn from my palm and reminded myself not to get soppy about a rose bush. If no one had
been inside, waiting for me, I would have walked through the garden, snipping heads from browning asters, clearing away the pulpy
nasturtiums. It was almost an ache in me, needing to touch the
plants. We'd already had a killing frost. Anytime now, I could finish mounding those rose bushes. They were so ugly, gnarled and

black, with not a sign of a rose. Amazing to me, what nature can do. The going to sleep, then spring resurrection. Thoreau said the ring of the woodsman's axe was buried in the acorn. And in us—life swirling in the genes, all possibility, all trembling verges. No one, ever, had the right to put an early end to a life. No one had the right to disturb the ordained cycle. I looked at my drowsing garden and thought of the two women, their shock at someone wanting to kill them. What was in their eyes? What was written on their faces? What did it feel like to die because someone else wanted you dead? I hoped I'd never know.

I looked out at the yard behind the house where another arbor led to the brick garden walk I'd installed myself. A patchwork of leaves covered the ground. In the ragged lilac bush, a cardinal sat, singing at me. His mate clung to a branch above him, nervously cocking her head at him, then at me. They would stay with me all winter. I would look out one January day, when the snow was over three feet deep and I was at my most depressed, and I'd see a flash of red and know color and life were coming back. It was all a matter of holding on and believing, for me, and for the birds. Winter, up here, was no joke. Animals starved. People went crazy.

Taking a deep breath of the cooling air, I went into the house.

Sorrow ran to meet me, his nails scrambling on the wooden floor, his white and black head thumping against the hip I thrust out at him. He danced in circles around me, until Jennifer clucked at him and he slunk away, giving me a reproachful look over his shoulder.

Jennifer had recovered from her near disastrous headlong run down the drive with Sorrow. He hadn't. I noticed Sorrow kept his distance from her, still suffering, no doubt, from the string of profanity aimed at him. I had the proud feeling that Sorrow was an extremely sensitive and keenly intelligent dog.

They'd had no dinner, they said, not wanting to raid my refrigerator, though I'd explicitly told them to help themselves. I didn't have much in the house anyway, so I took them to Buster's Bar for a burger, which tickled Jackson because he could wear the cowboy hat and boots he'd brought with him, confusing northern Michigan with Texas.

The little bar, a low, wood building set halfway back in the woods, was smoky. A country western song whined from the jukebox. Two old guys sat at one end of the high bar, backs hunched, fingers around their cans of Bud Light. They stared at us when we walked in, pausing to take in Jackson's shiny new boots and cowboy hat. I got a nod, then they went back to their conversation about the electric company coming through and trimming somebody's trees, which made that somebody so mad he went into his house and got a gun, which landed him in jail overnight. Both agreed a man ought to have a chance to defend his own trees, then they went quickly on to "that Dave Rombart's going around bragging some big magazine's doing a spread on 'im. Fool. Who'd want to give him publicity? Writer must be pretty hard up for something to write about."

I ignored the remarks and led Jackson and Jennifer to a table at the far side of the room, right under an overhead TV where a wrestling match happened in silence.

At the next table, a man and woman were deep in conversation. He had his hands behind his head as he leaned back, chair tipped up. She frowned at him. I thought maybe it was a juicy affair going wrong. Maybe she was an angry wife, ready to walk out. Which points out a problem with writers—an excess of imagination—

since she was saying, "Well, I'm going to New York whether you like it or not. There's that new production of Brecht…"

My usual miscalculation. Up here you never knew who was who. There was the guy who'd finally come to take my phone wire out of the tree where it had been wrapped for six months, and hook me to a telephone pole. Sometimes things take awhile up here. The guy looked at the beginnings of my garden and stayed an hour, walking slowly around and around my beds, offering plant advice, fertilizer information, and critter control. He'd been a horticulturist in Midland, wanted to live in northern Michigan, he said, and paid the price that meant in no jobs. I thought I'd learned my lesson, about pigeon-holing people, still I kept being surprised. They might all look the same, but people, up in the woods, had different skills and different reasons for being there. Maybe a lot like me.

Jackson asked Sally, our pretty waitress with long, brown hair caught up in an amazing ponytail, for the wine list after he'd settled his boots on the chair rungs and put his big hat carefully on the table beside him.

"I'll give you the list, mister," Sally said, then rolled her eyes at me. "We got red. And we got white. Which will you have?"

Jackson looked appalled, then asked to see the bottle of red, which she brought over.

"Boone's Farm," she read off, holding it out to him. "August."

Jackson waved it away and ordered a Sam Adams. Jennifer wanted spring water and got a glass of water Sally said was, "Right out of a spring. And for free, too."

Hamburgers and frozen pizza were on the menu so they ordered hamburgers and let it go at that. There weren't going to be embellishments like lettuce, or tomatoes. Just hamburgers. But thick, and good.

Back at home, after our dining adventure, our thrilling three-some shared a glass of the Cabernet Sauvignon Jackson'd brought with him. We remained magnificently interested in each other throughout the rest of the evening, even though Jackson did absorb a larger portion of all available air, space, and time. I yawned hard at nine thirty, then again at nine forty-five, and we were off to bed by ten.

Somehow they managed to get the bedroom door open all the way, pushing the dresser back far enough to expose my shamefully defaced drywall, which occasioned expressions of surprise from them and chagrin from me. They went in and closed the door hard behind them.

I woke sometime during the night to Sorrow growling. I sat up in fear of attack, at least something terrible being thrown at my house. It took awhile to fix the locale of the thumping noise. Grateful that it was nothing but Jackson's energetic lovemaking in the next room, I fell back to sleep with only the minutest pang of jealousy nibbling at my brain.

Sunday morning Jennifer went off for a long run around the lake while Jackson and I put on warm sweaters and took our coffee cups out to the front deck to sit in the warm, morning sunshine. A flock of migrating geese honked their hearts out on Willow Lake. A pair of frantic black squirrels dashed from oak to aspen, chasing each other as if spring-maddened instead of facing months of claustrophobia down in tiny holes. Chickadees sat on a maple branch hanging just above the deck and peeped insistently until I got up and filled the feeder by the steps.

"You seem quite content," Jackson said as he stretched his legs and leaned his already overly tanned face back to the sun. A late hummingbird hovered just above his head. Jackson swatted at it as he would a fly.

"I am," I said, and settled down in an Adirondack chair beside him.

"And the books you were going to write, what happened to those?"

"Never fear, Jackson. I'm writing them."

"Anything about to come out?" He raised his eyebrows into question marks.

I only smiled and sat forward in my chair, certain I'd heard a car at the top of the drive, and glad of it.

Dolly. I was never quite so happy to see her.

"Good morning," I called cheerfully across the railing, grateful for her chunky body and flat head, as she walked around from the drive. No police uniform today. I'd never seen Dolly in street clothes before and had to admit that Deputy Dolly, off duty, didn't look bad at all. She had on a blue fleece jacket, navy pants, and a yellow, scooped-neck sweater. A big brown shoulder bag hung over her arm. Her hair was fixed so it curled a little around her small, round face. I could even detect a hint of pink lipstick, and was that ... no! ... blush?

I figured her curiosity about Jackson got to be too much for her. She bent forward when I introduced them, told him she was our local law enforcement and gave him a brisk handshake. She pulled a metal chair from around the umbrella table and sat, legs spread too far apart, fixing one of her steady looks on Jackson. I went in to get her a cup of tea and when I came back she was pulling a stack of flyers from her purse, handing them to him, and explaining they were rentals.

"Just trying to help out," she said, frowning up at me as if about to be accused of interfering. She took the teacup and set it on the wooden table beside her.

"Any one of these probably just what you're looking for," she said to Jackson, then turned back to me. "I was telling your friend about some of the places around here for rent. Stopped at a couple of the real estates in town. Thought that might help you both out."

I nodded.

"Hmm." Jackson looked at one flyer after another, then turned to blink hard at me. "Not quite what I had in mind."

He handed back the brochures, smiled, and leaned over to pat Dolly's hand. "Thanks for the thought, dear, but I'm looking for something private. Closer to Traverse City. For the library, of course. And I will need some diversion. Restaurants. Theater."

"Thought I heard you brought a girlfriend," Dolly said, gathering her brochures together and wiping the back of her hand on her jacket. "Should be 'diversion' enough."

"Hmm," was all Jackson said again. He excused himself, got up, and went into the house.

"What in hell do you think you're doing?" I hissed when I could. "You're being rude."

"What do you care?" she hissed back. "You want him and his buddy hanging around forever? I'm telling you, Emily, I know people like this. That guy'll move in and write his book at your expense if you don't put your foot down."

"I'll handle it. Just get off . . ."

Jackson was back, looking tall and lean and only slightly dissolute, with his morning tousled hair and his thick, Irish sweater. A photograph album was tucked under his arm. "Thought you both might like to see photos of my trip to England." He smiled at me, then at Dolly. He sat down between us and set the album on his lap.

I'd known Jackson a long time. He didn't have a whole lot of moves. This was his "charm the masses" ploy. For whatever reason, he wanted Dolly to like him. He opened his album and quickly drew her in close, pointing out places in England he'd been, recounting funny little stories, putting an arm around her back when he had something he especially wanted to share with her. Once, he even stooped so low as to whisper in her ear, some *bon mot* that made her blush. Poor Dolly. I watched with amusement as she received the full Jackson treatment.

When Jennifer got back from her run, she acknowledged Dolly with a dismissive half-smile and stood stretching and arching in front of us. "I simply have to get out to look around," she said, mewing at Jackson. "Let's take a ride, Jack. Please! It's such an absolutely beautiful day. Let's not waste it just sitting around . . ." She looked from me to Dolly, and back. "Here," she added.

Dolly and I begged off the drive though Dolly looked unsure for a few seconds.

"We've got things to discuss," Dolly finally told Jackson, her face deadly serious and self-important. "A case we're working on together."

Jackson's eyebrows shot up. "A case? Really Emily, I didn't know you went in for police work."

"There have been two murders," Dolly said. She sniffed and gave him a smile I'd never seen on her face before. If I didn't think it impossible, I would have sworn she was flirting.

"Emily writes for the newspaper in Traverse and since I'm with the police department out here, well, we're kind of hoping to solve

202

this before anything more happens. Nobody knows the people back in these woods the way we do and ..."

I interrupted before she got stuck in the whole speech about our superior qualifications, and gave Jackson and Jennifer a shortened version of the story. They sat round eyed, asking questions and giving little shivers. But soon they were off on their Sunday afternoon diversion, while Dolly and I sat for the next hour mapping out what we knew, and where there were holes to plug. We made lists of the people we'd learned something about, and what we still had to discover. At a little after one, Bill Corcoran, from the paper, showed up and Dolly was wowed again, this time almost speechless.

Bill was a great-looking guy, big and rugged, with a head of thick blond hair. He wore horn-rimmed glasses, which endearingly slid down his nose as he spoke in a deep, halting voice. The glasses kept having to be hoisted with, unfortunately, his middle finger. Bill was one of the hunched-over, hands-clasped-in-earnest kind of guys who radiate sincerity, intelligence, and loyalty. Just the kind of man most women overlook in favor of the charmers like Jackson—to our eternal discredit.

I'd met Bill a few months after moving to northern Michigan. I'd gone into the busy paper one morning and brought a sheaf of stories I'd done. He'd read my stuff carefully and told me he didn't have a full-time job right then. Maybe in the future ... I told him I only wanted occasional work. Stringer stuff. I said I needed to keep my hand in, that I was writing a book ...

Bill had leaned back in his chair, pushed his glasses up his nose—which I didn't take personally—and said he was glad to have me with them. Since then I'd done stories on fires, on an airplane that came down and got stuck in a tree out near Arnold's Swamp, on a rabies scare, on a couple of new businesses, on the effects of a snow-free winter on Shanty Creek Ski Resort, on the White Pine Stampede out in Mancelona, and a couple of parades and things. I kept busy and I liked working for Bill. He was a nonchalant boss. Funny and earnest at the same time. Just the kind of hands-off guy I needed right then.

I handed Bill the notes Dolly and I had made, catching him up with what was going on in town, including the memorials at Murphy's and the funeral service at the Church of the Contented Flock.

We sat in the afternoon sun, flicking half-dead flies off our cheese and crackers, and downing the last of Jackson's Cabernet Sauvignon—which served him right since he and Jennifer hadn't bothered to return from their sightseeing tour of the countryside.

"Pastor Runcival," Bill said, and he bit at his lip, deep in thought. "You said he preached against the women?"

I nodded. "But he said he was put up to it by some people in his church."

"You know who?" Bill squinted at me and gave me the finger—or lifted his heavy glasses.

"He didn't seem to remember," I said.

"Don't you think that's important? I mean, find out who had something against the ladies, maybe that's where you'll discover the murderer."

"We've already got this Survivalist guy—Dave Rombart. They called the cops on him for snooping—Lucky Barnard says poaching—on the Henry property. Then there's my neighbor, Harry Mockerman. Mrs. Poet was mad at him for kiting the price of her firewood. She let a lot of people know she was unhappy. Harry's not especially ... well ... he's not ordinary. He could have gotten mad enough, I suppose, to do something to her. But why Mrs. Henry? Unless she'd figured out what he did. Maybe she went to see him."

Bill hummed under his breath. "How far have the state police gotten? Are they telling you anything?"

"Just what I've passed on to you."

"No snitches? Usually there's somebody noticed something, heard something. You know how folks are up here. They know more about each other than anybody wants to think."

"Nothing yet," Dolly finally spoke up, getting over being intimidated by Bill.

"To tell you the truth, Emily." Bill was looking straight at me now, glasses firmly in place, his green eyes, behind the glasses, large. "I kind of came today to talk you out of following the story any further. I can get the briefings from Gaylord myself from here on in. It just isn't safe. I think what you've got here is a maniac. Somebody who looks harmless enough, who acts sane enough, but who goes nuts when there's a full moon, or when he drinks, or when his wife hollers at him. Whatever it is, this one's dangerous and you've been targeted twice."

"I don't think…," I started to say, but he held his hand up to stop me.

"Not only that, you live right out here where the murders are happening."

"We don't know where Mrs. Poet was killed," I interrupted.

"Still, she was disposed of here in your woods. That has to tell you something."

Dolly said nothing through all of this. I thought the least she could do was stand up for me, declare me a necessary part of her investigation. Something.

"You could be right," she finally piped in, sucking at the inside of her left cheek. "Maybe I shouldn't let Emily get any more involved. If she were in law enforcement, well, that's different. We're trained for things like this. It was just because she wants to write mysteries. I thought maybe it'd help her to be on the inside of one."

"Is that enough reason to get yourself killed?" he asked, looking straight at me, worry written in lines across his forehead. It felt good, his concern for my well-being.

"I appreciate what you're saying, Bill, but would you pull a male reporter off the story because you were worried about him?"

"I would," he said, nodding hard. "Sure would. And I have."

"And did that reporter listen?"

Bill shook his head, shook it again, then chuckled.

"There. If I give up now you'll always think it was because I got scared. That stinks. And I'm not afraid. Dolly, here, can't quit if she gets scared. It's her job. So, it's my job, too."

"You've already been threatened—in a half-assed way," he pressed on. "This guy's committed two murders. What's to stop him from committing more?"

"Me and Dolly," I said.

"Oh." Bill settled back in his chair, hands going up in a gesture of surrender.

We spent the rest of our time, before Jennifer and Jackson got back from their drive, in small talk about local politics and a couple of scandals. Bill had details that didn't make the paper and Dolly listened hard, eating up being on the inside of things, along with this newspaper man.

When Jennifer and Jackson returned, extolling the virtues of a ten-mile run up a small cliff they'd come across in the Jordan Valley, I left them to entertain my two guests and drove in to the IGA in town for Italian sausage I could grill, the best bread I could find, plenty of salad, a big sponge cake, and fresh strawberries. I was going to cook—an unusual occurrence in my house.

Jennifer and Dolly helped in the kitchen, cutting up cheese cubes and tomatoes, and bread to grill for croutons. Jennifer nudged me. "He's cute, Emily. Your friend."

I let her think what she wanted about my journalist "boyfriend." Dolly rolled her eyes and asked Jennifer when she was going home to her parents' house. Nothing if not direct, I thought.

"I don't know. Emily's made it such fun right here. I thought," she smiled a winning smile at me, "well, I thought maybe I'd stay a few days. Just to get Jack settled."

Dolly's face went from slightly pink to deep crimson. "You going to help Jackson look for a place of his own, aren't you? He can't stay here with Emily, you know. She's got a book she's working on. She needs a lot of peace and quiet."

"Oh, we wouldn't think of intruding. We'll be busy. Jack definitely wants his own place. This house is much too small. His work requires space."

I thanked God for my negligible quarters.

"I'll just hang out until he gets settled. Wherever that is," she added. She gave me a wide smile with a territorial gleam behind it.

Dolly made a noise deep in her throat. A kind of Sorrow sound. I busied myself slicing strawberries in half.

Bill stayed for dinner, grilling the sausages while Jackson and Jennifer disappeared into their bedroom to change for dinner. I looked down at my jeans and my red cotton sweater and decided I was dressed enough. Sorrow kept Bill company at the grill, receiving a few sausage snippets I was sure would make him throw up about midnight. The two of them seemed to like each other. I didn't bother questioning Sorrow's loyalty anymore. He didn't have any.

Dinner went well, though I'd forgotten the onions and peppers that usually accompany grilled Italian sausage. I made a good salad. Jackson graciously had to admit my salads were what he missed most about me. Bill left soon after dinner, stopping long enough in the driveway to suggest I think over what he'd said.

Dolly drove out right behind him. I was left alone with Jackson and Jennifer, huddled together at one end of my sofa. I remembered I had some writing to do—that article for the magazine was due by Wednesday, my novel ... anything. Sorrow looked from me to Jackson and Jennifer snuggled together on my couch, watching television. He flopped down on the rug in front of them, winked at me, and left me—my disloyal friend—to make my way alone, in the dark, out to my studio.

TWENTY-THREE

EARLY THE NEXT MORNING, I awoke to thumping in the next room. And to Sorrow growling from the foot of my bed, where he'd decided he must sleep, draped over my legs. The growling was like a low motor in my ears, a vibration through the mattress. I whispered to him to be quiet. I didn't want them to know we were awake—me and my dog. It was terrible, lying there listening to the two of them—their occasional whispers, laughter, the squeaking of that infernal bed.

Stupid—that I'd tried to be so civilized, so sanguine about having him back in my house, now with one of his "girls." It was the "Jennifers" that had broken my life into bits. It was the "Jennifers"— no, that was too neurotic: blame the other women, exonerate the asshole. It was Jackson and his unconscionable lust, now his almost pathetic need to prove himself young by feeding off youth. He had to believe deep inside his head that to fuck a young woman was his only way to immortality. I didn't know who I felt sorriest for: Jennifer, Jackson, or me.

I didn't have a choice but to stick my head between two pillows and try to keep their noises out of my mind. I kicked at Sorrow, who then yipped and jumped down to lie on the rug where he could sulk in peace.

I fell back to sleep and didn't hear the phone when it rang. Jennifer came in, lifted the pillow from my head, and yelled in my ear, "Emily, the phone's ringing. It's three o'clock in the morning. You want me to answer? I didn't know …"

I mumbled something nasty and swung my feet around to the floor. It wasn't easy to get up. I'd had dreams earlier of a hanging, so though I was happy to be awake, I was also disoriented enough to have trouble placing myself in my home.

The phone on the living room desk kept ringing. I found it, finally, and answered. Dolly, her voice angry, then insistent, yelled at me to wake up.

"Murphy's Funeral Home is on fire!" she screamed. "You hear me? Completely on fire. One end to the other. They think Mary Margaret's in there. They don't know anything yet. Come on into town, Emily. Get here quick. This is awful. Just awful."

"Where'll I meet you?" I asked, still dim, blinking, trying to think.

"Where the hell you think I'll be?"

"Give me a little time …"

"I'm not giving you anything. Get in here. It looks like another one of our women has just gone up in smoke."

———————

Driving into town along US 131, I could see the sky above Leetsville lighted like a winter sunset, all burnt umber and bloody red. Above the brilliant color hung a mushroom-shaped cloud. As I got to the place where houses began and the woods ended, I could see embers shooting into the air, settling slowly down on rooftops. People were out with hoses, wetting down their homes. People stood along the sidewalk. One man fought a small blaze in his yard. It was a vision straight out of hell: the fires, the shadowy figures. I had to drive carefully. The dogs were frantic, running into the street and back. Children stood on the sidewalks in their pajamas, holding on to their parents who gathered in knots, straining toward the fiery horizon, leaning close to talk.

I was stopped by Lucky Barnard waving me down on Main Street. Mitchell Street, leading over to Griffith, where the funeral home stood, was closed. I pulled up and asked Lucky where Dolly was. He pointed toward the fire, and let me make a left turn.

The smoke and heat were thick before I got to Griffith Street. I had to park two blocks beyond and make my way back through crowds of people and standing fire engines, red lights flashing like sparks from hell. Hoses snaked everywhere, leading toward clouds of black smoke billowing from the listing funeral home. Flames shot up through the roof and outlined the windows. The sound was a terrible roaring from the fire, and the shouts of men, calling orders all around. There was no getting close. I looked for Dolly and finally spotted her at the other corner, directing traffic coming down Divinity Drive from the north.

She looked efficient and in control, using her flashlight to wave cars back out of town, yelling when she had to give information. I ran closer and hollered for her attention. She yelled back over her shoulder. "Nobody's seen Mary Margaret. They think she's still in there."

"She's not coming out of that alive!" I yelled back.

"I think that's the point, don't you?" She waved as a car crept toward her.

"Where's Gilbert and Sullivan?" I called. The noise behind me grew deafening. It sounded like the crashing and creaking and bellowing after a bomb. I turned to face a shower of sparks and smoke.

"My God!" I shouted. "The roof fell in!"

We had to hunch down. The air filled with hot cinders, with lighter-than-air ash, with terrible, choking smoke. She made her way over to me, bent and small. "Think the whole town's going to go up. I've got to get around and see who needs help."

She ran a yellow police tape across the road and shouted that it would have to do until some of the county or state police got there. We leaned forward and scurried, not away from the fire, but toward it, though the smoke grew so thick I had to pull my shirt over my mouth and nose in order to breathe. We found the fire chief, Ben Hamilton, with his arms waving as he yelled orders left and right.

"It's got Gertie's beauty shop!" the tall man shouted at us. "Maybe you should make sure everybody in the houses beyond there is out. Never know where this thing is going to go now. We're working on the adjacent buildings. Firemen keeping them dampened down. Praying the wind doesn't pick up."

Crouched and gagging, we made our way around the fire trucks, over the hoses, through the running men, to the other side of Mitchell Street, rushing past Bob's Barber Shop to the houses beyond, up porches, knocking, yelling. No one could have slept through the thundering noise, the sirens, the shouts. Everybody was out on the sidewalk, all watching in horror as a piece of their town went up in flames. When we could finally stop to stand with the others and watch the building burn, I leaned close to Dolly and asked again,

"Where are Gilbert and Sullivan? I thought they were staying close, to watch her?"

She shook her head, her face sorrowful. "Nobody knows if they're in there, too, or if they went out tonight. Just like both of them to sneak off, with those bad habits of theirs. Hell, now I hope they did."

"Why are they so sure Mary Margaret's still in there?"

"You see her anywhere around? Where else would she have been in the middle of the night?"

"That means…" The horrible thought hit me. "Joslyn Henry and Ruby Poet—their bodies were in there, too."

"All of them, together. Like some joint cremation." She nodded.

"But not Flora Coy."

Dolly shook her head. "I saw Flora a little while ago."

I couldn't help but think how lucky for Flora, and wonder what we knew about her. The last woman standing. Hmm, Agatha Christie: *And Then There Were None.*

We watched as morning came on. First the trees stood out in black relief, then the smoldering buildings: the funeral home, Gertie's shop behind it. As the light grew, the buildings darkened, becoming smoking piles of unrecognizable rubble. I couldn't bear to think of Mary Margaret in there. Why hadn't she awoken? I'd heard that people died of smoke inhalation before the flames ever got to them. The thought of her in there, dying, with her two friends in the basement, or maybe off to the crematorium. I hoped it was that— they were already gone. One more insult to those poor women was almost too much to think about.

Dolly, standing beside me, was silent and tired. She had smudges under her eyes and across her cheeks, as if she'd been in the fire, too. Her walkie-talkie crackled at her waist. She stepped away from all of us, who stood and stared at nothing, then came back and whispered, "We've got to go. The chief wants to see us over at the station."

I nodded and followed her, walking through deep mud puddles left behind by the streams of water that had showered the funeral home. The air was filled with the stink of fire. I didn't dare think of what else was mixed into that stench. There were times, I found, when thinking too deeply only hurt.

At the station, the chief looked as tired as Dolly, his hair oddly singed at the front. He sat at his desk with his shoulders slumped, his head down. He looked up as we walked in and settled on metal chairs in front of his desk, and shook his head.

"The state police were here already. Seems they have reason to think the fire wasn't accidental. Their lab boys will be out in an hour. Somebody smelled accelerant when the firemen first got there. The fire chief's been in. Everybody's going to be looking into this." He hesitated then ran a hand over his face. The man was exhausted.

"I've been just about ordered to keep you two out of it now," he said. "For your own good."

Dolly sputtered and sat forward on her chair. I slouched down. I didn't blame any of them. It was like I'd been playing, as if it were a game to keep my mind occupied, or a class in mystery writing. What I felt most was shame. Three women horribly dead. No game. No nice little diversion to keep my mind off failure and an ex-husband and his "Miss Thing."

"Are they getting anywhere?" Dolly demanded, her little body up straight and tight. "Are we bothering them?"

The chief shook his head again. "It's not that, Dolly. They just think maybe you're stirring things up that shouldn't have been stirred. They work kind of quietly. Looking at things scientifically, making inquiries into backgrounds. You're right out there. Know what I mean? I'll tell you, what we're most worried about now is you and Emily becoming targets. You go talking around town, listening to gossip. You're making yourself the only visible law in town. That's not such a good thing when you've got a murdering lunatic running around."

"That's my job, Chief," Dolly complained. "I'm supposed to be the law around here."

"Yes," he said. "You and me. Together. I've been distracted with Charlie's trouble but he's back home in a few hours. I think I'd better handle things from now on. What I mean is we've got to back off and not get in the way. They're calling in guys from other departments to work on this. It's the most serious thing we've had happen since that kidnapping a few years ago. I'm telling you, Dolly—and you, too, Emily—you've got to stay out of it now. Stay away from the people involved ..."

"Chief, when I was hired on you said I'd make a good officer, didn't you?"

"And you are a good officer, Dolly. Just those little accidents ..."

"Then what's going on? You don't like the state police sticking their noses in our town any more than I do. Something else's happened."

Lucky Barnard looked directly at Dolly, then at me. He hesitated. I hadn't picked up on what Dolly had gotten right away. Something more here. The man didn't want to come out and say what he obviously had to say.

"It's gotten worse than I thought it could get, Dolly."

"You mean with the fire? I didn't see that coming either or I would have warned Mary Margaret somebody could be after her.

I guess that means we'd better see to Flora Coy. Maybe she could stay at my house …"

"How would that help? You're gone most of the time. No better than staying at her own place."

"Then Emily's. People there now, and Emily could keep an eye on her."

I started to complain. I had a house full at the moment. Maybe it was better to find a safe place far away from Leetsville, with someone who wasn't known to be as involved as I'd gotten myself.

The chief interrupted. "That's not what I was talking about. Just be quiet a minute and let me get this out, OK?"

He was angry and way past losing his patience. "Somebody called and said they saw you running out of the funeral home just before the fire started."

"Me?" Dolly clapped a hand at her chest. Her mouth dropped open. "I was home in bed. How could I have been at the funeral home? Why the heck would I have been there …"

Understanding dawned. "My God! Somebody's saying I set the fire! Who was it? That's who's doing this. Me and Emily are getting close. He wants me off the case. That's it, Chief. You've got to see that's it."

He nodded. "I know that's what it looks like. But it was a woman who called me. Not a man. And Dolly, it wasn't anonymous. I know the person." He nodded a couple of times and looked sad.

She sat back, stricken. "Was it Dave Rombart's wife? You wouldn't trust that woman would you? Take her word over mine? She's just …"

He shook his head. "Not her. Somebody who doesn't want it out that she called. Not a troublemaker either, Dolly. Sorry as I am about this, I have to look into it."

"Was it somebody from Pastor Runcival's church?" I asked. "He's got women in his church who'd protect him. Even Amanda Poet carries on about 'Pastor' this and 'Pastor' that. Somebody here in town just wants Dolly and me to back off. That's obvious."

"I can't tell you what's going on until I look into it. Anyway, the focus is on Officer Wakowski and I don't like it. I can't protect her. We're the whole police force. What's going to have to happen is that you take some time off, Dolly. I mean, you know this is going to get around town like lightning. People will be looking funny at you. These things tend to feed on themselves. Before you know it, I'm going to be getting calls from every crackpot saying they saw you doing this and that. As it is, Officer Brent wants to talk to you. I had to tell him about the call."

"So now I'm supposed to leave you alone, when we've got all of this going on? What'd you hire me for in the first place? I'm either a police officer or I'm not."

"Now, Dolly," I reached over and put my hand on her taut arm, "Lucky's just thinking of your safety."

"Why?" She glared at me. "We're going to finish this, Emily. If we leave it to the state guys, it'll get shelved. They do a good job when they know the territory, but I'm telling you this isn't like Gaylord, or even Grayling. And certainly not like it is in Traverse. These people won't tell them anything. This is a closed-in place. We protect each other—even from outsiders who might do us some good." She turned back to Lucky, who looked miserable. "What if we played along? I mean, I'll talk to Officer Brent. I want to. You can tell everybody I'm on indefinite leave. But don't tie my hands, Chief. There's one to go, don't you see? One more of the women. They've got to get Flora. She's the last of 'em. If I keep her with me, maybe force whoever it is to come after her with me around, we can finish this."

Lucky was shaking his head. "That would mean I'd have to lie; cover for you. That's not how I operate."

I liked Dolly's idea. We could work full time. She could be watching Flora Coy, who was worrying me even as we sat there. The word would get around that she was relieved of duty. Whoever had called would think they'd settled that problem. It sounded good to me.

"Chief," I said, "you've never been up against anything like this before. Neither has Dolly. I certainly haven't. But I'd like to see it through. Not because of my mystery writing. Nothing like that. Dolly and I must be close to something. They're after her. They've been after me from the beginning, when they put Ruby's head in my garbage can and threw her arm on my porch. I don't think either one of us will be safer now by being shut out. We're in deep, for whatever crazy reason. We need your help, that's for sure. But we can't be pushed away. We're as much a part of this as any of the old women."

Lucky stared hard at me. Finally he nodded. "You're right, Emily. OK. As of now Dolly's officially off duty, but I'm not stopping you from going right on with what you've been doing. Word will get around soon enough that you're still working the case. I'll deny it; tell them you're on your own, if that's what you're doing. Make sure you take care of Miz Coy. That's the biggest job you've got. Keep the woman safe, for God's sakes. I'd lock her right up in my jail if I thought that would do it, but I can't."

Dolly sighed hard and beamed at her boss. "Thanks, Chief. I won't let you down."

She looked over at me and grinned. "We're still in business. First it's Mrs. Coy. You want to come?"

"I've got guests at home, remember? Probably sitting there waiting for breakfast to appear. Why don't you pick her up and bring her out for lunch? I've got to call Bill. I saw a reporter from the paper at the fire, and a photographer, but I'll bet he doesn't know they think it's arson. I want to get on the story right away. I need to talk to Mrs. Coy. She's got to have some information, something she's noticed, even if it's only the odd way someone's been looking at her.

"No memorial services now. And no funeral," I added. "No bodies all over again. Did you see Amanda around the fire?"

"I wasn't looking for her."

"Funny if she wasn't there. Wonder what she and Ernie are going to do about a funeral. If I were them I'd give up and hold a memorial later." I thought of something and turned back to the chief. "What about Gilbert and Sullivan? Were they in there with Mary Margaret? They were supposed to be watching out for her."

Lucky looked disgusted. "Yeah. Gilbert said he was gambling up at the Soo. Sullivan was home and he's lucky to be alive. Got himself out a back upstairs window. Drunk when we came on him. Standing there looking back up at the building like he was expecting his mother to leap out after him. They're both with the state police now. I've asked for them to drop in here, too, when they can. Guess they've lost their home as well as their mother, and their jobs. Can't see either one of them doing this. Too much to lose."

Dolly and I left, then parted outside the police station. It was raining, mirroring how I felt as I drove back home. Downcast. Gloomy. All wet.

TWENTY-FOUR

ANOTHER MONDAY MORNING. COLDER overnight. Roiling, black clouds above. Rain coming. There could even be snow. I'd seen thick, cottony snow collect before on colorful, fall branches. It was a trick of nature, maybe like a seasonal joke—to show us what was coming, what we couldn't avoid; to remind us of icy roads and whiteouts and blizzards where the wind blew straight across in front of you and stung your skin as bad as sand.

The crows were back, greeting me as I drove in even though I had no garbage can and might never dare set my garbage out again.

I walked in my house as the northern cardinal sang out nine from my bird clock.

Jennifer and Jackson weren't exactly waiting for breakfast, but the counter was littered with plates and cups, the sink filled with pans and spatulas, and the two of them sprawled in front of my TV, watching Murphy's Funeral Home burn on a news bulletin.

Sorrow was the only one happy to see me. He leaped and yapped as if scolding me for leaving him alone with that pair. I checked his dish, which was empty, and gave him water.

"That what they called you about?" Jackson looked up from the TV.

I nodded, too horribly tired to watch the fire again, in miniature.

"Awful thing," Jennifer said, showing sympathy.

I got a cup from the cupboard. Unfortunately, they'd left me no coffee so I made a cup of tea instead, without asking anyone if they wanted any, or needed anything, or asking if they were comfortable, laid out together on my sofa. I didn't have the heart for sarcasm.

"The owner didn't get out?" Jackson asked, rolling his eyes back to look up at me. I stood behind them, watching the flames devour Murphy's Funeral Home, though I had no stomach to go through it again.

"No," I answered, determined to be uninformative.

"Those places must have a lot of chemicals in them. An old building like that could be a death trap."

"It was," I said.

"Oh, by the way," Jennifer smiled up at me after stifling a yawn, "somebody was here to see you. An old guy in a funny suit. Woke us up before eight. Brought a bunch of dried-up vegetables he said were leeks. I stuck them in the refrigerator, though it doesn't really look like something you would want to eat."

"My neighbor," I said and then blew at my tea, wishing I could take it somewhere, anywhere, else, without seeming too antisocial. "From across the road."

"Strange duck," Jackson said. "I didn't want Jennifer to answer the door. Looked like a derelict to me."

"Just different. Harry does odd jobs for me. He say anything?"

"Said he hoped you could use the leeks and that if you got a chance he'd like you to drop over. Something he wanted to talk to you about," Jennifer said.

I figured later would be soon enough. What I needed right then were a few hours of straight, hard sleep. I thought longingly of the futon in my studio. Away from the house. Quiet. I'd work if I wanted to, finish the Survivalist story. I had to get into Traverse City and drop the story off to Jan Romanoff, along with the roll of photos I'd shot, since I didn't do digital. Jan would call later for cutlines. It wasn't difficult to deal with the newspapers and magazines up there. Either I sent my stories in electronically, or I drove to town and dropped them off.

I had no idea what time Dolly might come by with Mrs. Coy. She was probably as tired, as defeated, as I felt and would go home and sleep. Poor Mrs. Murphy. Another one of the harmless old ladies gone. What good were Dolly and I, if we couldn't stop what was happening? Maybe we were a part of it. Not the way they said about Dolly, but just sticking our nose in. I shook my head. First some sleep, then I'd suffer all the guilt I could muster.

So, at least a few hours.

I made excuses to my guests, who didn't seem to understand that I was leaving the house, and started out toward my studio, my lone beacon of sanity. I could almost feel my body begin to relax, one limb at a time. I pictured the lumpy futon and a pillow with my head on it.

A yellow SUV came tearing down the drive and my whole body sagged.

Simon and Gloria. Sorrow, who'd reluctantly accompanied me out to work, went into spasms of joy. He leaped on Simon, chest-high, and barked, then backed off because I'd been telling him leaping on people was unacceptable. He twirled in the air instead. Simon laughed and scratched Sorrow's ears and patted his head, then crouched down to talk to him, man to dog, letting him know what a wonderful animal he was and how lucky Emily was to have such a fine creature living with her.

"Awful about Mrs. Murphy, isn't it?" Gloria put a fist to her mouth, looking as if she might cry. "Everybody feels so bad. And they're saying it might have been set—the fire. We just can't believe it, can we, Simon?"

He agreed. If anything, his eyes welled up faster than Gloria's.

"Who do you suppose would do such a thing, Emily?" Simon stood, leaving Sorrow to sit with his tongue out, hoping for more attention. "We came because we heard you and Dolly got run off the case. Everybody in town's fighting mad over it. Nobody but a few nuts believes she had anything to do with the fire."

"Three dead women." Gloria shook her head. Her face was drawn. I had the feeling Simon and Gloria had been in the crowd outside the burning building, standing there half the night. What did they have to say that was so important it brought them out here when most of the town wasn't moving, was home sleeping?

"Me and Simon would help you both out if we could. You know we've been telling you every last thing we hear around town."

"I know that. You've been a big help. All it takes is one small fact: something somebody said about the women, something somebody let drop—a reason for murder. Just about anything."

"Well, that's what we were thinking," Simon said, standing taller, like a soldier, arms behind his back.

I hadn't asked them in because I wasn't in a hurry to introduce my company around. We stood near the middle of my drive. I thought of asking them out to the studio, was about to make a motion for them to follow me, when Gloria elbowed Simon and hissed, "Go on, Simon. Tell her what we came out to say."

"You tell her. You're the one told me," Simon hissed right back at her.

Gloria took a couple of deep breaths, looked off, then back at me. Her pretty face was earnest with her news. "I know who called the police and said she saw Dolly coming out of the funeral home. She told me herself."

"Who?" I demanded, sure if this fact were clear we would be straight on to whoever was doing these terrible things.

"I hate to say it. It seems so disloyal of me." She made a face, then looked back at me. "Don't tell anybody it was me, OK? I mean, I like my job..."

"You don't mean Eugenia?" This wasn't the direction I'd imagined.

Gloria nodded. "She told me right there at the fire. Said she was driving by. I guess she fell asleep in her office, doing the books, and didn't wake up until almost two o'clock in the morning. She thought she might as well get home because she had Nancy coming in to open and could still get some sleep. She drove by Murphy's and swears she saw Dolly running out. She thought it was funny and almost stopped to ask her what was going on, but she didn't want to get into one of Dolly's long stories so she went on home to bed. The sirens woke her. She got dressed and went to where she saw the engines going and there was the funeral home already up in flames. Eugenia asked me if I thought she'd better call somebody about what she saw. I told her to talk to Dolly, but she said with what's going on in town, maybe she'd better call Lucky Barnard. Then afterwards she told me she was afraid, with all that's happened, well, who knows but maybe Dolly and the chief are both mixed up in it. I mean, we're all scared to death now. We don't know who's going to be killed next."

I was angry with all of them. Poor Dolly. She'd been working her head off to bring this terrible tragedy to an end. Judged and found guilty—on what? "What did Eugenia see anyway? I know it wasn't Dolly. She was home in bed."

"She says it looked just like Dolly. Kind of a dumpy person in a uniform. She swears it was a police uniform."

"But she didn't see her face? Or his face?"

Gloria shook her head.

"She's sure it was a woman? Not a small man—somebody like Ernie? How about one of the boys—Gilbert or Sullivan?"

"I'll ask her. Don't think it could be Gilbert or Sullivan. That's their mother."

"But if the person was running hunched over. Could have been anybody she saw. Why did she automatically think it was Dolly?" I asked.

"The uniform, I guess. Maybe you should talk to her," Gloria said. "Just don't tell her who told you."

Gloria fell to chewing her lip, thinking hard.

"You know, Emily, I was thinking about a story for you," Simon said, his face lighting up. "About a guy who's really crazy. I mean, this guy kills people right and left. Then you could have maybe a federal agent come after him. Only make it a woman. That will be a surprise ..."

"Hannibal Lecter," I said.

"Who?" he said.

"It's already a book. And a movie."

"You mean the story I'm telling you?"

"Un-huh," I said.

"I didn't see anything like that."

"Bet you did. With Jodie Foster?"

"Who?"

"Jodie Foster. She was the federal agent in the first one. Julianne Moore in the second."

"I never see movies."

"Then somebody told you the story."

He shook his head. "I don't think so. Just kind of came to me."

"Somebody told you," I said.

They drove back out and I was almost to my studio, already feeling my head on the pillow I kept out there for emergencies, like writing until it got too dark to find the house and spending the night on my futon. I didn't make it. Dolly arrived, a little lady whose eyes barely peeked over the dashboard, beside her. It wasn't just that I wasn't going to get any sleep now, but everything was going to be hashed over again and again, and in front of Jackson and Jennifer, who would keep asking dumb questions. Unless I could think up an errand for them, I thought, ever hopeful. Unless I could make up the perfect place for Jackson to go see. Hmm ... out on Torch Lake, maybe. He'd like that. Snobby enough for him. *Just heard about it, you two. Better get over there fast.* I made up an address on a road that didn't exist, and walked along behind Dolly's car, back down toward my house, not nearly as tired as I had been.

TWENTY-FIVE

JACKSON AND JENNIFER WEREN'T interested in Dolly, nor in the odd little woman with a fluff of white hair, pink-framed glasses with moist, frightened eyes behind them, thin lips that snapped down on her words, pink cheeks, a deep voice that sounded like it was coming up from a cave, and a merry laugh that wasn't much in evidence that morning. Flora Coy was shaking when she put her hand out to take Jackson's. Shaking when she nodded to Jennifer, who was only too thrilled when I told them about the possible house for Jackson on Torch Lake. I noticed that Jackson wasn't quite as excited. I was getting the feeling Jackson liked things just the way they were, as Dolly said. All familiar and comfortable—for him.

The three of us—me, Dolly, and Flora Coy—sat lined along my sofa, smiling, waiting for Jackson and Jennifer to find their car keys, Jackson's wallet, their shoes, a map, a piece of paper with the mythical address on it, and finally leave, with Jennifer running back in for her water bottle—in case she should dehydrate between here and there, and Jackson's hiking boots, in case they found a great trail along the way.

Finally they were gone.

Dolly got up and made all three of us a pot of tea. She knew where everything was now, very comfortable in my house. I thought how all of a sudden I had more people familiar with my life than I was.

We stayed in the living room. Dolly put the teapot, cups, cream, sugar, and a plate of cookies on my big square coffee table. She poured tea and passed cookies. What a sweet little tea party we were having.

Dolly waited until she finished her tea and cookies to tell me about the phone call she got that morning, from the state police. They were looking into her background, they told her.

"I told Brent to go right ahead. And if he finds out anything, I'd like to know. I been here for the last fifteen years. Before that it was Kalamazoo. Before that a bunch of foster homes I'm still trying to forget. Last fifteen years I haven't hardly been out of Leetsville. Nothing to find out about me."

We sipped our tea like perfect ladies. Dolly's face was sad and closed in. There were things written there I didn't want to know about, and Flora Coy had so much on her mind I could tell she couldn't absorb any more.

After a while Dolly gave a short laugh. "Then I got a call from some nut. Phone rang right when I walked in the door, like he was watching my house. Said if the police couldn't stop me, he would. Ranted on about the corrupt police department and how Lucky is covering up for me. Somebody saw me set the fire and I'm going to pay for it. Crazy stuff like that."

"Awful," I said.

"Somebody actually believes I'd hurt Mary Margaret." Dolly lowered her head.

Flora Coy reached over and patted her hand. "Nobody who knows you would think such a thing, Dolly," the old woman said. "You've been the soul of kindness to me."

Dolly nodded listlessly.

"I know who called Lucky about you," I said.

Dolly's head snapped up.

"You mean the one who said they saw me coming out of the funeral home?"

I nodded. "Eugenia. She was on her way home. Fell asleep in the restaurant."

"Eugenia said that about me?" Dolly made a face then put a hand to her mouth. "For goodness' sake. Why would Eugenia say a thing like that?"

"Don't have a clue. You know how notoriously undependable eyewitness accounts are. And how nervous everybody is. She must've seen somebody who looks like you. Or was dressed like you usually dress?"

"In a uniform?"

"Yup."

"But, Eugenia! That's awful. I'd better have a talk with her."

"Yeah, I think so. I mean, she was half asleep. It was dark. Something gave her the idea."

"What if I call her? Who told you it was Eugenia? Couldn't've been the chief."

I felt funny, ratting out Gloria and Simon. I shrugged and she caught on. She nodded and bit at her lip.

"This is getting terrible," Flora Coy spoke up. "My friends all dead. Neighbor turned against neighbor. Everybody scared to death."

"How about some new ideas?" I took Flora's cramped hands in mine. She looked like a mouse caught in a trap. She snapped her lips a few times, shook her head, and seemed unable to speak. Her eyes behind those pink-framed glasses were magnified. She blinked again and again.

"Any idea who could be doing this to you and your friends?" I asked, eager to move straight to a place where we could help.

"Got a couple of ideas but Dolly here says you've already been looking into them. I mean, that Pastor Runcival. He spoke out against us in church, like we were the spawn of the devil. And that man out in the woods. You shoulda seen his face when we caught him spying on us that time. Well, maybe not spying so much as waiting for us to move on so he could get back to poaching deer. Joslyn was mad as a wet hen at him. She says she caught him in her woods more than a few times. Ernie took a shot at him once—it came to that."

"I've been thinking about Ernie," I said. "Could he be involved? I mean, was he mad at his mother and the rest of you for your little … er … ceremonies? We don't know where he really was when his mother was killed."

"Tractor pull," Dolly said.

"But, we don't know."

"State police'll look into it, I imagine."

"Good," I said.

Flora gave me a stunned look. "Ernie? I wouldn't think so. He could get mad. Yes, that's true. Joslyn told us about times he was mad at her for things, but it was ordinary stuff. Like she forgot to buy peanut butter. Just things like that. Nothing that would make him kill her."

"Didn't Ernie ever leave home? Joslyn, Ruby, and Mary Margaret all had grown kids living with them. Did any of them resent it? You'd think they'd have wanted to move on."

"Gilbert and Sullivan were gone for a while. I remember Mary Margaret wasn't too pleased when they came back home, but she got used to having them around. At least she didn't complain much; though, to tell the truth, we all knew what a trial the boys got to be. You know, nobody was keeping any of them there. Ruby got a little fed up with Amanda. The girl went to college but wouldn't get out and get a job. Kept going on how Ruby needed her there. A couple of times Ruby came right out and shook her head and said she wished the girl would get some gumption and go off on her own. Amanda wanted things—all the time. Talked about moving. Talked about a new house. Talked about taking trips. Anything she could think of to devil Ruby. But that's kids for you, I guess. Still, I never once heard Joslyn say a word against Ernie. When he'd get mad she'd just say it was because he had big plans when he was a boy but nothing ever panned out for him. Joslyn always blamed George. George was her husband. He left when Ernie was twelve years old. Left and they never heard from him again."

I gave Dolly a look. *Never heard from him again?*

"Now don't go looking like that. That's what people know, that George up and left. That's all Joslyn wanted folks around here to know of her business. She told us, in confidence, that George called a few times, from someplace out west. Didn't want to be tied down anymore, is what he told her. Wasn't coming back and had no intention of staying in touch either. So don't go getting ideas about poor Ernie. It's enough his father deserted him and now his mother's been killed so horribly. You look somewhere else for your culprit."

231

Duly chastened, I switched targets. "OK, but you said Ruby and Mary Margaret were fed up with having their kids at home. Did they say anything specific? I mean, were they trying to get them out?"

"Well, I know Mary Margaret had all kinds of trouble with the boys. Sullivan's a heavy drinker, likes to party—and he's hardly a teenager. Boy's in his forties. And Gilbert, well, he's not much better, only with the gambling."

"What happened to Mary Margaret's husband?"

"Poor man. Died young. Same with Ruby's husband. Mine, too. That's what kind of brought us all together. Our husbands were gone. I was the only one with no children. Seems like losing their father young is very hard on kids. That's what poor Ruby thought. Saw Amanda just curl up and turn into somebody who was afraid of everything."

"I wouldn't say Amanda's afraid. She seemed very much in charge when we were there the other day. She was the one planning the funerals," I said.

"Well, yes, I've seen it before; when the parents are finally gone the kids come out of their shell. To tell you the truth, I never saw it the way Ruby saw it, that Amanda was so weak. It was just that Ruby hoped for grandchildren. I guess they all did, and not one of 'em had a chance of having any. Funny, you would've thought one of them would have had some. Not one grandchild in the group."

"And Gilbert and Sullivan? Would you say either one had a reason to kill their mother? Gilbert—maybe gambling debts. Has to be insurance on the funeral home."

"But kill the others? Sounds a little far-fetched to me," Dolly put in. "I still think we've got to look at something way out there. Somebody totally nuts."

"You're back to my neighbor," I said, not wanting to face it.

"Harry Mockerman?" Flora Coy looked fast from Dolly to me. "Why that's not possible. I've known Harry since we went to grade school together. He's always been what you might call an odd boy, but Harry wouldn't hurt a soul."

"He kills everything that gets within a foot of his house," Dolly said. "And makes soup out of 'em."

"Well, that's just the way old-timers are up here. Most of my family lived off the woods. Our way of life. Harry can't help it if he's kind of a leftover. You know it's like the old farmers, collected junk in their yards, left one trailer and moved into another, left the old one to rot. Nobody thought anything of it until the new people started moving up here. Suddenly there was loud complaining about junk left around the old houses, and too many cars, up on jacks, rusting out. Just the clash of the old with the new. Always been like that. Always be like that."

She smiled indulgently, not meaning to flummox any ideas ranging around in our heads, but doing a pretty good job of it.

"Still." Dolly wasn't one to be stopped. "Was there anything from the past? Maybe it goes back to when you were all in school? Did he have a crush on any of you girls? Any of you spurn old Harry? Could he have been nursing a grudge for the last fifty years or so?"

"Harry Mockerman? And us? I'd say not. Never was a thing between any of us and Harry. Not that we didn't like him OK. He just wasn't, well, you know. I don't think Harry ever went for girls." She waved a hand hurriedly. "Not that he went for the boys. I don't mean that, though we didn't even know about things like that in my day. Never heard of such a thing. It was just that Harry didn't seem to go for anybody. He always kept to himself. Had a lot of dogs. Lived back there since I can't remember when. Always, I'd say."

Remembering something, I turned to Dolly. "He was here this morning, looking for me. Jennifer said an old guy in a funny suit dropped off wild leeks and wants to see me."

Dolly nodded, then nodded again.

"Should I go over there?" I asked.

"You worried about going alone?" she asked.

I thought a minute, then shook my head. "No. I don't think so."

"Want me to come with you?"

"You scared him last time. And anyway, we don't want to leave Flora."

"Why don't you go on then? I'll give you, oh, say twenty minutes. If you're not back by one thirty, we'll come get you."

I nodded, not liking to think Harry presented any danger, but still I knew that danger could hide anywhere up here now.

TWENTY-SIX

Not being a mother, I didn't know if what I felt toward Flora Coy and Dolly was motherly instinct or not. I was wishing I could keep them right at my house, dump Jackson and "Miss Thing," and take the two women in; keep them safe. Only, since I wasn't very good at keeping myself safe, why did I think I could take care of two wily women who were probably a lot braver than I was? Maybe I wanted them with me for just that reason. So ... no motherly instinct at all, just self-protection.

I was telling myself all sorts of things, while I walked over to Harry's. I'd lied to Dolly. I was nervous about going there. Not that I suspected Harry of doing any of the terrible things that were going on, but even the woods made me nervous. A million eyes followed me. There wasn't a tree that didn't threaten. Like *The Wizard of Oz*, when those trees threw apples at Dorothy, I had the feeling the trees were watching, and at any moment they would reach out with scaly arms and grab me.

Harry's dogs began to bark when I was halfway up his driveway, or pathway, or whatever. A true early-warning system. I'd heard his dogs when they were loose in the woods, baying after something or other, barking like *The Hound of the Baskervilles*, with enough tremolos to set the hair along my arms straight up on end.

Harry's old hybrid car was parked at the side of his house. Either he was home or out in the woods. I knocked on the front door and got no response. If he was in there, he wouldn't hear me shouting over those dogs. But then, with the dogs so loud, he had to know somebody was around.

I gave up knocking at the front door and walked to the back.

Harry leaned over a stump with a hatchet in his hand. I didn't mind the hatchet. I was relieved to see his scrawny figure in that sprung black suit. I'd had enough of finding dead people.

"Emily," he said without so much as glancing up at me.

"Harry," I said, mimicking his monotone.

He held a dead skunk in one hand and the hatchet in the other. He was skinning the skunk. Not a pretty sight. Something about the bloody half-bare carcass that unsettled me. I wanted a little distance between me and that dead skunk and between me and Harry with a hatchet in his hand, but it was too late. I couldn't sneak out of the clearing and come back some other day, some other week, some other eon.

"Glad to see ya, Emily," he said, still without looking up. He was at a critical point, I could see, where the hatchet had to be used delicately, around the joints of a leg. I had to admire his skill even while wishing I didn't have to look. "You get the leeks I brought over? Good in soup. Salad. Anything you cook. Strong flavor, this time of year. Don't use too much of 'em at once."

"Thanks Harry." I got as close as I felt my stomach could take then stood standing on one leg, looking anywhere I could look, examining the dogs in their cages as they threw their bodies at the chicken wire. I checked out Harry's wood piles, now extending all around the clearing. He was ready for winter while I hadn't even thought about things like wood and preserves and putting plastic over my windows—all those practical things people up here knew instinctively to do. Three years and I still didn't have good sense when it came to the elements.

"That skunk's not going to stink, is it?" I asked finally, shifting my feet in the trampled weeds of Harry's yard. Like Harry, there was the smell of fresh wood and decaying leaves out there. The small, leaning buildings were picturesque, not simply old. Boards peeled, roofs slanted, doors hung crookedly—it was a fairy tale place. I thought, any minute now I'll be guessing Harry's real name. *"Rumpelstiltskin, sir."*

Harry looked up at me, his wizened face moving around into what I took for a grin. "Wouldn't catch me skinning 'im if I didn't get the sacs out."

"I just don't want to be smelling like skunk for the next three months." I think I was whining. Sounded like whining.

"Yeah, know what you mean. I got into one when I was a kid. Had to sleep outside for a few weeks before my dad let me back in the house. Then he made me take a bath in tomato juice every day. Went through a lot of tomato juice, I'll tell ya. Good way to get rid of unwanted guests though. In case you're looking for something." He was really grinning now, pleased with himself. He'd met Jennifer, maybe Jackson, too. "But you don't need to be afraid of this guy." He held the almost skinned skunk up by one bloody leg. "Ain't gonna do nothing. Killed 'im clean. Didn't have a chance to get his tail in the air."

I edged away as if that dangling black and white pelt could rear up and get me, dead or not. I'd heard of bees stinging after they died. Why not a skunk spraying *post mortem*?

Because the day was chilly, Harry had a red plaid jacket on over his funeral suit. It was funny how the suit jacket hung down at the bottom and yet, on Harry, it didn't look out of place. Maybe I was beyond finding things odd up here. Or maybe I'd grown just as odd as my neighbors and friends. I looked down at my sneakers with torn toes, then at my jeans with holes at the knees. *For God's sakes*, I told myself. It was one thing to go native, but quite another to simply let myself go to hell. And with Jackson there, too. What a contrast I must be to Jennifer of the long slim legs and blond hair and lispy laugh, despite my one-colored hair and chewed lipstick.

"If you're sure." I edged closer again.

Harry set the hatchet aside and got a knife from his jacket pocket. He switched a long blade out and went to work. The knife moved fast, scraping the inside of the hide, whisking at it, removing tiny pieces of flesh until the hide was stripped clean. I couldn't help but think how good he was with that knife. An expert. The kind of man for whom dissection of a body was probably second nature.

I shuddered and crossed my arms over my chest. I was getting like everybody else; suspecting Harry though I'd never thought he could hurt anyone. Not really. Not human beings. I guess I thought that was because human beings weren't fit for the soup pot, but here he was skinning a skunk. No soup there.

"What'll you do with the hide, Harry?" I asked.

He gave me a funny look, as if the question was a dumb one, or outside his understanding.

"What does anybody do with a skunk hide?" he said, laughing at me.

238

"I haven't a clue," I said.

"Why, tan it, then I sell it to some boys in town that like 'em. I don't know what they do with 'em. Maybe just use the tail. Sold a bunch of 'em awhile back to Jake Anderson who owns the bar in town. He tacked 'em up all over the walls behind the bar. Said it's what you call a conversation piece. That's why he called it the Skunk. You know that? The bar's called that because of me? Well, you'd be surprised what people buy around here."

I shook my head. No, I thought, I wouldn't be surprised at all.

Working expertly, Harry slid the last of the black and white pelt off. I winced and looked away as the bare, bleeding carcass fell down to lie on the stump.

"Geez, Harry." I made a face. "How can you do stuff like that?"

He gave me an astonished look. "You mean kill a few things?"

"More than a few. It seems you've always got something simmering."

"A man's got to live. This one's not going into a soup pot. I got my standards, you know."

Yeah, I wanted to say. Standards that fell just short of cooking a skunk.

I turned away while Harry finished his job. I looked off at his woods, which he kept thinned, almost park-like. He'd told me once he could manage my wood lot like he did his, taking down the bad stuff, the useless stuff, for firewood, and giving strong trees, like my oaks and basswood, a place to grow tall. I'd said "no" because I still had a romantic notion of me and the woods as a thing that would grow tall and old and thick together. Now I knew better. Now I knew that Harry was right. If my woods weren't taken care of soon, some of the big trees would topple and rot where they fell. I was considering taking Harry up on his offer; have him come cull the dying trees, some of the weaker trees, some of the crowded trees, to make room for the others. I thought maybe, if he'd do the work, he could have the wood and I would have a better forest. I just hadn't gotten around to discussing it with him yet, and this murder stuff had driven it right out of my mind.

"If you ever feel the need of a good skunk hide, why, now you know where to come." He wiped the knife clean on a rag he whipped from his jacket pocket.

I gave him a weak smile, not certain if my leg was being pulled or not. I had a sneaking suspicion it was, the way I had a sneaking suspicion a lot of people made fun of me up here.

When he'd finished with the knife and put it back in his pocket, he pinned the hide to a board to dry, then pulled the board up off the ground. "Keeps the dogs and things away from it," he said. I followed him to his shed where he got a big ax, ran a wet finger over the blade, set a log up on another log and began whacking away, making himself some kindling.

"Thanks again for the leeks," I said between whacks. "I'll make a stew one of these days and have you over."

"'preciate that." He looked sidewise at me, grinning. "But not while you got all that company. Don't understand people needing other people hanging around."

"What did you want to talk to me about?"

He shrugged. "Just came over to see how you was doing. I heard about all the stuff happening. The fire last night." He shook his head. "Another poor old woman. Heard you was all upset."

"Of course," I said. "Who isn't?"

"Not the fire. I'm talking about the other things. Those things you found. Seemed like it would be right up your alley, being a writer. That's what I told Simon the other day but he said all this

240

was doing everybody in. What with Joslyn Henry. Now Mary Margaret. Fire get those boys of hers?"

"Nope. Almost got Sullivan but he got out a back window."

"Too bad," he said. "If poor Mary Margaret had to get caught in it, a shame to have those boys of hers profit. Terrible shame. This whole thing. Can't imagine what's happening around here."

"You mean profit from the funeral home?"

"Insurance. Those boys won't be unhappy they come into some money. Life insurance. Building insurance." Harry shook his head. "Money's what does it to people. Makes 'em terrible."

"You hear anything else being said around town?" I moved closer and leaned against a tree, out of range of the flying bits of wood.

He stopped midair and gave me a look. "I don't pass on stories, Emily. If that's what you want."

"I'm here because you said you wanted to see me."

He nodded once, then again. He gave a log a powerful whack, sending shreds of tree sailing. "I got two things on my mind."

"What two things, Harry?"

"First I was thinking maybe you need protection over there to your house. The way things are going now, and with you putting yourself right into the middle of it, well, I was thinking… I got this tent I could put up in your front yard. Bring a few of my dogs over. You know, kind of camp out and watch things."

"Why Harry, that's very nice of you."

He reddened and lowered his head so I couldn't see his face. "Just using common sense. Seems to be in short supply around here."

"I've got a dog," I said, not following who was the one without common sense.

His head snapped up. "Thought so. About time. I was thinking of giving you one of mine, but I just couldn't make up my mind which one didn't belong. Came to the conclusion there wasn't a one of them I could get rid of."

I looked again at the panting faces behind the chicken wire fence keeping them from me, and was grateful for their master's indecision.

"You like him—yer dog? Kinda cute. Saw him this morning. But, Emily, he's only a pup." Harry scowled and shook his head. "What in hell good's a pup to you right now? Shoulda got yerself a grown dog."

"Sorrow's friendly. He barks."

"You don't want 'im too friendly. Take my dogs, here. Tear a leg off you unless I tell 'em 'NO.'"

"I don't want Sorrow biting anybody."

Harry shook his head again and set his ax down.

"Whatever pleases you," he said.

"Was there anything else?" I leaned away from the tree, stretching, figuring I'd better get back quick or Dolly and Flora would arrive with guns blazing.

He hesitated. "You know those state police were over here to see me? A couple of times so far."

"I knew they were interviewing people around here. In town, too. Anybody who knew Joslyn Henry, or Ruby Poet. Now they'll be looking into Mary Margaret's death."

"That's everybody," he said. "They been here too much. Seems to me they should be over to those Survivalist folks. Strange things going on back there. I seen it with my own eyes. I been hunting these woods since I was born. Not going to stop now just 'cause they put up signs and point guns at a man. That goes two ways, ya know. The gun pointing. Seems to me the police should be looking into them a lot closer. I know some things..."

"What things, Harry?"

"Well, just things. Like I seen that Rombart guy in Joslyn's woods, watching when the women were out there at their fire pit. Silly old women. Dancing around. Flowers in their hair. Singing songs. More than one time I asked Ruby Poet what in hell they thought they were doing. That's what got her mad at me, not what they're saying, that I wanted too much for my firewood. I told her they were damned stupid, flitting around the fire the way they was. Ruby said they were sick and tired of men spying on them and I said it wasn't spying, just that I was always out there. She blew right up and said to stay off Joslyn's property and she was going to have a talk with Ernie and Joslyn. That's what our argument was about. Thought you should know the truth and maybe put a bug in that state policeman's ear about looking more at that Dave Rombart. I'd put my money on them. I think they're trying to take over this whole North Country. Maybe start a war on the government, turn this place into a battle-ground. Maybe that's why they're killing off people."

"Why Ruby Poet? She doesn't own anything out here."

"Who knows why? Maybe she said something to one of them like she said to me. Don't ask me why they're doing it, you just better take a long look at those folks, is all I'm saying."

Harry was angry now, whether at me, Dave Rombart, the state police, the dead women—I couldn't quite figure out.

I told him I'd pass on his suspicions to Deputy Dolly, who was leading the investigation for the Leetsville police. He shook his head, his shoulders slumped. I guessed Harry was thinking we were all doomed for sure. "Thought she was out of it," he said. He was busy picking up pieces of kindling from the ground and cradling them in his arms.

Even Harry, I thought. Old Harry, alone back in these woods with his dogs. He knew things like the rest of them.

"She's not." I turned to go, but hesitated. "And Harry," I said sweetly. "If you hear anything else you think we should know, please come on over. You'll tell me won't you?"

I got a grudging nod from Harry and headed back toward home.

TWENTY-SEVEN

DOLLY HAD ONE HAND on her gun. Her head was down, lips moving, as she plodded up my drive, grumbling, long-faced, and in no obvious hurry to save me from Harry Mockerman. Poor Flora tiptoed along behind, huffing and puffing. This was my cavalry.

They spotted me at the edge of Harry's drive, emerging from the brambles and pulling fat, thorny pickers from my jeans. Flora waved and smiled. Dolly almost smiled, but caught herself. She scowled and yelled, "You took too damned long...what were you thinking? Had the two of us scared to death. Thought I was going to have to come shoot my way into Harry's house..."

And on and on.

"I'm fine," I said, meeting them in the middle of the road, in the shadow of one of the rolling dark clouds overhead. The day was starting to match my mood: threatening, gusty, and not to be trifled with.

"Harry and I got talking. I forgot you were coming to get me in twenty minutes." I looked pointedly at my watch. "Hmm. That

245

was forty-five minutes ago. I could've been dead by now. I'm not depending on you two again."

Flora had the good grace to give a sheepish laugh. Not Dolly.

"So? What'd he want?" she demanded, stepping out of the middle of the road so a car could pass.

"Want to go back to the house and talk? Or just stand here waving to the neighbors, who don't have enough to gossip about already?" I put my hands on my hips. The only way to deal with Dolly was to out "indignant" her.

Flora huffed and puffed. Her eyes, behind her pink-framed glasses, were large and uncertain. She looked down the drive, then off into the woods. "It's so peaceful out here. I don't think it's going to rain, do you? Could we just go sit someplace in your woods?" She took a deep breath that turned into a sigh. "Somewhere close by. I feel at home here. Despite what's happened, it's not the forest doing these things. Never is. It's Man. Or Woman. We just don't know, do we?"

Dolly and I looked down. A little ashamed, I thought, that we hadn't put an end to this awful business, weren't even close to knowing what was going on, and that Flora Coy had a better outlook on life, despite everything, than either of us.

I figured Flora was out of steam after climbing the steep hill so I guided the women to a bench in front of my studio, where we could watch the leaves fall, smell the rich autumn smells, and turn our faces up to the sun, or clouds, or whatever happened by. Maybe, for just a minute, we'd forget the horror going on around us and sink back into what northern life was all about.

We settled along my wooden bench with a big, black metal eagle at the back. I'd put the bench on a bluff up from the small pond outside my studio windows. Here I watched fox and coyotes and, once, a blue heron circling overhead, casting a wide shadow around and around until it was gone. Here I learned I was put on the earth for sunny days and shining leaves and a huge buck drinking at the pond, furred rack of horns made golden by the light. Here I'd learned to stop thinking for a time and simply be.

Flora worked her way onto the seat on the other side of Dolly, settling like a hen, plumping her bottom down, wedging it around for maximum comfort, then folding her hands in her lap. She heaved a huge sigh and let her legs dangle in the tall, dead grass. There we were, lined up like a row of ducks, staring off at nothing much.

Dolly sat forward, shoulders working together under her dark, wool police coat. She wasn't giving up her anger easily.

"What was it Harry wanted to tell you? You gonna tell us or not?" She turned her body slightly toward me but looked out to the meadow where tall, yellowed grasses lay matted in a wide circle. A deer's bed. Many deer.

"He wanted to come over and pitch a tent, bring some of his dogs, and protect me," I said.

Dolly gave me an openmouthed stare. "Isn't that like putting the fox in charge of the hen house?"

"Now Dolly," Flora chided. "There's nothing wrong with Harry, and I don't believe the man had a thing to do with killing anybody. He's been odd for years. No odder now than when he was a boy. Nobody pays him any attention."

"He wasn't happy with you and your friends out there in the woods, dancing around the fire. He said he thought you were all crazy," I said, thinking I had to keep everybody right down to earth, dealing with what was, not life as they wished it could be.

Flora leaned up and looked around Dolly. I'd hurt her feelings. "Oh Emily," she said. "That's not nice at all. Poor Harry. Anything out of the ordinary for him is dangerous, I suppose. When you're not, well, not quite like other people, you need your life very orderly, you see. That's the way it is with Harry. Always has been. That's why he keeps so much to himself. Poor man can't handle what seems strange to him, though he's strange to just about everybody else. I mean, for heaven's sakes—his funeral suit? As if somebody couldn't find the thing in that tiny house." She stopped, sat back, and bounced her hands in her lap. "Just listen to me being mean about Harry Mockerman because he found fault with our little circle of women. Isn't that the end of everything though? You see what all this is bringing us to?"

She leaned out again and looked straight at me, hard. "You heard it was Eugenia said she saw Dolly coming out of the funeral home? Well, of course you did. Can you imagine? I told Dolly to go right over there and get it straightened out. People are calling Dolly and saying terrible things. Me and my friends getting threatening letters. This isn't the same Leetsville anymore. We've always been such a friendly place. I don't care if it was a blizzard, a fire, or that tornado came through the north end of town once, why, everybody was out as fast as the wind was gone. With their chain saws, with food, with ladders—whatever help anybody needed. Taking folks into our homes."

We sat and listened to Flora Coy mourning the place she used to know before death came to town in a big way.

"I've been thinking." her voice fell. "What we were doing in Joslyn's woods, me and my friends—well, you think we brought this on in any way?"

Dolly looked around at her. "What do you mean? In what way?"

Flora dropped her voice to a whisper. Her eyes nervously searched the nearby bare trees around us. I got the distinct feeling Flora was frightened.

"I mean, I wasn't into 'being in touch with nature' the way Ruby and Joslyn were, but I was a part of the ceremonies we had. You think we touched something evil without knowing it? Could there be evil spirits in these woods that we somehow got a hold of and let loose after all? I'd hate to think…" Her hands were at her lips. Dolly reached over and awkwardly patted the woman's knee.

"Not a chance," I told her. "Whoever is doing this—it's not an evil spirit. Evil, yes. But very human. What we've got to figure out is why? Who would commit murder? Who benefits?"

"There's only me left." Flora Coy was talking to herself.

I couldn't come up with any comforting words because I was too busy trying to figure my way back through the horror of the last week, trying to find some thread to hold on to, a way through the maze of events.

"You know, girls," Flora sighed, "we really had the loveliest circle. You should've seen us. Just because we're old we figured we didn't have to give up living, having adventures. Why, we'd put flowers in our hair and hold hands and circle the fire under the stars. Sometimes we'd just throw back our head and dance around by ourselves. It was like being a child and circling while you watched the stars. Remember doing that?"

Dolly and I nodded, remembering only too well. She was making me wistful for the times I'd felt that free.

"And we had songs. Didn't do anybody any harm. It's just that we'd been friends since back in that one-room school over to School House Road. Girls together. Used to have sleepouts. Sing songs around a campfire. Dance if we felt like it. Tell stories. We wanted some of that back, and maybe bring peace to the world, or show Mother Nature we were grateful for our blessings. That's not bad, is it?"

Dolly and I made demurring noises. We let her talk. Overhead, geese veered off and away south. It seemed ominous, everything leaving us behind.

"We all loved Ruby maybe best of everybody. Gingrich she was then, back before she married Wally Poet. Such a true lady. And so smart. Ruby should've been a teacher or something instead of marrying Wally. But that's neither here nor there. She married him and that's that. Anyway, when one day Ruby got mad at the pastor over to the Baptist church, she said no religion let any woman have a God that looked like us. She said: Why did God have to be male when, to tell the truth, the males we'd had in our lives weren't all that hot. Ruby said we aren't male and she said God was really no more than a way of looking for a perfect self—that's what we were all looking for, and how could a woman's perfect self look like a man? She said we could find our spirit in nature and that's what we did though it turned out only Ruby could see her. Mother Nature, I'm talking about. Gray-haired old woman, Ruby said, with a happy face. Ruby said she could see her, smiling and clasping her hands to her breasts while we sang and danced. Well, at least that's what Ruby said. I liked the dancing and the being together the way we'd always been. Ruby said maybe one day we'd have a lodge by the fire, a kind of chapel all our own, so we could keep meeting in the woods right on through winter. Not have to skip the winter solstice 'cause of our arthritis."

She sighed and looked around, eyes damp behind her thick glasses. "Wouldn't that have been nice? Ruby thought maybe word of what we were doing would spread one day, and we'd have this place people could come to from all over, take part in our singing and dancing, sit by the fire and tell their stories."

She sighed again and wiped away a single tear running from crevice to crevice down her old cheek.

Dolly pulled a wad of Kleenex from her jacket pocket, peeled one off as if it were a dollar bill, and handed it to Flora. Flora sniffed, blew, wadded the Kleenex up and handed it back to Dolly, who stuck it in her pocket.

Flora's voice went on, wearier now, with a waver to it. "Mary Margaret always made a fine poppy seed bundt. Ruby made us moon cookies. We had the best times. Sometimes their children didn't understand. Ernie and Amanda, well, they'd complain, but then children always complain, don't they? I mean, just carry on if their mother isn't plain and ordinary so nobody notices her and nobody comments or disagrees with what she's doing. They didn't like that people criticized and made fun, but not one of us gave a tinker's damn. Excuse my language.

"I think it was always more important to Ruby than the rest of us—the Mother Nature business. She was more serious than me and Mary Margaret. Joslyn, well, I think Joslyn went along with Ruby more. She thought what we were doing was the beginning of a huge movement that was going to start right there, in her woods, and spread around the world. People honoring the earth. People honoring Mother Nature as if she was real. I went along with it because I loved my friends. But I wasn't as ... well ... as close to nature as those two. Now look, they're gone. Mary Margaret's gone. And what'd we try to do? Bring some peace to the world, is all. Honor the place we live. Nothing bad. Don't see why my friends had to die."

Flora Coy fell silent. I could see, being out here in the woods, the need to love a place where you lived this close to nature. I already knew things I'd never known before. How trees had different personalities. How flowers of the same species could be different. How birds lived within their own small orbits. The nature of the dragonfly. Knowledge I treasured; things I'd learned while living up here. Who knew what more I'd learn if I really paid attention? Dancing in the woods around a blazing fire, honoring this place—it seemed eminently sane to me at that moment, and eminently sad that four women who engaged in such a gentle pastime should be singled out for death.

"Harry thinks it's Dave Rombart and that group," I said after a while. "Said he's seen them in the woods doing odd things. He thinks it's them and their goofy games. Maybe all of you saw something you shouldn't have seen."

Flora didn't answer right away. She was deep in thought.

Dolly looked around at me and smirked. "He thinks it's Dave and his wife? Well, guess what? The chief called me on my way out here. He got a call from Dave Rombart. Said one of his men reported he saw Harry back in the woods with what looked like a human head in his hands. You know what I think? I think Harry and Dave are squabbling over the same hunting turf and are looking to knock each other out."

I had to smile. So here we were, caught up in more internecine warfare. Tiresome, if not worse.

"What's the chief doing about it?" I asked.

"Told me, and he called Officer Brent. They'll be over to see Harry today."

"Then we'd better call them and tell them what Harry said. I mean, just to be fair."

Dolly nodded and got up. "I'll go call in." She turned to Flora. "You'd better stay with us 'til this is over …"

Flora shook her head as fast as she could shake it. "No sir. I won't be chased out of my house. I've got my birds to take care of. Can't leave them unprotected. I'll be very careful and I'll call you if I hear anything around my house or if I get a single phone call that seems the least bit funny, or if I get another letter."

It was Dolly's turn to shake her head. "I don't think …"

"You don't have to, young lady. I'll do the thinking for myself." Flora stood up. "Now, if you ask me it's time for you two to be talking to Eugenia about what she saw at the funeral home. You know it wasn't you, Dolly, so why don't you find out just what was going on outside there? And then you can take me home and check my doors and do whatever detectives do."

She smiled brilliantly and straightened her pink glasses. She stood as tall as she could get and looked resolute. I was thinking maybe Dolly should move into Flora's house. Seemed like the best idea for both of them. Dolly could be away from insulting phone calls and protect Flora at the same time. I wished I could move the two of them right in with me but I already had a houseful, though I hoped to get rid of Jackson and Jennifer as soon as I could think straight again. Any minute. Maybe after they discovered the address I'd given them didn't exist, they'd get the hint. It was a faint hope. Not one in which I put a lot of faith.

TWENTY-EIGHT

THE WHITE JAGUAR PULLED in directly behind us, as we came down the drive. An unspoken meanness between me and Dolly made us ignore it though Flora looked over her shoulder, and gave a flustered "*Ooh, ooh*," warning we could get run over. Jackson gunned his motor, frightening Flora, who stumbled off to the side. Dolly and I turned in unison, a chorus of two, pretending surprise, jumping out of the car's way, smiling as wide as we could smile.

"Swine," Dolly muttered under her breath, her smile clamped grimly in place. I reached out and punched her arm. At that moment, I didn't need her making things worse with my fishy-smelling guests.

"Never found that house!" Jennifer yelled cheerfully out the car window and waved as they drove on past.

At the bottom of the drive they got out and waited while we choked our way through their trail of dust. Jackson pulled off his sunglasses, threw back his arms, and stretched hard. I recognized the move. Kind of a strut for women who could only look, but never have him. All I noticed was his stomach, which used to be so flat but wasn't anymore—at least not what it once was. And I noticed that his shoulders sloped more than they had. When you know where to look for fault in an old lover, the discoveries can be pure pleasure.

"We had the most unbelievable picnic," Jennifer gushed and folded her hands over her heart, or between her perky breasts, almost visible beneath a wide-weave, champagne-colored sweater. "Bread and cheese and wine and fruit. One of those events most people only get to read about in *Gourmet Magazine*."

The three of us—the "most people" Jennifer was talking about, (well, at least Dolly and I; Flora Coy wasn't really in this tug of war)—went on smiling, saying nothing much.

In the house, Sorrow lay in the middle of the living room oriental with a piece of leather hanging rakishly from the side of his mouth. Oh, oh. I recognized what was left of one of Jackson's shoes. At least I imagined it was Jackson's shoe, though now it was in bits: a lolling tongue hanging off in one place; laces, like little worms, in another; and small chewed pieces of leather scattered all around a busy Sorrow.

"Sorrow!" I shouted, making him cock up his ears and look at me funny, as if he would never understand how to make me happy. "You bad dog."

Jackson and Jennifer lugged in a wicker picnic hamper clanking with empty wine bottles and glasses. Jackson's mouth fell open when he saw the destruction of his shoe. He set his end of the hamper down and stood with his hands on his hips, scowling.

"My God!" Jennifer gave a shout and ran into the living room, whirling in circles as she searched for, then found, the other shoe. She grabbed it up.

"You beast!" she screamed. "Look what you've done! Stupid, stupid animal."

As the rest of us stood transfixed, watching, she brought the shoe down on Sorrow's head.

I heard my dog yip in pain and I was off. I think Dolly was right behind me. I grabbed Jennifer's upraised arm. She was about to hit him again because he hadn't the brains to drop the shoe completely from his mouth, or maybe a tooth was still hooked in the leather. All I knew was I had to stop her. The quickest thing I could think of was to hip check her, sending her on to the sofa, arms flailing, mouth and eyes opened wide. She hit with a whoosh of breath and bounced, coming to rest in a slide off the sofa to the floor where she lay with her tiny skirt up around her waist. Teeny thong panties, for which I was grateful, were shoved up into her crotch. Her arms were stretched wide, unfettered breasts at their fullest, and the offending shoe lost from her hand.

"Emily!" She lay where she was, shocked, the air knocked out of her. Her big blue eyes filled with astonished tears.

"Don't you ever, ever hit my dog like that." I bent over her, my face as threatening as I could get it. What I wanted to do was laugh, or help her up. Anything to lighten the moment. I was stuck with indignation and didn't know where to take it next.

Dolly held Sorrow back. He saw what I was up to and wanted to leap on Jennifer now that she was down. Flora Coy stood away from all of us, behind the kitchen counter, hands to her cheeks. I heard Jackson sputtering behind me. Soon he elbowed me aside, helping Jennifer, who was crying, to her feet, soothing her, saying something about how kind it was of her to protect his property, that it wasn't necessary ... just another shoe, after all. Surely Emily is sorry ...

My face was frozen. Flora Coy scurried off to the bathroom. Dolly disappeared through the door to the porch, dragging an incensed Sorrow beside her, bits of chewed leather still hanging from his muzzle.

"I'm sorry, too," Jennifer said between sniffles as she tugged at her skirt. "I was just so mad at what he did."

She turned big, wet eyes on me. "I didn't mean to hurt your dog. I wanted to save poor Jack's shoes was all. They're expensive."

She leaned on Jackson's arm and sniffled again. He pulled his handkerchief from the back pocket of his Bermuda shorts and held it out for her. She took it, tenderly holding the precious gift, then blew her nose.

I chewed at my bottom lip. For one thing, I needed to stop myself from laughing at the silly scene. The other thing was, I was really pissed off. I didn't sic my dog on "poor" Jackson's shoes. I didn't leave the shoe where a puppy could find it. I didn't …

Well, I couldn't think of any other way I would have been smarter, but certainly I'd never let my girlfriend bean my hostess's pet. Especially if that hostess was my ex-wife.

It didn't take me long to work back up to a good sense of outrage. When I stood straight, I was almost in Jennifer's face. Maybe a little shorter than the statuesque beauty. Still, I was sure I looked impressive as I forced the two of them to back away and give me room to stomp off with dignity.

"I'm very sorry my dog chewed Jackson's shoes," I shot over my very stiff shoulder. "However, if he'd put them in the closet where they belonged, it wouldn't have happened."

"Emily, that's outrageous!" Jennifer, taller than I by a good four inches, grabbed back her indignation and looked down her nose at me.

I smiled a nasty smile and waited just long enough to be sure I was going to say exactly what I wanted said. "You know, Jennifer,

I don't like people who hit animals. It's time for you to get over to your parents, or wherever you're going. In the morning, Jackson, you drive her where she needs to go, OK?"

"I … eh … don't know what to say, Emily." Her full lips went into a full pout. "I'm really sorry. I didn't mean … if I offended you … it was just … well … poor Jack …"

The best I could come up with was a flounce off to my bedroom and a solid slam of the door behind me, leaving Jackson to get his shoe, or leave it, to soothe his grieving girlfriend, or leave her.

I couldn't stay in my room for long. Dolly was alone with Sorrow. Flora Coy couldn't hide in the bathroom forever. But getting out was going to be a little tough. My pride was on the line. First I opened my door and peeked around it. The bedroom door across the hall was closed. I could hear voices. Jackson soothing Jennifer, who wailed that she couldn't go and leave him here, where he wasn't appreciated.

I tiptoed into the hall and back to the living room. Dolly and Flora sat on the sofa, Dolly hunched forward, hands between her knees, head bent. Flora was taking a nap, chin on her chest, glasses slipping down her nose. She snored softly, little bursts of breath rippling her thin lips. When Dolly saw me, she put a finger to her mouth and motioned for me to join her outside.

I got a Diet Coke and followed her into the garden where we walked along slowly, looking down at my flower beds, most buried under leaves now, ready for winter despite me.

The day had cleared again. Probably not for long. Up in northern Michigan, weather changed every hour. Kind of like my life was going. The sky was one of those fall blues almost impossible to believe isn't painted on. I called them Rembrandt skies—enough gold to make each one a treasure. Everything around us, trees, grasses, knobby roses—all with a crisp edge to them. If it hadn't been the bloody—and beyond—time of year, I might have enjoyed the walk.

If I hadn't been such a shit to a guest…

I felt sad, and small, that I'd taken such pleasure in throwing Jackson's "friend" out of my house. It didn't matter that there was damned good reason behind it. I still saw Jackson's face. A rare kind of disappointment etched there. I guess I'd always been above the psycho/sexual dramas he'd indulged in. Now I'd matched him in vileness. When he had his affairs, while we were married, I didn't have many meltdowns. Well, not until my one spectacular dish-throwing fit. I guess even now he expected better of me.

I expected better of me. I hoped this wasn't about him at all, but really about my black and white mutt with sad eyes, who didn't deserve being hit, or hurt. I hoped I wasn't one of those sick, jealous women who'd do anything for revenge.

"I'm sorry…about all that." I motioned toward the house.

"Yeah," Dolly said, and she took a swipe at her nose with the back of her hand.

"I shouldn't have gotten that mad," I said. "It wasn't right to hit her. Maybe I'm just jealous. I don't know…"

Dolly stopped at the top of a set of brick steps leading down through a wild strawberry patch turned a soft bronze fall color. The steps led to the bottom garden where tall, pink foxgloves grew all of July.

Dolly made a face at me. "Do all of you smart people wear hair shirts? Hey, sometimes a duck is a duck, you know? That duck you got back in there…" She snapped her head to point to where I lived. "That duck's a conniver without the good sense God gave a pumpkin."

I had to grin. It felt good to have somebody angry on my behalf. I couldn't remember the last time a friend had been so solidly on my side. Maybe not since grade school, when Claudia Jarvis decked a boy for hitting me in the face with a snowball. That was loyalty, too.

"Think he'll go now?" She walked ahead of me, out to what an etched rock I'd found in Traverse City proclaimed as my "Secret Garden." Really it was just a mass of weeds growing up through creeping thyme. Another one of my garden dreams gone bad. It was supposed to be tranquil, with a bench, a birdbath, a flowering crab, and a ring of lilacs.

I said nothing. Something about my house being that empty didn't appeal to me. Jackson might be a pain in the ass, but at least he was a familiar, and reassuring, pain.

"Time you got your head back to what we're supposed to be doing." Now she scolded me; standing in front of my leaf-choked birdbath, feet planted in my weeds, hands on her hips, the harsh look on her face finding me seriously lacking.

I opened my mouth, but I must have run out of comebacks and insults. My lips hung slack while she waited for a zinger. She looked disappointed in me yet again as I gave a sputter, then another sputter, and finally gave up.

"You want us to leave? Get out of your hair?" Dolly asked, stopping beside a lilac bush still decorated with small, brown blossoms at the top, where I hadn't been able to reach last spring.

I shook my head.

"Then why don't we get the heck out of here? How about Fuller's? I'm hungry and we need to talk to Eugenia. If she's the one said she saw me coming out of the funeral home, we'd better find out why."

I stopped between a bent-over butterfly bush and a cascading spirea. "Let's go to Flora's, too. She needs clothes and stuff."

"Should feed all those damn birds." She hesitated. "Think she'll come back here to stay?"

I shrugged.

We went in and woke Flora. The other two were nowhere in sight. I didn't care if they left or stayed. It felt good to have more important things on my mind. Flora Coy was ours to keep alive. Mine and Dolly's. We were her guardians. Like it or not, we'd be the Three Musketeers until this thing was over. That meant I had no room in my life for errant strings attached to my past. If Jackson was gone when I returned, let that be the finale, the *coup de grace*, the overdue ending to my marriage.

———

When we got to Fuller's, the parking lot was almost empty. While Dolly and Flora went on in, I stopped to check the latest of Eugenia's genealogical sheets, almost as a way of forestalling this confrontation between Eugenia and Dolly, and anyway, I was always curious about Eugenia's latest.

The new sheet had a big gold star attached, the way Eugenia did with her favorite ancestors. But something was wrong with this one.

William H. Bonney, Jr. died in 1881, the sheet said. Dead at twenty-one.

Un-uh, I thought. I knew the name and he almost certainly never married—so therefore no descendants—and though he was certainly a bad guy, he wasn't hung, as Eugenia claimed in big bold letters. The guy had been shot, I thought, by a sheriff in New Mexico.

I knew Billy the Kid, and he sure wasn't part of Eugenia's family tree, or almost anybody's family tree (except for maybe a brother or two), and had no place in Eugenia's vestibule.

I took a look at some of the old charts. Nothing jumped out until I uncovered Belle Starr. How had that one gotten by me? It looked as though Eugenia claimed every outlaw who ever lived. I was disappointed. I guess I'd wanted her infamous family tree to be real. I wanted that touch with a rowdy past, which Eugenia had been claiming, to exist. To lose that big, wide wayward family felt like a personal loss. I felt sad for Eugenia.

I went on in but said nothing to the others. I hugged my guilty knowledge to myself.

Eugenia was nowhere in sight when I entered the main dining room of the restaurant. I knew most of the waitresses working. They waved through the haze of smoke and one waitress, a middle-aged woman named Nancy, yelled, "Sit on down, wherever ya want." She hurried over to slide much-used menus across the table at the three of us.

"How ya doin', Flora?" she leaned over close and asked, ignoring me and Dolly.

"Eugenia here?" Dolly asked, keeping her eyes on the menu.

Nancy, with little tight brown curls all over her head and tiny, almost no-color eyes, looked away from Dolly and said, "In the back."

"Could you ask her to come out?" Dolly asked sweetly.

The woman frowned. She nodded reluctantly, then disappeared through the swinging doors to the kitchen.

"Guess I'm pretty famous in town," Dolly muttered, checking out her pudgy fingers one by one. She picked at a raw cuticle, then at another.

Flora Coy straightened her glasses. She patted Dolly's arm. "Don't you worry, Dolly. Everybody knows you wouldn't do such a thing."

We ordered the meatloaf and mashed potatoes with a side salad then sat waiting, not talking.

Eugenia's face wasn't any happier than Dolly's when she came through the double doors from the kitchen. We exchanged an embarrassed "Hi, how ya doing," and Eugenia sat down on the fourth chair at our table. She heaved a sigh and called back to Nancy to bring her a cup of coffee.

That cup of coffee took a lot of attention—with sugar pouring, three small creamers, and a lot of stirring. Our food came while she stirred. That took up more silent time. Finally Eugenia looked over at Dolly, watched her steadily, and said, "You heard it was me told the chief I saw you coming out of Murphy's."

Dolly nodded. "I just want to know why you'd do that, Eugenia? You know it wasn't me."

"I don't know who it was. That's my problem. I saw somebody I sure as hell thought was you running hell-bent for leather right out of there."

Dolly, face blossoming with bright patches, pushed her chair back and made a move with her hands that must have meant *look at me, see me*. "You saw me there? Then how come I was home in bed?"

Eugenia shook her head. "There's a monster here in town doing this. All I know is I saw somebody in what looked like a police jacket and hat running out of there. The chief's too tall. This person was kind of squat—sorry, Dolly—and had on a hat and a jacket. I didn't see the pants or anything because I wasn't thinking about somebody doing anything wrong right then. To tell the truth, I was tired. You know, seeing a cop at a funeral home isn't so different. Maybe, I thought: Oh, oh, looks like somebody died … but that's all. Until I heard the fire engines. Then it all came together, and I thought I'd better mention to the chief that I saw you there. I imagined he'd say you was the one discovered the fire and were running out to report it or something like that. I didn't know I was getting you in trouble. At least I didn't think about it."

Her voice was a little grudging. Wrinkles along her jaw wiggled. I couldn't help but think of her rogue's gallery of relatives and imagine Eugenia didn't have it in her genetic makeup to knowingly help the police.

"It's not about getting me into trouble. This is murder," Dolly said, pulling in close to the table and picking up her fork again to poke at the meatloaf. "I know it wasn't me so what we need to know now is who it really was ran out of there last night."

Eugenia shrugged. "Thought it was you. That's all I can say. If I start saying different, I'd be making it up."

"OK," Dolly said around a mouthful of mashed potato. "Somebody who's kind of built like me. You don't know if it was a man or a woman?"

Eugenia shook her head.

"Maybe it was Sullivan. He was there. Got himself out but not his mother."

Eugenia raised and dropped her shoulders. "Why would Sullivan be wearing a police uniform?"

"I don't know," Dolly said. "That's what I'm trying to find out."

"Well," Eugenia pushed her chair back and stood, "I'm really sorry if I caused you trouble, Dolly. I hear the chief took you off the case. That's too bad, if it really wasn't you I saw."

"It wasn't," Dolly almost growled.

"How come you're still going around asking questions if Lucky took you off duty?"

"Because I want to know who's trying to make folks think I'm a killer."

Eugenia nodded. "Good for you. Don't blame you. I wouldn't lay off either. If I think of anything else, or I hear anything in here, I'll get right to you."

She turned to Flora and me. We'd been silent through all of this. "I'm really sorry, Flora. I guess Mary Margaret's the last of your friends."

Flora teared up then wiped at her eye with a paper napkin.

"Hope you're staying with Emily here. It looks like somebody's after all of you Ladies of the Moon. Can't imagine what's going on."

"Me either," Flora said, her deep voice cracking. "Just don't have a clue."

Eugenia got up to go back to her kitchen. I acted as if I'd just thought of something, got up, and followed her.

"Eugenia?" I stopped her halfway through the swinging kitchen door. I couldn't help myself. I didn't think I was getting even for Dolly, but sometimes we just don't know why we're doing things. "Those relatives of yours out there in your vestibule, they're not really related to you are they?"

Eugenia paused, one hand holding the door open. Her face went through a series of changes, searching through possible comebacks. At last she softened, even smiled.

"Busted," she said and then gave a short, almost barking, laugh.

"Come on—Billy the Kid? Belle Starr? How'd you get away with it this long?"

"Don't think many but you reads 'em."

"Why do you bother, if they aren't your relatives?"

She shrugged. "Everybody needs somebody, I guess. They're my somebodies. Don't be so surprised, Emily. Lots of things aren't what they seem to be." She looked back at Dolly for a minute, then shook her head. "I did it just for fun. First because I liked looking 'em up. Then just to see how long I could fool people. If you don't go around telling on me I'll keep it going. It's like a game. I'm not hurting anybody. A few others know. That's what kind of separates the people who come here: the people who know and the people who don't. You just got yourself into an elite club, Emily." Eugenia smiled and her wrinkles smacked together like dominoes.

"I don't get the point," I said.

Eugenia made a face. "Lots of us don't get the point of other people's lives. Most hiding secrets far worse than my little gag. As I said, sometimes things aren't what they seem to be. Some can hurt us. Some can't." She shrugged and went through the swinging door.

I walked back to our table and didn't say a word. It wasn't that I wanted into Eugenia's "elite" club as much as I felt a kind of secret guilt, maybe at taking three years to figure it out, maybe at knowing something Dolly didn't know and not sharing it. Anyway, I wasn't telling on Eugenia. She was right, lots of things weren't what they seemed to be. Including me and Dolly.

266

TWENTY-NINE

FLORA KNEW SOMETHING WAS wrong with her house before she got the front door open. "My lord, my lord," she whispered frantically as she fumbled the long, metal key into the old lock. "Listen to my birds. Oh dear, now what?"

She threw the door open to a room filled with shadows and chaos. The house had been ransacked. Books and papers lay everywhere. Sofa cushions were slashed, Styrofoam filling thrown around like clumps of old snow. It was the kind of nightmare no one wants to walk in on.

Poor Flora moved from room to room with her hands clamped over her mouth. She absorbed the damage slowly, more concerned for a flock of parakeets flitting from chandelier to ceiling molding than for her broken furniture.

"My poor birds," Flora cooed, putting her thin arms up high as if she could gather the parakeets together.

"Are they all here?" Dolly asked, concerned, following Flora from room to room. "How many do you have? I'll try to get them back in their cages."

"Oh no, Dolly. You might hurt them. I'll do it." The poor woman wasn't crying anymore. Her drained face looked too worn for crying, too worn for more tragedy. I never felt sorrier for anybody in my life. How I wanted to get my hands on whoever did this.

I picked up a few things and tried to set others right, but there was no easy fix for the mess the intruders left behind them.

"Where are their cages?" I asked, giving up on quick fixes.

"Out in the kitchen, Emily. Oh, would you please get them? They'll be so happy to be back in their homes. My little sweet ... oh dear ... I never thought anybody could be this mean."

This mean seemed an understatement considering what had already happened. I went for the cages standing in a row along the kitchen windows, all with their doors hanging open, as if yanked free. They would have to be wired shut, I imagined.

It was a relief to get the birds settled, to have the twittering and peeping and fluttering cut to a minimum of complaint. Flora was thrilled to find every one accounted for—six of them—as if it were a moral victory not to have her birds murdered, too.

I wanted to get busy and clean the house, to make Flora feel better about what had happened, but Dolly shook her head, warning me not to touch anything more than we'd already touched. "Gotta call Lucky," she said. "He'll get the state police out here. They'll have to go over everything."

Flora moaned and plopped down into one of her still-standing spindle-backed kitchen chairs. She sat very still, offering no resistance, doing nothing but sighing and shaking her head.

This whole thing was getting to me in a way I couldn't separate myself from any longer. This was very personal. I wanted to move, do something, go after somebody.

"Why do you think this house and Joslyn Henry's house were searched?" I asked Dolly, keeping my voice low because Flora was stressed enough.

Dolly motioned me back into the living room where we could talk. We settled on the floor, not wanting to disturb the disturbance. "This has all got to be tied together," I said, impatient now. "Somebody is desperately looking for something. It's the only thing I can think of that connects what's been happening—the women and these searches. What is it somebody wants? What did one of the women have that was important enough to kill for?"

Dolly nodded and thought awhile. "You think the funeral home was burned down to hide something?"

"What good would that do? If the women had something the killer or killers needed, burning down the funeral home without finding what they were after wouldn't make any sense."

"Maybe they found it, that's why they burned the place down."

"Then why search here?"

We looked around at the overturned furniture, the dumped drawers, the disrespectful flinging of an old woman's belongings.

"And why wasn't Ruby Poet's house searched?" I asked.

"Let's ask Flora if she has any idea," Dolly said.

Flora sat where we'd left her but now she was peeping up at her birds, smiling at them, ignoring the mess around her. I asked gently if she could think of anything she had valuable enough to cause what had happened, but Flora shook her head. "Never had much," she said. "There was my Grandmother's Limoges. Maybe they heard about the cup collection ..."

I looked around the kitchen, broken dishes thrown out of the cupboards, a cereal box emptied on the floor, flour and sugar canisters dumped. This wasn't about a set of Limoges cups.

"Look," I whispered to Dolly. "You wait with Flora. I'm going over to talk to Amanda. That fluff-head routine of hers just doesn't impress me anymore. It all started with her mother. Maybe it's the money from the oil her mother was expecting. I can't think of anything else, can you?"

Dolly shook her head. "Sure you want to do it now? You've got to be as tired as I am."

"Yeah. But somebody doesn't want us to rest."

I promised to return for them.

"We'll head back to my home when the police finish here," I told Dolly. I left her leaning against a kitchen counter, trying to keep from stepping on pottery shards. Flora Coy stood peeping at her parakeets.

―――――――

The first thing I noticed at Amanda's, though it was dark by the time I got over there, was the for-sale sign on the lawn. There were lights in the front window and a blue Dodge Dart parked in the side drive. She answered the door after turning the porch light on and peeking out from behind the curtain. It took awhile but I didn't blame her for being cautious. I imagined people all over Leetsville were being very cautious and that Jehovah's Witnesses would have a hard time getting anybody to answer a door until this was over.

I waved through the front window and smiled at Amanda. I tried to appear nonthreatening though I was nervous myself, standing in the bright light of the overhead porch globe where anybody passing by could see me. Amanda opened the inside door but held on to the storm door. "Emily. Why, what could you be doing here at this hour?" she said in a loud voice.

"So many things have been happening, Amanda. Dolly and I had some more questions we thought you might be able to help us with." I put my hand on the door handle, fully expecting her to unlock it. She didn't.

"I heard Dolly Wakowski was put on indefinite leave," she shouted, though it was only glass she spoke through. "Word around town is she was seen setting the fire at the funeral home."

"That's not true at all," I said, and I rattled the door handle slightly, letting her know I expected to be invited in. "It was a mistake. Eugenia saw somebody who looked like her coming out of the funeral home, but Dolly was home in bed. Eugenia saw somebody else. We're trying to find out who that could be and now there's been a break-in at Flora Coy's house. I'd like to talk to you ..."

She hesitated for a bit longer, than flipped the lock and pushed the door open.

"Well, I certainly hope you haven't come here to murder me in my bed," she said over her shoulder as I followed her into the living room where she sat in the plaid rocker and eyed me. I wasn't offered a chair, so I stood, and with the state the room was in, I was just as glad.

"You are right to be cautious, about everybody," I said. "We just wondered if you could think what it might be somebody's hunting for. Joslyn's house was ransacked the day she died. Now Flora Coy's house. Maybe the funeral home, too, for all we know. Have you missed anything here?"

Amanda frowned and shook her head. "My house certainly hasn't been ransacked."

I looked around the messy living room and wondered how she would know. "Anything about that money your mother was going to receive from the oil company? Did she get a check and give it to one of her friends for safe keeping?"

"Why would Mother do a thing like that? There's a perfectly good bank right here in town. And the first thing she would have done was show it to me. All I know about the oil lease money is that she signed an agreement guaranteeing her so much on every barrel of oil they bring in out there. Could be a little. Could be a lot. That's nobody's business but ours … well … actually mine now."

"So, she wouldn't have maybe made a loan to one of the other ladies, or offered one of them some of the money?"

"For what reason?" Amanda looked shocked. "Mother knew I wanted to move out of this town a long time ago. Leetsville isn't the cultured kind of city we should've ever been living in. We have plenty of use for our own money."

At least I wasn't getting the fainting daisy routine this time. There was certainly a practical bone down somewhere in Amanda's body.

"I see you've got your house up for sale. Kind of fast, isn't it?"

Amanda's lips tightened. "None of this is your business, Emily. All I'll say is that I think I've found a place I like better. Now, especially, with all the bad memories here, I'm sure you can understand. You're from the city. You're more cultured than most of the people around here can ever hope to be. It's a matter of what we want from life, don't you agree? I mean, maybe you choose to live out in the woods, but some day you'll see, you'll head back to the city. Mark my words."

"You're moving south? Grand Rapids? Detroit?"

"Oh no." She waved a hand at me. "Nothing like that. Just up to Petoskey. They've got better shops and a decent hairdresser."

"Cultural centers," I said, being deliberately mean.

"Are you making fun of me?" Her hurt look deepened.

I shook my head, ashamed. "Not at all," I assured her falsely.

"Well," she sniffed. "Since you're here you might as well know the plans we've made for the funerals." She sighed. "I, for one, just want this behind us."

"You mean you and Ernie Henry?"

"Yes, and now you can add in Gilbert and Sullivan Murphy. They've got their mother to bury, too, or what's left of her." She made a noise in her throat. "Anyway, we're having a service at the Church of the Contented Flock on Wednesday. No bodies to bury. Who knows whose ashes would be whose? I was a little upset with Ernie, I don't mind telling you. The man is cheap. Didn't even want a nice cake after the service. But the rest of us voted him down. It will be very well done. I hope you plan on being there to celebrate the lives of these wonderful women."

I assured Amanda I wouldn't miss it and left her poring over what she said was a new list of hymns "Pastor" had given her, since she hadn't been happy with the last list he'd provided. I noticed the list was printed on paper and wondered, on my way out the door, the lock snapping shut behind me, how the minister who preached against books and the printed word explained his printed lists and signs and being listed in the phone book. I guessed, as I stumbled through the garden gate, that people believed what they wanted to believe, and never what was right in front of their nose.

Then it occurred to me Amanda Poet was a perfect example of a myopic human being who could erase anything from her mind when it didn't suit her to take notice. After all, she'd asked nothing about the break-in at Flora's house, and seemed unconcerned for the safety of the last of her mother's friends.

THIRTY

Dolly was staying the night at Flora's house. Flora refused to leave her birds alone again.

"Just look what happened," she'd demanded. Neither of us could disagree.

And there were the police to handle. Then the cleanup. I was happy to get away after Eugenia and the women from the restaurant arrived with their buckets and bags, alerted by their usual extra sense.

Dolly and Flora couldn't be in better hands.

All I wanted to do when I got back home was sleep. Jackson's car was in the drive. I smiled as I walked in and peeled off my sneakers, but it was written there on Jackson's face, my rudeness to his girlfriend, my audacity, the ever-lengthening litany of my sins against him. A big, sinking boulder hit my stomach. I smiled again—hoping to avoid the worst of it. I thought my sheepish grin, after a day as rough as mine had been, the height of gentility.

"I took her to her parents' house," he said to me through a fog. I watched his lips move. I knew words were coming out. I just couldn't hear them. I nodded and nodded again. All I could think about was moving the few extra feet from my living room, where he sat stiff-kneed on the sofa, to my bedroom. Sorrow understood. He leaned into my legs and made odd, burping sounds. I thought them sympathetic noises, sleepy noises.

I blinked a few times at Jackson, whose face was drawn and earnest, and, if I wasn't mistaken, more than a little accusatory. I backed away because I couldn't take accusation, nor guilt, right then. I kept backing through the kitchen, my smile firmly in place. I backed all the way down the hall and through my door to my bed with Sorrow nipping at my bare feet.

Six sad parakeets chirped in my head as I fell across my bed and pulled the white fuzzy comforter to my chin. Sorrow leaped on the bed and settled with his head on the other pillow. I remember smiling at him as I fell asleep. I think he smiled back.

———

In the morning, when I awoke, the house was still. I thought for a minute I was alone. I lay wallowing in the thought: *alone.* Maybe I'd pissed Jackson off and didn't remember. Maybe I'd said something terrible when I got back the night before. I was almost hoping. I'd had all I could take of shame for a while.

Jackson sneezed. He was in his room, talking on his cell phone in a low monotone. I groaned and rolled over, burying my head under my pillow. Sorrow, thrilled to see I was awake, landed on my back and bit at my hair until I got up.

The woman who stared back at me from the bathroom mirror looked awful. What a pathetic human being. Kind of brown hair standing on end or laid flat against her head. Eyes puffy and red. I yawned at my image just to see how truly ugly I could get, then said the hell with it, peed, washed what I could reach comfortably, and went out to smile a bleary smile at Jackson, no doubt reminding him why infidelity had been a necessary option to our union.

I made coffee for Jackson, a pot of tea for me, and some toast. My body didn't feel like moving and cooking, and my mouth didn't want to talk, but when you have a guest you move, you cook, you talk, and then you stand still, teacup in hand, or lean against the refrigerator, paste a smile on your face, and nod every once in a while as your company drones on and on and on.

Poor Jennifer. I'd hurt her feelings. Jackson said he knew he should leave, too, but seeing I'd gotten myself into the middle of this murder mess, well, he didn't think it right of him to leave right then. And since I was so involved with this Dolly person, well, I wasn't, after all, using my studio and he would just as soon set up his work out there, out of my way, where he could begin his book and be there to see to my safety at the same time.

"I'll be working in the studio this morning," I said. I watched a look of hurt shock move across his face. "I'm almost finished with the mystery I'm writing."

"Mystery?" That might have been a sneer around his lips. I hoped not. "Why, how … eh … enterprising of you, Emily. I had no idea you wanted to write fiction."

"Really? Hmm … seems I mentioned it a few dozen times."

"Well, then, what about this? You work in your studio now, and I'll work out there when you're not around."

"What about finding a place of your own?"

"I will. That's what I want. It's just that there is nothing suitable available."

"I'm sure there must be … we'll look in the paper today."

"Good idea." He went to stand at the large front window with his back to me. His back looked wide, and comforting. I had to admit it was good to have a strong male essence in the house. Not that Sorrow didn't do his job just fine—but having Jackson there was like knowing I had someone who could wield an ax, if necessary, or pick up a gun and kill an intruder instantly. He was male and could beat his chest, if he wanted to, and swing from a tree, and rescue me as I swooned.

I stopped myself. He wasn't there to protect me. *I* was there to protect me. And he wasn't going to get his hands on my studio. I'd have to be careful, watchful, or I'd come home one afternoon and find my things sitting in the sun outside the door with Jackson fully ensconced inside.

I called Dolly at Flora Coy's house. She was busy helping Flora figure out what was missing. She wanted to know if I was coming in to help.

"Not today," I said. "I've got to write this morning. Get a story in."

Her disappointed "Oh" didn't change my mind. I needed time away from Dolly, from Flora Coy, from Jackson, from just about everybody in my life at the moment.

"I'll see you tomorrow, at the memorial," I said and then hung up before I could hear how we had work to do and there was no time to lose and what in hell did I think I was doing, leaving her in the lurch like this?

Or something close to all of that.

My morning was wonderful. Maybe it was because I could sense Jackson salivating in the house, wanting to get his hands on my studio. Or maybe because I finally had a couple of hours to think. Whatever it was, the novel moved along brilliantly. The first thing I had to do was knock Martin Gorman, my protagonist, off the wagon. I got him roaring, soaring drunk and then I had him feel sorry for himself and suspicious of Catherine Martel, the writer who may or may not be the murderer he's after. I really screwed up Martin's life. A great couple of scenes. I had him fall off a stool in a sleazy bar, then run his car off the road. A cop he knew, a buddy of his, pulled up and yelled at him for being so stupid as to start drinking again. I really let Martin have it ...

Then I wondered if Martin was my substitute for Jackson again. I liked the writing so much I told myself I didn't care. If Jackson was my depraved muse, than so be it. I was going to take good writing wherever I could get it.

When I got back up to the house, Jackson had spread his books and papers across the kitchen counter. He made one listless move to collect them. I told him it was fine, just fine, if he wanted to leave his things there until he found a house. As I made lunch for us, he spread the newspaper over his books and searched the Houses for Rent columns. I kept my fingers crossed but soon he was shaking his head and commenting on how little there was to choose from in the way of rentals.

"Must be because it's off-season," he said.

I agreed and made a mental note to put "House for Jackson" at the top of my list of things to see to. After lunch, I washed the dishes, changed into town clothes, ran off a copy of the Survivalist story, and headed into Traverse City.

Jan Romanoff sat at her neat desk in the offices of *Northern Pines Magazine*. She looked over the tops of her half-glasses and waved me to a chair. "What in hell's happening out there in Leetsville?" she demanded in her lady editor, probing voice. "I've been reading about the carnage you folks are caught up in. You found a head in your garbage can? Geez, girl, I thought it was quiet back in the woods."

I smiled the brightest smile I could come up with. Now I would forever be known as the girl with a head in her garbage can. I wasn't going to mention the arm. Notoriety wasn't my thing.

"Bad," I said in my best Clint Eastwood voice. I shook my head.

"Well, I'd say." She could see I wasn't in the mood to discuss atrocities at the moment. At least, not anything beyond the Survivalists.

"That your story?" She reached for my manuscript, then gave it a cursory glance. "How many words?"

"About 1200. That enough? They aren't exactly a scintillating group."

"Figured. Got photographs?"

I handed her the roll of film and left with an assignment on a llama farm.

I still had to get over to the *Northern Statesman* offices to see Bill and hoped I didn't have to run a gauntlet of curiosity there, too.

I was greeted with no interest whatsoever. Ever since they redid the offices and sealed the workers from the public after an incident at a paper farther north where an angry reader shot up the place, it was like walking into any office building anywhere. No immediate excitement of breaking news. No overworked reporters following leads in whispered phone calls. Only a receptionist and a waiting area with stock, off-the-showroom-floor chairs for guests.

Bill was summoned and came to greet me, giving me a big hug, which sent the receptionist's eyebrows soaring. We went back to his office—more what you would expect from a newsman, papers everywhere, stacks of books, file folders, notes.

"Get rid of the ex yet?" was his first question. Refreshing.

I laughed. "I got the girlfriend out. She hit my dog and I blew up."

"Don't blame you." He pushed his glasses up his nose and chuckled deep in the back of his throat. "Now if only Jackson would do something equally despicable." He scratched at his chin. "He didn't find a place?"

"Still looking," I said.

"Here." He got out of his chair and grabbed a paper from a pile on the file cabinet behind him. "Tomorrow's rentals. If there's nothing there I'll see what I can come up with. Anything new on the story?"

"Not since the break-in at Flora Coy's." I'd called that in already.

"You talk to Gaylord? See if they've got anything?"

I shook my head. My mind had been on the novel. I forgot I should've been following up, maybe doing a few interviews.

"Call now." He motioned toward his phone.

I took care of that, being told that Officer Brent would return my call as soon as he was free. Our story had hit the national news. He was probably being besieged by networks and papers from across the country.

"I've got something I found for you," Bill said, and he pushed a paper across the desk at me. "It's on Ernie Henry. You know he was picked up last year in Grand Rapids?"

I shook my head. No one had mentioned anything bad about Ernie.

"Lewd and lascivious. Busted in a prostitution sweep."

"You mean his tractor pulls and his small-engine shows . . . ?"

Bill smiled sheepishly. "Looks like it. I don't know if this has any bearing . . ."

I shrugged, disappointed in Ernie. "Everything does, I imagine. You think I should tell Brent?"

"Up to you. Don't know if it has a thing to do with what's happening out there. I don't see how, do you?"

I shook my head. I was beginning to know more about my Leetsville neighbors than I wanted to know, or felt I should know. "More pathetic than ominous, don't you think? You find anything else?"

"No, but I can look up the others if you want me to."

I thought awhile, not sure I should. Then I figured I didn't start this mess and what was happening transcended mere good manners.

"How about Gilbert and Sullivan Murphy? Could you see what they've been up to? And if by any chance there's anything on the Reverend Runcival of the Church of the Contented Flock, I'd like that, too."

"The Murphys are the funeral home twins? It was their mother who died in the fire, right? OK. Are you staying in town awhile?"

I was going to shop. Give myself an afternoon off.

"How about an early dinner?"

Sounded good to me. We agreed on La Cuisine Amical down by the State Theater. Five o'clock. Early dinner.

I bought new jeans at a downtown store, and a smashing velour top in iris blue. I bought new tennis shoes at Plamondon Shoes on

281

Front Street. I'd throw out the old ones with the holes in the toes when I got home. I bought nice-smelling soap for my bathroom and did girly things all afternoon. Still I arrived early at the restaurant, but I wasn't the only early diner. As if I was being haunted by nasty spirits from a past I was trying to forget for a single day, the Murphy boys and Amanda Poet were at the last table along the wall.

The Murphy boys sat with their backs to me. Amanda saw me as I walked in. At first she looked anything but happy. She leaned forward and said something to the Murphys, who turned to stare over their shoulders. She raised a hand in greeting and broke into a wide smile.

"Yoo-hoo, Emily."

Reluctantly, I walked back, near the fireplace, greeting the trio.

"What are you doing in town today?" Amanda asked brightly.

"Turning in a story." I nodded to the twins, noting they weren't any happier to see me than I to see them.

"Aren't you the busy writer. Got a finger in every pie, I guess, hmm?"

I smiled then remembered I hadn't seen the Murphys since their mother's death. I hadn't said how sorry I was about the fire, and their mom. I told them now, almost choking at the thought of the last time I saw Mary Margaret, standing on the porch of the funeral home, waving to me and Dolly.

The boy's faces darkened. Gilbert glowered. Sullivan looked as if he might cry. I thought I caught the faintest whiff of alcohol drifting off him, like cheap cologne.

"I'm in town finding a black dress," Amanda said. "I didn't have a thing I could wear tomorrow for the memorial and I want to do my mother proud."

I admitted I was shopping. Not for a black dress, but new clothes.

"I suppose you're in the public eye, working with Dolly the way you have been. Doesn't do to appear dowdy."

I said, no, it didn't do.

"The boys here are staying at the resort until they figure out what arrangements they're going to make about the funeral home and all. They're homeless, I guess you could say."

I thought—the Grand Traverse Resort? Quite a swanky place to be homeless in. I could think of closer and cheaper motels they could have moved to. Including, I imagined, the home of just about anybody in Leetsville, since neighbor tended to neighbor there.

"My doing," Amanda said, giving a *mea culpa* bat of her eyelashes. "I told them they'd been under enough stress as it was. Better to be away from town. Tomorrow will be hard on all of us."

The nasty thought that there were more bars in Traverse than in Leetsville and that the Resort was awfully close to a casino, shot through my head. I hoped my face didn't show what I was thinking.

I said I'd be at the memorial, and took a table as far from the group as I could get, burying my face in a menu until Bill Corcoran arrived, looked over the restaurant, and came to sit across the table from me.

I saw his eyes move to where the Leetsville contingent sat eating their pasta, downing their wine.

"That the Murphy twins?"

I nodded. "And Amanda Poet, too. Ruby Poet's daughter."

"What are they doing in town?" he asked, keeping his eyes on the menu and his voice down.

"Amanda's shopping for a black dress for tomorrow. The boys are staying at the resort."

Bill's eyebrows shot up. "Guess they're counting on the insurance from the funeral home."

I refused to be mean. I said nothing.

Bill cleared his throat and leaned across the table toward me. "You know how you asked me to see if I could come up with anything on the Murphys and Reverend Runcival?"

I nodded.

"There was a Leetsville paper up to about five years ago. When it went out of business we inherited their files, all the back issues. I put a couple people at the paper on it. They found what you would expect on the pastor. Church doings. Nothing on Amanda Poet beyond some social stuff—she attended a tea for Hillary Stroud on the occasion of her bridal shower. Things like that. But maybe something on Sullivan Murphy. There were funeral home stories. Even stuff back to when the twins played football for Leetsville High. One I thought you might be especially interested in because of what you told me happened to your friend, Officer Wakowski, the night of the fire. You know, someone saying they saw her run out of the funeral home. At least saw somebody in a police uniform."

I frowned, waiting for him to get to the point.

"Yes?" I nudged him along.

"Seems Sullivan moved away for a while. Left Leetsville. Lived down in Saginaw. Know what he did for a living?"

"Can't imagine." I wished he'd get on with it.

"He was a cop."

"A cop?"

"Yeah. You know. A cop. With a uniform. Wonder where that uniform is now."

I looked back to where Sullivan was pouring the last of their bottle of wine into his glass, then looking down the neck of the bottle, and scowling.

Me too. I wondered, and hoped, for Dolly's sake, I could find out.

THIRTY-ONE

I stood at the back of the church trying to be inconspicuous, though I knew I never was, and never would be, inconspicuous in this village of people who'd known each other all their lives, people who could sense the "Outsider" with the backs of their heads, as if they had antennae, or the kind of intuition that warns small women of big men nearby. I wanted to see who came for the memorial and who didn't. Not that I expected any grand revelations, but there was always the chance whoever had murdered the three women would have an attack of conscience and stay home. Absence could be telling. So could a shouted confession from a guilt-ridden miscreant. But I didn't really expect it.

The Church of the Contented Flock had the plain, bare look of all country churches: vaulted, pine-paneled ceiling that came together high in the middle, like praying hands; stretching, I imagined, all the way to heaven. The windows were tall and narrow, recalling the old chapel at Greenfield Village. Spartan. Puritan. Spare. Small panes of glass, like tiny pursed mouths, let in little light or air, or much of anything to distract from the message of God the good pastor would proclaim. There were no pews in this church, only brown folding chairs—rows of them, with breaks for aisles. The altar was bare except for a tall lectern of plain pine. Flowers, in fall colors, were set in baskets across the front of the church, from the lectern to the far walls.

Up high behind the altar hung a plain, black, wooden cross. Empty. No Christ. A stark, lonely, symbol. Impressive and moving.

Eugenia Fuller, Simon, and Gloria passed me, entering together. They nodded in my direction but kept going down the center aisle, as eager as everyone to get a good seat. Doc Crimson, dressed in a Western shirt and old boots, walked in with his wife, Harriet, whom I'd never met but who seemed like a proper lady in her beige wool coat and beige oxfords. People from the Skunk were there, and the cashiers at the IGA. Harry Mockerman walked by me, resplendent in his funeral suit and black bow tie. He'd brushed his long, yellow/white hair so it laid across his scalp in rows, hit his jacket collar, and flipped skyward. His white, grizzled beard was neater than usual. Harry, I imagined, had bathed, or at least washed up, for the occasion. Gertie came in with her head freshly lacquered red despite her recent troubles. She sat at the edge of her seat like a pert redbird, turning to eye old customers, to see where they were going now that she wasn't open for business. Outrage etched her heavily made-up face every time she spotted a new "do," as if she'd expected flat, curl-less heads, signifying a proper mourning among her friends for the burned beauty shop.

Officer Brent stood inside one of the double doorways to the hall, watching the townspeople troop in. He looked at me once, his round eyes under that unibrow like icy marbles.

The folding chairs filled quickly. As far as I could tell, everybody in town was there, along with people I'd never seen before, all greeting each other in subdued, church voices; plumped up in their best Sunday dress; whispering and waving. They craned their necks, one to the other, sharing the latest "Have you heard?"

The four chief mourners passed me on their way down to seats in the front row. Amanda led the procession, trailing Eau du Bois and black chiffon. Sullivan, his back wide and straining under his dark, wool jacket, gave me a glassy-eyed look. His red eyes flicked over me then ahead, down the aisle. A faint trail of Jack Daniels wafted past in his wake, as if he'd splashed on a jigger after shaving.

Gilbert was in his best funeral director's outfit of dark suit and white shirt, incongruously opened at the neck to show his many gold necklaces—probably gotten with all that gambling money, though word was he didn't have much luck, for all of his practice. When he turned in my direction, his round face was hard and mean, dark, small eyes sweeping over me then back. He nodded, settled his head down into his neckless body, and left his eyes on me a fraction too long for comfort.

Ernie Henry came in behind the Murphys, looking uncomfortable in his baggy, blue suit with no oily rag hanging from a back pocket. He tucked his head down and scurried to catch up with the others, down to the front row.

Amanda took her seat beside the men, then perched at the edge of her chair, body turned to the congregation to take nervous stock of the growing crowd. She waved to someone just entering the church and pointed to a pair of empty chairs; she directed another couple to seats at the side. There was managing to be done here; a single-minded lurch out of her chair, a flutter of a finger, and a sail up the aisle, hem of her black dress in hand, every once in a while stopping to dab at her eyes with a lace-edged handkerchief.

Amanda'd certainly found herself a dress in Traverse City. There must not have been much left in Macy's funeral collection. This one was sheer black chiffon. Not quite right for the occasion, I snottily judged. Maybe for a back alley tryst. Maybe for swishing into a cocktail party. Maybe for a second act entrance.

I gave up being nasty about Amanda and watched her work the crowd instead.

She exuded thrill—of attention, of being dressed in her new outfit. Amanda Poet was obviously a woman unchained. Her hair had been poufed—not by Gertie, but in Traverse City. It wasn't sprayed to the full, upstanding glory Gertie would have achieved, but still poufed to a size no normal head of hair should ever aspire to. And blonder, if I wasn't mistaken. But then who was I to cast the first stone, with my single-colored brown glory?

Dolly, when she joined me at the back of the church, wore a black pantsuit that looked suspiciously like a uniform. She carried a large purse. I would have bet anything there was a .38 in there since she swore it never left her side. Flora Coy was tight behind her, fluttering, handkerchief to her nose, eyes red-rimmed and nervous.

"They don't like that I'm here," Dolly leaned toward me and whispered.

I tightened my lips and scowled indiscriminately at the people around us.

"They're all giving me the eye," she said.

"I've never known Leetsvillians to be so mean." Flora Coy hugged in close, standing taller than normal in her black, heeled shoes. She wore a plain black dress with a plain jacket. A lovely cameo hung at her puckered neck. She, or Dolly, had fixed her hair, but she didn't seem to have her heart in looking nice, or looking anything, here at the funeral of all her oldest friends.

"Everybody's afraid of everybody," I said, soothing.

Dolly shrugged and tried to look smaller, hugging the wall in a very un-Dolly-like attempt to disappear. I felt bad. If I could have, I'd have liked to puff up my chest and stand in front of her.

"Everybody from Fuller's is here. Harry Mockerman's here." I leaned close so she could hear me above the crowd noise that resembled the low rumble of approaching thunder. "I saw Amanda snub him, too. Only one I haven't seen is Dave Rombart. His wife, Sharon, came. She told me she was representing her husband. Show they aren't the monsters the town thinks they are."

"She tell you they're selling out?" she whispered from the corner of her mouth.

I shook my head. "Didn't say a word."

"They are. Heard they got big, handmade for-sale signs everywhere around their wire fences."

"Guess they don't feel welcome anymore."

"Know the feeling," Dolly said, and she gave me a quick, rueful smile.

"The chief's here," she added. "He'll be directing traffic after the service." She cleared her throat. "Usually that's my job."

We agreed to sit on opposite sides of the church, keeping our eyes open in case someone screamed out a confession and made a break for it. Flora, who'd been visiting with neighbors, took a chair beside Dolly in a show of support. When the Reverend Runcival entered from a side door, Amanda quickly took her seat, signaling the others to face forward and stop talking.

The room grew warm. Too many close-packed bodies. Too little air, after the doors were closed. I had to take a few deep breaths to keep myself seated. I was too used to space, and fresh, almost potable, air and no people around me. I settled back as the pastor

she wanted tucked in; Ruby Poet's favorite kind of pie; Joslyn Henry's taste in library books. They were all dear people wanting their voices added to the accolades being sent heavenward. Around me people sniffed and snuffled and dragged hankies from pockets and purses. I had trouble keeping my own eyes dry. Though I'd barely known any of the women, I saw, through the memories of their friends, women who'd lived quiet, helpful lives. Women who'd given a neighbor shelter when she was afraid of a storm. Women who took in a child running away for fear of a parent's wrath. Women who taught night school parenting classes at the high school, who planted petunias down the main road of town every early summer, women who loved their gardens and shared their flowers with passersby, who taught little ones the names of the flowers they'd picked. These were women respected for their kindness, their knowledge, their love of beauty in a not-so-beautiful place. Women who in no way deserved the deaths they'd been condemned to suffer.

At the end of the service Pastor Runcival invited everyone down to the church basement for light refreshments. Cake and coffee. Amanda, in the front row, struggled to her feet quickly, catching her dress in the folding chair, frowning. She yanked her dress loose with an impatient, unladylike jerk to the fragile material then reached out for Gilbert Murphy's hand to steady herself. She threw her arms into the air and called out, "PLEASE, EVERYONE!" As she spoke, she motioned for the other three to stand with her.

We all craned our necks around the heads of those in front of us.

"Ernie, Gilbert, Sullivan, and I would like to thank you for coming to support us in this, our hour of supreme desolation." She smirked at the gathering, straightened her shoulders, sniffed, and added, "The pastor was a little shy about the refreshments. To fully honor our mothers, we've planned a full buffet lunch for everyone.

You're all invited to break bread with us in the dining hall downstairs. Don't be shy. We want to meet and thank each of you personally for your flowers and for coming here today."

I thought I saw a look of pain cross Ernie's face at the mention of an expensive full buffet, but I could have been wrong.

The line snaked out of the church proper, through the hall, around to the head of the basement stairs. Harry Mockerman and Sharon Rombart were the only ones I saw slip out the front doors without going for the buffet lunch. I imagined this was far too many people, in too tight a space, for Harry, and understood how he felt. With Sharon, I figured she'd accomplished what she'd come to do and was needed back in the woods to skin a squirrel, or grind some grain, or whatever she did for her brother survivors.

Dolly joined me and we fell in with the others, some talking to us, others pushing along, talking to family members. If I could have bet, I'd have said there were a lot of people here who didn't even know the dead women. This was the biggest thing to hit Leetsville ever. I didn't imagine anyone within forty miles was about to miss it.

The chief mourners made an informal receiving line at the bottom of the stairs. The three men stood beyond and behind Amanda, nodding, making a comment here or there, but it was Amanda who carried the day, accepting condolences, thanking people for coming, directing them to the next line—for the buffet, and encouraging them to taste the macaroni and cheese she'd had made with three cheeses, a Martha Stewart recipe.

Flora Coy drew her own circle of friends and neighbors around her. She was safe for the moment.

I made sure I stood with Dolly all the way down the stairs and through the receiving line so people would have to snub me, too, if they were going to be mean to Dolly. Flora and Eugenia made sure to stand with us, and Simon and Gloria. Eugenia kept repeating, in a loud voice, how she'd never understand how she mistook Dolly for the person running out of the funeral home that night. "An awful mistake," she said again and again, eyeing the people around us, making certain they heard and would repeat what she'd said. At one point she leaned in close and apologized again to Dolly. "It was that damned police uniform. Who else would be wearing one, do you think? Sure wasn't Lucky Barnard."

Dolly shook her head.

Sullivan, his plate filled with ham and macaroni and cheese, passed behind us on his way to a seat at the main table. I stepped back, almost knocking his plate from his hands.

"I hear you used to live down in Saginaw," I said, keeping my voice low, putting a hand on his arm to hold him in place.

He nodded, then decided he could be a little friendlier than that, and almost smiled. "Used to," he said, his jowly face quivering, his red eyes taking in the people with me. He nodded to everyone and pointed to his plate. "Great food Amanda's got here. Why don't you folks get on into that line before everything's gone?"

"Weren't you with the police department in Saginaw? I thought I heard that," I said.

Sullivan looked taken back, as if he hadn't given a thought to such a thing in years. He nodded after giving me a long, slow look. "I was. Four years. Then Mother needed me up here to help run the business."

"Well, I was just wondering. You don't still have your old uniform, do you?"

By this time Dolly's face was perking up and the others nearby were standing at attention.

Sullivan looked as if he was thinking hard, then moved his neck uncomfortably inside his too-tight shirt. He looked around as if searching for the nearest place he might grab a drink. "Somewhere. We had to buy 'em. No sense in leaving it behind. Burned up with everything else, I suppose."

"I'm asking because of what Eugenia saw the night of the fire."

Sullivan looked suspicious, then sad. "Yeah. Somebody running out." He turned on Dolly. "I heard that was you, Office Wakowski. I wondered why you were here today, if that was the case. I mean, not that I think you set the fire but until everything gets cleared up …"

"It wasn't me," Dolly said loud and clear, puffing herself to old Dollyesque proportions.

"That's why I was wondering about your uniform," I said. "Wouldn't have been you, would it, Sullivan? You wouldn't've been wearing it that night? Or maybe grabbed it when you jumped out the window, wrapped yourself in the jacket. Anything like that."

"Are you asking did I put on my old uniform then set fire to the funeral home?" Now he was mad. He stepped away from us and squared off his shoulders. "Don't try to shift blame to me. If it wasn't Dolly, you'd all better get busy finding out who it was. If I get 'em first they won't be alive long. If I get 'em first you may never hear who it was either. All I want is that person dead."

He walked off calling a last, firm "That's all" over his shoulder. Maybe I shouldn't have accosted him at his mother's funeral. I felt bad until Gilbert wandered over while we were eating, and leaned in and warned in a low voice, "I wouldn't be botherin' my brother if I were you, Miss Kincaid. It's our families affected and none of us wants you sticking your nose in. Not you and not Dolly Wakowski either. We don't need two silly women mucking around, making people think there's wrong where there isn't."

He leaned back, uneasy on his feet. Nobody at our table said a word. Gilbert went directly to where Sullivan sat, leaned down and whispered something in his ear.

Lucky Barnard was halfway down the stairs, bending forward to look around. Dolly waved to let him know where she was. The tall man made his way through people at the dessert table, eyeing the elaborate funeral cake Amanda had ordered, with white and black icing and a huge black cross standing upright at the middle.

Lucky nodded to everyone at the table then crouched down between me and Dolly. I knew more than a few eyes around the room were on him. He looked at the faces turned his way, then at each of us. "Might be all over, ladies."

First, being called a lady, in that tone of voice, always got my back up. Made me feel as if I should be wearing a hoop skirt or a couple of crinolines. Second, his face looked as if the news he was bringing wasn't what we'd want to hear.

"What do you mean?" Dolly demanded, her look as mistrustful as I was feeling. "What is it, Chief?"

"I got a letter this morning," he said, trying to keep his voice low. "From Mary Margaret, herself."

"What do you mean, 'from Mary Margaret'? The woman's dead."

Lucky moved around on his haunches, uncomfortable in his squatting position. "Sent it before she died. Sunday night. Maybe sometime Sunday afternoon. Went out Monday, Dorothy at the post office said. I didn't get it until today."

Flora heard and leaned around Dolly. "Sent to you?" she demanded. "Mary Margaret sent you a letter before she died?"

He nodded, then put a finger to his lips, signaling her to lower her voice. People were already craning their necks our way.

"What'd she say in the letter?" Dolly hissed in a half whisper.

"Well, this is hard. Maybe you don't want to hear, Miz Coy." He raised his eyebrows at Flora.

"What more can there be, Chief? I can't think of a thing Mary Margaret would have written to you that could hurt me."

He was well aware that people around us were listening. He took a folded sheet of paper from his pocket and held it out. Dolly took the paper. Flora and I leaned in as close as we could get.

"That's not her handwriting." Flora dismissed the letter with a flick of her hand.

"I know," Lucky said. "It's mine. I made a copy. The original went to the state for fingerprinting."

"Was hers handwritten?" I asked.

He shook his head. "Typewritten."

"Do you have the envelope?"

He nodded. "I already turned it over to the state."

"What color was it?" Dolly asked, squinting hard at him.

Lucky nodded. "Just what you're thinking. Pink, like the envelopes the threatening letters came in."

We leaned in to read.

> *Chief Barnard,*
>
> *When you read this letter I'll be dead. I've got too much on my conscience to live. It all started because I needed money to fix up the funeral home or I'd have to shut it down and have no income left for me and my boys. When Ruby told us about her good luck with those oil wells I just thought I'd ask her for a loan since we'd*

*always sworn to help each other out. Ruby didn't want
anything to do with it. She said there wasn't enough
for doing things like making loans. At first I was just
surprised. Then I got mad. We always vowed to help
each other when we needed it and here I was asking a
favor and being turned down. She was at the funeral
home because I called and asked her to come on over.
I don't know what happened. I must have hit her with
something because the next thing she was laying dead
on the floor of the viewing room. All I could think to
do was get her downstairs. There was no problem after
that. I've taken care of dead bodies all my life. The
only thing I could think of was to get her out to Joslyn's
woods and bury her. I did that in parts. Taking a few
pieces at a time. But Joslyn found out. She accused me
when we were out at our fire place where we'd gathered
in happier times. What could I do but silence Joslyn too?
I don't know how this all began but I'm going to finish
it tonight. I'm going to kill myself because that's the best
I can do for my boys, now that I've ruined their lives.
I hope everybody can forgive me or at least pity me.
Something evil just crawled into my soul. I hope it had
nothing to do with our ceremonies out there at Joslyn's,
in the woods. I hope we didn't let loose things we didn't
know how to control. Tell everybody how sorry I am for
everything I've done.*

*Signed,
Mary Margaret Murphy*

THIRTY-TWO

"SHE NEVER DID ANY such thing," Flora Coy said in her deepest, angriest voice. She was loud and looked about to lose her grip. "Look at that letter, will you? Doesn't sound a thing like her. Why, you all knew Mary Margaret. Does that sound right?"

"She sign it?" Dolly asked, as bewildered as the rest of us.

"Signature was typed."

"There, that proves Mary Margaret didn't write that thing," Flora said, dropped her hands in her lap, and fell back in her chair. "You think if a word of that was true she wouldn't have signed it herself? That's crazy." Tears filled her eyes. "Imagine saying Mary Margaret murdered Ruby and Joslyn. As if she had one mean bone in her whole body. I can't imagine. Why, I just can't imagine ..."

Flora dissolved in tears. Others sprang up around her immediately. It was bad timing. The wrong place. I wished Lucky would have called us outside. Anything but this. Flora was sputtering mad. She looked into the faces of her neighbors and demanded if any one of them thought Mary Margaret did any of this herself? People began shushing her, patting her back. They were caring, but curious, looking to Lucky, demanding what that paper was he'd shown to poor Flora. Gilbert and Sullivan were there, asking to see what they'd heard was a letter from their mother. Amanda hurried over to shush everyone, telling them to go back, have more of the macaroni and cheese, then demanding in an urgent voice to know what on earth was going on *now*. Lucky looked from me to Dolly but we were no help. He'd gotten himself into this, I thought. Let him disentangle.

Dolly and I got out of there as Sullivan sputtered that the letter was a pack of lies, how his sainted mother never hurt a soul in her life. The only reason she was in the funeral business at all—despite her soft heart—was that their daddy'd started it long ago and when he died she had no other way to make a living. He staggered as he made his points, red face almost purple with anger.

Gilbert was silent, standing behind all of the others, glowering.

"Well," Dolly said once we were outside, away from everyone. She glanced around the packed parking lot, so full that cars had spilled out along Divinity Drive. "You'd have to admit Mary Margaret was one who could take care of a dead body."

"Yeah," I found myself agreeing reluctantly. "But would she dismember one friend and strangle another?"

"And why'd she search Joslyn's house?"

"Maybe looking for a letter? Something Joslyn had written to implicate her in Ruby's murder?"

"What about Flora's house? That was after the fire." She shook her head, bewildered.

"Right," I said, feeling the same. "Somebody was looking for something and it wasn't a random robbery. Couldn't have been Mary Margaret. She was dead. This doesn't make sense."

We weren't outside long before people began pouring from the church. I guessed the luncheon was over. Amanda stomped out with her face dark and angry. She kept going, across the street to her house. We could hear her front door slam from where we stood. Evidently Amanda didn't like having her festive occasions ruined by bad news, especially when she'd sunk so much money into a really elegant buffet.

Gilbert and Sullivan weren't far behind Amanda. Sullivan spotted me and Dolly and thumped over with his arms out at his sides, his shoulders tight. Sullivan had gotten ahold of something to drink in the church. He was unsteady and looking for trouble.

"You two better not take this any further, you hear me!" He shouted before he even got close. Dolly moved in front of me, her hands patting the air, trying to calm him.

"We only want to get at the truth here. Same as you," Dolly said in her best authoritative voice. Sullivan wasn't having any of it.

"My mother was as pure as the driven snow. Somebody's trying to sully her memory. I'll kill the son of a bitch if I get my hands on him. Mother no more sent that letter than she killed her two friends. I got money. I was gonna fix the place. It was just I needed a little time. Things were turning around for me. We were going to be fine. She never asked Ruby Poet for nothing. That's not the kind of person Mother was."

Sullivan wiped at his mouth where spit had landed on his lower lip.

He faltered by the time he got to the end of his speech. He teetered in place. I felt sorry for him. Sullivan Murphy, like his brother, was a small, squat man who wanted people to think he was big, tall, impressive. He wasn't. Even less so now, with his hands clenched, his face contorted, eyes blurred and red, his bright cheeks shiny with tears.

Gilbert followed his brother out of the church, but stood apart while Sullivan yelled at us. Gilbert kept his head down, listening. He didn't come over, or try to get his brother to leave. He didn't make a move to join the tirade. He waited, like a bystander, for the show to end. Sullivan broke down completely and stood with his shoulders shaking, unable to say another word. Dolly helped him to his car, a rented van. Gilbert turned his back and walked to where his hearse stood at the front curb. He got in and drove off while his brother sat behind the wheel of his van, sobbing. Dolly talked to Sullivan through his open window and finally convinced him that Ernie had better take him back to Traverse City. He was in no shape to drive.

Lucky brought Flora out to us. Friends and neighbors were gathered around her, having their say over the letter, how nobody believed a word of it.

We went back to Flora's house. I made tea for all of us while Dolly sat with Flora and calmed her down. The old woman was as upset as I'd ever seen her. Even more than sadness, behind the tears was outrage.

"How could anybody do that to Mary Margaret's memory?" she asked me and Dolly again and again as we sat over tea and cookies, with the backdrop of squeaking parakeets. "Why, if she'd asked Ruby for money, Ruby would have moved heaven and earth to help. I know…knew…Ruby well enough for that. All poor Ruby talked about was helping people. That was her whole life. She offered to get me as many birds as I wanted but I told her I had all I could handle. She talked about helping the world by what we were learning out there in the woods. How you treat Mother Nature. I told you Ruby said she could see her, didn't I? When we were out there dancing? Ruby was the kindest..."

Flora wiped at a stray tear and looked up, beseeching us to understand what she and her friends had been about.

"Mary Margaret said something about an envelope she gave each of you..."

Flora blinked as she thought. "Well, my goodness, yes. I do have a note from Ruby. How nice. Now I've got something to remember her by. A nice poem, I'll bet. A few words against the dark days. Ruby was good at things like that. Better than me."

She gave a sad smile.

"I remember when she gave it to us. One for each. And said to keep it and someday it would come in handy. It was important that we thought about what we were doing when we weren't together. Ruby's little notes would do that. Sometimes it was clippings from a newspaper or magazine. Sometimes even a secret letter about us. Said it was our connection to each other, to our humanity, to our womanliness, to what we stood for..."

Flora took a long, deep breath and sat with her head down. Dolly and I looked at each other and waited.

"Don't know where I put it now. But it'll surface. And I'll bet you it will be on just the right day, when I need an encouraging word from Ruby."

Dolly and I exchanged a look. "Maybe you should look for it now, Flora. Whoever's after all of you, it's about something you were in together."

She looked up, thought a moment, then stood. "Well, this might be the right time after all. I could stand a dose of Ruby's good sense about now."

"You know where it is?" Dolly asked.

"Hmm." Flora frowned. "Only one place I ever keep anything, I suppose. Put everything in my desk in the front room."

"Or"—she hesitated—"it could be in the refrigerator. I read where burglars don't ever think to look for valuables in the refrigerator. That's where I keep my wedding ring when I'm not wearing it—in an ice tray. But I don't think I put Ruby's letter in an ice tray. I mean, it wasn't valuable. Just precious to me, you could say."

"Why don't we take a look at it," Dolly urged gently.

Flora looked over at me. I nodded, too.

"If you think so." She sighed, got up, and left the kitchen.

While she was gone Dolly and I didn't say a word. Not a hope. Not a hint. Nothing about thinking it was time we got a break.

Flora was back, her hands empty. "I looked in the desk and it's not there. Then I looked in the bedroom dresser and it's not there either. You think I should check the refrigerator, just in case?"

Dolly nodded and offered to help but Flora waved her off. She searched shelf after shelf, then the freezer, ice trays, the crisper drawers.

"I didn't think so." She straightened. Her shoulders fell. She looked her seventy-plus years. "They must've got it. I don't understand any of this. All just too much..."

"The people who robbed you? You think they took your letter?"

She nodded, miserable. "Who else?"

"You all had one? You're sure?"

Flora nodded, her flushed face sad.

"You. Joslyn Henry. Mary Margaret," I said.

Finally, it looked as if we were onto something connecting the three dead women, beyond their moon cookies, beyond their dancing. A poem. A clipping. Not likely, but we didn't have anything else.

THIRTY-THREE

I TRIED TO WORK on the novel the next morning while listening to Nina Simone; that voice with all of life still throbbing in it. Sorrow lay beside my desk on his back, four feet in the air. Every once in a while he gave a subdued "Woof" and his legs made running movements. The guy was busy chasing dreams.

"Here comes the sun, little darling...," Nina sang.

Ohh, the woman could see into my soul and sing healing.

That voice hurt. Sometimes too much. I switched to Satie. Nothing personal there, in his music. Oh no ... just those long notes that got me down where I lived. Dragged out emotion, dark and deep and so very slow.

I turned off the music, figuring it was a day of too much imagination. Then turned off the computer, making Sorrow scramble up, thinking we were finished. I motioned for him to lie back down, that we weren't ready to go. I occupied my studio to protect it from "Jackson invasion," but the stress was making me unhappy and nonproductive. I lay on the futon for a while in the complete silence of early October. It was my period, I figured. That's why the emotion, the melancholy. First day stuff. Cramps in my back gave me an excuse not to sit at my desk pretending to write. I felt sad about four old ladies who wanted to make the world a better place before they left it. Three of them murdered. I lay on the southwest-design cover of the futon and stretched my arms high, stiffened my body. I closed my eyes and imagined being out there in the woods, dancing around a fire. I imagined lying back on the earth and opening my eyes to the universe, wondering if I could feel at one with all of that, with a loving spirit around me, watching and smiling.

I envied Flora Coy, Ruby Poet, Mary Margaret Murphy, and Joslyn Henry. Three of them might be dead but for a little while they'd had that, what I thought of as a perfect friendship taking in everyone and everything. No jealousy. No meanness.

Their deaths grew larger than their lives had been. Larger than the way they'd died. A good revelation, though it didn't diminish my fervent desire to get the killer. It just made him less important, of only momentary interest, eclipsed, when we got him, by what the women had known.

As usual, with the strange twists my life took, and the loss of that aloneness I used to have, a car pulled down the drive, bringing me out of my reverie and out of my studio before anyone thought to join me and spoil that place, too. Sorrow, who loved company, bounced into me, getting out the door. He did his dance and barked a welcome.

Bill had come to see how I was doing, he said, after getting out of his car and patting Sorrow's head. It felt good to have Bill standing in my driveway. It was a day for a big man with a big chest and funny glasses that he pushed up his nose with his middle finger. I wanted so badly to hug him, but I stopped myself.

"I came to talk to Jackson," he said, walking into the house behind me.

That wasn't what I needed to hear right then. Jackson wasn't supposed to fit into this equation. My equation. My job. My friend.

"Brought him some news."

Jackson jumped up, as men always do, to shake hands. They settled on my sofa, two large, healthy male animals, while I made coffee. I did it quietly, not wanting to miss a word.

"A friend of mine, he's a pilot with Northwest up here. He's being transferred for ten months and wants to rent out his place." Bill stopped and watched Jackson's face as he listened. "I thought you might be interested."

Jackson nodded. "'Course I am. It's just that it might not be a good time to be leaving Emily. With this problem she's got herself into ..."

"Don't worry about me," I called from the kitchen. "We're close to the end now. I can feel it."

"Still ..."

"Anyway," Bill pressed on. "He's got this house just outside of Traverse, on Spider Lake. Bigger than Emily's."

That opened Jackson's eyes. He glanced toward me. Me and my matched cups and saucers, my sugar and my creamer, my little life and littler house. He smirked. "Well, hmm, that does sound like what I've been looking for."

Bill nodded and rubbed his big hands together. "I thought it might."

"How much does he want for it? I don't have a lot ..."

Bill went on smiling. He shook his head. "Oh, no. Not a lot. He just wants somebody reliable in there. You'd be kind of watching the place for him."

Jackson nodded slowly. "So, in a way, I'd be doing your friend a favor, right?"

Bill nodded, a little more slowly. He was onto Jackson faster than I'd ever caught his twists and turns. "I could take you in right now to see it. If you want?"

"Great." Jackson stood, rubbing his hands together. "You want to ride in the Jag?"

"We'll take two cars." Bill hesitated, smiling at me. "After Emily's coffee. Wouldn't want to miss that."

They drank. They left. I was relieved. Quiet. And a sunny afternoon. I could walk. I could sit down by the lake and swear at the last of the fleeing geese. I could work ... without Nina.

I didn't get to any of those things. Another car pulled down the drive, almost before I'd finished waving Bill and Jackson off. Sorrow was thrilled. Two in one day!

Sorrow didn't like Officer Brent much. The policeman got out of his car, stretching, pulling up his trousers. He looked around him, removed his big dark glasses, and smirked at Sorrow, who gave one halfhearted woof and one tepid leap in the air before slinking off, tail wrapped up between his legs.

"Emily," Brent called out to me and made a face—as if he smelled something bad, or was bringing me more bad news. I got the strangest chill. Something about the uniform, the car, the glasses, that way big cops have of doing things slowly.

"Officer Brent," I answered.

"I was just over to see your neighbor, Mr. Mockerman. You heard what that Rombart guy says he saw out in the woods, right?"

I agreed.

He nodded again. "Not home. All his dogs are back there. His old car's parked behind the house. But no Harry. You seen him lately?"

"Yesterday," I said. "At the memorial. He was there for the service. He didn't stay for the lunch."

He looked around slowly, his mine-sweeper eyes going over my garden, the house, the woods.

I invited him in. He filled the doorway, then the kitchen. He settled on one of my kitchen stools, much the way Dolly always settled. Something about packing a gun, I supposed. It required legs spread, a hand on one hip. This man was a big, big presence in my little house.

"I thought it was time I came to see you," he said. "And since I was out here anyway..."

I poured coffee and waited.

"I have to tell you, I'm stumped. People here act friendly then they clam right up. I don't know who to believe and who not to believe. You having the same trouble?"

I shrugged. "I suppose so. They're really good, honest people. It's just that everybody's upset. Wouldn't you be? I mean, with something like this going on in your town?"

"Certainly would." He drank his coffee slowly. He took it black, the way I imagined he would. "So, I was thinking. You know these people better than I do."

"Yeah, me and Officer Wakowski."

"Well, yes, her, too. People like this Harry Mockerman. I thought we should get together and talk about it. There's this supposed confession we've got now. I got word from Grayling, no fingerprints they could pinpoint on that confession letter from Mrs. Murphy. I tend to doubt it's real, don't you? I mean, what are people in town saying?"

"Forged," I said.

"What I thought. So I guess we can discount that. What about your neighbor?"

"Harry?"

"Yeah."

"I don't know. I really don't. It doesn't feel right to me but I guess you never know."

"Those oil leases Mrs. Poet signed awhile back? Going to bring her some money I understand. I went in to Traverse to see her attorney. He said there's already a good sum accruing. She left a will. Everything goes to her daughter, Amanda. She'd have no reason to kill anybody. Rules her out."

"What if she wanted everything before her mother was ready to give it to her?"

"Hmm. A possibility. But what about the others? Can you see that little woman burning down the funeral home?"

"To tell the truth, I can't see her doing that to her mother either. Maybe Joslyn Henry. I suppose anybody could strangle someone if they took them by surprise. But not the funeral home. Setting a fire?" I shook my head. "I can't quite … What do you think about Ernie Henry?"

"I had a talk with him. There was no tractor pull or small-engine show or anything over in Leland those days he was gone. Won't say where he really was."

I told him what Bill had said about Ernie's arrest down in Grand Rapids.

"Prostitute, huh?" Brent chuckled, then shook his head.

"He makes frequent trips out of town. My mailman thinks he's with the CIA."

"I'll go see him again."

"What about the Murphys?"

"They'll get the insurance, eventually. Their mom didn't claim she was setting fire to the place. If it turns out she did do it, murder the other women, well, still, the fire could've been an accident. Couldn't begin to tell you—though they're still calling the fire suspicious in nature," he said. "I wouldn't put anything past either one of the Murphy men. Dumb-shit bunch—those two. One's a drunk and the other one's a gambler. You never know. Probably both need money. But what reason would they have to kill all the women? Their mother, I could see. Get her insurance. Fire insurance—as long as everything's OK. But not the others. No reason at all."

I nodded, agreeing.

"Could there have been another will?" I asked. "I mean, Ruby Poet. Maybe she made a new will and left Amanda out."

"Why? Then we're right back to: could Amanda Poet have done any of this?"

"Geez," I said. "Everybody's guilty and everybody's innocent. What do you think of one of Dave Rombart's guys? You know Harry had some things to say about them."

He nodded. "Again, we're right back to: why all three women?"

"Maybe he was mad at all of them, for siccing the cops on him. You never know with nut cases like Dave."

We both shrugged.

"That business about Dolly running out of the funeral home. You know that's not true, don't you?" I asked.

He made a face. "Figured it wasn't her."

311

"I found out that Sullivan Murphy used to be a cop. Down in Saginaw."

"Why didn't you tell me?"

"No time. Then I had other things …"

"So, maybe it was Sullivan ran out when the funeral home burned. Killed his mother. Figured if he was seen, Dolly'd be blamed."

"Brings us right back to: why the other women?"

"Hey, but, this is an interesting development." He perked right up. "If we solve one of these we'll solve them all. You watch. I think we should go talk to Sullivan. How about you?"

"I already mentioned the uniform to him and he got furious."

"Let's see if he does the same with me. You want to go along?"

"Me? A reporter?" I snickered.

"You won't be reporting things until the right time. I've learned that about you. I think I can trust you."

"I'll call Dolly."

Officer Brent made a face. "She's off the case."

"Not really," I said.

He shrugged. "What the hell."

I made the phone calls. First to Dolly, who said she'd wait for us to pick her up, though she was puzzled what I'd be doing with Officer Brent. I called the Grand Traverse Resort. The Murphys had checked out. I called Lucky Barnard to see if he knew where the Murphys might have gone. He said he'd just passed the two of them, over at the funeral home, picking through the wreckage and throwing things into Gilbert's hearse and Sullivan's rented van. We had our target, me, Dolly, and Officer Brent. I climbed into yet another police car as if this was my new life's path, and we were off to town.

THIRTY-FOUR

LIKE A GOOD NANNY, Dolly had Flora in tow when they met us a block from the funeral home, where Officer Brent parked his car. They'd walked over from Oak Street. "I'm not leaving her for a minute," Dolly said, and she held the woman, white hair flying, pink glasses fogged from exertion, by the hand, as if she were a child. Flora, maybe still in shock, said nothing. She didn't greet me or Officer Brent, nor even smile. It was as though her eyes, who she was, all that spirit, had stopped being with the latest death of a good friend.

Gilbert and Sullivan Murphy were both at the ruins of the funeral home when we got down there. Gilbert, squat, rounded shoulders slumped, leaned against the family hearse not doing much of anything, though he was wearing a painter's hat and gloves, both still very white and clean. Sullivan was moving fallen boards and blackened furniture; grunting and stumbling as he threw things back to the sidewalk. He had a dirty rag wrapped around his head, filthy gloves on his hands. The smell of wet burned wood was strong. In places, wisps of smoke or ash curled upward as Sullivan moved a board, lifted the frame of what had been an overstuffed chair, or pulled away a burned wooden rectangle that might have held a painting.

The men saw us coming. Sullivan put a hand to his back and stretched. He scowled and said something to Gilbert, who didn't look around.

Flora stopped when we stood in front of the ruin. She put her hand to her mouth. "Oh dear," she said, near tears. "That's where they all were … cremated." She shook off Dolly's grip and turned her back to the men and the building.

"Tough job," Dolly said when we joined the Murphys, who squinted up at us then looked away. Sullivan nodded to Officer Brent and made noises that sounded like a greeting.

"Saving whatever we can," Sullivan offered, halfheartedly, his eyes with their usual watery, disconnected look. I couldn't decide if Sullivan was always drunk or if he was one of those people who just looked that way. I didn't pick up the scent of Jack Daniels, so maybe he was only tired, or sad. I'd give him that—a profound reason for sadness.

"We're moving on pretty quick," Sullivan said, turning to look at the destroyed house, pillars across the porch hanging at acute angles, not a part of anything. "Too many memories here. If we re-build, it won't be in Leetsville, I'll tell you."

Officer Brent shook his head slowly. "I wouldn't be too quick to move if I were you, Mr. Murphy. We've got three murders here, and a case of arson." He motioned toward the house.

"Nothing to do with us," Gilbert muttered from behind.

Officer Brent turned on him, taken aback a minute. "Your mother was murdered, sir."

Gilbert shrugged. "Won't bring her back to find out who did it."

314

"You don't want to know who did this to your family?" He let incredulity creep into his voice.

"Of course we do." Sullivan turned on his brother, a touch of disgust surfacing.

"All we've got left us is the insurance money," Gilbert went on, lifting his chin as a way of pointing at the life they'd lost. "Nothing's going to bring back my mother."

We all nodded. True enough.

"Your insurance agent tell you it could be awhile?" Brent asked.

"Said something. Because it's a suspicious fire. And he said something about that letter. That maybe Mother set the fire. Never heard of such a thing," Gilbert said, his face mottled by anger. "We're getting a lawyer."

"You can't profit from arson. Not one you set yourself, or a member of your family. They won't be paying off too soon."

"She didn't send that letter," Sullivan said, and he wiped a dirty sleeve across his nose, leaving a streak of soot on his right cheek.

"That's for sure," Gilbert said.

"Lab's checking for fingerprints. Should know soon if she did."

"What do you mean, 'fingerprints'? How can a letter have 'fingerprints' on it?" Gilbert scoffed. "Anybody could have touched that thing."

Brent shrugged and left it at that. He had other things on his mind and turned back to Sullivan. "About that police uniform, Mr. Murphy. Whoever set the fire was seen running out of here by Eugenia Fuller. I hear you were on the police force, down in Saginaw."

"Yeah. So what?" Sullivan growled. "Years ago. Who the hell knows what happened to my old uniforms? Probably in there." He gestured behind him. "Burned with everything else. You worried about a police uniform, you just talk to Dolly here. I know what Eugenia said."

Beside him, Gilbert was still shaking his head and scoffing, "Fingerprints. Yeah, sure."

Dolly said nothing.

"Mind if we look through your stuff in the van?" Brent asked.

Sullivan made a face. "Why the hell should I care? Got nothing but whatever clothes I bought since the fire. There's some stuff I found here. Not much left. I sure as hell don't have anything to hide. Though, come to think of it ... maybe I should call that lawyer. I don't trust you ..."

He looked from Officer Brent to Dolly to me.

"You guys may be trying to protect the deputy." He narrowed his red-shot eyes at us and shook his head. "Yeah. Don't be too fast touching that van ..."

"Don't let 'em do anything, Sullie." Gilbert stomped around behind his brother, agitated. "'Cause a them we won't get the money right away. I don't want to be hanging around. No reason."

"Yeah," Sullivan growled at Officer Brent then included the rest of us.

Officer Brent shrugged and walked away. As if remembering something, he turned back to me and Dolly. "You two wait here. I'm going to make a call and get a search warrant for that van. Don't let these men out of your sight."

We nodded seriously. I doubted Officer Brent had any way of getting a search warrant issued with nothing to go on but suspicion. No judge would fall for it and nobody was going to give him a warrant over the phone. Sullivan said nothing. He swore and paced the sidewalk, faster, working himself into a sweat.

"We don't want trouble." Gilbert had his hand on his brother's arm. His face was skewed up, eyes blinking fast. "Maybe you should let them go ahead, Sullie. You've got nothing in there, have you? Nothing you don't want the police to find?"

Sullivan stopped pacing to frown at his brother. "What do you mean? What would I have? What have I got left?" He swept an arm out to include the burned building.

Sullivan thought a minute then called after the slowly retreating Officer Brent.

"Go on and look!" he yelled. "I got nothing to hide. Go right ahead and search all you want to."

Brent was back—he hadn't gone far.

"Hurry it up," Sullivan said, chin stuck out at Brent. "And you better not damage one damn thing or I'm suing you, all of you, personally."

Officer Brent went to the van and began lifting out boxes, opening them, poking through the contents, closing the box and setting it aside on the curb. Dolly and I stayed where we were. I had no official standing here and I was well aware of it. Dolly let Officer Brent do the job while she kept an eye on the Murphys.

Brent went through ten or twelve boxes, then bags of clothes. He found nothing. He searched the front of the car, feeling under the seats. I watched him hesitate, leaning over, his hand half under the front seat. When he straightened, he pulled something dark out. He unfolded whatever it was on the front seat, refolded it, picked it up and walked over, cradling it in his arms.

Gilbert watched him. Sullivan's eyes bugged out of his head.

"What's that?" Sullivan demanded.

"Uniform." Officer Brent seemed deep in thought. He bit at his bottom lip.

"What kind of uniform?" Sullivan demanded. "I didn't have any uniform in there."

"Police uniform, from the look of it." He stretched the cloth open to show an insignia on the shoulder. Saginaw Police. "Looks a little singed. You forget you put it there?"

"I didn't put it there or anywhere. I don't know where it came from...," Sullivan sputtered then ground to a halt. He looked very serious. His shoulders hunched forward. He licked at his lips.

"Maybe it would be best if we talked about this over at the station. We can go here, over to see Lucky Barnard, or you can come with me into Gaylord."

"What the hell...!" Sullivan backed away. "What's a uniform prove? I'm not going anywhere. This is a frame-up. You're trying to pin this..."

"Why hide the uniform?" Brent asked.

Sullivan sputtered. "I didn't know it was... Nothing to do with me."

Gilbert watched his brother.

"Hey Gilbert." Sullivan turned to him, hands out. "You know I didn't do anything like..."

Gilbert shook his head again and again.

"You, too, Gilbert." Officer Brent called and gestured. "I think it's time we all went in and had a good long talk."

———————

We went back to Flora's house. She seemed to gather strength from the physical exercise while Dolly and I wilted the more we talked about what was wrong with the Murphys as murderers and the more we realized our job wasn't finished.

The light on Flora's answering machine blinked three times. Three calls. Flora frowned at it and backed off. "I'm not answering that thing ever again, I know it'll bring me no good," she said, flapping her hands as if to keep the devil away.

Dolly punched the button that brought a tirade of abuse. The same high-pitched woman's voice, screaming obscenities, then, "Your fuckin' friend the cop did this, old woman. And you know it. Murdered three of our best people. You better watch out—idol worshipper. You hear?"

All three calls. Same woman's voice. Same abuse.

Flora backed up to the sofa and sat down, face buried in her hands.

Dolly scrolled through the numbers on the caller ID the police had installed for Flora's safety. "One number." She read it off. "Familiar?" she said.

"It should be," Flora said, sniffing, hands down, anger written across her elderly face. "That's the Church of the Contented Flock. They're the ones been calling me."

"It's not the pastor," I said. "This is a woman."

"Bet he put 'er up to it," Flora said. "Why don't you get over there, Dolly? Find out who's doing this."

I looked hard at Dolly. "You think the pastor's involved?"

Dolly shrugged. "I'm not thinking anything anymore. Sure not Sullivan Murphy's voice though. Could be anybody, I guess. Maybe the pastor's behind it all. If so, then he's just nuts, and that's as good a reason as insurance money to kill people."

THIRTY-FIVE

THE REVEREND RUNCIVAL WAS alone in his office, down the hall in the church building, beyond the steps to the basement, before the doors to the church itself. We surprised him sitting quietly, hands behind his head, deep in thought. The man looked even smaller indoors.

He smiled tentatively, sat up, and nodded formally to Flora, who nodded as coolly back to him.

"Writing my sermon for Sunday—in my head," he said pointedly, giving a little laugh. "No trees die when I'm writing." He smiled at me. "What can I do for you ladies?"

He didn't rise. He leaned back in his chair again and twined his hands together over his chest.

"Mrs. Coy's getting threatening phone calls," Dolly began.

"Terribly sorry," the pastor said to Flora and clucked his tongue a few times. "Awful things going on. I can assure you I haven't said a word to stir up any…"

"There were three while she was out this morning. Just a few hours ago," I said.

He lifted his eyebrows and waited to hear how that should be significant to him.

"Her caller ID listed this number as the phone they came from."

He settled his chair forward. His mouth flew open. "You're not accusing me ..."

I shook my head. "It's a woman's voice. We'd like to play the tape for you ... and find out who was here a few hours ago. Maybe some woman working in the church, or here in the office, or ... well, she'd have had to be here alone, I suppose."

Dolly plugged in the tape player we'd brought, and fiddled with buttons. The tape played and that same voice burst out. One time. Two times. Three times.

At first the man shook his head, then he looked puzzled, then he sat forward, started to say something, but stopped himself.

"You recognize the voice?" Dolly asked. "We're protecting Flora here. If something more happens, well, you could be held as an accomplice."

The pastor frowned as if he found her silly but still there was a worried look behind the frown. "I don't really know who that is. All I can tell you, there was only one woman here today."

"Who?" I asked, keeping my voice even, the excitement at bay.

"Well, that was ... I don't know if I should be saying anything. Perhaps I should have a talk with her first."

"Why?" I asked. "If she's mixed up in it, do you want to protect somebody like that?"

He shook his head, thought awhile, then decided something. "No, I can't. Not until I've spoken with her myself. It's what a good pastor would do. She deserves a chance to explain to me first. If I'm not satisfied, well ... then I'll call Chief Barnard."

"You could be taking your life in your hands," Dolly said.

He laughed and brushed away the idea. "That's not a murderer," he said. "That's a hysterical woman. If I'm right, it's the same person who first warned me about the old women dancing out there in the woods, holding the Pagan rituals. I was of a tendency to ignore it but she didn't think it would go away unless I spoke out against them. She lets herself get all excited. I'll handle it." He turned to Flora. "You don't have to worry, Mrs. Coy. I know for a fact it's got nothing to do with your friends' deaths. Sometimes it's an attack of religious zeal. Sometimes it's a personal problem they can't handle. Ministers see more than you'd imagine." He shook his head and actually chuckled. "Nothing to worry about. Not at all."

We left the church with his hollow assurances fading behind us.

"Hope she doesn't get him, too," Dolly said, more glum than usual.

I nodded. So did Flora. Somehow we weren't sure of anything anymore. Not anybody's safety. Certainly not the pastor's ability to handle what was coming at him.

Over dinner at Fuller's, Dolly was all for keeping an eye on the pastor, for his own good. I was all for returning to my house to see if Jackson was back yet. There was something unsettling about my ex-husband and a man I worked for spending an afternoon and evening together. I hoped all they'd talked about was football, or the stock market. Usually I could depend on Jackson to talk about himself for hours on end. I prayed he was still that dependable and wasn't showing signs of thoughtfulness. Still, I wanted to see his face. I was eager to hear if he would soon be gone from my life.

We settled on Dolly calling Lucky and reporting what had happened at the Church of the Contented Flock. She held her radio out across the table so Flora and I, and Eugenia and Gloria, and just about everybody else in Fuller's EATS, could hear. This wasn't much of a secret investigation anymore. Never had been, not with the uncanny ability to communicate over long distances the people in Leetsville enjoyed. Lucky said the Murphys were gone, released. Nothing to hold them on. Officer Brent didn't have anything to charge them with until he'd had Sullivan's police uniform tested for gasoline—something that would connect it to the fire.

"Even with that, he'd just claim he pulled it out of the building," Lucky said.

He left the radio for a minute, then came back. "I spoke to Brent. He says he'll get on to the pastor in the morning. Find out who the woman on the phone was. At least scare her off, if she doesn't have anything else to do with this.

"And," Lucky went on, then stopped, speaking to someone in the room with him. "Wait a minute, Officer Brent's got something he wants to say to you."

The voice changed. "Officer Wakowski? Sorry I had to let the Murphys go. Wish I could have held them. Me and Lucky think you two might be in deep trouble with them out there somewhere. Look, if all three of you want to get the hell out of town, that's fine with us. Dolly's still officially off duty, Lucky says. Why don't you go someplace until we wrap this up?"

Dolly pulled back from her radio. She looked worried. "What do you think, Emily? I don't want to get you or Flora hurt ..."

Flora pooh-poohed Dolly's fear and muttered something about not leaving her birds to killers. I thought a minute then said, "We've got to see this through. It sure didn't look as if Gilbert was too happy with Sullivan. They've got their hands full right now."

Dolly nodded. She passed the message to Brent. I reached out and grabbed her hand. We held on a minute, in something like a pledge.

"Tell them we're all going out to my house … ," I said.

Flora started to complain again but I shushed her with a finger at my lips. "We'll take your birds," I said. "Can you fit four cages in the back of your car, Dolly? OK. They'll be fine at my house."

"What about that dog?" Flora hissed across the booth at me.

"Sorrow loves birds," I lied, figuring it was worth it to get a good night's sleep, on my own floor—if it came to that. At least my friends would be safe under my roof. Then, too, I was the only one among us who could offer a big male presence. Well anyway, I had Jackson, just in case things got bad. Like they used to do with virgins, I could throw him as a human sacrifice if the Murphy twins came after us with hatchets or ropes or flaming torches, or Pastor Runcival decided on an exorcism, or Harry Mockerman thought we'd make good soup.

———

Since I'd ridden into town in Officer Brent's big blue police car, I rode out of town in Dolly's big white and gold police car, with Flora in the back surrounded by bird cages. The parakeets weren't thrilled. There was much twittering and loud squawking. We had to shout to be heard above them.

It was dark by the time we were on our way. Along our country roads, that meant very dark. Especially on overcast nights that threatened rain. The deer were unusually active because it was autumn. They were getting ready for winter and about as nervous as they got in spring, when they had their minds on something other than hunting season. A couple of does ran across the road in front of the car. Dolly missed them by swerving to the right as they ran to the left, into the woods.

We were just coming up on the turn to Willow Lake Road, passing the place where a stream drained into Arnold's Swamp. I already had my mind on how much bread I had in the house for morning for my guests, and if there was enough tea, and if I'd let the milk go sour again.

I looked out the front window, worrying about where I'd put everybody. Dolly's headlights picked up the tall, furry-headed dead reeds lining the road and then a huge, slow raccoon, the biggest I'd ever seen. He parted the reeds on the swamp side of the road and crawled down the embankment. I pointed him out to Dolly and Flora Coy, who craned their necks in the direction of the swamp. We were all pointing and laughing when we were hit from behind. A huge jolt. No time to say anything. Dolly grabbed the wheel and held on. We were hit again. Metal crunched and squealed. I'd never heard or felt anything like it. My instinct was to keep myself from going forward but my body was propelled. The seat belt restrained me just before my chest hit the dash. I couldn't catch my breath. Dolly yelled as the car veered, then teetered at the edge of the embankment. We were going over, down into the swamp. I felt a strange sense of displacement, being where we shouldn't have been. Air bags came out, making a sound like a shotgun. My face was covered; my chest slammed with what felt like a solid board. There was another bang into the car and with sudden speed we sailed up and over the embankment, plunging headlong down into Arnold's Swamp, stopping with a jolt as the car met soft earth and dug in with sounds of folding and snapping and groaning.

My head felt as if it was going to come off my neck. I didn't have breath to breathe. The car was stopped but the groaning went on. I couldn't tell if it was in or outside of the car. The headlights were on but, when I pulled the air bag away from my face, I could see the light was diffused, pointing out over dark water.

I gulped for air and made a noise. A release of terror. There were no other sounds in the car. My feet were getting oddly wet. Cold water seeped up through the floorboards and under the door. I sat with my eyes closed for I didn't know how long, trying to catch my breath, make sure I was alive, that I could feel the various parts of my body. My head and neck were hurting more than I wanted to think about. Everything else was intact.

"Dolly? Emily?" I heard Flora's weak voice coming from the back seat. I wanted to cry with relief. At least she was alive.

"I'm OK, Flora," I called over my shoulder, pushing at the air bag, wondering how I could deflate the thing and get it away from my face. "Are you OK?"

"I ... I think I got hit with one of the cages. I feel blood on my face."

"Oh, God. We'll get out of this. Give me a minute." I called back. "Dolly, can you open your door?"

No answer.

"Dolly?" I called louder. I couldn't see anything because of the dark. Even when I pushed the air bag down and held it there, I couldn't see anything. I felt across the seat, toward where Dolly had to be. Her arm was beside me, warm, limp.

"Dolly!" I called again, grabbed on to the arm, and shook it.

No answer.

"Oh no," Flora moaned in the back. "Is she all right?"

"Maybe knocked out," I said, keeping my voice steady. It looked as if I was the one who had to get us out of there. We'd been hit. I knew that. Something big. A truck. A huge car. For an instant, though I'd seen nothing, I had a vision of that hybrid vehicle Harry Mockerman drove. Half truck. Half car. The front end a rusted-out black pickup, the tires from a car, the back a hand-built flat-bed. Big enough to knock anything over, I imagined. But I'd seen nothing. It was all imagination, my way of giving a face to what had been done to us. Or maybe I'd recognized a sound. I couldn't think. Nothing wanted to fall into any kind of order. All I knew was that I had to get us out of the car. Had to take care of Dolly.

"You see who hit us?" I yelled back to Flora as I maneuvered myself from the seat belt, away from the air bag. I pushed at my door and it gave, but stopped, wedged against something I figured had to be dirt. We'd sunk down into the muck. I pushed harder. The door gave enough to snap the overhead light on.

"Thank the good Lord!" Flora called. "Oh, my poor birds. Let me see here..." I heard her moving, straightening cages, talking to her birds. "See to Dolly, Emily. Oh, please see to Dolly. Dolly? Dolly?"

Still no answer.

"You getting out, Emily?"

"Un-huh, trying," I said, pushing harder, widening the opening far enough for me to strain my body through. My feet sank into cold swamp muck. Without being able to see where I was putting my feet, only able to sense the icy water climbing my legs, under my jeans, over my skin, all I could think of was water moccasins and beetles and blood suckers and whatever else lived in swamp water. Thank God it was October instead of August, I kept telling myself as I picked one foot up after another and set it down again into the ooze, feeling my way, hand over hand, around the car to Dolly's side door.

She lay with her head against the window, slumped down. I tapped, but she didn't move.

The car motor was still running. I could hear a burbling at the back, as if exhaust was escaping into the water. I pulled on Dolly's door then had to catch her when I got it open. She fell hard against me. I glanced into the back seat. Flora was lost in a pile of bird cages.

I put the back of my hand to Dolly's face and slapped her slightly. "Dolly," I whispered near her ear. "Dolly. You OK?"

No answer. I felt her chest. There was a slow rise and fall of breath.

"She's OK. Just knocked out!" I yelled back to Flora, who began to moan again about her birds.

"I've got to find Dolly's radio," I said, feeling around beyond Dolly for the switch to her car radio. "Maybe it's still working."

"Oh, I hope. Hurry. Hurry. Are we sinking? I feel water. Oh Emily, we're going to die. Somebody wants us to die." Flora was hysterical. I had to calm her down and get us help.

"Count your birds, Flora. Make sure they're all here. Count 'em, Flora."

I heard her moving the cages, pulling them off her. She began to count. "Trigger. Samson. Delilah ..."

"I've got it." The switch moved and the radio came to life.

"Yeah? That you, Dolly?" A voice came at me.

"Lucky?"

"Yeah. Who's this? What are you doing on my deputy's radio?"

"It's me. Emily."

328

"Emily? You shouldn't be playing games with the equipment..."

"Lucky. Somebody hit us. Threw us down into the swamp."

"Oh, my God! Dolly with you?"

"Yes, but I think she's knocked out. She's breathing. I've got Flora Coy, too."

"Where the hell are you? I'll get an ambulance. I'll be out..."

"You know where Double Lake Road nears Willow Lake?"

"Sure."

"There. Down in Arnold's Swamp. The car lights are on but I'll get up to the road."

"I'll be right there."

Leaving the car and making my way through the cold water and up the embankment, feeling my way with my hands, touching things I didn't want to know about, wasn't easy. But neither was leaving Flora Coy behind me naming birds; and Dolly, coming to, moaning.

The ambulance got to us first. Lucky wasn't far behind. He set up portable lights while the paramedics pulled out stretchers. I crawled into the back of the ambulance as directed and sat down, my head in my hands, exhausted, dirty, wet, and shaking. They got Flora and then Dolly out of the car and into the ambulance with me. We were going to Munson Hospital in Traverse City, one of the paramedics told me. Flora screamed she couldn't leave her birds to drown. Lucky promised to rescue Flora's birds and get them to my house, then come straight into Traverse. I told Lucky where a key to the house was hidden, in case nobody was home.

"I'll see to the car, too," Lucky said, making Dolly moan louder.

"I screwed up another one," she said—her first coherent words—and put an arm up over her eyes, hiding.

"Well ... we'll see. Have to get a look at the damage. Don't worry about that now." Lucky leaned across the stretcher, assuring her. I knew the only thing that really terrified Dolly was the thought of patrolling backwoods two-tracks, for the rest of her life. That, and doing it on a bicycle.

THIRTY-SIX

I don't want to get out of bed...
Don't want to open my eyes...
Don't want to get up today...
Don't want people in my house...

I LAY STILL, EYES closed, and told myself what a sellout I was. Everything I'd come up north for, all gone. The peace. The quiet. The absolute aloneness I needed. The writing time. Gave it away. Smiled and lied that *no, I didn't mind*. Not me.

Nina's voice in my head: *"... she aches just like a woman..."*

I felt sorry for myself and for my aching body. Through a shroud-like veil of self-pity, I tried to recall how I'd gotten involved in these ugly murders. The reasons came back fast enough, vividly enough. Not just Deputy Dolly, but the deaths of good people, the woman's head and arm so terribly dumped on me. "Like it or not," I remembered my dad saying after he'd gone through a bad time when Mom died, "there are times we don't pick to live through,

Emily. They pick us." Our job, Dad told me, was to get through those times with a little courage and dignity. *"Like it or not."*

I didn't know about the dignity, but my courage was OK, if dented. There were moments from the previous evening that made me wince, memories of fear, of those sickening, grinding jolts, the seeping water, poor Dolly knocked out cold then in pain with what turned out to be a broken ankle.

They kept Dolly at the hospital overnight.

Lucky showed up in the emergency room and took down everything that had happened. Who might have hit us? Who did we think it could be? Did we hear anything?

"Just that awful jolt," I told him. "Then another jolt and we were down in the swamp."

I couldn't bring myself to share the terrible feeling I had about Harry—that it had been his car that hit us. Maybe I didn't want to believe he'd do something like that to me. Maybe I didn't want Lucky thinking I was as fey as the other folks in Leetsville, knowing things I couldn't know, thinking things were true that couldn't be true.

I planned, instead, to get a look at Harry's car myself. There was no way he escaped without a caved-in front fender. Not after hitting us as hard as he had. At the very least, he would have white paint all over some part of that hybrid thing he drove. I had no intention of siccing cops on Harry, not unless what I was afraid of was really true. No matter how confused I was, how suspicious of everyone, I prayed hard it wasn't Harry.

More than anything, I'd wanted to go home. Flora and I were just bruised and bumped, so they let us go, but not before Flora made sure Lucky had saved her birds, got them safely to my house.

"They're just fine, Miz Coy," Lucky assured her.

"Phew!" She gave a long sigh, took a deep breath, then put her hand on Lucky's arm.

"And Charlie's fine, too?" she asked. Lucky dropped the tough cop stuff, got teary-eyed and nodded. His son was doing just fine, too.

I could collect Dolly in the morning, I was told. She didn't take to the idea of me and Flora leaving without her, but the doctor didn't fool around. She gave Dolly a shot and in a few minutes Dolly was out cold, snoring, with a tiny smile coming and going across her face, as if she'd sailed off to a very happy Neverland.

I flipped over in bed, my nose touching something cold and wet. I forced my eyes open to find Sorrow with his head on the pillow next to mine, eyes closed. He gave a snort and his jowls rippled. Sound asleep. I pulled my nose away and thought "yuck" though I didn't say it. His eyes shot wide at my movement. He lifted his head, reared up, and stared at me as if I had a colossal nerve, bothering him like that. Didn't take more than a shove to get him down to the floor and on his feet, leaping with joy. Unlike me, he was happy that it was morning, that we were alive, that it was time to eat.

I narrowed my eyes, meaning to instill guilt in the brazen dog; a little shame for sharing my bed. He had the good grace to look slightly shamefaced, but joy knocked guilt right off his radar screen. He leaped up, stepped on my chest, then off again before I could swat him. He hit the floor and stood there yipping at me. Time to run outside, time to pee, time to see who'd done what to his property overnight, time to get going, time to …

Dogs have a full agenda.

Oh, but I ached. I sat up and put my head in my hands. There was immediate pain in my neck and across my shoulders. Whiplash, I thought, and pictured the neck brace they should have given me at the hospital. If I ever got my hands on whoever did this to us I would...but I couldn't come up with anything dire enough. It was too early for devices of torture to dance in my head.

Someone, other than me, was up. I heard them—him or her—out in the kitchen. Flora. I groaned again. An early bird. And speaking of birds, I heard twittering and singing that wasn't just inside my head. Six parakeets to face that morning. And Dolly to face. I had to go into Traverse and pick her up at Munson by noon. Bring her back and wait on her until she was OK to go to her own house. And take care of Flora Coy until it was safe to take her home—with all her birds.

Take care of Jackson, unless—here I put my hands together and rolled my eyes heavenward—unless he liked the place Bill found for him.

And another thing I hadn't let myself think about—Harry. I had to get over there and take a look at his car. If yet one more rustic I'd learned to trust and like turned out to be lethal—well, I wanted it over, once and for all. I wanted him behind bars. I wanted him put away forever. Him and his Trojan Horse possum stews.

First, some sort of breakfast. Then Dolly. Then I'd see about Harry Mockerman.

I had a plan for the day though I would rather have had none.

Dolly looked much the worse for wear. She was sitting at the side of her hospital bed when we got into town to retrieve her. A black eye had developed overnight. She sat hunched forward, crutches half pushed up under her arms. Her cast ankle stuck straight out as she examined it, maybe for a way to crack it open.

"They taught me how to use these damn things." She waved the crutches at Flora and me. "But I still bounce all over and land on the cast, which they told me not to do, at least until later. They had to redo it this morning. Something about the other one being only temporary. When this one hardens I'll be able to walk on it. Which I told them had better happen because I was going to be walking on it anyway."

"I'm glad to see you too, Dolly." I smiled and greeted her. Flora clucked and looked sad. Dolly glowered like a kid about to tear the room apart.

"They get who did it?" she demanded.

I shook my head. I'd called Lucky but they didn't have much to go on except dark paint, black, on the back of the white squad car.

"Hmm ... black. Could be anybody? They check cars in town?"

"Lucky said he was doing everything he could."

"What about Brent? He must be on it, too."

I nodded. "I called him and he said they were going out today to look at your car. Had it towed into town."

"I'll find 'im. The bastard who did this to us."

Flora gave a cluck of disapproval.

Dolly looked at her but didn't apologize or look very sorry for her language. She was beyond niceties. Dolly was fuming.

"You're coming to my house to stay. You want to swing by yours first? Get whatever you need?"

I got grudging agreement. A nurse came in and handed Dolly her release papers. The nurse looked relieved and left the room without a goodbye or a have a nice day or even a *get that crazy woman the hell out of here.*

All the way back to Leetsville, Dolly complained about having to keep her leg up, about the pain, about being hampered at a time she most needed speed. "Lucky say much about the squad car?" she asked after a while, looking at me sideways. "I'll bet he's mad. All that's left is the two-tracks back in the woods after this. Maybe I won't even have a job."

"He didn't say," I told her. "But don't worry about Lucky, Dolly. He's on our side."

"Yeah," was all she said. When I turned her way, she was sunken in on herself with un-Dolly-like misery.

At her house she got the hang of the crutches and swung her body up the walk, then up the steps, and through the front door. Flora got a ham Dolly wanted us to take out of her refrigerator. "Might as well use it up," she said, holding a carton of milk to her nose, sniffing, making a face and putting the carton back on the shelf.

I admired her walls of pictures. Just as she'd said, all kinds of pictures. Many of them good-looking men. More like a rogue's gallery than decoration. But then, this was Dolly's house.

I noticed her answering machine blinking. Many calls.

"Want me to see what's there?" I asked, pointing to the machine.

"Probably more people thinking I torched the funeral home," she said. "But go ahead, if you have to."

The callers were townspeople who'd heard about the accident and were calling to leave good wishes for her to get well soon, to get better. One guy said, "Get those murderin' bastards, Deputy Dolly. The whole town's behind you."

Eugenia Fuller called, and so did just about everybody else. By the time I'd run through the messages, Dolly was beaming. "Well, what do you know," she said, leaning back hard on her crutches. "Suddenly I'm Joan of Arc instead of Lizzie Borden."

"Lizzie used an ax," I said.

She shrugged. "Well, whatever ..."

"I told you people in this town are good people," Flora said as she bundled Dolly's clothes into a black garbage bag, twisted the top, and held it out for me to carry.

I took the bag and slung it over my shoulder. Flora carried the canned ham. We were off.

———————

By mid-afternoon Dolly was ensconced on my sofa. Flora watched a soap opera on my miniscule TV, her chair brought up directly in front of it, one hand to her ear so she could hear over our talking. I sat with a teacup in hand and my feet up on my coffee table.

Dolly had insisted we pick up her uniform at the cleaners before leaving Leetsville. When we got to my house, she had to put on that jacket. The pants wouldn't pull up over the cast so she stayed in the sweatpants I'd taken to the hospital. Even without the pants, Dolly said she felt more on duty.

Jackson went in and out of the house, packing his stuff into the Jag. A welcome sight.

"Loved your friend's place," he'd said first thing that morning, eyes clear and happy again. "Bigger than this. And a wonderful room for writing. Huge windows. Great desk. You'll have to drive over, Emily. Come for a visit. I insist on buying you dinner in town one night—when you've finished with … eh … when your friends go home."

I smiled and said how pleased I was for him. I said I knew he'd be able to write so much better in a more congenial atmosphere.

"Well, that's true," he stopped, suitcase in hand, and smiled a crocodile smile. "I never imagined, when you said you lived out in the woods, how much company you'd have, how awfully busy this house was."

"Not usually," I almost growled.

"Not that it isn't wonderful." His bright, insincere smile fell on each of us, one after the other.

"Of course," I said.

"This place I've found will be so much better for my work."

"I'm sure." I ground my teeth together. Flora made a face at me. Dolly glared.

"I'll acknowledge you in the book, you know. For all your help." He stood in the doorway, screen door open. He was back to being Jackson: tight black tee shirt, jeans, a white scarf tied at his throat. Today he was something between a matador and a gondola driver.

"I've done nothing, Jackson." I smiled ever so sweetly.

He looked unsure, as if I'd convinced him of my negligible contribution to his oeuvre.

"Well, I'll see that you are at least mentioned." He nodded again and again, convincing himself he could do that much without compromising his academic integrity.

I smiled—well, moved my lips up—and wondered how one goes about snapping one's teeth. Since I was afraid he might find a reason to stay longer, that a twinge of conscience might strike him, that he would never get in his car and go, I followed him out to the studio where he packed all his books and papers and notes and CDs. He'd taken the disks out of my CD player and knocked over another stack as he gathered his. He apologized but didn't stoop to pick them up. He apologized again for the coffee cups and paper napkins and sandwich ends he'd left in my trash basket. Then he stopped, smiled sheepishly, and held his arms wide. This was the big moment. His grand finale. He would give me a continental kiss—one to each cheek, and be gone.

I steeled my back and let myself be hugged, then kissed—not twice, but three times—as I glanced over my beloved studio. Have to get his spirit out by smudging the place with sage, I told myself. Maybe find a local shaman to do some drumming. Might take a priest—and an exorcism. Anything, I thought. Anything was worth a try.

Jackson was almost gone. He made a last promise to keep in touch, to take me out for a wonderful dinner as soon as he'd settled in. I helped him carry his bags and briefcase from my studio. As a final thought, with one leg in his car and one on the ground, he leaned out and said, "Maybe what I can do is send you chapters as I finish them. Let you do a line edit." He gave a short laugh. "After that I can mention your contribution without either of us feeling it wasn't warranted." With that I received a final flip of his hand—a wave, I think. He shut the car door, and was gone.

I waved and waved and waved until he disappeared from the drive. I waved on, listening to the receding sound of his motor up on Willow Lake Road. I waved some more then looked down at Sorrow who sat looking up at me, tongue hanging from the side of his mouth. I smiled a new, wide smile. Sorrow smiled right back.

THIRTY-SEVEN

Dolly didn't like my idea.

"That's crazy, you going over there alone."

I shook my head at her. "I'm not taking Flora, and you make too much noise." I nodded toward her crutches.

"Call Lucky. He'll check it out without letting Harry know."

"No, he won't. Harry will know. He's like everybody else in town. He can smell things happening before they happen."

"You're nuts. They've got police scanners, is all. It's like the biggest hobby next to bowling." She laughed hard at me.

I thought awhile then disagreed. "It's not about police business. They know about me. About things that happen."

I got an exasperated look back from Dolly. "If one person knows something, they all know it. I'd just say, be careful who you talk to."

———

I took a long, circuitous route through Harry's woods, over to the old logging road that ran behind his house, a two-track worn down by the huge wheels of the horse-drawn carts that once brought logs out from the deep woods in winter. The old logging train ran just a ways off, through a clearing where the logs got dropped, then loaded on flat cars and taken down to Grayling. Much of the road and rail line was obliterated by new growth but still the ruts ran true, as clear as an animal trail; places where the big wheels had been pulled along by a team of horses, and places where the iron rails ran. Once in a while I still picked up a hand-forged spike when I walked through here. Some winter nights, I swore I heard men yelling "Timber!"

Today there was no adventure involved in my walk. As I neared the back of Harry's place I walked slower, quieter, careful on the crisp, dry leaves, not wanting to alert his dogs.

The leaf mold was deep and soft. In places, trees, nature-pruned by last spring's winds, lay in disjointed heaps, hard to get around, impossible to get through. When I stepped on branches and broke them with a snap, I froze, waiting for the dogs to start barking. From where I stood I could see the back of the kennel. I saw a dog or two get up from where they slept near the fence and walk over to a food dish or a water bowl. One or two gave a sharp woof, as if to keep in voice. They hadn't seen or heard me yet.

Harry's half-breed car/truck was parked off to the side of the kennel. Too close to the building for comfort. The only thing I could imagine doing was sneaking around the far side, to the west, and circling back in a direct line with the vehicle between me and the dogs.

I stole on beyond the kennel keeping deep in the trees. I started my loop around, back toward the west side of Harry's property. I kept as close to the ground as I could get and still stay on my feet.

There was little breeze. I came up on the back of the car/truck, parked with its nose facing Harry's house, its handmade flatbed toward the woods. It stood directly in front of me, but angled enough so I couldn't see the front fenders. I had to get closer.

I got to the truck without the dogs taking notice. I knelt down and waited, not daring to breathe. I was close to the house now. I could see Harry's windows, and then could see Harry in his kitchen, moving near the sink. I swallowed hard. What would I say if he caught me? How did I step from behind his car and pretend I was just out for a walk? Harry moved away from the window. I had to go then or never. I stood and leaned out to get a look at the front of the car. The metal was pushed in, dented, as if it had hit something hard. The right fender was smashed.

"Hey!" Harry called from his back porch. Dogs began to bark.

I ducked down and hid, scuttling back on all fours, away from the car. If only I could get to the cover of the trees, I thought. Then I would run, hiding behind one tree after another. I'd have a head start.

"Hey!" Harry shouted again. "You, over there! What the hell you think you're doing by my car? You bent on stealing, you little shit? I got my gun. Come on out of there."

The dogs barked full force. I stood and ran as fast as I'd ever run. Harry was after me, and he had his gun.

I heard the dogs, but different. Baying now, as they did when on the loose, hunting an animal in the woods, running it to death.

I could feel my heart against my ribs. My head was filled with sounds that couldn't be there. All around me: voices, I thought, but it was my own heavy breathing. My feet hit the ground and sometimes slipped on the light leaves that weren't part of the earth yet. I caught myself with a hand on a tree trunk. I fell to my knees and leaped back up, running down through hollows and up hillocks. I tripped again and again, then toppled forward, onto my hands and knees. I stayed a minute, head bent, trying to catch my breath and stop the panic. I needed to think.

The logging road was behind me, back where I could hear Harry calling to his dogs. Once, I was sure I heard a gunshot and waited, very still, to see if I'd been shot, if I was going to fall, if blood would begin to spread. I'd heard that people didn't always know when they'd been hit. That there was a time of shock to the body, when the body protected itself the way a body protects itself from profound trauma, with amnesia. I stood behind a thick tree, listening, checking myself for blood.

Where were the dogs? Where was Harry? I put my hands to the coarse bark of the maple and tried to become part of the tree, invisible, a thing pasted to its backside.

The barking got closer. If he found me, I would die. This was the perfect place to get rid of my body. No one would find me buried out here. Not in this century, maybe not in the next, until some developer wanted to make a golf course in a future time and turned up a few inconvenient bones, which he might hurriedly rebury, thinking to save himself the trouble of archeologists and investigation.

I heard a faint whooshing and thumping farther off in the woods. An oil pump. Maybe there. Could be people. Someone. I pushed off from the tree and ran headlong down an embankment. At the bottom was a tangle of raspberry canes I couldn't penetrate. I had to get around them, down to the small creek running at the base of the hill. I'd go along the creek, come up the other side. Get to that oil pump.

I ran, hit slippery rocks and skidded, falling again, landing on a knee, which immediately let me know I was hurt, that I'd lacerated the skin beneath my jeans, that blood was going to soak through my pants leg, probably give the dogs something stronger than my faint scent or sound to follow. I got up and hurried on though I was no longer running. It wasn't possible.

I knew I couldn't run, couldn't walk, couldn't move much farther. I looked for cover. Anything. I thought of crawling into another thicket of raspberry bushes. I found, instead, a kind of cave dug into the hillside. The home of an animal, I imagined. A fox hole. A bear den. Last year's, I hoped, as I crawled into the depression in the earth and pulled leaves over me. I stopped breathing to listen. I couldn't hold my breath for long. The dogs came closer. There was snuffling in the leaves at my head and the sudden, sharp bark of a discoverer dog.

The next thing, I was being poked with the barrel of a shotgun, the gun nudging into my hiding place, then whipping leaves away.

"Gotcha," Harry said above me, triumphant, pulling leaves off faster, tapping my arms in my heavy jacket.

Harry hushed the dogs. There was a moment of silence. I didn't dare look up.

"Emily?" The voice was quizzical. "Emily Kincaid? Is that you?"

I took a long, deep, difficult breath and kept my eyes tightly closed. "Yes," I said.

"What the hell...? What were you doing at my place? Hanging around my car? I thought you was some kid come to steal it. What'd you run for? Damn dogs could of took yer leg off."

"Don't kill me, Harry," I begged. I pulled in air. "I thought we were friends. Why would you do this to me?"

"Me? Do what? You're the one was skulking around my house."

I dared open one eye and peek up at him. He was hunkered down in front of me. His rough face was perplexed. He put up one hand and scratched at his chin. The gun lay beside him, in the leaves. Clearly, Harry wasn't about to kill me. At least not at the moment.

"I saw your car, Harry," I said, sitting up and brushing at my jacket, my pants, where leaves and dirt clung. "I know what you did."

"Yeah." He stood now and reached down to help me. "You're not turning me in though." His voice was matter-of-fact. Harry had to be a raving lunatic if he thought I'd keep his secret.

I shivered and waited, not knowing what to say. How could he not kill me? What choice did he have? I sure wasn't going to protect him.

I stood beside him, huddled in on myself. I looked for a way to run but the pack of slathering, heavy-breathing dogs sniffing around my feet wouldn't make it easy.

Harry shook his head. "Couldn't help it."

"Why would you do such a thing? I can't believe it was you."

"Nothing I could do about it. You won't tell. I know you."

"Not tell? Christ, Harry, I can't cover for you on this. I was in that car. It was me you almost killed."

He stepped back and gave me an odd look.

"Nope. Wasn't you."

I nodded. "Yes it was. I don't know which one of us you were after, but I was in there. Me and the others—Dolly and Flora Coy. And you left us to die like that." I shook my head, feeling so sad—for me, for Dolly, Flora, but most of all for Harry.

He took a step away and stared harder. "I don't know what the hell yer talkin' about. I killed a deer. Ran right in front of me yesterday. I didn't call nobody, the way I'm supposed to. Stupid state law. The thing was dead. I didn't see nothin' wrong with bringing it home. Already got it cut up and in the freezer. I'll have meat right through the winter without doing another bit of hunting. Now if you think you got to report me, well you go right ahead. They'll have to come and take it. I've got my rights and ..."

"A deer?" Something wrong here. "I'm talking about last night."

"Yeah."

"When you ran Dolly's police car off the road out by Arnold's Swamp. Nearly killed us."

Harry stepped back and gave me a stupefied look. "You're nuts. I done no such thing. I killed a deer. That's what happened to my car. I figured if I had to fix my car, least I could take the meat. Thing was dead, as it was. No sense leaving it by the side of the road for the crows to get."

I couldn't take in what he was saying. My legs buckled under me and I sat down fast, sending Harry's dogs in all directions, barking and snarling.

"You OK, Emily?" Harry knelt beside me. I nodded, not sure I was telling the truth. He was talking about hitting a deer, not a police car. He was talking about illegally taking the deer home without reporting it, the way he should have. I was talking about something different.

Harry stayed beside me. "What in hell is this all about? Me trying to kill you. I didn't hit no police car or any other car. Somebody did, it wasn't me."

I told Harry what happened and how I'd been at his house to get a look at his car, because it was big and black. I told him I saw the damage to the front of his car and naturally assumed ...

"Well, you 'naturally assumed' wrong," he said, then was quiet, picking up a golden leaf, sticking it into his mouth, and chewing at the stem. "But, I got something I've gotta say. Should've said it earlier, but didn't."

346

I waited.

"You know Miz Poet?"

I waited.

"Well, that head and that arm?"

I waited again. Harry turned his face away, looked off at his dogs that all looked back at me.

"Wish my dogs woulda found the murderer instead of Miz Poet. Poor woman. It was my dogs dug her up, I guess. They brought home her head and dropped it on my doorstep. Same with the arm. Thought they had something. Guess they did."

"Oh no, Harry. You're the one put it in my garbage can?"

He nodded, still turned away from me.

"Why didn't you call the police?"

"And have 'em out here nosing around? Have Lucky Barnard and those state boys all over this place? Why, what's to say they'd believe I didn't kill her myself? I'm not like you, ya know. You're from the city. A writer and all. Nobody's gonna think you'd kill an old lady. But me? Crazy Harry Mockerman?"

"Oh, Harry."

He made a noise and chewed harder at his leaf. "Sure they'd blame it on me and that would be that. I didn't know what to do. Just took it up to the road, saw your garbage can, and put it in there."

"And the arm?"

"Had to get rid of it. Couldn't let 'em find it on my place. I knew you'd take care of everything, writing mysteries and all. Being a reporter. Coming from down below. Nobody was gonna suspect you of a killing. But me ... well ... maybe they'd take my dogs away. Who knows?"

"They wouldn't take your dogs, Harry."

"You never know anything anymore. Things are changing up here in the woods. People don't want us to live the way we're used to living. I don't trust nobody."

"You know one of Dave Rombart's militia men saw you with the head?"

He gave me a dark look. "You don't say? Why didn't he turn me in? No love lost between them and me."

"Dave called the state police. I told them what you said about Dave Rombart and his group—that they were up to no good. I don't think anybody took either side seriously."

"Hmm. Well, they were up to no good. Poaching. Saw 'em myself."

I suspected Harry saw them poaching when *he* was out poaching, but I didn't want to say so and didn't want to laugh. There were still more important things to think about.

"Who's been doing this, Harry? Who's been killing the women?"

He raised his back and shoulders then dropped them. "I don't know. Wish I did. Can't figure it out either. Wish my dogs would've got 'im that first day. Wish they woulda got him while he was burying Miz Poet. Woulda stopped it right there. But they didn't. And he didn't stop. And I just don't know who's doing it. All I know, it's not me."

THIRTY-EIGHT

ODD, HOW I FELT happy, almost skipping down my drive, kicking at fallen limbs and wind-tossed leaves. Harry hadn't tried to kill me. A tremendous relief. Who did it was almost beside the point. At least it wasn't Harry.

The afternoon had turned dark while I was over at Harry's making a fool of myself. Rain and wind were predicted. Cold. Maybe some sleet thrown in to make things interesting.

I thought about the winter to come. How it would be so quiet. Snow would pile against my house walls and wind would blow, and inside I'd curl up in a quilt, in front of the fireplace, as if I lived in a cave. Across from me—and I could almost see his house in winter when the bushes and trees were completely bare—would be Harry, with his dogs, his possum stews, and his freezer filled with purloined meat.

How happy that made me. Just knowing he would still be there, wishing me no harm. I forgave him his aberrations. I forgave him— head and arm. He was still as I believed him to be—my friend, my caretaker, my goofy neighbor. How I wished the others could still be there—all the dead dancing women.

Safe in their alabaster chambers.

Emily Dickinson flew into my head the way she could when I needed to see things clearly, when I needed to sail above all things plaguing me.

> *Untouched by morning and untouched by noon,*
> *Sleep the meek members of the resurrection,*
> *Rafter of satin, and roof of stone.*

How sad. Our poor women without even their own *"Rafter of satin, and roof of stone"* to comfort them. No neatly lined-up graves in Leetsville cemetery. No geranium circles around their resting places. Joslyn Henry. Ruby Poet. Mary Margaret Murphy. They'd taken such pride in their closeness to nature. Now denied a final resting place. How angry that made me. *Damn*, but I was going to find out who'd done this. Before last night, this whole thing had been a puzzle, a sad story to report. Now it was more than personal—not just me, but all women who dared to be different. All women ... whew, I was on a crusade. Me. And Deputy Dolly.

I couldn't help but smile.

OK, I told myself. If not Harry—then who? If not Harry ...? Someone with something to gain. Someone with a reason to have the women gone.

Not Harry.

Not Dave Rombart and that crew of his. Poaching and peeking rights didn't seem reason enough for one murder, let alone three.

The others ... Sullivan Murphy. An alcoholic. Used to be a cop. Probably the alcohol was the reason he wasn't one any longer. It was logical for him to have a uniform, and for him to be the one

Eugenia saw running from the funeral home before it burst into flames. But if he'd been running from the fire—why didn't he save his mother? Too drunk? Too ashamed to admit it?

No doubt Sullivan needed money. Mother sick to death of him and needing money herself. Maybe there'd been a blowup. Maybe she did ask Ruby for money, at Sullivan's insistence. What mother wouldn't do terrible things for her children? Maybe Sullivan thought of another way to get it. Burn the funeral home and kill off his mother.

Ernie Henry. Money again? Or something more sinister. Something to do with that arrest down in Grand Rapids. Something to do with porn. Something to do with ...

I kicked stone after stone then watched them fall downhill in quick, arcing bounds. Things followed their nature. The nature of a stone was to roll downhill. Leaves to fall. Dogs to bark. Human nature, too. Follow nature, I told myself. Look at the nature of the people. Something clicked in my brain. Follow nature ...

A blue Dodge Dart was parked at the bottom of the drive, just behind my jeep.

I was in no mood for company, least of all in the mood for the woman I found sitting in my living room, a cup of tea in her hands, a pinky finger duly shot straight up in the air.

Amanda Poet sat across from our recuperating Dolly and a rather tired-looking Flora Coy. She looked at me and made a sad face, as if I'd interrupted a eulogy.

"Why Emily," Amanda turned in her chair to face me. "I was hoping to see you before we left. My ... well ... look at you ..."

I brushed at the last of the leaves clinging to my jacket and jeans. I knew my hair was a mess.

Sorrow lay prone with his nose resting on his front paws, surprisingly subdued. His eyeballs moved from me to our guest. He didn't greet me.

"I came to offer Flora the safety of my house—such as it is. I mean, with all that's happened ... I've been so distraught. But it was awful of me, not thinking of this before. Mother would be so mad. Of course Flora's got to come stay with me. We'll be a comfort to each other. I just won't hear of anything else ..."

"I told her we're charged with keeping Flora safe. Can't let her go." Dolly hauled herself up straight, leg stuck out in front of her, resting on the coffee table.

"Well, yes," Amanda said, and she looked pointedly down at Dolly's cast. "But now that you're incapacitated, I think Flora would be much better off with me, in town, where Lucky can keep an eye on us both. Don't forget, I might be in danger, too. I mean, when will any of us be safe in our beds again?"

"How'd it go?" Dolly shut out Amanda's voice and gave me a meaningful look. She snapped her head in the direction of Harry's house. Flora fixed her big myopic eyes on me.

"Fine," I said, and I gave each a smile meant to bring them peace.

Dolly wasn't buying it.

"Was it his car?"

I shook my head, no. "He's got damage. But he hit a deer."

"You believe him?" Dolly demanded.

Flora gave her an angry glare. "Of course she believes him. We all know Harry Mockerman wouldn't do a thing ..."

"Is this about what happened to you last night?" Amanda sat up straighter. "You think it was Harry Mockerman who ran you off the road? With that what-ever-you-call-it thing he drives? Well,

352

of course. Harry lives out here where they found Mother. Harry is very, very strange. Really, the worst of the types that live back here ... well, no offense, Emily."

I stared her to silence. At least she was nervous, even sputtering when she went on.

"I hope you've called the state police about this."

"No need," I said. "It wasn't Harry."

"I don't think you should take it on yourself, miss."

"And I don't think you've got any business coming out here to my home and ..."

"Stop it!" Flora Coy stood up, hands in the air, waving at all of us. "Amanda's right. I'd be safer in town, near my own house. And who better than our own precious Ruby's daughter, Amanda, to watch out for me and my birds."

"That's ... that's ... that's ..." Now Dolly was sputtering. I was confused, not sure I wanted Flora out of our sight. Still—we'd been on the job last night and look what happened to all of us.

"Oh no." Amanda set her teacup down on the floor next to her chair and put her hands to her cheeks. "The birds will have to stay here, Flora. Elvira Pederson is going to be bringing people over to show the house, prospective buyers, you know, and birds make such a mess."

"Why, Amanda." Flora straightened her back and stuck out her chin. "My birds make no more mess than ... than I do."

"Oh, dear." Amanda struggled out of my rather sprung old chair and put a hand out to Flora. "Don't get mad at me, Flora. We don't want any trouble between us ... not after everything. I just want you with me. These two ... women ... well, they aren't like us. No refinement, you know. They never would have understood mother like we do."

It was getting to be a familiar song, this imperiousness, then contrition. I was getting mighty tired of Amanda Poet and her better-than-everyone airs. "'Course not, Amanda." Flora was still angry but getting ahold of herself. "You mind keeping my birds another day or so, Emily?"

I wouldn't have denied that embarrassed face of Flora's anything. She was mad enough to bite the head off a chicken but wanted to honor Ruby Poet's memory. It wasn't her first choice of sanctuaries, being with Amanda. But I could see she was doing her duty.

"You got plenty of seed. Anyway, you two will be better off without me hanging on to you. This needs to be settled, once and for all. I hope you get whoever's doing…"

Dolly and I gave our best we-sure-will nods though I didn't like the idea of Flora being out of our sight. I tried one last time to persuade her to stay but she was adamant. She was going home with Ruby Poet's daughter.

On their way out the door, Flora was offering to clean up Ruby's garden for Amanda. Get the beds ready for winter.

"Oh, no need of that, Flora," Amanda, hand on the little woman's back, hurrying her along, said. "It doesn't matter anymore."

I carried Flora's things out to the car. When I came back in Dolly and I exchanged a look.

"Wonder if we should've done that," she said, glowering as the expected rain started hitting my front windows.

I shook my head. "Something's making me very uncomfortable."

"Me too."

"But it's not our choice. Flora's a grown woman." I busied myself in the kitchen, washing teacups and thinking about a sandwich. Maybe a ham and Swiss sandwich out in my studio—which I still had to smudge with sage to get Jackson's spirit out of there.

I thought about a sandwich, my novel, about the quiet out in my own place.

Maybe a nap on the futon. Maybe I'd take a walk in the rain. Dark was coming earlier now. How much time did I have left? Hmm … I considered the existential element of that question.

"Maybe I should get back to town, too," Dolly said from the sofa.

"And who's going to take care of you?" I demanded, the way people do when they really like the idea but know they're only being selfish.

"I don't need taking care of. My ankle's broken, not my head. I can get around good enough …"

"Don't be a jerk." I slammed the last cupboard door.

Fuming, Dolly struggled up at the edge of the sofa and grabbed her crutches. "I don't need to hang around here and be called names."

"Yeah, you can go back to town and be called names there." Now *I* was mad. I wasn't looking for a fight with this chicken-little woman, just trying to do the right thing.

"What in hell does that mean?" She hung on her crutches and glowered in my direction.

"Oh … nothing." I waved a hand at her and made for the bathroom where I closed the door and sat on the toilet, muttering until I'd calmed down, could put on a smile, and go back out to face the wounded dragon.

The phone rang, flushing me out of the bathroom. It was Bill. I'd called my story in earlier. He wanted some clarification. And he was worried about me—which was good to hear. I assured him I was fine and would get back to him that afternoon.

Dolly was at the sink, jacket on, gun belt strapped over her sweat-pants. She ran cold water into a glass then downed a pill I knew was for pain.

Guilt. Awful thing about living alone for a few years. You forget other people have feelings, too.

"You'll have to drive me in," she said, back turned, head down. "Don't have a car."

"And you won't have one in town either. How are you going to get around? And how will we ever finish this thing if you're in Leetsville and I'm out here?"

"Lucky'll think of something." She turned. "Look. I'm the professional police officer here. I shouldn't have asked you to get into this in the first place. Big mistake. Put your life in jeopardy, along with Flora Coy's. Now I'm going after who did this full-throttle. I believe you—it's not Harry. It's sure no outsider. What I need to do is sit down where it's quiet, which sure as hell isn't this place. And I want to see what we've got."

"That's what I've been doing—in my head. Going over what's been happening. And I keep coming back to human nature. I think we've got to follow nature …"

"And that means … what?"

"You know … who could kill so easily? Who would know how to dispose of a body? Think about who would be able to cut up …"

Dolly's mouth fell open. "And who would always need money? A gambler. And who supposedly wasn't home when the funeral parlor went up in flames—with his brother and mother inside?"

"And who drives a big black car?"

"And who could get his hands on his brother's police uniform?"

"And who might come up with a harebrained scheme to kill his mother's friends, to cover up the real target?"

"And who's going to get at least half the insurance money—unless he gets Sullivan first?"

"Gilbert!" We shouted simultaneously.

"I gotta call Lucky." Dolly lurched to the phone. She dialed, listened, then slammed the receiver down. "Nobody answering." She shook her head. "Let's just get in there."

I agreed, then stopped. "You think Flora and Amanda are all right?"

Dolly shrugged. "We'll go warn them. But first I've got to find Lucky. And we've got to get to Sullivan. Didn't somebody say they checked out of the resort? Damn! I wish I had my patrol car. I wish I had my radio. I wish I wasn't on these friggin' crutches." She thumped them hard on the floor, making the startled Sorrow leap up, bark, turn over his water bowl, and pee at the same time.

"That's three wishes. You're finished," I said, pushing her out the door, ignoring my overexcited dog, and leaving all that mess behind me.

THIRTY-NINE

IT WAS DARK WHEN we got to town, having dodged four deer happily prancing their way from one side of the road to the other, and one of the mangiest coyotes I'd ever seen. The deer were already into their dark fall coats. Sad, because it marked their way of dodging the bullets of November. I pointed this out to Dolly, who looked over at me as if I were crazy.

"We've got a killer on the loose. Friends alone there in town. Can't get ahold of the chief. And you're worrying about those deer? Who almost just killed us, by the way. Running out like they did."

"You're just mad because you don't have a siren."

"Damn straight, I'm mad. That's Gilbert's fault, too. My siren. And my ankle. These damn crutches. If I didn't have 'em I'd be driving and we'd be there by now."

With monumental restraint, I didn't indulge myself in a comment about her driving—and the cars she'd wrecked.

We avoided conversation the rest of the way into town.

The windows of the Leetsville Police Station were bright squares against the dark. I parked in front and we could see a woman inside, taking off her jacket and hanging it on a corner coat tree. But no Lucky.

"That's the chief's wife. I'll run in and find out where Lucky's got to. You wait here."

I didn't have time to argue. She was out of the car, up on her crutches, and in the station. Dolly'd gotten the hang of the things and they weren't holding her back. In a few minutes she came flying out of the station. She got in, swinging the crutches dangerously near my head as she tossed them in the car.

"You'll never believe where Lucky is?" Her mouth fell open as she waited for me to guess.

I shrugged.

"Out at Sandy Lake." Dolly's eyes were wide. "Damnedest thing. The Mitchell boys found a car with the back end sticking up out of the lake. Somebody wanted to sink it and failed. The boys tried to get it out. I'll bet to go joy riding but it was stuck down in the lake bottom. They told their dad and he called Lucky. It's a hearse, Emily. Gilbert's hearse. I radioed Lucky. They just pulled it up on shore. Got white paint on the right front fender. Lucky's called Brent already. The state cops are on their way over from Gaylord to help us hunt for Gilbert. Could be he's stole a car and long gone. Or maybe he's around. But somebody helped him out there at Sandy Lake. Had to get a ride back. Maybe Sullivan. Lucky says be careful. I told him we'd be over to Amanda's. He said that was a good thing. Don't know what's going to happen next."

I put the car in gear and backed out, squealing my tires loud enough to make Dolly smile.

"You see that?" Dolly whispered and pointed at something.

The Poets' house was dark except for a dim light in one of the front windows. Amanda's Dodge Dart was parked in the gravel drive beside the house, so we knew they were back. We'd been sitting in my car, lights out, discussing how to handle the situation, how much to tell the women. We didn't want them scared.

I'd seen what she was pointing to. Darkness against darkness. A figure moving out from the trees, around behind the house.

The figure was furtive, bent forward. Thick bodied, but impossible to tell whose body.

"What do we do?" Dolly whispered, bent down as if to hide, though we were in complete darkness.

"Can't leave," I said.

"Can't get ahold of Lucky. Damn, why didn't I think to take a radio with me?"

"Do we just sit? What if he's breaking in? They're alone in there."

"He probably wants Amanda's car."

"What if he takes them hostage?" By this time we were hissing at each other.

"I got my gun."

"You going to take him on crutches?"

"Won't need to chase him down if I've got my gun."

"And if he runs? What then?"

"You want to chase him?" she demanded. "Look, what's important are the women. Let's get up there to the door. We can maybe look in, see what's going on. I could stay here then, keep the place covered. You go back to the station. Find Lucky."

"I'm not leaving you."

"Don't be an idiot."

"Yeah. I'll prop you up against the house with your gun and leave."

"OK. OK. Let's fight later. Slide over here and come out my door so we don't keep slamming doors and having the overhead light come on. We'll do it once. Get the crutches out of the back for me."

We coordinated the whole thing, opened the door, and slid out as gracefully as we could.

Dolly stationed herself beside one of the front windows, body balanced on her crutches, gun in her hand. I was going to creep around to the porch and look in the door window. I made a move in that direction just as the front door opened.

The first thing we heard was Flora Coy crying and begging the person behind her, pushing her out onto the porch, not to hurt her. "You know I won't take it now." Flora's words were interrupted by snuffles. "I can't do what Ruby wanted. That's not me. No chapel. That was always more Ruby's dream. Ernie owns the property. There's no more Women of the Moon. It's all yours. All yours."

"All you had to do was tell me where it was," the person behind her, still inside the house, hidden by the door, growled at her.

"I didn't remember. Why, you know…" Poor Flora was hanging on to the banister, looking down the steps as if afraid of being pushed again. "I forgot she told me to put it near something I loved. All that's been going on … right out of my head. You know I wouldn't have kept any…"

Dolly and I braced our bodies against the house, staying out of sight. I could have bent down, hidden behind the bushes under the window, but not Dolly, not up on the tree trunks she was swinging from. We held our breath.

From behind Flora, Amanda Poet emerged. She stumbled on the door sill and grabbed the storm door.

"Watch yourself." It was a man's voice, behind her.

Gilbert. Taking hostages, as we'd feared. And here we were...

I felt Dolly pressing something into my side. It was her gun.

"Take it," she whispered faintly at my ear.

I thought I got the picture. I was to step out with the gun and stop him. She'd remain back in the shadows, pretending she had him covered, too. It was all we had.

I was ready to take a step forward when Amanda spoke again.

"None of you old witches needed to die, if you weren't so greedy."

"Nobody was greedy, Amanda." Flora, at the bottom of the steps, looked back up at Amanda Poet. "I didn't even know about the will. Now it doesn't matter."

"Joslyn knew. Came over here and told me right after they found Mother. Threatening me. She said that was the way Mother wanted it and that was the way it was going to be. Imagine, leaving all that money to the bunch of you."

"We wouldn't have..."

"Gilbert, shut her up. I just can't listen to any more of this. Now we've got to go back out there to that awful writer person's house and get those damn birds."

Gilbert Murphy stepped forward, around Amanda Poet, who stood with her hands to her ears. He pulled Flora's arm and started dragging her toward Amanda's car when I grabbed Dolly's gun, took a deep, shaky breath, and stepped out into his path.

The three of them stopped where they were, frozen in place.

"Not another step," Dolly said from back by the house. "We've both got guns."

I stood in what I imagined was gun-holding stance, legs apart, hands—with gun—straight out in front of me. I didn't say a word. I couldn't. I just stood and pointed—not sure which one of them I pointed at.

"My goodness!" Flora was the first to speak. "Emily? Is that you?" She turned. "And Dolly? Well, am I glad to see the two of you. This pair, why they're in cahoots. Both going to get money from their poor mothers. Murdered them. "

She walked between me and Gilbert as she spoke, coming right at me.

"Get down, Flora!" Dolly yelled as Gilbert made a move to grab her. Flora dodged his outstretched arms, and fled behind me, where she held on so hard I could barely keep my hands out straight.

Gilbert stopped where he was. He raised his arms, which made me feel better.

Amanda hadn't moved. Now she took her hands down from her ears. All I could see in the light from the doorway were the whites of her eyes.

"Why, Emily. We were coming back out to your place...," Amanda began to speak. She took a few steps forward.

"Stay right where you are, Amanda. The chief's on his way with the state cops. You're not going out to Emily's or anywhere."

"Don't be silly, Dolly. This can all be explained..."

"No, it can't," Flora, peeking out from behind me, said. "Our dear Ruby left a will giving us those oil leases. She wanted a chapel built in Joslyn's woods, by the fire. So all women could come and join in, maybe make our little group grow. That's what Amanda wanted from me. Mine's taped to the bottom of one of my birdcages. I just forgot because ... well ... I just forgot."

"That's OK, Flora," I said. Her voice was shaking, and her hands weren't steady either.

A block or so away, I heard sirens blaring. Lucky. I hoped he was on his way. No doubt somebody in town had seen and called him. Somebody knew Dolly and I were standing out here with two killers held at gunpoint. Something this big couldn't have slid under the town's infallible radar.

"Get down, Gilbert," Dolly ordered.

"DOWN! On your face!" she shouted when he didn't move fast enough.

Dolly limped from the dark shadows of the house, whipping her handcuffs out as she came haltingly forward. She handed the cuffs to me and pointed toward Gilbert, now docile and face down on the ground. She took the gun from my hands and kept it trained on Amanda while I cuffed Gilbert—which wasn't as easy as it looked on *COPS*.

"Why Dolly!" Amanda's voice was disappointed. "You lied to us. You don't have a gun at all."

"Sorry, Amanda," she said just as Lucky, siren blaring, pulled up on the grass. "I guess some of us don't know how to be a lady."

Gilbert and Amanda disappeared into the back of the chief's car. Amanda scolded Gilbert when he didn't step aside and let her get in first. Gilbert growled at her and she finally shut up.

———

Later, when she'd finished filing her report and been congratulated by Officer Brent and the other state cops, and been assured by Lucky Barnard that she was back patrolling in town—as soon as they got her car fixed, Dolly joined the rest of us at Fuller's EATS, where most of Leetsville had already gathered.

Over coffee, Flora preened when she was called a hero and patted on the back. Simon said she'd probably get Ruby's money now.

Flora shook her head. "Well, no use to it, is there? I can't build that chapel. Land's Ernie's and he won't want anything like that out there." She thought awhile. "Seems I could build a shelter for women. That'd be the ticket. And I can tell them about Ruby and Mary Margaret, and Joslyn. Maybe one of them will start up Women of the Moon again." She looked at the avid faces around her and nodded, again and again.

"I figured just today it had to be Gilbert doing this," Gloria announced to anyone who would listen. "Always about money. You should've known that, Emily." She stooped to fill my cup with coffee—though I'd ordered tea. "All you have to do is watch *Law & Order*. And when Eugenia mentioned she thought the two of them had a thing going on, well, that was it. Amanda'd get the oil lease money. Gilbert the insurance. And they'd get out of Leetsville like Amanda always wanted. Just don't understand, with his connections, why Gilbert cut up poor Ruby and buried her out in the woods. Why didn't he just put her in a box and bury her properly at the cemetery?"

Nancy, another waitress, made a noise. "That's easy," she snorted. "'Cause his mother would've seen the order to open a grave. If she looked, she woulda seen he paid for the plot himself. With Ruby missing, you can bet Mary Margaret woulda been asking questions."

"I figured all along it had to be Gilbert, too," Simon, not to be outdone, spoke up, leaning back and running a hand through his long, blond hair. "He's the one did the bodies at the funeral home. 'Less it was Mary Margaret. Personally, I figured he put poor Ruby out there to make it look like old Harry Mockerman did it—over a load of firewood. Once he started killing, guess Gilbert figured he'd do in his mother and brother and burn down the funeral home for the insurance money. Maybe by then he'd decided, with all that money, he could live in Vegas and get himself a showgirl." The men in the place snickered. The women eyed them coldly. "Well, I guess that was until he messed up the hearse and needed Amanda to help him hide it and get him out of town."

"That's where you two come in," Eugenia said, pointing at me and Dolly.

All Dolly had to add was that the day we saw an angry Joslyn Henry heading into Amanda's was the day she'd found Ruby Poet's hand-written will, leaving everything to the women in order to perpetuate their love of nature. "To Amanda and Gilbert," she said, a hint of self-satisfaction in her sniff, and in the set of her shoulders, "that meant all the women had to die, and all copies of a second will had to be destroyed."

"Good thing Lucky Barnard was on the job—besides me and Emily, of course," Dolly added, giving a slow, serious look at the people gathered around us. "And Pastor Runcival, too. He finally called Lucky to say it was Amanda who'd been at the church. Amanda's voice on those awful phone calls to Flora, here. It was her sending the letters, too. She admitted it to Lucky.

"Found Sullivan Murphy, alive and well," she added for our spellbound crowd. "Or what passes for alive and well with Sullivan. Found him over at the Skunk—drunk as one."

"Poor Sullivan." Eugenia shook her head. She moved from table to table, doling out skinny pieces of apple pie, cigarette hanging from the corner of her mouth, smoke curling up into her eyes. "Got himself a good excuse to drink now. Mother gone. Brother in jail. And all that insurance money coming to him. There'll be a lot of sorrow to drown, but with all that money, drowning it is going to get a lot easier."

She sighed and stopped talking only long enough to give me a warning look. "No big secret why people do the things they do. Two of them had a thing going on for years. I saw 'em at Dill's in Traverse once myself. Like lovebirds. Amanda, uppity old maid the way she was, and Gilbert, a gambler—well, I didn't know which one to feel sorriest for. All of it's human nature, ya know. Take my Great Aunt Lizzie Borden, out there..."

EPILOGUE

I BURNED THE SAGE and wafted the smoke to all four corners of the room, then the ceiling, then the floor—for all the compass directions, the heavens, and the earth. I did a dancing circle with it, to cover any direction I'd neglected. I hoped for a complete wipeout: Jackson gone, voice and spirit.

After he'd read that morning's newspaper, with my story in it, he'd called to say how happy he was that it was all over for me, and to say how wonderful his new place was, how spacious. "Too bad you don't have something this nice, Emily. Away from all those..."

I'd gotten off the phone pretty fast, promising I'd try to get around to editing any pages he sent me—when I took a hiatus from my own work. That left him sputtering about his time being of the essence, and me leaping in air, singing a little Nina Simone, puzzling Sorrow who watched me with his head cocked, tongue hanging out.

All my morning euphoria ended with a thud when I sat down at my desk and began going over the chapters of my book. I looked at my main character—a writer. My detective—the alcoholic who thinks the writer is the murderer, but falls in love with her. I read where I had him fall off the wagon, become a suspect himself . . .

Faces danced before my eyes: Sharon Stone, Michael Douglas.

Oh no . . .

Basic Instinct!

How could I be so dumb!

All over again . . .

What an idiot! Wasn't I ever going to get it right?

I got up and stamped my way around the room. I took a slap at my computer as I passed, then at the funny painted head I'd picked up in Santa Fe. I stood over Sorrow, giving him a slant-eyed look, warning him not to say a word. He lifted his head, opened one eye briefly, and went back to sleep.

Here I was. Still a failed mystery writer, though now one with an aptly named dog—Sorrow. Sorrow floats . . .

Does it ever! Floats and follows right along behind and chews up ex-husband's shoes, as if on command.

Back to basics, I told myself firmly, with no inkling of irony.

Write what you know. Every writing teacher's mantra.

But what did I know? Just the trees. My garden. Sorrow.

I sat back down at my desk and began to type:

> *Something in the shivering trees. I could feel it*
> *overhead, and around me in the woods; and in the late*
> *September air with needles of cold at its heart. Autumn.*
> *Prelude to death, I'd always thought. Death of my*
> *garden, of the trees, the animals, ferns, grasses, the last*
> *of the purple knapweed clinging to sheltered places on*
> *the hills of my home. All of that . . .*

Karen Youker

ABOUT THE AUTHOR

Elizabeth Kane Buzzelli is a creative writing instructor at Northwestern Michigan College. She is the author of novels, short stories, articles, and essays. Her work has appeared in numerous publications and anthologies.

WWW.MIDNIGHTINKBOOKS.COM

From the gritty streets of New York City to sacred tombs in the Middle East, it's always midnight somewhere. Join us online at any hour for fresh new voices in mystery fiction.

At midnightinkbooks.com you'll also find our author blog, new and upcoming books, events, book club questions, excerpts, mystery resources, and more.

MIDNIGHT INK ORDERING INFORMATION

Order Online:
• Visit our website www.midnightinkbooks.com, select your books, and order them on our secure server.

Order by Phone:
• Call toll-free within the U.S. and Canada at
   1-888-NITE-INK (1-888-648-3465)
• We accept VISA, MasterCard, and American Express

Order by Mail:
Send the full price of your order (MN residents add 6.5% sales tax) in U.S. funds, plus postage & handling to:

> Midnight Ink
> 2143 Wooddale Drive
> Woodbury, MN 55125-2989

Postage & Handling:

Standard (U.S., Mexico, & Canada). If your order is:
> $24.99 and under, add $3.00
> $25.00 and over, FREE STANDARD SHIPPING

AK, HI, PR: $15.00 for one book plus $1.00 for each additional book.

International Orders (airmail only):
> $16.00 for one book plus $3.00 for each additional book

Orders are processed within 2 business days. Please allow for normal shipping time. Postage and handling rates subject to change.